THE BORGIAS

Nateese

New St. B'ham - 1st Nov 1981

Also by Sarah Bradford:

CESARE BORGIA

Sarah Bradford

The Borgias

based on the television scripts by
John Prebble and Ken Taylor

Macdonald & Co Publishers

A Futura Book

First published in Great Britain by
Macdonald & Co · London and Sydney
and George Weidenfeld and Nicolson Ltd

ISBN: 0 7088 2019 0

Printed in Great Britain by
Richard Clay (The Chaucer Press) Ltd,
Bungay, Suffolk

Macdonald & Co Publishers Limited
Paulton House
8 Shepherdess Walk
London N1 7LW

Contents

Dramatis Personae

THE BORGIAS

RODRIGO BORGIA Born in Jativa, Valencia, in April 1431. Elected Pope Alexander VI in 1492, and father, by his Italian mistress Vannozza Cattanei, of –

CESARE Born September 1475.

JUAN Later Duke of Gandia, born 1476.

LUCREZIA Born April 1480.

JOFRE Born 1481. Rodrigo frequently refused to recognise Jofre as his son.

Their husbands, wives, mistresses, children and servants, etc.

VANNOZZA CATTANEI CANALE Mother of Rodrigo's four children, at the time of the action married to her third husband, Carlo Canale. Aged about 50 in 1492.

ADRIANA DE MILA ORSINI First cousin and female confidante to Rodrigo Borgia, married to Ludovico Orsini, Lord of Bassanello, and mother-in-law of Rodrigo's mistress –

GUILIA FARNESE ORSINI Wife of the one-eyed Orsino Orsini, and mother of Rodrigo Borgia's illegitimate daughter. Aged 19 in 1492.

JOHANN BURCHARD Papal Master of Ceremonies, and keeper of a secret diary chronicling the Borgias' activities.

PEDRO CALDERON, *known* as 'PEROTTO' Rodrigo Borgia's favourite Chamberlain, murdered by Cesare in 1498.

MIGUEL DA CORELLA, *known as* 'MICHELOTTO' Bastard soldier of fortune from Aragon and Cesare's right-hand man, known to contempories as his executioner.

RAMIRO DE LORCA *or* LORQUA Cousin of the above, also Cesare's henchman, later Governor of the Romagna, executed in 1502.

GIOVANNI SFORZA Lord of Pesaro, Lucrezia Borgia's first husband. Divorced in 1498.

ALFONSO OF ARAGON Duke of Biselli, bastard son of Alfonso of Naples, married Lucrezia as her second husband, in 1498, murdered on Cesare's orders in 1500.

ALFONSO D'ESTE Son of Duke Ercole of Ferrara, married Lucrezia as her third husband in 1502.

SANCIA OF ARAGON Princess of Squillace, sister of Alfonso of Aragon (above), wife of Jofre Borgia.

GIOVANNI BORGIA Son of Lucrezia and Rodrigo, born 1498.

RODRIGO BORGIA Son of Lucrezia and Alfonso Biselli, born 1499.

CHARLOTTE D'ALBRET A French noblewoman, married Cesare in France in 1499.

DOROTEA CARACCIOLO Cesare Borgia's mistress, illegitimate daughter of Roberto Malatesta, Lord of Rimini.

VASIA A Greek girl, Cesare Borgia's last mistress

OTHER MAIN CHARACTERS
CARDINALS, CONDOTTIERI, AND
ITALIAN NOBLEMEN AND WOMEN

CARDINAL GIULIANO ROVERE Rodrigo Borgia's life-long enemy and rival for the papacy. Aged 49 in 1492.

The Sforza family (rulers of Milan)

CARDINAL ASCANIO SFORZA Wealthy Cardinal, sometimes a supporter, sometimes an enemy of the Borgias, younger brother to –

LUDOVICO MARIA SFORZA Regent of Milan.

CATERINA SFORZA Ruler of Imola and Forlì, bastard niece to Ascanio and Ludovico.

The Sforza brothers were also uncles to Giovanni Sforza (see above) and related by marriage to Alfonso of Aragon (see above).

The Orsini family (with their enemies, the Colonnas, the most powerful of the Roman noble families)

PAOLO, GIOVANNI *and* GIULIO ORSINI Sons of Virginio Orsini (who was probably put to death on Rodrigo Borgia's orders in 1497), all three were Captains and then enemies of Cesare Borgia. Paolo and Giovanni Orsini also met their deaths at the hands of the Borgias.

CARDINAL GIANBATTISTA ORSINI Head of the house after Virginio's death, died in Castel Sant'Angelo, probably poisoned on Borgia orders, December 1502.

PROSPERO COLONNA Roman nobleman and soldier, hereditary enemy of the Orsinis, in the service of the Kings of Naples and Spain.

GIAN PAOLO BAGLIONI Member of the ruling Baglioni clan of Perugia, friend of Cesare's youth, his Captain and later his enemy.

VITELLOZZO VITELLI Lord of Città di Castello, Cesare's Captain and leader of the conspiracy against him. Executed in 1502 on Cesare's orders.

Kings of France

CHARLES VIII Undertook the first French invasion of Italy in 1494, died 1498.

LOUIS XII Cousin and successor to Charles. Established French power in Italy with a second invasion in 1499, and was an important instrument in Cesare Borgia's rise to power.

YVES D'ALÈGRE An experienced Captain in the service of Charles and Louis.

VENICE

Milan

MILAN

MANTUA

Venice

GENOA

FERRARA

MODENA

Bologna
Imola
Faenza Forlì
Cesena
Rimini
Pesaro
Urbino Sinigallia
Città di Castello

LUCCA

Pisa

Florence

FLORENCE

Siena

Perugia

SIENA

Orvieto

PAPAL
STATES

Spoleto

Rome

Ostia

KINGDOM OF NAPLES

Capua
Naples

Italy in 1492

Italy in 1492, when the Borgia story begins, was the centre of the civilised world, home of the Papacy which rules Christendom, and of the city-states like Venice, Florence and Milan which dazzled Europe with their learning, industry and luxury. It was also a patch-work of smaller independent lordships, whose rulers, interlinked by a network of family marriages, lived lives which, though frequently charged with violence, were also gilded with magnificence. This was the cultivated, aristocratic world which was soon to be disrupted by the passions and ambitions of a rapacious clan of outsiders — the Borgias.

1

The Pope

ROME. 26TH JULY 1492. The sun shone down on the huddled roofs of the medieval city that was no longer the glorious Rome of the Caesars and had not yet become the magnificent Rome of the Popes. The ancient walls still stood, although the town within them had shrunk to a nucleus round the Tiber, leaving fields where cattle and goats grazed among the ruins. The monuments of imperial Rome stood out white like ancient bones, often with rickety tenements of wood and stone clinging to them like sparrows' nests. But Rome was growing again, expanding since the Papacy had returned to the city some fifty years before after more than a century of 'Babylonian Captivity' in Avignon at the hands of the Kings of France. The air rang with the sound of stonemasons' hammers building gleaming palaces of the luminous Roman stone, travertine, to house the enormous retinues of the Cardinals, the Pope's courtiers, Princes of the Church.

For Rome was a parasite city sucking blood from the veins of Christianity, living off the pilgrims and churchmen who flooded the town at all seasons of the year, a huge floating population serviced by an army of whores and tavern-keepers, purveyors of necessary luxuries and expensive necessities. For the Romans life was pleasurable, but it could also be violent. The dark streets and winding alleys were unsafe at night while the henchmen of the great nobles carried out their vendettas, throwing their victims into the Tiber as the lesser citizens did their refuse. Even in daylight the partisans of the two great families of Orsini and Colonna fought each other in the streets.

The real ruler of Rome was the Pope, Bishop of Rome, spiritual leader of the entire Christian world, and worldly Prince of the lands of the Church, called the Papal States, which straddled Italy. And on this hot July morning the city seethed with excitement; all eyes were turned towards the Vatican, where Pope Innocent VIII, born Gian Battista Cibo of Genoa, lay dying, sustained, it was whispered, by the milk of nursing mothers, and even by the blood of young Christian children injected into his ageing veins by a Jewish physician.

*   *   *

Although the Romans did not know, Innocent was already dead, lying waxen in the darkened vaulted chamber in the medieval palace. The sickly smell of death filled the room, wrinkling the fastidious nostrils of Raffaele Riario, the Cardinal Chamberlain, and competing with the summer smell of rotting refuse and the river which filtered through the shuttered windows. Mechanically, Riario went through the formal rites, tapping the dead man on the forehead with a silver mallet, and calling his name, before formally pronouncing Innocent VIII dead.

Riario was not grieved by the death of Innocent, an easy-going man who had allowed his chamberlain to keep and increase the vast wealth he had amassed as nephew to the previous Pope, Sixtus IV. Like everyone else in Rome, his thoughts were on the coming Conclave of Cardinals which was to choose the new Pope. For him, as for the rest of the Christian world, the election was of vital interest. A Pope could found a dynasty, raise his family from the humblest beginnings such as the Riarios themselves had had, he could make noble marriages for them, endow them with rich fiefs from the territories of the Church, or, if they were churchmen, he could create them Cardinals to ensure that their power would outlast his death, and give them lucrative offices and rich benefices to sustain their position. Would the next Pope be a strong, rapacious pontiff in the mould of his uncle, Sixtus, Riario wondered, who would, like Sixtus, enrich his family at the expense of the Church, or might the choice fall upon a more saintly man, such as the elderly Portuguese Cardinal Costa, or the Venetian Zeno?

Riario was a shrewd man and a politician; in his opinion the times were not made for saints, still less elderly ones. Behind the election of the Pope lay the tangled web of international politics, the rival claims of the powerful Kings of France and Spain to the kingdom of Naples whose ferocious old ruler, Ferrante, must soon die, and the ambitions of Ludovico Sforza, Duke of Bari and Regent of Milan, who coveted the state of his nephew, the feeble Gian Galeazzo Sforza, nominal Duke of Milan. The next Pope, as spiritual referee of these quarrels and temporal overlord of a great part of the Italian peninsula, would have to be able to withstand intense international pressures, to pick his way through a minefield of conflicting claims and intrigue. No, Riario did not think the successful candidate would be a saintly man, but a politician, a player of power games. It could be his cousin, Giuliano Rovere, a man of great abilities and violent passions; or it could be Ascanio Sforza, a member of the powerful Sforza clan and brother to the Regent of Milan, whose interest in politics was only equalled by his passion for hunting; or it could be the man who, as Vice-Chancellor of the Church, was second in rank to the Pope himself, and reputedly the wealthiest Cardinal of them all, the Spaniard, Rodrigo Borgia. Rodrigo Borgia too was the nephew of a Pope, Calixtus III, whose election just over thirty years before had founded the family fortunes. Another Borgia Pope – Riario repressed a shudder. . . . The great bell on the Capitol began to intone the death of the Pope.

The sound of the bell brought a smile to the sensual lips of the man kneeling at the *prie-dieu* in the rays of the morning sun. Rodrigo Borgia was powerfully built, with a great hooked nose and heavy jowls, olive-complexioned, dark-eyed, his grey head heavily tonsured. The Cardinal Borgia was a formidable man, in mind as well as body. The son of a relatively obscure land-owning family in Valencia, his keen

3

brain and instinct for survival, combined with initial good luck, had brought him from the olive groves of his native Jativa to a Roman palace and to the threshold of the Papacy itself. He had been only eighteen when he left Spain to accompany his uncle, Alonso Borgia, a clever lawyer who had been rewarded with a Cardinal's hat, to Italy; twenty-four when that uncle, to everyone's surprise, had been elected Pope, taking a title of Calixtus III. Within a year, his uncle had made him a Cardinal, two years later he appointed him Vice-Chancellor of the Church, and two months before his death he had lavished upon Rodrigo the see of Valencia, the richest in Spain, with a yearly income of eighteen thousand ducats. Rodrigo's astonishing good fortune seemed to have changed when his uncle died in August 1458, and a wave of anti-Spanish feeling broke over the late Pope's Spanish family and adherents. But Rodrigo used the prestige of his position as Vice-Chancellor so that the next Pope, Pius II, owed his election to Rodrigo's support, and he maintained that position through the reign of Pius, and of the two succeeding Popes, Sixtus IV and Innocent VIII, increasing in power, wealth and influence as the years went by, always working towards the ultimate goal, the Papacy for himself. He had fought for the papal crown once eight years before on the death of Pope Sixtus, against Giuliano Rovere, Sixtus's nephew. The ballot had ended in stalemate, and the cunning Giuliano had contrived to have one of his own party, Cardinal Cibo, elected as Innocent VIII. Now the tolling of the bell announced the death of Innocent, and for Rodrigo Borgia at sixty-one this would be the final throw for the great prize and, very probably, the last round with Giuliano Rovere, twelve years his junior.

But at sixty-one, Rodrigo still felt himself to be in the prime of life, with enormous vitality for everything, for politics, for hunting, and for love – especially for love. Rodrigo was possessed of a formidable sexual drive, physically attracted to women as they were to him. Even at eighteen, as a young cleric, his tutor had noted enviously that beautiful women were drawn to Rodrigo in the most

4

remarkable way, 'more powerfully than iron by a magnet'; and at twenty-five, as a young Cardinal, his licentious behaviour at a wedding party in Siena had drawn down upon him a rebuke from the Pope himself. At over sixty, Rodrigo was still the same, with all the qualities women love, a boisterous gaiety, a quick sense of humour, a hon-eyed eloquence, a majestic presence, and, above all, unashamed sexual power.

Women, Rodrigo knew, were his weakness, he could not resist them. Even now, with his body in an attitude of prayer and his mind leaping ahead to the prospects of the Conclave which the bell announced, he subconsciously relished a sensation of satisfied desire. He could not resist turning his head to look at the girl who lay in his bed.

Giulia Farnese Orsini — how beautiful she was, he thought, with the sunlight catching her rich golden hair, her smooth nineteen-year-old body glowing against the heavy brocade hangings. Rodrigo rose from his knees and, picking up a peach from a silver bowl which his favourite Chamberlain, Perotto, had placed on a table, went over to the bed. He looked down at her. Any man of his age would be proud to bed a girl like that, he thought, fondling her body. Giulia looked up at him through thick lashes, her blue eyes kindling with greedy expectancy. Rodrigo's power had already helped her family, penniless nobility from the Roman Campagna — now, if he were to become Pope, perhaps he would make her young brother Alessandro a Cardinal, and the family fortune would be made.

She moved Rodrigo's hand to the flat of her stomach. 'Does it show?' she asked petulantly.

Rodrigo did not answer, instead he fed her the rest of the peach, kissing her as she ate, licking the peach juice from her chin, caressing her.

Giulia pouted. 'I don't want it.'

'And if it were mine, not your one-eyed husband's?'

'No.'

Rodrigo looked at her fondly, almost paternally. He was sure it was his child and not that of her feeble young

5

husband, Orsino Orsini, son of his first cousin and close confidante, Adriana de Mila. He was sure of his own virility, having already fathered seven bastards, four of them by the same woman. He was passionately fond of those four children, perhaps too much so. The thought of them recalled him to the business at hand. If he succeeded, he could be the founder of a Borgia dynasty in Italy.

'Get up, my child,' he told her, 'there are many things I must do today.'

Giulia slipped out of bed and pressed herself against him. 'Will you now be Pope?' she asked.

Rodrigo folded her in his arms, the great red sleeves of his Cardinal's robes engulfing her. 'That depends on what I hear, say and do over these coming days,' he said. 'You must forgive me if I neglect you now.'

He released her. 'Now go, Giulia, I must work.'

Giulia pirouetted in the doorway leading out of the bedchamber. 'Am I still desirable?' she asked coquettishly. When she received no answer, she pouted childishly and disappeared through the door into the adjoining chamber. Rodrigo's attention was no longer upon her, his hand was already on the bell to summon his secret Chamberlain.

Pedro Calderon, known as Perotto, came quickly. A handsome young man in clerical dress, dark and curly-haired, he was a Spaniard, as were all the trusted servants of Rodrigo's household. Although it was now more than thirty years since Rodrigo Borgia had left his native Valencia in the train of his uncle, Alonso Borgia, a newly-made Cardinal, he was still a Spaniard at heart, and liked to be surrounded by Spaniards, using Spanish as a family language with his children, Cesare, Juan, Lucrezia and Jofre.

Perotto glanced automatically at the rumpled bed, as if expecting to see Giulia still lying there.

Rodrigo saw the look and said sharply, 'What news?'

Perotto cast down his eyes respectfully, 'Your Eminence may be confident of success this time ...'

Rodrigo cut him short impatiently, 'So I thought before. I need not remind you of the saying that he who goes into

6

the Conclave a Pope, comes out a Cardinal still. How many Cardinals do not come to the Conclave?'

'Four, Your Eminence.'

'So I must be assured of fourteen votes ... What news of Cardinal Rovere?'

'They say the French have offered him two hundred thousand ducats to buy his way to the Holy Chair ...'

'A heavy sum for Charles of France to wager upon his horse winning the race. But then he could hardly have offered them to me, a good Spaniard.'

'Will Your Eminence then treat with Giuliano Rovere?'

'Useless, Perotto. Giuliano hates me. Have you forgot the insults we exchanged over the deathbed of Pope Innocent? We have wrestled for this prize before – this will be the final round.'

Rodrigo stopped and stared down at the great emerald episcopal ring on his finger. 'Giuliano may have his two hundred thousand ducats, he will need twice that to satisfy a man like Ascanio Sforza, and then there are others just as greedy as he ... I think I shall have more to offer, I am Vice-Chancellor, I have this palace, the finest after Riario's, I have my bishopric of Porto, my abbey of Subiaco ... Yes, I think I can outdo Giuliano. And then again, these French ducats may prove like millstones round his neck, there are Cardinals who will not like this French alliance of his. How came you by the news?'

'Your Eminence, I know a wench who creeps into many beds, and that of the Cardinal Rovere's Chamberlain among them ...'

'So let her spread the tale. If it were known to come from me, it would be said that I invented it to discredit Giuliano. I shall deny it. With horror. Let it thrive upon denial until I am forced ... at a favourable moment ... to acknowledge its truth. So speed your wench upon her way, with my blessing – and what encouragement you deem necessary. Be economical, Perotto, not more than one servant in each Cardinal's house – but for the Cardinal Sforza, he is the key ...'

*   *   *

Cardinal Ascanio Sforza, a thin, dark man with a look of cunning about him, sat facing Giuliano Rovere across a table in a room of Rovere's fortress at Ostia dominating the mouth of the Tiber. Between them stood an exquisite flagon of rock crystal and two intricately-worked silver goblets. Ascanio took a sip of wine from his goblet and made a wry face. Giuliano Rovere was a connoisseur of art, not of food and wine. But the luxury-loving Ascanio had not come to Ostia to enjoy the pleasures of the table, but to seek advantages of a more permanent nature. Although he knew he had no real chance of the Papacy, he could command a number of votes and he was determined to sell them for the highest price. He looked over the rim of his goblet at Giuliano sitting opposite, impassive, impressive, a man not to be underestimated, still less to be crossed.

Giuliano had the mind and body of a giant, the face of a Roman Emperor and the soaring ambition of an eagle. He was a subtle politician who had known how to survive the collapse of the Riario family fortunes on the death of his uncle, Sixtus, who had made him a Cardinal. He was a man of violent and ungovernable rages and he was also a great hater. Above all men he hated Rodrigo Borgia. A sudden fit of anger gripped him at the thought of Rodrigo. He got up abruptly and began to pace the room with long strides. 'We've had one Borgia Pope in his uncle, Calixtus,' he told Ascanio fiercely, 'another would destroy the Church.'

'You underestimate its resilience.' Ascanio was calm, waiting.

'And you the greed of those Catalans,' Giuliano retorted. 'Money, women, and family ambition are all Rodrigo Borgia cares for. He uses the privileges of his Vice-Chancellorship to sell pardons to murderers, saying that it's not God's will that they should die, but that they should live and pay ...' Catching the ghost of a smile crossing the younger man's face, he stopped his tirade, turning to the business in hand: 'Is the richest Prince of the Church to make himself Pope because a Cardinal's vote can be bought for two mule-loads of silver?'

8

'Your revenues too are great, Giuliano,' Ascanio said quietly.

There was no need to say more, the subject had been introduced and both men understood each other. But as a Sforza, Ascanio was interested in power as well as money, and there was something which he wanted more than a share of Giuliano's French ducats: the greatest office in the Church would be at Giuliano's disposal should he become Pope. Silence fell upon the room, as the two men looked warily at each other, sizing one another up.

Now it was Ascanio's turn to rise from the table. He crossed to the vaulted window, looking down on the sea shimmering in the summer heat. 'It's said your cousin, Domenico, will be given the Vice-Chancellorship should you be elected,' he said casually, turning in time to note a tightening of the muscles of Giuliano's jaw. 'An able man ...'

Rovere was tight-lipped, 'Indeed he is.'

'But in poor health and the office will be burdensome.'

'Should he be given it.'

'He would bring you but one vote. The office would be a positive inducement to one with a greater following.'

There was a long silence. Giuliano said nothing. So that is it, Ascanio thought. For all his protestations of caring only for the Church, Giuliano intended to follow the well-established tradition laid down by his uncle, Pope Sixtus, and the Borgia Pope, Calixtus. Power was to remain with the family. Very well then, he would accept nomination as a papal candidate and sit on the fence at the Conclave. Unwise, perhaps, to commit himself so early anyway, and it was Borgia after all who presently held the office he coveted. To discomfit Giuliano he voiced his last thought aloud.

'It is, after all, the Cardinal Borgia who holds the office at present,' he said evenly, moving towards the door. 'He too will be a strong candidate ... And now, Giuliano, I fear it is time to take my leave of you. Business calls me to Rome.'

'Ascanio,' Giuliano put a hand on his shoulder almost pleadingly, 'do not trust Rodrigo Borgia. Remember that

9

he too has a family, a brood of bastards. Already I have heard reports of the Catalan arrogance of his first-born, Cesare Borgia, whom he has made Bishop of Pamplona, although he is only seventeen. At Pisa, where he attends the university, the luxury of his household rivals that of the young Medici, Lorenzo's son, and they say that he is surrounded by Spanish cut-throats. Take care that the bull-calf may not be worse than the bull who sired him.'

* * *

Cesare Borgia, Bishop of Pamplona, was hawking in the hills near Siena when he heard the sound for which he had been waiting – the bells announcing the death of Pope Innocent. In looks he did not resemble his father Rodrigo in the least, having inherited the fine features and fresh complexion of his Roman mother, Vannozza Cattanei, together with her dark hair with its reddish glint. He was tall and well built, a powerful athlete who delighted in riding and swordsmanship. He liked too to show off his strength, wrestling with the peasants in the country villages and running races with them. Like most noblemen of his time he was a passionate hunter and proud of his string of hunting dogs and coursers; indeed his horse was favourite to win the race for the Palio at Siena, even against the Marquis of Mantua's famous stable of Gonzaga horses.

With these accomplishments he had inherited his father's brains and was acknowledged to be the most brilliant student of his year at Pisa, but there was little of the churchman about him; he liked to wear rich velvet and silk as his contemporaries did, and to carry a sword at his belt. His only concession to his episcopal status as Bishop of Pamplona, which he had never visited, was a tiny shaven spot on the crown of his head, a token tonsure. He had a hardness and fierceness in his temperament that did not come from his father, a nature that did not forgive insult or injury, and he bitterly resented the contempt he knew the young Italian aristocrats at the university felt for him. Medicis, Orsinis, Estes, they were all related, and looked down on him as an outsider, a Catalan bastard. His fine lips curved in a vindictive smile as he heard the bells. Now he would show them all. Now they would have to bend their proud necks and come crawling to him – if his father were to become Pope. With a gesture of defiance to all Italy, he threw his hawk from his wrist and watched it spiralling upwards in its cruel flight.

Gian Paolo Baglioni, riding beside him, looked at Cesare intently. He had heard the bells, and he too knew what they could portend. Although Gian Paolo belonged to the ruling house of Perugia, a family known for its savagery and quarrelsomeness, Cesare had dominated him since they had first met there as boys at the Sapienza. Gian Paolo was a little afraid of him. Although he could be the best of companions – charming, witty, good-natured – there was a black side to his character which Gian Paolo had occasionally seen and preferred not to remember. Still, there was something about him that made men follow him, and, if his father were to become Pope, who could tell where destiny might not lead Cesare Borgia, and Gian Paolo Baglioni with him?

Three horsemen approached them, cantering through an olive grove to their right. As they came nearer, Cesare's face darkened. 'The brothers Orsini,' he said contemptuously.

Giovanni Orsini reined in his black gelding beside Cesare. 'So, it's the young bull-calf,' he said sarcastically.

His brother Paolo, more tactful, said appeasingly, 'Good-day, My Lord Cesare.'

Some distance behind the servant accompanying them, a huge, powerfully-built Spaniard, Miguel da Corella, known as Michelotto, watched the scene intently.

Giovanni Orsini went on, recklessly taunting Cesare, 'The Borgia bull-calf with a discreet tonsure between his tiny horns.'

'Your brother's manners have not improved, Paolo,' Cesare said with a cold smile.

Giovanni gave a mocking bow, 'My humble apologies, Your Grace. Will the learned Bishop of Pamplona forgive me, and grant me his blessing?'

Paolo Orsini and Gian Paolo Baglioni exchanged nervous glances, but Cesare appeared unmoved. Lifting his left hand, he made the reverse sign of the cross to Giovanni. 'May Lucifer go with you, my son. In the name of the goat, the toad, and the serpent,' he said.

Furious, Giovanni's hand moved to his sword-belt. Behind him, Michelotto moved his horse forward, quietly menacing, his eyes always on Cesare. Paolo Orsini, putting out a restraining hand to his brother, pleaded with Cesare, 'Do not provoke us, My Lord.'

'I have no quarrel with you, Paolo Orsini,' Cesare answered, 'you were a friend when we were children at Montegiordano.'

'And would be still.'

'While his father beds our cousin's wife,' Giovanni interrupted.

There was a meaning note in Cesare's voice as he replied, 'No doubt your cousin will profit from her experience.'

In the silence that followed, the bells of Siena could be heard, underlining Cesare's words.

'You will wager against my horse for the Palio, Paolo?' he said lightly.

'A hundred ducats,' Paolo smiled with relief.

'And against my father for Pope?'

Slowly, Paolo Orsini shook his head.

*   *   *

In Rome the preparations for the Conclave were already taking place, supervised by the Vatican Master of Ceremonies, Johann Burchard, a fussy, punctilious German cleric. Carpenters were erecting wooden cells for the Cardinals in the Sala Reale, while Burchard checked off the articles considered necessary to make their eminences' lives bearable during the nights they would have to spend there until a Pope should have been elected. It was Burchard's second Concalve and he was well versed in his role. No one knew more about the workings of the Vatican than he. Alert to all the gossip and intrigue of the papal court, he had been noting down the doings of the palace in a secret diary which he had kept through the reigns of the last two Popes. Now, naturally, like everyone else, he was speculating as to who would be his next master in the Vatican though, like the cautious German he was, he was not laying bets on the outcome as many inveterate Roman gamblers did. Burchard simply kept his ear close to the ground. He had heard all the rumours: that in the first Conclave the Portuguese and Venetian Cardinals would be nominated, but that for the second round the choice might lie between Rovere, backed by France, and Sforza, backed by Milan and Venice. Like most shrewd observers, he considered Rodrigo Borgia's chances good, since he was bound to no man. The neutral Italian Cardinals would dislike the thought of France as much as they would the dizzy promotion of the Sforza family. And it must not be forgotten that the Cardinal Borgia was the richest of them all, and would therefore have more to give ...

On 6th August, the Conclave assembled in the Sistine Chapel, a room of noble proportions built some twenty years before by Rovere's uncle, Sixtus, and as yet not glorified by the frescoes of Michelangelo. Against the white walls the Cardinals' robes blazed out scarlet as they sat in ranks under canopies of green and purple. In the centre of the chapel upon a table was placed a golden chalice containing the voting papers of the assembled Conclave. The Cardinal-Deacon was reading out the results:

'Upon the second vote of the second day, the votes cast this morning for Cardinals Zeno and Costa having been transferred to the second preferences on the papers, the figures now are ...' with a bow in the direction of Rovere, 'for the Cardinal-Presbyter of San Pietro ad Vincula, nine votes.' Then, bowing towards Ascanio Sforza, 'For the Cardinal-Deacon of San Vito and San Modesto, seven votes.' And, finally, bowing towards Rodrigo Borgia, 'For the Cardinal-Bishop of Porto and Santa Rufina, Vice-Chancellor of the Holy Roman Church, five votes. There being no majority of two-thirds, the papers will be burned, and the voting will be resumed tomorrow morning.'

While the useless papers were ceremonially burned, the Cardinals retired with a rustling of silken robes to their quarters in the adjoining Sala Reale where the real business of the Conclave would begin.

Fourteen votes. The magic figure was emblazoned across Rodrigo Borgia's mind as he knelt at the *prie-dieu* in his cell, apparently at prayer. Perotto's domestic intelligence had told him much that he wanted to know: one aged Cardinal was deeply in debt – that could easily be remedied; the Cardinal-Deacon of Santa Maria Nuova, the representative of the Orsini, offered the fortresses of Soria and Montecelli by Rovere, had set his heart on the rich revenues of the cathedral of Cartagena which were in Rodrigo's gift; the Cardinal Colonna had his eyes on the prestigious abbey of Subiaco, also Rodrigo's; the Cardinal Sanseverino, a Sforza supporter, could, he thought, be bullied rather than bought. Then there was always Ascanio...

* * *

While Rodrigo bought votes, Cesare in Siena was making certain in his own unscrupulous fashion that his horse would win the Palio. He could not bear to lose, not even a horse race, and least of all the Palio, a prize coveted by every horseman in Italy, and usually won by the famous stable of the Gonzagas at Mantua. He had set guard over his horse to prevent the henchmen of other owners as unscrupulous as he from tampering with the animal or its harness, and he had taken care that several of the more fancied runners would not stay the course. Mantua's stable was, however, impregnable, and it was Mantua's horse that he had to fear.

In the stable the night before the race, Cesare was giving his final instructions to his jockey, Luigi: 'If the race is all but over, and the Mantuan pressing you hard...'

'He'll not get close,' Luigi assured him.

Cesare made an impatient gesture. 'You misunderstand

me, fool. If he does, then fall against him as if by accident. Bring him and his horse down, if you can. With you astride or not, my beast must win.'

As he spoke, a dust-covered messenger entered the stable. Seeing the Borgia bull embroidered on the man's chest, Cesare knew it must be a message from his father. His heart leapt as he gripped the man's arm. 'My father sends for me?'

The man shook his head. Cesare dropped his hand, attempting to mask his disappointment. 'No message?'

'My Lord, you are to remain here, or ride no nearer Rome than Spoleto.'

Cesare spoke through clenched teeth, 'Is my brother Juan in Rome?'

Reluctantly, the messenger nodded. With a muttered curse in Spanish, Cesare pushed him aside and strode out of the stable, his eyes clouded with jealousy and anger.

Rage blunted his normal wariness; a wise man with powerful enemies does not walk the streets alone at night. Suddenly behind him Cesare heard the soft steps of an assassin. Before he had time to turn round, the man's arm was round his neck, a dagger at his throat. But Cesare was young and strong, and the attacker seemed half-hearted and was easily overpowered. With his own dagger at the assassin's neck, Cesare saw that his assailant was the burly Orsini servant, Michelotto. 'In the name of Christ, Señor, do not kill me!' he cried out in Spanish. Momentarily taken aback, Cesare relaxed his grip. Michelotto sprang upon him and pinned him to the ground, his knife once more at Cesare's throat. 'You've much to learn, My Lord Bishop,' the Spaniard said grinning. 'Never hesitate when the knife is drawn.'

'Then why do you?' Cesare was puzzled. 'I saw you riding with Giovanni Orsini. Did he . . .?'

'A tight-purse master. How generous are you?'

'I'd be wise to outbid him then,' Cesare said, relieved. He had thought this man was sent to kill him on Orsini's orders.

'I would join your household, My Lord. You see I know my trade.'

Cesare nodded. He had no choice. Besides, this man might be useful. 'So let me up,' he said. 'A Bishop may sometimes have need of a strong arm – and a quick steel.'

Michelotto helped him respectfully to his feet. Feigning weakness, Cesare leant wearily against the wall before springing upon the man, the point of his dagger beneath Michelotto's chin. 'So you want to join my service, do you?' he said grimly. 'Who are you, and why do you want to serve me?'

This time Michelotto was genuinely afraid, sensing the ruthlessness and wariness of the man whose knife was at his throat. 'Miguel da Corella, My Lord, from Aragon, called Michelotto. I am a Spaniard and have no love for these Italians. Besides, I am ambitious, and they say your father will be Pope.'

Cesare released him, sheathing his knife. 'So he may be, Señor Michelotto. But in my service you must heed your own precept, never hesitate when your knife is drawn . . .'

*   *   *

In Rome, the third day's voting had ended in stalemate, with none of the three candidates having the required two-thirds majority. Rodrigo Borgia, having gained the vote of Sanseverino and another Cardinal, now stood with seven votes in second place to Rovere with eight, Sforza having fallen back to third place but still controlling six votes. Seven and six equalled thirteen. Rodrigo thought the time had come to offer Ascanio Sforza what he wanted. That night the two men met in Rodrigo's cell. Ascanio drove a hard bargain. Rodrigo offered him the castle of Nepi and his own splendid palace on the Banchi Vecchi, the revenues of Agria and three mule-loads of silver. Ascanio still held out for the Vice-Chancellorship. Rodrigo was well aware what that would mean should he become Pope – a public demonstration of his support for Ascanio's brother, the intriguing ambitious Ludovico Sforza of Milan. Mentally Rodrigo shrugged his shoulders. If he accepted Ascanio's terms, he would be virtually certain of the Papacy with only one vote left to go.

'Very well. The Vice-Chancellorship,' he said quietly. 'Is that all?'

It was not, and Rodrigo knew it. Ascanio spelt it out, 'My brother Ludovico hopes that a new Pope will acknowledge his title to the dukedom of Milan,' he said pointedly.

'Your nephew, Duke Gian Galeazzo of Milan, is gravely ill?' Rodrigo enquired with an air of innocence.

'We fear he may be.'

'Then I see no obstacle, your brother is Regent,' Rodrigo replied with a tone of finality.

Undeterred by Rodrigo's manner, Sforza still had more to ask. 'The Duke, my brother, would rejoice to see our alliance pledged in a marriage bed. Your niece, the Lady Lucrezia, with our nephew, Giovanni Sforza, Lord of Pesaro.'

Rodrigo frowned. 'She is already betrothed...'

'To an insignificant Spaniard. Dissolve it.'

There was no point in hesitating further. With Ascanio as Vice-Chancellor, the world would know he had committed himself to the Sforzas. 'So be it,' he said.

As the door of the cell closed on Ascanio Sforza, Rodrigo stifled a shout of triumph. He knew that he had won. The prize he had coveted for over thirty long years would be his. He would become the most powerful man in the world. He fell to his knees and thanked God with sincerity.

*   *   *

On the morning of 11th August 1492, under a leaden sky lit by fitful flashes of lightning, and to the constant background rumble of thunder, the crowd waiting outside St Peter's saw a window open, a cross held high. In the sudden hush, a voice cried: '*Pontificem habemus* ... We have a Pope!' Rodrigo Borgia had become Pope Alexander VI. While the Orsini and their friends grumbled, and the aristocratic families of Italy looked down their noses at the Borgia Pope, the people of Rome rejoiced. The new Pope was popular, jovial – and generous. Indeed the coronation was the most splendid within living memory, and Rodrigo's reception by his new subjects rapturous. As he rode on a white horse from St Peter's to the Lateran basilica, through streets adorned with triumphal arches and decorated with the Borgia bull rampant, the crowds roared 'Alexander! Alexander the Great!'

Sweating under the heavy papal tiara in the blazing August heat, tears of joy mingling with the sweat, Rodrigo's eyes sought those of the people he loved the most, discreetly assembled on a balcony above St Peter's square. His cousin Adriana de Mila, mother-in-law of Giulia Farnese and guardian of his beloved daughter Lucrezia, stood in the foreground, middle-aged but still handsome with her dark Spanish looks. Beside her stood Giulia, her wonderful golden hair caught back in a glittering net of gold thread and precious stones, and twelve-year-old Lucrezia, the darling of his heart, the child, he thought, who most resembled him, even if she were fair where he was dark. Behind the women his second son Juan lounged, affecting nonchalance in his peacock clothes, a large diamond blazing in his hat, and next to him the youngest, Jofre, yet a child and unable to keep still with excitement. In the background, as usual, stood the cuckold Orsino Orsini, Giulia's husband, glaring sullenly with his remaining good eye. One figure was notably absent, that of Cesare. A shadow crossed Rodrigo's face at the thought of his eldest son. He knew Cesare would not understand his refusal to let him come to Rome, that he would bitterly resent it. But then the boy was after all a Bishop, and as such would have had to be present at the ceremonies – an embarrassment. Besides, he would have resented the lowly position he would have had to occupy, and when Cesare's pride was hurt there was always the devil to pay. Rodrigo sighed to himself, why was life always so difficult when Cesare was there?

Cesare *was* furious. Even the fact that his horse had won the Palio (although the victory was contested by the Marquis of Mantua who claimed that Cesare's jockey had cheated) could not compensate for the bitter fact that he alone of all the family was excluded from his father's triumph. And on his father's explicit orders. As if to underline the insult, he had been intercepted at Spleto by Perotto, whom he had never liked, with a second instruction to proceed no further. Brushing aside the compensatory promises of the archbishopric of Valencia with its sixteen thousand ducats yearly revenue, and of a palace of his own in Trastevere, Cesare exploded in fury against the terrified Perotto, 'But *I'm* not to come to Rome! To the devil with appearances! They're all there already, all of them but me!'

At that moment he hated his father, hated his authority over him, hated him for his favouritism towards his younger brother Juan. Cesare ground his teeth in rage and frustration, but he could do nothing else but obey. He would wait. One day his time would come.

*　　*　　*

'Where is your beloved Cesare?'

Giulia Farnese's voice held a note of spite as she addressed Lucrezia Borgia. The two girls were sitting in a long gallery hung with tapestries in Adriana de Mila's house, the Palace of Santa Maria in Portico. Formerly the residence of a Cardinal, it was now the seraglio of the women whom Rodrigo Borgia loved, and, like a harem, it was situated conveniently – adjoining the Vatican.

Lucrezia shivered as a cold March draught pierced the gallery, rippling the tapestries along the walls. Eight months had passed since her father's coronation, and still he had not allowed Cesare to come back to Rome. She bit her lip to conceal the vexation Giulia's question had caused her. 'At Spoleto,' she replied shortly.

Now almost thirteen, Lucrezia was already a woman, and although she did not have the ripe golden beauty of her father's mistress, she possessed the animal grace and sexual magnetism of her family in full degree. She was fair, blue-eyed, her profile having a slight suggestion of Rodrigo's powerful nose and receding chin, giving a strength and interest to her appearance which Giulia's classical features lacked. Her neck, unlike Rodrigo's, was long and graceful, her hair pale blonde where his was dark, but her expression had the same quick mobility as her father's, and her nature, like his, was essentially buoyant and joyous. She did not like Giulia, of whose relationship with her adored father she was well aware, and she knew too that Giulia was jealous and resentful of the passionate affection which Rodrigo lavished on his daughter. With deliberate insolence, she opened her big blue eyes wide and looked at Giulia, letting her glance travel critically over the other girl's figure, still heavy with the after effects of having given birth to a child, Rodrigo's daughter.

'Cesare wrote to me the other day,' Lucrezia went on, affecting innocence; 'he calls you the Bride of Christ, isn't that amusing? He says other people call you other names which he scruples to write to me until I am a married woman...'

'Take care, Lucrezia.' Giulia's voice was malevolent.

But Lucrezia continued, enjoying herself. She liked baiting Giulia who was slow and, despite her seven years' advantage in age, no match for the younger girl's quick wit.

Apparently changing the subject, she went on innocently, 'Cesare says that when women become fat they lose their wits as well as their beauty ... I shall not become fat.'

'So that your dear brother Cesare will still love you.' Giulia's voice had an ugly note.

Lucrezia rose from her seat and went over to the window, not wishing to expose herself further to that hateful girl's insinuations. Giulia Farnese with her sensual body and mercenary mind could never understand the love between her and Cesare, an intensity of feeling, a unity of mind and body that made the two of them as one being against the world. She closed her eyes. Cesare's dark young face, as it had looked in their childhood days in the Orsini palace at Montegiordano, rose before her; she seemed to hear his fierce voice whisper in her ear as they clung together in the great bed the night before he was to leave for the university at Perugia. '... The two of us, Lucia, against the world ...

Together we can do anything. We must be faithful to each other . . . for ever and ever. You must be faithful to me alone . . .' She shivered again; this time it was not because of the cold wind. She adored Cesare, loved him above everyone else, yet sometimes the strength of his feelings for her frightened her, and she felt a subconscious urge to escape from his domination of her. Still, she longed to see him, and wondered whether he had yet arrived in Rome, for he had written to her that he would come soon, with or without their father's permission.

*   *   *

Cesare was already in Rome, at their mother Vannozza's house in the Piazza Pizzo di Merlo. Vannozza, whose fine Roman features still retained traces of the beauty that had held the fickle Rodrigo Borgia in thrall for twelve years, greeted him warmly; the bond between them was strong. Cesare was her favourite son, indeed her favourite child of the four children she had borne to Rodrigo Borgia, possibly because of his strong physical resemblance to herself, possibly also because they both seemed to suffer from the withdrawal of Rodrigo's love. The second son, Juan, handsome, curly-haired, vain, charming and indolent, had always been his father's favourite among the boys. Jofre was the runt of the litter, whom Rodrigo, for reasons of his own, had always been unwilling to acknowledge as his son. As for Lucrezia . . . Vannozza felt sorry for the girl who was so much a Borgia that she seemed to have nothing of her mother in her, the object of the passionate devotion of both her father and eldest brother and yet another source of the rivalry between them. Indeed the unnatural strength of their feelings for Lucrezia disquieted Vannozza; Rodrigo's passions, she well knew, were uncontrollable. Once he had loved her as passionately, although she had been over thirty when she met him, and therefore no longer young. But in the end his physical needs had driven him to younger women, and in the year of Jofre's birth, 1481, he had married her off to a suitable husband, then, when he died, to a second convenient candidate, Carlo Canale. Poor insignificant Carlo, she thought as she saw her husband come forward, nervously rubbing his hands and grimacing welcomingly at Cesare who, as usual, ignored him. He kissed her mother's hand, then folded her in his arms. Vannozza gently pushed him from her, standing back to look at him admiringly. How handsome he was, she thought, and so much a man. Not like Juan whom Rodrigo loved. She sighed, aware of Juan's eyes upon them, jealously.

'Why are you in Rome?' Juan interrupted them. 'You were not given leave to return.'

Cesare ignored him. 'When is Lucrezia to be wed to Sforza?' he asked his mother.

'In the summer,' Vannozza replied, a shadow clouding her face. It was not the marriage she would have chosen for her only daughter, still so young. But in this, as in all other matters regarding her children, she had no choice. Rodrigo's will must be obeyed. This ill-matched marriage was but the price of the Papacy.

Her youngest son, Jofre, a dark, ill-favoured imp who enjoyed exploiting the rivalry between his older brothers, could contain himself no longer. 'Cesare,' he said, 'did you know that Juan is to be Captain-General of the Church?'

Everyone was silent, waiting for the explosion, but Cesare said nothing, only tightening his grip on his mother's hand so that she winced. Juan saw this, and smiled mockingly. He knew how much it hurt Cesare that he should be the soldier and Cesare the priest. It had been decreed so by their father since they were small children, while their elder half-brother Pedro Luis was still alive, fighting in the service of the King of Aragon, as befitted the eldest son. Thus Cesare, the second son, had been destined for the Church, even though he wanted to be a soldier more than anything in the world. Juan himself had no taste for fighting, caring only for clothes and pleasure, but the panoply of war pleased his vanity. He liked the idea of himself, in glittering armour and plumed helmet specially

22

made for him by the finest armourer in Milan, riding at the head of a magnificently-equipped procession, with the great banner of the Church floating above him. He had no notion of war, and pictured his role as Captain-General to be very much what it was now, when he caracoled on a fine courser caparisoned with silver bells in procession before his father, with his intimate friend, the Turkish Prince Djem, beside him.

'Juan will be a General when soldiers pluck flowers,' Cesare said between his teeth.

Jofre laughed, and Juan started forward angrily.

Vanozza put her hand anxiously on Cesare's arm, but her voice was firm and authoritative when she spoke. 'He's your brother, and this is my house. You'll not depart from it in anger, either of you.'

Cesare shrugged his shoulders; the look in his eyes was veiled, concealing any emotion. 'My father's a fool to favour him.'

'Your father loves you,' she reassured him.

'And tried to keep me from Rome,' he replied sardonically.

'Be patient, Cesare, he will make it up to you, I know it.' She held him at arm's length, looking at him intently. 'What is it you want of him — and of life? Love...? Riches...?'

Cesare spoke softly, so that only she could hear. 'No, mother mine. Power.' He kissed her hand. 'And now I go to see Our Holy Father...'

*　　*　　*

Rodrigo received Cesare with cold formality, seated on the papal throne in the Sala del Pappagallo, as if to emphasise the disparity between their respective stations. He was displeased with Cesare for having come to Rome without leave, and before he had had time to complete his plans for Lucrezia and Juan which he wished to take precedence over any arrangements he might make with regard to his troublesome eldest son. Cesare, he was sure, would try to

23

force his hand. Rodrigo's voice, therefore, was distant when he asked, 'Your mother is well?'

Cesare nodded. 'Yes.'

'Where are you lodged?'

'In the palace of the Borgo.' Cesare raised his eyebrows enquiringly, 'Am I welcome?'

Rodrigo said sternly, 'You come to Rome without our permission. You wear silk and velvet and carry a sword. You've hired an assassin, Perotto says. None of this is seemly in an Archbishop. Even at seventeen.'

Cesare bent his head to display his small tonsure, indicating it lightly with his hand. Then he lifted his head and smiled. 'Any man with the courage to stand above me may see that I'm a servant of God.'

Rodrigo smiled in spite of himself. He rose to his feet and stepped down from the dais to take Cesare by the shoulders, embracing him. 'Cesare ... Cesare ...' he said, 'what other man has such a son?'

'What other son must call his father uncle?'

Rodrigo released him, a look of disappointment tinged with embarrassment on his face. 'Aye, your mother said ... I'll not buy your love!'

'I want a Cardinal's hat,' Cesare demanded.

'I was twenty-five before I became a ...'

'You're giving one to Alessandro Farnese. Do I come second to the brother of your whore? Are you afraid of me?'

Rodrigo defended himself. 'You're not eligible for the Sacred College. You're illegitimate.'

'I'm what my mother made me. And may be what you choose. You are Pope.'

Rodrigo turned away from him wearily. When he spoke his voice was that of an old man weighed down with the cares of the world. His histrionic ability had served him well throughout his career. He used it now to ward off a difficult issue, and to gain his son's sympathy. 'Yes, we are Pope,' he said heavily, 'and carry the world upon our shoulders like a patient ass. We hold the future of Holy Church in trembling hands. The fate of Italy to us appears dark and we weep for it. When King Ferrante of Naples dies, as he soon must,

24

France and Spain will surely grapple in the belly of Italy, unless I prevent it. Pray for us, my son...'

'Bravo.' Cesare's voice was ironical. 'Is the Duke of Gandia to be your Captain-General in the face of this future?'

Rodrigo evaded the issue, his manner becoming suddenly brisk. 'Your brother Juan goes to Spain when Lucrezia's wed. As our envoy, and will himself marry anyone they have to offer in Aragon. A royal bride, perhaps, or one of King Ferdinand's family. So much for Spain. As for France, Lucrezia's marriage to a Sforza will protect us from the French, Ludovico of Milan's dear allies ... You see, I take you into my confidence and trust.'

'What trust? I'm kept from Rome, while Juan attends your court, holding hands with an Ottoman savage.'

'Prince Djem is a hostage. The Sultan pays us forty thousand ducats a year to keep him here.'

Cesare said fiercely, 'I've a better way with Turks. Release me from my see and I'll offer my sword to the Knights of Rhodes.'

Rodrigo was impassive, calling his son's bluff, 'If you wish.'

'You know I do not!'

Rodrigo shook his head in mock despair. As he moved over to a desk and took up a paper lying upon it, a faint triumphant smile played about his lips. 'This,' he shook the paper in Cesare's direction, 'has kept you from Rome. The Cardinals have been examining your legitimacy and have decided that you are the lawful son of the Lady Vannozza by her first husband. We shall issue a Bull accordingly.'

Cesare interrupted rudely, 'And I shall nail it to the door of a brothel!'

Rodrigo continued as if he had not spoken. 'By a second Bull, private and unpromulgated, we shall acknowledge you as our son. It will give us great joy...'

'And myself a Cardinal's hat?'

'You shall be Cardinal of Valencia, my son. Does that not please you?'

His voice pleaded with Cesare for some sign of gratitude

25

or affection. But Cesare merely bowed. 'In anticipation of your paternal kindness, Holy Father,' he said, 'I have brought you a gift...'

Cesare moved to the door to admit a young page dressed in green velvet, who knelt before the Pope. As the page did so, Cesare, grinning, swept the cap from the boyish head, releasing a wave of dark hair that was undoubtedly a girl's. She was exquisite, slim, olive-skinned, and not more than sixteen.

'Enjoy her, father,' Cesare said, amused.

*   *   *

Three months later, in June 1493, Lucrezia, now just thirteen, was married to Giovanni Sforza, Lord of Pesaro, in fulfilment of Rodrigo's pledge to the Sforzas before his election. The marriage was celebrated in the Vatican, and was followed by a banquet in the papal palace to which only the most beautiful women of the Roman nobility had been invited, along with the wives of the envoys whose presence could not be avoided. It was the first of those Borgia family festivities which were to cause such scandal throughout Italy, and indeed the whole Christian world, much of which could be attributed to the boisterous, some might say licentious, behaviour of the Pope.

Rodrigo was enjoying himself hugely. In high good humour he moved among the dancers performing alongside the tables ranged round the Sala dei Misteri, jesting with the envoys and courtiers, flirting with their wives, and scattering the slivered sugared almonds called confetti over the guests. One audacious woman pelted him with a handful of the sweetmeats, to be rewarded by a papal hand filled with confetti thrusting into the cleavage between her breasts.

It was a warm night, and most of the guests had been eating and drinking heavily, their faces flushed and sweating. In contrast, the thirteen-year-old bride was as white and cold as the unmelted snow chilling the wine in the great silver buckets. Dressed in silver and white brocade, with a fillet of silver and pearls entwined in her blonde hair, the only live thing about her seemed to be the glow of the rubies round her neck, the Sforzas' wedding present. Beside her, the bridegroom, Giovanni Sforza, looked sulky and uncomfortable. Sulky because his bride remained unmoved by his tentative advances, uncomfortable because he could occasionally catch obscene references to himself made by the more uninhibited and intoxicated wedding guests. Lucrezia hardly noticed him, or the warmly clammy touch of his hand; she was thinking of Cesare, sure that his misery at this marriage was as great as hers. The heady scent of bergamot assailed her nostrils, she felt rather than saw Giulia's cheek, now the colour of an over-ripe peach, heard her voice hiss in her ear, 'Where is your brother Cesare?'

Lucrezia stared straight in front of her as if she had not heard.

Giulia continued to vent her spite. 'Does he love you no more now that you are a bride?'

Receiving no answer, she said in a voice loud enough for others to hear, 'I saw him at your nuptial mass – sick-green at the thought of your nuptial bed...'

There was the sound of a sharp slap. Adriana de Mila had come to the rescue. 'Hold your tongue, you slut,' she whispered fiercely to her daughter-in-law.

Many hours later, as Lucrezia was dancing with Juan, she almost fainted from exhaustion. Swiftly, a concerned Rodrigo was at her side, cradling her in his arms. Drunken voices shouted for a bedding, the public climax of any wedding celebration, which was much enjoyed by the guests. But Rodrigo shook his head, as he looked at the sulky Giovanni Sforza. 'Have you forgotten the contract, my son?' he asked.

'The contract?'

'It was stipulated, was it not, that the Lady Lucrezia being too young for the duties of marriage, no consummation was to take place until a year had passed ... Enough!' he called to Lucrezia's ladies. 'Take her to bed.' He bent his head and kissed his daughter tenderly on the lips, his mouth seeming to linger on hers longer than was necessary for a paternal caress. Adriana de Mila drew in her breath disapprovingly, while Giulia looked venomous. Giovanni Sforza turned away, all too aware of the grinning faces about him, seeking his uncle, Ascanio, for comfort.

Ascanio Sforza, representing his family at the feast, watched the scene wearily. He had been an unenthusiastic participant in the celebrations, not from any sense of outraged propriety, but simply because, from the Sforza point of view, this alliance was already out of date. There were rumours that Rodrigo intended other marriages for his family which would place him and thus the Papacy in the opposite camp. It was said that an envoy from King Ferdinand of Spain would shortly arrive in Rome with offers of an advantageous match with a member of the royal house of Aragon for the Pope's second son, Juan Borgia, who, moreover, was already Duke of Gandia and thus a grandee of Spain. Worse still was the rumour that the Pope's third son, young Jofre, was to be betrothed to a bastard granddaughter of King Ferdinand's kinsman, King Ferrante of Naples, sworn foe to Ludovico of Milan. Ascanio had no need of a soothsayer to predict which way Rodrigo Borgia's loyalties would turn in the event of a struggle between France and Spain over the kingdom of Naples in Italy. Once a Spaniard, always a Spaniard, Ascanio thought contemptuously. It might yet turn out, he reflected, that in allying himself thus closely with the cause of Spain and Aragon in Naples, Rodrigo Borgia would find that he had paid too high a price for the marriages of his bastard sons. It was time for the Sforzas to make common cause with Rodrigo's old enemy, the restless Giuliano Rovere...

*   *   *

Ludovico Sforza's dark handsome face bore the same look of cunning which distinguished the meaner features of his younger brother Ascanio. For once in his life, however, this born intriguer had decided to be frank. Giuliano Rovere was too wily a man to be easily deceived. He leaned back in his chair with a sardonic smile. 'Come, Giuliano,' he said,

28

'we each know what the other wants. I, the dukedom of Milan. You, the Papacy.' Rovere did not answer. Ludovico took his silence as acquiescence and continued. 'For both of us that means supporting France – in Naples.'

'Ferrante of Naples is not yet dead, Ludovico, and yet you would disturb the peace of Italy...'

'By reminding that nasty little ape, Charles of France, of his dynastic right to the kingdom? Yes. He will be grateful to me – and my nephew, the Duke, is delicate.'

'His health is as poor as that of his grandfather, King Ferrante?'

Ludovico gave a wolfish smile, as he nodded. 'When Ferrante dies, there will be war in Italy. He has nominated his son, Alfonso, as his successor.'

'Yet Charles of France has the stronger claim.'

'And will assert it – at lance point. So if Ferrante obliges us by dying before Christmas, we'll have French lancers in our olive groves by spring. And France will crush Naples like a nut...'

'All roads to Naples must pass through Rome,' Giuliano said musingly. 'That means Rodrigo Borgia.'

'Exactly. And Alfonso of Naples is kinsman to King Ferdinand of Spain. Borgia is a Spaniard at heart, whatever else he may pretend.'

'He's not declared himself.'

Ludovico shrugged angrily. 'Naturally not. But these marriages planned for his bastards show clearly enough which way the wind blows...'

'And the wind from France may blow strongly enough to topple Rodrigo Borgia from his throne.'

'I can assure Your Eminence that it will be irresistible.' Ludovico said dryly. 'Charles of France is already talking of crossing the Alps with the greatest army seen in Italy since Hannibal. You and I will be on the right side, I assure you.'

'And Rodrigo Borgia?'

'Must pay the penalty for having backed the wrong horse. You will remind the King of France that this Borgia Pope stinks of corruption. The papal throne must be cleansed – in favour of a worthier candidate. When

Ferrante dies, Giuliano, you will open the campaign. And earn your two hundred thousand ducats.'

* * *

Ferrante did not die before Christmas, as Ludovico Sforza hoped, but soon after, on 27th January 1494. Events moved rapidly towards the inevitable conclusion predicted by Sforza. Rodrigo Borgia showed his hand by sending his Legate to crown Alfonso as King of Naples in return for the marriage of Jofre to Alfonso's illegitimate daughter, Sancia, with the title of Princess of Squillace, while Juan Gandia, now safely married in Spain to Maria Enriques, kinswoman of King Ferdinand, received a principate and two counties in Naples, and Cesare numerous rich benefices. Giuliano Rovere, for his part, resolved to show himself publicly on the side of France, opening the campaign against Rodrigo with a furious speech in Consistory denouncing Rodrigo for nepotism and corruption.

'Thus has the authority of the Church become debased!' he thundered. 'We have seen the Pope's son, Cesare Borgia, made a Cardinal against the will of all good men of this sacred College. We have seen a dishonest bargain made for the marriages of the Pope's other sons. Even a goat-herd on the Capitol knows that the price the Pope has paid for these marriages in Spain and Naples is the blessing of the Church on the false succession to the Neapolitan throne. All this to aggrandise his brood of bastards...'

Cesare leapt to his feet, 'God burn your tongue, Rovere!'

Rodrigo, impassive on his papal throne, motioned him to be silent. 'You may continue, Cardinal Rovere. But be cautious,' he warned.

But Rovere had deliberately thrown caution to the winds. He had come prepared to have his say, and he was determined to do so. 'We were promised honesty,' he bellowed, 'and we've been fed with lies. We were promised an end to corruption, and we choke in its stench. We were promised peace, and we must now endure war...'

Rodrigo interrupted him, 'Rovere!'

Rovere appealed to the assembled Cardinals, 'May I not speak?' There was a sympathetic murmur. Encouraged, he proceeded. 'You know that the cities of the north are already in revolt. In every village poor priests cry out against Rome's wickedness, and call for an avenging sword. It will come! This morning I received news that the King of France will enter Italy when he has gathered together the greatest army we have yet seen...' A wave of shocked exclamations rippled round the room. 'Yes!' Rovere shouted, 'and he will advance upon Naples to remove the usurper Alfonso. If he is opposed by the Holy See...' He turned theatrically towards Ascanio Sforza, 'Speak, Ascanio!'

Ascanio rose from his seat with apparent reluctance and some nervousness, his voice barely audible above the babel of arguing Cardinals. 'My brother Ludovico...' he began. The Cardinals fell silent. 'My brother Ludovico, as Regent of Milan, has asked me to inform this Consistory that, as a true servant of God and of his conscience, he feels obliged to give the French all assistance to ... to...'

'To cleanse Peter's chair!' Rovere bellowed.

Cesare stood up, shouting above the clamour, 'I accuse...! I accuse Giuliano Rovere and Ascanio Sforza of conspiracy, schism, heresy and treason!'

'God in heaven turns his face from this corrupt church!' Rovere screamed.

'Silence... silence!' Rodrigo thundered. The hammering of Burchard's staff on the floor at last producing a semblance of quiet, he rose from his chair, beside himself with rage. 'Have none of you been paid enough?' he screamed at the Cardinals. 'Will you get more from France? Will you? You yelp and squeal like deflowered virgins! Am I to be frightened of that? I am Pope ... I ...! I ...! I can create a hundred new Cardinals to replace you. Test me! Test me – and you shall see what manner of man is a Borgia Pope!'

Blind with rage, he blundered from the chamber, swiftly followed by a grim-faced Cesare.

2

The King

THE LEAVES WERE turning gold on the vines as Charles VIII of France rode through the rich Tuscan countryside towards Florence in the late autumn of 1494. Behind him his thirty-thousand-strong army trailed in a huge cloud of dust that whitened the fields as they passed; while the eighty pieces of heavy artillery which so astounded the Italians lurched in its wake over the deeply-rutted roads. The sun glinted on the ten-foot pikes of the King's Swiss and German mercenaries, touched a forest of longbows, carried by his personal guard of Scots archers, and reflected from the gleaming armour of the heavy cavalry, the nobility of France, who rode with the King. At their head, beneath a huge silken standard embroidered with the lilies of France floating proudly against the blue Italian sky, rode the King himself.

Charles was only twenty-three, an insignificant, misshapen figure on his splendid charger; the circlet of gold covering his mousy hair surmounting a face so hideous that the Italians said he was 'more like a monster than a man'. His forehead was low and sloping, his nose huge and heavily hooked, his pale eyes slightly protruding, and his chin bony and long-jawed like a pike's. The splendid suit of armour wrought in Milan covered his hunched shoulders and spindly shanks, but for all his ugliness and the gentle beauty of his Queen, Anne of Brittany, Charles was an inveterate lecher. His eyes widened in pleasurable remembrance as he recalled the beauty of the women who had yielded to him at Milan, their perfumed flesh and jewel-encrusted dresses seeming so exotic after the staider ways of the French court. Why even the Milanese whores lived as richly as any French countess, he thought, and as for the ruler of Milan – the luxury of his court surpassed anything Charles had ever seen, let alone imagined. His eyes rested on the swarthy countenance of Ludovico Sforza riding at his side, clad in a cloak of purple silk embroidered in gold with his emblem, the mulberry, over a suit of armour far more splendid than the King's.

Ludovico's thoughts as he rode beside the King on a superb charger given him by his sister-in-law, Isabella d'Este Gonzaga, were far from complimentary to Charles, and indeed to the French nobility as a whole. The King was not only ugly, but half-educated and not very intelligent, indeed it was rumoured that he could scarcely read. The poor fool had only one idea in his head, Ludovico thought scornfully, and that was Naples – apart from women, that is. Which suited him perfectly. Ludovico had a superlatively high opinion of his own intelligence, and, in consequence, a passion for intrigue, mainly to prove that he could outwit his enemies – and his friends. Ludovico smiled to himself. It was proving no difficult task to control the King and guide him in the direction he wanted him to go, away from Milan and south to Naples. Which meant, of course, crossing the Papal States, the fief of the one man in Italy whose intelligence could be thought to approach his own, but then Rodrigo Borgia had already chosen the wrong side. The reign of the Borgia Pope was likely to be a short one. Ludovico shrugged, what should he care for the ruin of an upstart family, when he was so close to the realisation of his own dynastic plans. His nephew, Gian Galeazzo of Milan, would not last long, probably no longer than Rodrigo Borgia...

His thoughts were interrupted by the high-pitched voice of Charles. 'What is that monk saying?' he enquired, pointing to a mendicant friar who stood at a wayside shrine, his eyes and hands lifted up towards heaven, his voice intoning an hysterical chant.

'He is praising you, Sire,' Ludovico replied suavely, addressing the King in his nasal French, for Charles had no Italian and his Latin was poor. 'He is a follower of the monk Savonarola, who cries your name from his pulpit in Florence, calling you the new Cyrus, the saviour of Italy. Why even the power of your name was enough to drive the Medicis from Florence, where the mob have looted their palaces, shouting "Viva Francia!"...'

'Truly God is with us,' Charles responded with a self-satisfied smile. 'They say too that he is against his wicked servant, Pope Alexander, who opposes us...'

* * *

Rodrigo knelt at his *prie-dieu* in the papal bedchamber, his shoulders hunched in weariness and despair, tears of hopelessness welling into the palms of his hands which covered his eyes as if to ward off visions of advancing armies. There was the sound of quick footsteps and the clang of halberds outside the door as the guards saluted someone of importance. Cesare came in, dressed in hunting clothes, a sword at his side; Rodrigo rose and went towards him, his hands outstretched, wordlessly pleading for some comfort from his son. Instead, Cesare pulled a sheet of folded parchment from the cuff of his gauntlet, and threw it at his father's feet, almost as if he would have liked to have thrown it into his face. 'Charles demands free passage through the Papal States, and threatens you with deposition if you refuse. The Medicis have given up their castles to him without a fight, and run off with their tails between their legs like the cowardly dogs they are. Charles is in Florence, and no one stands between us and him. What will you do?'

Rodrigo sat down heavily in his chair beside the window, gazing down upon the meadows outside the Vatican walls, as if he saw them already teeming with French soldiers. He shrugged his shoulders. 'What can I do? But pray...'

Cesare made an impatient gesture, 'What good will that do? You've no force to resist them.'

'No, I believe they may conquer Rome with no more than the sticks of chalk they need to mark their billets...'

Cesare moved over to the table in front of Rodrigo, and

34

taking up a quill and paper put them in front of Rodrigo as he stood over him. 'I will tell you what you shall do.' His voice was eager, persuasive, yet with a hint of a threat. 'You will write to Alfonso of Naples and tell him to give me command of his army.' He picked up the pen, as if to press it into Rodrigo's hand, 'Go on, write.'

But Rodrigo continued to stare out of the window, appearing not to notice his son's outstretched hand. There was a silence. Finally he said, 'It has commanders. With my approval . . .'

Cesare's hand holding the pen shook perceptibly. 'Who?' he asked.

'Virginio Orsini. His sons Paolo and Giovanni.'

There was a long pause, as if Cesare could not believe he had heard aright. Then he said between his teeth, 'I'll not credit you could have been such a fool. The Orsinis are treacherous dogs like all the Italians. They'll turn on you at the first opportunity, just like the rest. Did you learn nothing from Sforza's treachery? You fool. You old dotard . . .!'

There was a rustle of silk; Giulia appeared in the doorway, smiling seductively. Turning, Cesare flung the pen in his father's face and strode furiously from the room, pushing roughly past Giulia as he did so. Giulia pouted with dislike at his retreating back, not daring to reproach him with his rudeness. Instead she moved over to the Pope's chair, inviting his caress. Rodrigo pulled her hungrily down to him, enfolding her in his great sleeves. Laying his head on her soft shoulder, he began to weep as his hand automatically stroked her.

'Little father,' Giulia's voice was gentle, 'are you weeping for me? Please, please, let me stay with you . . .'

'No, my child,' Rodrigo raised his head, 'I weep for Italy.' His voice took on a dramatic tone, as if he were addressing the world from the papal chair. 'Although I am a Spaniard, not the less for that do I love Italy, nor wish to see her in the hands of any but Italians.'

Giulia was unimpressed, continuing her pleading, 'Please, Rodrigo . . .' Then, as Rodrigo made no response, gazing out of the window to the north from whence the French must come, she became angry. 'It's all Cesare's fault,' she burst out; 'he hates me because of his mother. They're plotting together to separate you from me. They don't want anyone to have any influence with you except themselves. They're all the same that she-devil and her brood, Cesare and Lucrezia...'

The shrill malice in her voice roused Rodrigo from his thoughts. How beautiful she looked quivering with anger. Lust overcame him. Desire for her could still blot out unwelcome thoughts. He pressed her yielding body tightly against him. 'No, no,' he said, soothing her, 'it is not Cesare but I who love you who says you must go. Would you have the French drag you from my bed? You will be safe in Pesaro with Lucrezia and Giovanni...'

But Giulia still thought she could bend him to her will, use his desire for her as her only weapon. 'That worm Giovanni Sforza,' she said viciously, 'he cannot defend his own honour, so how do you expect him to defend mine?'

Rodrigo affected not to notice the slur against Lucrezia 'Giulia,' he said, pushing her before him towards the bed, 'we have not much time left together. Come.'

*   *   *

'So, Giulia, you have obtained a farewell blessing from our Holy Father, have you not?' Cesare said ironically, as the flushed girl joined the party about to leave for safety in Pesaro. He seemed to have recovered his composure as, dressed in his Cardinal's robes, he waited to take his leave of his father's women in an anteroom of Adriana de Mila's palace of Santa Maria next the Vatican. He lounged against the panelled wall, eyeing the assembled group, Adriana de Mila, in travelling dress, composed as usual, Lucrezia and Giulia on the verge of tears. Lucrezia's husband, Giovanni Sforza, sulky and resentful, avoided Cesare's eye. He had heard that Cesare thought him to be expendable, and the knowledge made him more than a little apprehensive. He was afraid of his brother-in-law.

A knock sounded on the other side of the panelling.

Turning, Cesare twisted an elaborately-carved rose, and the panel swung back to reveal Rodrigo, attended by Perotto.

'Good ... good ... You are ready.' Rodrigo was brisk, anxious to avoid further emotional scenes. 'Cesare, the road is still open?'

'It is.'

'Giovanni, you know what you must do?' He turned from Sforza to Perotto. 'You've written it for the Lord Giovanni? It's all been written down? Clearly?'

'Yes, Your Holiness.'

'Well, then ... there's no more to be said ... Yes, Giovanni, what is it?'

'Holiness, if I may not join my kinsmen, I would wish to stay in Rome...'

Cesare interrupted him, 'So you may crawl on your knees before the French? With your uncle, Ascanio? Do not be afraid, Giovannino, I'll send Michelotto with you as far as Spoleto.'

'No, no, please, not that!' Giovanni wailed. 'Holiness, he ... he ... plots to have me killed!'

'Be still, foolish boy, no one wants to kill you.' Rodrigo's voice was imperious. 'We have commanded you to escort these ladies to Pesaro until it is safe for them to return to Rome.'

'Not I,' Giulia broke in defiantly. '*I* shall stay here.'

Rodrigo smiled at this display of petulance. 'Pretty Giulia, do you truly wish to be ravaged by a Frenchman — or a German, or a Swiss? Perhaps even His Most Christian Majesty himself...'

'Holy Father.' Anxiety overcame Giovanni Sforza's timidity. 'I beg you ... My duty obliges me to...'

Rodrigo turned on him angrily, 'Duty? You would instruct us in that? Your duty, Sforza, is to obey us. No more.'

Giovanni stuttered, losing his head, 'My Uncle Ascanio tells me...'

Lucrezia caught her husband's arm, warning him to go no further.

Rodrigo's voice was stern, 'We know what your uncle has been telling you. And all your Sforza brood. That you must spy upon us and betray us. Do you think we've not read the letters?'

Giovanni was aghast, 'Holiness ...' he stammered.

Cesare cut in, 'Let the fool stay. He can share a cell with his Uncle Ascanio.'

White-faced, Giovanni turned for protection to Lucrezia. For a moment no one spoke, letting the threat hang in the air.

Rodrigo stared briefly at Cesare, as if he were about to protest. Then, as if nothing had occurred, he pulled Lucrezia and Giulia to him, kissing his daughter's mouth in a long embrace, so passionate that the jealous Giulia pouted, until he kissed her in turn in the same way. Then, holding their hands, he addressed Adriana, his voice trembling with emotion, 'Madonna Adriana, here are my eyes and my heart. Guard them for me. Keep them safe, until the blessed time comes when we shall all be together again in peace ... Now go, all of you. May God go with you. But remember an old man who loves you, and write to me, often.'

Cesare's face was contemptuous. 'Jesu,' he muttered under his breath.

Giovanni made one last desperate stand. 'No ...' he said mulishly.

Lucrezia moved forward to him, calming him. 'Husband, you will take us to Pesaro. We'll be safe there and it will be carnival time. With hand on heart, I promise you we'll be happy there.'

Rodrigo was reassuring, his jovial self again, 'Of course you will. Has she told you why? Fortunate boy, you have our permission at last. You may now consummate your marriage...'

Cesare gave a short derisive laugh. As the women moved towards the door, he embraced Lucrezia, whispering in her ear. Lucrezia smiled, but said nothing, as she pressed herself against him, then she turned and followed Adriana downstairs.

38

Cesare and Rodrigo watched from a window as the party rode out of the courtyard. Rodrigo's mood had changed again to one of maudlin tenderness, tears stood in his eyes, as he watched them go. Cesare gave him a glance of distaste.

'How beautiful she is ... still only a child ...' Rodrigo murmured fondly.

'She's a whore.'

'Your sister!'

'Not her.'

'Giulia! Cesare ... No, no, it can't be true. You wouldn't dare ... Would you? Have you ...?'

Cesare smiled, and said nothing. Rodrigo turned away to the window once more, his shoulders shaking. When Cesare did speak, his voice was coolly matter of fact. 'Father,' he said, 'what of Ascanio Sforza?'

Rodrigo's voice was cold in return, 'The order has been given. Tonight he will be taken to Sant'Angelo.'

'And Rovere?'

Rodrigo was once again perfectly calm, conscious of his superior position and experience. 'He I shall leave to fall into his own trap of treachery and ambition. Rest assured that he will run to the King of France to drip poison into his ear against us. Much good may it do him.'

'You are wrong,' Cesare said fiercely. 'He is our enemy and we must destroy him before he can harm us.'

'You're a boy in statecraft yet,' Rodrigo was condescending. 'If our enemy is about to make a fool of himself in the eyes of the world, then why should we prevent him doing so?'

'You are wrong,' Cesare said again. 'You must not let him go. I shall see to it that he does not escape ...' He turned to go.

'Your Eminence!' Rodrigo's voice was peremptory.

'Holiness!' Cesare turned back, his countenance deceptively meek.

'You will not presume upon our authority. You will walk in our shadow.'

'As Your Holiness pleases ...' He grinned savagely.

39

'As for Sforza, the plague is fierce in the cells under Sant'Angelo ...'

'No!' Rodrigo's voice was commanding. 'The Cardinal Sforza is a Prince of the Church, and shall be lodged accordingly. I have spoken ...'

*   *   *

Ascanio Sforza sat in a pearl-studded, leather-covered chair, watching Rovere stride about the chamber, making preparations for a hurried departure.

'I tell you, Ascanio,' Rovere said, 'that you would be wiser to come with me to Florence, to the King of France. Do not trust Rodrigo Borgia.'

Calmly, Ascanio took a sweetmeat from a small silver box, and put it in his mouth before answering. 'You may be right, Giuliano. But then you have never trusted Borgia, and you have no choice but to join the French. Your die is cast, mine is not.'

'But your brother, Ludovico ...'

'Ludovico will look after our interests with the King of France. Two Sforzas at Charles's side might be too many. I have been frank with Rodrigo Borgia and he has assured me of his friendship and his respect for me as a member of the Sacred College ...'

'And you believe him? You're a fool.'

'Not a fool, Giuliano, but a gambler, a wise one who does not like to place all his ducats upon one horse – and that horse the young King of France. Ludovico tells me he is a fool, and easily influenced ...'

'And shall be influenced – by me.'

'Perhaps, Giuliano, perhaps. But then perhaps not. Rodrigo Borgia is still the Pope. And I am Vice-Chancellor of the Holy Church and should be here to welcome the King of France when he should come.'

'From a Borgia prison?'

'Of course. I wonder you've not thought how advantageous that might be.'

'*Deus disponit*, Ascanio,' Rovere warned.

'Indeed it is as you say, God disposes, and I shall be prepared whatever His dispositions may be ...' Ascanio smiled philosophically, tracing the intricately-wrought surface of the comfit-box with a well-kept hand.

*   *   *

As Rodrigo had predicted, Rovere fled Rome to join Charles of France at Florence, resolved to persuade the King to depose Rodrigo Borgia and to replace him with himself, a well-known friend of France. On Rodrigo's orders, and to his own satisfaction, Ascanio Sforza was arrested and confined to Sant'Angelo, not in the dungeons below ground level where Cesare had wished to put him but in comfortable lodgings beneath the castle ramparts. Here he awaited the outcome of events, conscious that he would not have to wait long. The French were pouring down through the Papal States towards Rome, reaching Viterbo on the Via Flaminia where they had the good fortune to intercept the Pope's women and capture them. Shortly afterwards, the Orsinis, as Cesare had said they would, went over to the French, surrendering their arms and their castles. For the French, the way to Rome was open. The Borgias were at bay. Although they were not yet aware of the extent of the disasters that had befallen them, they knew that it was only a question of weeks before the French reached the city, and prepared to defend themselves as best they might.

*   *   *

Rodrigo and Cesare stood on the city wall above the gate of Santa Maria del Popolo where the Via Flaminia entered Rome, their faces grim. Cesare kicked contemptuously at the rotting fascines protecting an antiquated cannon. Below them, Juan's friend, the Turkish Prince Djem, caracoled on his fine horse, as though supremely unaware of any danger.

'Is Your Holiness satisfied?' Cesare complained angrily.

41

'The first Frenchmen to break wind will rival Joshua's trumpets.'

'Orsini and his sons still oppose them...'

'Until they smell the French King's money...'

'You believe I should flee to Naples, Cesare?' Rodrigo's voice took on a dramatic tone. 'No. I am still Pope and Bishop of Rome. I will not abandon my flock, nor yet my city to the barbarian...'

'Your flock will abandon you as soon as the first French-man arrives at the city walls. No. Let the French have the city. We can hold Castel Sant'Angelo until Your Holiness recovers his wits and delivers us.'

'Do you fear for my safety, Cesare? No one has yet killed a Pope.'

'You forget St Peter. There's a precedent for you...'

Yes, Rodrigo reflected, they had killed St Peter, and there was a more recent precedent in the forefront of his mind, the dreadful day at Anagni when the French had kidnapped Pope Benedict, and so maltreated him that he lost his mind. Not a pleasant thought. Never had Rodrigo felt so alone. Longing passionately to see Lucrezia again, or even Giulia, he was tormented by unsatisfied desire and besieged with loneliness. There was little comfort to be had from Cesare, he was so hard and unyielding. Not like Juan. Rodrigo looked down fondly at Djem. Cesare saw the look.

'Must you always have that Saracen at your skirts?'

'Poor Prince Djem. He's your brother's friend, and thus reminds me of Juan.'

'And me. Is that all you keep him for?'

'You forget, Cesare, that Djem is an important personage in his own land, the brother of the Sultan who hates and fears him. I have written to the Sultan that he may send us help, for if the French defeat us that vainglorious fool Charles will declare a crusade against him, and place Djem on his throne.'

Cesare laughed admiringly, 'A bold move, to save your-self from the Most Christian King with the help of the enemy of Christendom! How did he answer?'

'Like the Moslem infidel that he is,' Rodrigo smiled subtly. 'He would pay three hundred thousand ducats to hear that his brother Djem was dead. Come, let us return to the Vatican...'

As his father mounted his mule, with the respectful help of two of the papal guard, Cesare regarded Djem with new eyes. Three hundred thousand ducats – enough money to raise and keep an army, to sustain a man wherever his ambition might lead him ... Rodrigo's impatient voice cut across his musing... 'Come, Cesare. To the Vatican. There may be news of Lucrezia.'

*   *   *

At the Vatican all was confusion; even as Rodrigo passed into his private apartments, shouts indicated that the papal servants were already looting the palace in anticipation of his departure to escape the approaching French. From his own apartment, Cesare listened to the tumult with rising rage. 'This is not to be endured, Michelotto,' he said fiercely. 'Come.'

Even as he rose, buckling on his sword, there was an agitated knock on the door. It was Perotto, pale, his eyes fearful. 'Your Eminence, His Holiness ... There is news ... Please come ...'

Pushing Perotto roughly aside, Cesare strode out into the corridor, closely followed by Michelotto. As they rounded the corner, a servant, his arms full of stolen silver cups, blundered into Cesare. Caught in the act, he dropped his booty, his hand going to his dagger. Michelotto stepped forward and, with an expert thrust of his sword, ran the man through. Blood spurted from the wound onto Cesare's cuirass; he wiped it off with an expression of distaste, which Michelotto misinterpreted as squeamishness and put out his hand to reassure his master. Cesare reacted as if a snake had bitten him. 'Don't touch me! Never touch me, you toad,' he said menacingly. Astonished by the sudden cold fury in his eyes, Michelotto dropped his hand, saying nothing.

As they neared the Pope's chambers, they met Ascanio Sforza, hurrying in the same direction. Seeing Michelotto's bloody sword and Cesare's grim expression, Ascanio feared for his life. 'I have the Pope's safe-conduct,' he said quickly, holding forward a piece of parchment.

Cesare brushed it aside. 'You will wait here, Sforza,' he said curtly, and passed into his father's room.

The Pope's private apartments were dark, for the windows giving on to the deep Cortile del Pappagallo were small, but the walls glowed with the rich colours of Pinturicchio's recently completed frescoes, and the Borgia bull glittered on the ceiling carving, a rampant celebration of family pride.

Cesare saw his father, seated in a chair by the window, his back against the light, so that he could not distinguish his expression. At his feet was a kneeling figure, clad in mud-stained armour. It was Paolo Orsini. 'Tell him, my son,' Rodrigo's voice was expressionless. 'Tell your friend, the Cardinal of Valencia, how your family have kept faith with us.'

Paolo Orsini turned to Cesare, his face apprehensive. '... Eminence ... remember we were friends in our childhood...'

Cesare started forward, seizing Orsini by the neck of his cuirass. 'Why have you come here to snivel at His Holiness' feet?'

'Eminence, my honour ... my father has surrendered his castles and army to the French, and knelt before their King ... I could not ... our onetime friendship...'

'Which you have betrayed,' Cesare said evenly. 'Hang him, father. Like the treacherous dog that he is.'

Rodrigo made a restraining gesture. 'Listen to me, Paolo Orsini,' he said, with a rising note of passion in his voice, 'we release you now, because you came to us of your own free will. Go now, and bear this message to your sinful father and to all your faithless family, that we, the Pope, shall not forget what they have done, nor shall we forgive, and upon our certain vengeance we pledge our mitre, our lands and our life.'

44

Rising from his chair, he towered over the wretched Orsini, who cried out placatingly, 'If Your Holiness wishes, I'm ready to treat with the French Captain for the return of the Lady Lucrezia and the others taken with her.'

Rodrigo subsided abruptly into his chair, his face crumpled with shock. 'Taken ... how taken?'

'Your Holiness had not heard?' Paolo's voice had regained some confidence. 'Five days since at Viterbo.'

Cesare flung Paolo Orsini towards the door with a brutal gesture. 'Get out, dog, while you yet live,' he said between his teeth, 'the Borgias have no need of your help...'

The door opened to admit Perotto; Paolo Orsini took the chance to make his escape. 'Your Holiness, the Cardinal Sforza is at the door. He bears grievous tidings ... the Lady Lucrezia, the Lady Giulia...'

'He knows,' Cesare said rudely. 'Now get out, weasel.'

'Eminence, what shall I tell the Cardinal Sforza?'

'Tell him nothing. Let him wait. Now get out.'

Perotto disappeared. As the door opened running feet, shouts and the noise of furniture being dragged across stone floors could be clearly heard. So too could the aristocratic tones of Ascanio Sforza, his voice raised in outrage at such unceremonious treatment.

Rodrigo's self-possession had entirely deserted him. His mouth working and his eyes staring in panic, he seized Cesare's hands moaning, 'Anything, promise them anything, only give me back my Lucrezia. Tell Ascanio ... Bring Ascanio to me. He will tell them to release her. They will listen to him. He is the one ... the only one. I want to speak to Ascanio...'

Cesare drew away his hands disgustedly and seized his father by the shoulders as if to instil some of his own strength into him. 'What will you give them? Your crown and shoes?'

'All. Everything. We are ruined. Only give us back our beloved daughter...'

Cesare released him in contempt. 'Listen, old man, and try to become Pope again. The women are unimportant. They'll not be harmed. We are not ruined yet. We'll hold

45

Sant'Angelo till the stones rot, and show them all what it means to be a Borgia.'

But Rodrigo only moaned, refusing to be comforted, rocking to and fro in his chair in his anguish, his face buried in his hands, muttering, 'Lucrezia, Lucrezia.'

Looking down at the shuddering figure, Cesare shrugged. 'Michelotto!' he shouted.

Rodrigo looked up as Michelotto came in and, seeing the bloody sword in his hand, in his confused state he became frightened. 'Cesare, what is this? You mean to kill me?'

Michelotto, as became a devout Spaniard, knelt, horrified, to kiss the hem of the Pope's robe, sheathing his sword. 'Holy Father!'

'Come, Michelotto,' Cesare said brusquely, 'we are going to Sant'Angelo. Take his arm, you fool. He's only a man.'

As the Borgias hurried along the covered passage which linked the Vatican to Sant'Angelo, they heard the shouts from the streets below in the city, announcing the coming of the French, 'Francia! Francia! Rovere! Rovere! Open the gates . . . !'

*   *   *

Charles VIII entered Rome as a conqueror on 31st December 1494, the feast of St Silvester, the day for which, his astrologer informed him, the omens were most propitious. The weather, it seemed, was on the side of the Borgias. Charles rode through a welter of mud and rain to enter the city through the Porta del Popolo, where he was met by Burchard, whom Rodrigo had charged with the handling over of the keys to the city gates. The Master of Ceremonies was distinctly unhappy in his prominent role. The French had no idea of papal protocol, and he did not relish the prospect of stage-managing the meeting between defeated Pope and victorious King – whenever that might take place. Fortunately, the King seemed to be unaware that Rodrigo had shut himself up in Sant'Angelo; and Burchard was determined that this embarrassing fact should be concealed from him for as long as possible. 'A magnificent army, Sire,' he said ingratiatingly.

It was indeed a magnificent spectacle as the great French force defiled down the Via Lata to the Palazzo Venezia where the King was to lodge. Their entry lasted from three in the afternoon until nine o'clock at night, so that darkness fell and torches had to be lit, heightening the impressiveness of the long marching columns of armed men. The King's German and Swiss mercenaries came first, dressed in short multi-coloured uniforms, with plumed helmets, carrying short swords and the great ten-foot pikes which had made them the most dreaded infantry in Europe. They were big, powerful men, marching in perfect time to the sound of trumpets, their size and splendour contrasting with the small, soberly-dressed Gascon crossbowmen who followed them. Behind the infantry rode the heavy cavalry, the core of the King's army, the nobles of France, with gorgeous silk cloaks over their streaming armour, carrying lances and maces. Five thousand light cavalry armed with English longbows followed them, and behind them the King's guard of four hundred archers, including one hundred Scots, then his personal bodyguard of nobles, marching on foot with iron maces on their shoulders. Then came the King, flanked by Rovere and Ascanio Sforza who had ridden out to meet him. The fickle Romans, Burchard noted with disapproval, raised shouts of 'Viva Francia', 'Rovere', and 'Sforza' – there was not one cry of 'Borgia'.

Well satisfied with his reception, Charles settled himself on the throne prepared for him in the great *salone* of the Palazzo Venezia, surrounded by his nobles, gaping at the magnificent hangings, the chests laden with gold and silver vessels, with which the room was furnished. Burchard, bowing obsequiously, attempted to take his leave, but the King called him back. 'Messer Burchard, we desire to know when we are to be granted audience of His Holiness the Pope.'

'Sire,' Burchard stuttered, not daring to meet the King's eye, 'I know not ... His Holiness is indisposed ...'

'Indisposed to greet His Majesty,' Rovere interposed

47

sharply, glancing sideways to see what effect this sally would have upon the King. 'We hear he has taken himself to Castel Sant'Angelo, and remains there surrounded by soldiers. A most hostile attitude.'

'My guns will smoke him out of there,' Charles exploded, red with anger. 'Take that message from me to your master the Pope, and see if he will receive us. Go!'

The embarrassed Burchard was only too anxious to leave; backing hastily out of the *salone*, he found himself at the top of the stairway with Ascanio Sforza, who whispered in his ear, 'Tell His Holiness, Burchard, that the French Captain will surrender his prisoners for three thousand ducats. A small sum to pay for a speedy cure to his indisposition...'

*   *   *

'We are grateful for your intervention in this matter dear to our heart, Ascanio.'

Rodrigo was seated on a canopied chair of state in the vaulted and frescoed audience chamber of the Castel Sant'Angelo, with Cesare in his Cardinal's robes standing at his side, the walls lined with armed men with the Borgia insignia on their breastplates. Outside, the sound of the relentless French cannonade could be heard, the great stone balls from the King's mortars and bombards crashing into the walls of the castle which the Emperor Hadrian had built as his tomb. Ascanio bowed and made a sign to the guard to open the door, admitting Lucrezia, Giulia and Adriana de Mila. At the sight of them, Rodrigo rose from his throne, unable to restrain the expression of joy which crossed his face. Instinctively, he opened his arms to greet them then, remembering where he was, resumed his majestic attitude, holding out his hand to the kneeling women to kiss. Adriana's eyes were respectfully downcast, as befitted such a public reception, and Lucrezia's full of tears, as she rose and moved to embrace Cesare. Only Giulia, unsubdued, looked up with a wanton smile at her lover. Rodrigo resumed his seat, impassive. 'Yes, Ascanio?' he said.

'The King is distressed. He asks why Your Holiness will not return to the Vatican.'

'We have been greatly indisposed, Eminence.'

Ascanio replied gravely, without a hint of a smile, 'May I now tell His Majesty that Your Holiness is recovered?'

'God has restored our strength,' Rodrigo answered in the same tone, but he was looking at Lucrezia.

Ascanio was encouraged. 'So I may tell His Majesty that you will return to the Vatican?'

'No, we shall never yield to force against our holy person. As long as His Most Christian Majesty continues his impious attack upon us, we remain here.'

'I much regret, Holiness, that His Majesty insists that the bombardment of Sant'Angelo must continue until Your Holiness informs him that you will return to the Vatican.'

'It pains me to refuse the King's demands, Eminence,' Rodrigo answered, 'but we must remain here until the voice of God has spoken, and He has indicated his wishes to His servant...'

A louder explosion than before seemed to shake the room. Sforza started nervously, Rodrigo remained impassive. 'Fear not, Ascanio,' he said. 'God's voice will be louder than King Charles's cannon.'

*   *   *

Ten days later, a thirty-foot section of the outer wall of the castle collapsed in rubble, killing three guards. Further resistance was clearly impossible. Rodrigo summoned the Cardinal Sforza. 'It seems to us that God has spoken, Ascanio. He wishes us to return to the Vatican. Perhaps you would so advise His Majesty? Our Master of Ceremonies will inform him of the hour of our passage through the garden ...'

*   *   *

'The King of France is most favourably disposed towards Your Holiness,' Ascanio reported to Rodrigo as they knelt together at Mass in the Sistine Chapel two days later. 'It

49

seems that he was impressed by your saintly demeanour when he saw you pass through the garden, yesterday.'

'So I have heard, most gratifying news to our ears. It appears that His Majesty climbed onto the back of our Master of Ceremonies, the better to see us. Does he still wish to depose us and put Giuliano Rovere in our chair?'

'Holiness, Giuliano whispers poison against your holy person into the King's ear, but since yesterday His Majesty no longer listens as once he did. He wishes above all things to go to Naples. If you will no longer oppose his claim to the crown, he will support your right to keep the papal tiara.'

'What must we then do, Ascanio?'

'Temporise, Holiness. Believe that the people are already turning against him. The Princes of Italy. Many who welcomed him . . .'

'Like the Duke of Milan,' Rodrigo interrupted mischievously.

'My brother Ludovico wishes Your Holiness to know that it was never his wish to see you deposed.'

'Or to fight Spain in a French cause?'

A note of anxiety crept into Ascanio's urbane voice, 'Then Spain is indeed sending another force to Naples?'

Rodrigo smiled, giving nothing away, 'You Sforzas are indeed eager weather-vanes. But what if the wind does not blow as you expect, Ascanio? What if it unseats us?'

Sforza shifted uneasily and did not answer directly. 'Your Holiness will receive the King?' was all he said.

'Tomorrow, Ascanio, in the Sala del Pappagallo.'

*   *   *

Rodrigo Borgia presented an impressive figure as, seated on the ceremonial throne in the Sala del Pappagallo, flanked by Cesare and the Cardinals who had remained loyal to him, he watched the young King of France shamble awkwardly towards him across the inlaid marble floor. Charles had been well briefed beforehand by Burchard, who had found him an eager but inept pupil. Nonetheless, he was nervous and hesitant, afraid of doing the wrong thing, and overawed, as he was intended to be, by Rodrigo's display of papal majesty. As Burchard watched anxiously he approached the throne, knelt and humbly removed his cap. With paternal dignity, Rodrigo raised him, exhorting him not to uncover his royal head. As he bent to greet the King with a kiss of peace, the Pope seemed to stagger, and, as if faint, clutched at Charles's arm.

Charles was startled. 'Your Holiness is ill!'

'It's nothing . . .' Rodrigo's breath was coming in quick pants, '. . . I need air . . . the room . . . so crowded . . .'

'Another room,' Charles cried imperiously, 'We would be alone!'

Cesare moved forward to show them into the adjoining chamber. When they had passed through, the Pope leaning heavily on the solititous young man's arm, he followed them, pausing with a faint smile on the threshold to observe Giuliano Rovere's look of frustrated rage, before he closed the door on the onlookers. Truly, Cesare thought to himself, his father was a great actor, and the King of France an even greater fool. As Rodrigo sank back heavily onto a chair, he went over to the *credenza* where a rock-crystal ewer of Rhenish wine stood ready on a salver with silver goblets. He took them and placed them on a table beside his father, then drew back into the shadows to observe the scene.

Rodrigo opened his eyes, and, as if seeing Charles for the first time, beckoned to him to sit beside him. When he spoke, his voice was feeble, almost tremulous. 'You see, Majesty, I am an old man . . . weak and defenceless. Your guns have disarmed me . . . What does Your Majesty want of me?'

Charles was blunt, unskilled in the devious ways of diplomacy. 'Do you still dispute my claim to Naples, Holiness?'

A wave of faintness seemed to have overtaken Rodrigo again, he closed his eyes, gesturing feebly towards the flagon of wine. 'Forgive me . . . I am weaker than I thought . . . I spent the night upon my knees, praying to God for guidance . . . Your Majesty, please,. some wine . . .'

As Charles rose to pour out the wine, Rodrigo continued

in a firmer voice, watching the King from beneath half-closed lids, 'God has not abandoned us, this morning he enlightened me as to the significance of Your Majesty's arrival here...'

Charles was alert, suspecting a trap. 'What significance?'

'If you ask our approval of your claim to Naples, it must be that you acknowledge us as earthly Vicar of Christ.'

But Charles, too, had his weapons. 'That has been called into question, Holiness, by others...'

'By Giuliano Rovere?'

'At Ferrara, before a General Council which then deposed you.' Charles was triumphant.

Rodrigo opened his eyes, his expression almost apologetic. 'Alas, I fear Giuliano has ill advised Your Majesty...'

'A Pope cannot then be deposed?'

'By a General Council? Yes, Your Majesty.'

Charles became confused. 'Speak plainly!' he said angrily.

'Forgive me, Your Majesty. An old man's wits are not as quick as your own. I mean the convocation at Ferrara had no validity.'

'How so? No, I'll not believe it.'

'The Pope alone has the power to call a General Council.'

Charles looked stunned by this master stroke, his chief weapon now useless to him. Rodrigo smiled at him sympathetically. 'It was unpardonable of Giuliano to abuse your good faith, my son.'

Cast down, Charles stared at the floor, twirling the stem of the wine goblet nervously in his fingers, then he looked up slyly. 'Would you convene such a Council?'

'Would you, Your Majesty?'

There was a short silence, then the younger man's face broke into a rueful smile. 'The devil with it, then. But I march on Naples. You'll not oppose that?'

'Your Majesty will leave with my blessing.'

Charles was again suspicious, recalling that he had gained nothing from this interview. 'You wish to trick me,' he said petulantly. 'You want me gone from here, no more.'

Rodrigo smiled at him paternally. 'I was responding to Your Majesty's noble spirit. Having made yourself master of the Holy City, now, by returning it to God, you show yourself to be indeed the Most Christian of Kings...'

Charles was flattered, mollified. 'Your Holiness speaks the truth ... Then, when I am master of Naples, will you invest me with its crown?'

'Your Majesty may be confident that God will direct our conscience and our duty in the interest of Christendom's greatest Prince.' Rodrigo's voice was suave.

Charles frowned. He must have some definite pledge to show the world the Pope had not outwitted him. He stood up and began to pace the room, his prominent teeth biting at his lower lip. 'Words are not enough, Holy Father,' he said moodily.

Rodrigo was generous in victory. 'May we suggest a contribution to your campaign chest, a pledge of our support for Your Majesty? Say twenty mule-loads of ducats in gold?'

Charles continued to pace the room, but when he spoke his voice was triumphant. 'Excellent, Holiness, excellent. But I must also have hostages to your good faith. The Turkish Prince for my crusade ...' He stopped, facing Rodrigo with a cunning smile. 'And, for Naples, your son, Cesare.'

Slowly, Rodrigo nodded. 'So be it, my son,' he said.

Overcome with gratitude, Charles knelt at the Pope's feet to kiss his hand. 'Holy Father! Your blessing!'

As Rodrigo made the sign of the cross over the French King's bowed head, Cesare slipped silently out of the room.

*　　*　　*

Just over a week later, having taken a most filial leave of the Pope by whom he seemed quite bewitched, Charles rode south out of Rome down the Via Appia, with Cesare and Djem at his side, bound for Naples.

*　　*　　*

Charles was happy at Naples, happier than he had been at Rome, where, fearful of Borgia poison, he had always had his food tasted by a trusted servitor, and his wine stirred with a spoon containing a piece of unicorn's horn, the antidote to poison. The city had yielded itself to him willingly, and so too had its women. The book in which Charles had painted the women whose favours he had enjoyed took on voluminous proportions. In a letter to his brother-in-law, he called his new kingdom an 'earthly paradise'. But there were ominous signs which Charles, drunk with pleasure, preferred to ignore. The French army was becoming demoralised, debauched with wine and women and suffering from a virulent new disease, syphilis, which they, blaming the Italians, called *'le mal de Naples'* and the Italians, blaming them in return, called 'the French disease'. The Neapolitans, tired of having their women violated and their houses looted by drunken Frenchmen, were turning against the King. Most dangerous of all, an anti-French league was being promoted by Spain and the Empire which, it was rumoured, Venice, Milan and the Pope were prepared to join.

*   *   *

Charles stood at a delicately arched window of the Castel Nuovo, looking out over the Bay of Naples. His brows were knit together in an angry frown, his loose mouth closed in an unusually firm line, and his misshapen shoulders hunched in displeasure. Behind him stood a group of worried advisers, earnestly pleading with him. Foremost among them were Paolo Orsini and Giuliano Rovere.

'Sire,' Orsini's voice was apologetic, 'it would be impolitic to remain further in this kingdom. The people...'

Charles swung angrily round. 'The people? What people? I don't give a fig for your Italian peasants! I stamp on them!' He suited the gesture to the words.

Giuliano attempted to intervene. 'Your Majesty...'

Charles turned on him. 'You are an Italian too. Italians are not to be trusted. Delaroche,' he appealed to a grizzled old soldier, 'Delaroche, as a good Frenchman, tell me the truth!'

'Your Majesty has heard the truth. We may no longer depend upon the support of the people here. Your Majesty's army is becoming undisciplined, greatly weakened by sickness.'

'Yes,' Charles burst out, pointing at Orsini and Rovere, 'you Italians fight with the bodies of your women.'

Stung, Paolo Orsini retorted, 'It was Your Majesty's army that brought the sickness.'

Charles was beside himself. 'You lie! All Italians are liars, cheats, dirty dogs...'

Delaroche interrupted his tirade. 'Sire, the leaders of Italy are turning against us. There's not one Prince in Italy upon whom you may now rely.'

Charles's rage was unabated. 'I know about their Holy League ... It's the work of that devil the Pope!'

'Your Majesty.' Delaroche's voice was calm but firm. 'We cannot remain here. We must retire. Before a Spanish army stands between us and France.'

Charles stamped his foot, his mouth working. 'Spain! He tricked me. That Spaniard! That Catalan bull!'

Rovere stepped forward; he had had difficulty restraining his proud temper in the face of Charles's insults, but he had succeeded. The muscles in his powerful jaw were tight with the effort, but his voice when he spoke was even. 'May I respectfully remind Your Majesty that you still hold Cesare Borgia? And by that the arm and will of the Pope.'

Charles became calm, a grin of triumph began to spread across his irregular features. 'You are right, Rovere,' he said. 'Where is the bull-calf?'

*   *   *

Cesare's apartments were empty but for the lifeless body of Prince Djem, sprawled across the table at which he had shared a banquet with the Pope's son the previous night. A trickle of black bile mingled with blood had dried at the corner of his mouth; a few dead flies lay on their backs in the

55

stain of wine which had leaked from the overturned goblet. For a moment, Charles stared down at the body as if unable to believe his eyes. 'Delaroche!' he screamed. 'Where is Borgia?'

'Gone, Sire. I found a dead groom in the stables dressed in the Lord Cesare's clothes, stabbed through the heart. And a horse gone. No sign of the Cardinal, nor of his Spanish servant...'

'The chests, you idiot,' Charles shouted at him. 'The chests were still there? The gold...?'

'Majesty, the chests were there, but,' he paused, afraid of the effect his words might have on the enraged King.

'Go on! Go on!' Charles stamped his foot with impatience.

'They were filled with stones, Sire...'

It seemed as if Charles were about to have a fit. Momentarily transfixed by the news, his eyes bulged and choking sounds came from his throat. Then, his thin body shaking with rage, he turned on Rovere as if he were about to strike him. 'Priests ... priests!' His voice rose to a scream, as he beat his fists on the table in a paroxysm of helpless rage. 'You priests ... You Borgia priests...!'

3

The Family

THE SOFT LIGHT of a summer evening bathed the marble columns and frescoed façade of the Villa Belvedere in the Vatican garden, turning Rodrigo's white robes the colour of rich cream as he sat on a stone bench festooned with cupids, his hand caressing the hair of Lucrezia, curled on a cushion on the grass beside him. It glinted on the pearls at Giulia's neck, as she too sat on a silk cushion on the grass, watching Rodrigo and his daughter with jealous eyes, and caught the poppy-red robes of Cesare, as he lounged against a pillar, flamboyant against the stone. It was late June of the year 1495. King Charles had hurried back to safety in France, and the Borgias had returned to the Vatican.

'How good it is to be once again in Rome, surrounded by those we love,' Rodrigo said. 'Truly God has been good to his servant and has struck down the impious barbarian in his pride...'

'God has had nothing to do with it,' Cesare interrupted impatiently. 'Was it God who escaped from Charles at Naples, leaving him with nothing but a dead Turk and chests full of stones? Was it God who told you to lead Charles on through Orvieto and Perugia until he wearied of the pursuit and faced the armies of the League at Fornovo? We defeated Charles through the exercise of our own wit and our own will.'

'Two qualities with which the King of the French was ill-provided,' Rodrigo said. 'Peace be to him, now that he is safe back in France, he was a good son of the Church at heart. We may have need of him yet.' His voice became stern, rebuking his son. 'Do not take too much upon yourself, Cesare. Remember that after all you are a Prince of the Church, and that we are the Vicar of Christ, God's Vicar upon earth.'

With raised eyebrows, Cesare stared ostentatiously at Giulia, shrugged his shoulders and said nothing.

Rodrigo's tone became conciliatory. 'Be happy, my son. We shall be a family again. I've sent for your brothers. Juan comes from Spain, and little Jofre will bring his bride from the South. Is the Princess Sancia as beautiful as they say, Cesare?'

Cesare did not answer his father's light-hearted query. At the mention of his brother Juan's name, he stiffened. As so often, the darkness in him cast a shadow across his father's sunny mood. 'Who is to go against the Orsinis?' he asked meaningly.

'We are not to be questioned upon that,' Rodrigo replied haughtily.

Cesare was not to be put off thus easily. 'I'll not truckle to brother Juan!' he warned. 'Where was he when the French had us at bay?'

'Where his duty and our will obliged him to be.'

'And I was putting marrow in your trembling backbone.'

'Cesare!' Rodrigo shouted, suddenly enraged at his son's presumption. 'You will not question our decision. You will accept our authority in all matters of the Church. Swear to that, Cardinal of Valencia. Swear!'

For a long moment, the two men glared at one another, then Lucrezia's pleading voice broke the tension. 'Cesare ... please ...'

'No.'

With a swift movement, Lucrezia got up from the grass and moved to her brother. 'Sweet brother, please,' she breathed in his ear, stroking his cheek.

At length Cesare relented. 'So be it. As Your Holiness pleases.'

Relieved, Rodrigo held out his arms to embrace his son, 'Cesare ... Cesare ... my heart bleeds salt tears when we quarrel.' Grasping his shoulders he shook them as he might a sulking boy, but there was a hint of pleading in his voice which reflected the uncertainty of the relationship. 'We are too Spanish, all of us. Our blood is too hot. But we are Borgias. One family, one head, one heart. Is that not so, my son?'

'I've two fathers in one flesh,' Cesare said sardonically. 'Spiritual and temporal. Now that we are in Rome again, which will come with me to my mother's house?'

* * *

A deep bitterness and anger smouldered in Vannozza's fine dark eyes as she surveyed the wreckage of her ravaged house. That she, the mother of the Pope's children, should have been thus treated by those miserable barbarian French. Rodrigo no longer cared. She felt tears of helplessness pricking at her eyes, as she looked at the torn hangings, the floor littered with debris, broken majolica from her prized collection, shattered crystal, and human excrement. With a shudder of disgust, she plucked up the soiled hem of her gown. There was a clatter of feet upon the stairs and angry exclamations as Cesare, accompanied by Gian Paolo Baglioni and Michelotto, entered the room.

'Madonna ... Mother!' He bent over her hand.

'Cesare! My son!' She pulled him to her, almost crying with relief.

'Who ... who dared do this?'

'The French, upon Rovere's orders. He took it upon himself to occupy my house.'

'Rovere! I feared it, but my father promised he would protect you when I left Rome with King Charles ...' Seeing Rodrigo at the door, he took an angry pace towards him, 'You gave your word she'd be safe!'

But Rodrigo evidently preferred to ignore him; with majestic step he approached Vannozza who knelt to kiss his hand. With a cordial kiss, he gently raised her to her feet. 'Beloved Vannozza, I rejoice to see you again.'

'I prayed God Your Holiness might one day come. For the great love I bear you.'

Rodrigo was touched, a little guilty at his neglect of her. 'I'm a poor sinner, Vannozza, who never deserved your love ...' Then, taking her hand, he led her onto the loggia. 'Come let us breathe purer air than that which those pigs have soiled ...'

'This outrage must be avenged!' Cesare said between his teeth, turning to Baglioni. 'Take as many as you need of the Spanish Guard. Let them bathe their feet in the blood of every French soldier left in Rome...'

'No, My Lord, no! His Holiness will not forgive me for thus breaking the peace...'

'Whose orders do you obey, his or mine?' Cesare said savagely. 'Now do it. Or rather than face me again you had better run for your life back to Perugia.'

Baglioni looked at him for a long moment, then dropped his eyes. 'As Your Eminence desires,' he said woodenly.

Cesare turned to Michelotto. 'Go with him. See it well done. Meet me at my apartments after. I must attend His Holiness back to the palace.'

Rodrigo took a tender farewell of Vannozza. 'Wait for me outside, my son,' he ordered Cesare. 'I would speak with your mother.'

Cesare kissed his mother's hand, bowed and strode out, Vannozza's glance following him affectionately. 'Love him, Rodrigo,' she pleaded. 'He is a good son to me.'

'Would that he were to us also,' Rodrigo replied harshly, 'but let us not talk of that. I have happy news for you. Juan returns to Rome.'

'And Jofre? He is your son too.'

Rodrigo's face closed, as if the subject were embarrassing to him. 'Jofre too. You shall have all your children in Rome. Now tell me that this makes you happy, that I may take my leave of you.'

Vannozza bowed her head, 'Your happiness is mine, Your Holiness ... When shall I see you again?'

Rodrigo made a sign of benediction over her head, his voice vague. 'We are much occupied with the affairs of Holy Church, Vannozza. But we shall give orders that your house be rebuilt and furnished in a style that befits your honour. Farewell and God be with you.'

*   *   *

60

'A score of men killed! And before our holy church of St Peter's, at the very Vatican steps!' Rodrigo's rage thundered through the room. 'May God have mercy upon your wretched soul, Gian Paolo Baglioni,' he roared. 'You are no better than a hired assassin, like all your bloodthirsty clan.' Snatching a paper from the hand of Perotto, who stood watching the scene with ill-concealed satisfaction, he shook it at the frightened young man.

'They were but Frenchmen, Holiness,' Baglioni stammered. 'I was ordered...'

'We know that you were ordered, and by whom. But for that, you would have paid for this outrage with your life. Now get out of our sight, and out of our city. If you do not go at once, your life will be forfeit to any man who wishes to take it. Remove the wretch from our presence, Perotto.'

As Baglioni and Perotto withdrew, Rodrigo, without a word to Cesare, who stood impassive by his side, attempted to leave by another door. Cesare caught his robe as he passed. Rodrigo drew back in disgust. 'There's blood on your hand. Would you soil Christ's vestments with it?'

Cesare was unmoved. 'They despoiled my mother's house and called her whore! I avenged her honour. That is all.'

'And poor Djem...?'

Cesare smiled. 'A Muslim who drank wine in breach of his faith, and no doubt died of his sin...'

'Your brother's friend, removed so lightly.'

'Thus giving weight to our purse.' He gripped his father's arm, his face hard. 'Ask yourself if my brother, your beloved Juan, can be so resolute in your service.'

*　　*　　*

Juan Borgia, Duke of Gandia, gorgeously dressed in green velvet, an emerald glowing in his cap, gold chains around his neck, and his silk hose clocked with the sunburst rays of the house of Gandia, lounged beside his father, at the long table, loaded with wine, fruit and sweetmeats. The eyes of both men were following the sinuous form of Jofre's new

61

bride, Sancia of Naples, as she danced with the Spanish Captain of the Vatican Guard. Flame-haired, green-eyed and voluptuous, Sancia was several years older than her boy husband, Jofre, who, it was rumoured, was unable to satisfy her, his interests being exclusively in those of his own sex. Rodrigo, in particular, followed every sexual innuendo of her movements with a lustful interest, a fact which did not escape the notice of Cesare, a dark figure in plain clerical dress seated at his father's other hand. Juan, on Rodrigo's right, leaned towards his father and whispered something in his ear, which made him laugh and, taking his eyes for a moment away from Sancia, he gave Jofre an amused glance.

'Jofre,' he said, 'your brother Juan has paid you a great compliment.'

Jofre was eager to hear it. 'Tell me! Is it bawdy?'

Juan teased him. 'Bawdy? What do you know of bawds, little brother?'

Giulia, sulky at the attention Sancia was exciting in the Borgia men, joined in, but with malice. 'Less than he may know of boys.'

'You witch ... You ... *old* witch!' Jofre screamed at her.

Lucrezia intervened, soothing him, 'She teases you, Jofre ...'

'I will not be teased.' Jofre was petulant. 'I will hear Juan. What compliment?'

'That with such a wife as Sancia ...' Juan drawled, then stopped. 'No. You've enough conceit already.'

'Jesu. Tell him and be done,' Cesare cut in.

Juan turned his teasing smile on him. 'Are you impatient too, brother?'

'As any man might be with the hee-hawing of an ass,' Cesare retorted.

Juan only said silkily, 'Poor Cesare.'

'You need not pity me, brother.'

Juan's voice was suddenly full of a deadly meaning. 'No, only him who pleased me, and thereby offended you.'

Cesare rose, holding out his cup to a servant for more wine. 'Have you not found another to hold your hand?' he said insultingly.

Juan leapt to his feet, furiously facing his brother. 'If I had, would Your Eminence take wine with him too?'

Rodrigo stretched out his hands, pulling them gently down to their seats, his face troubled. 'Juan . . .' he said, his voice half pleading.

Lucrezia tried to turn the conversation. 'May we not hear the compliment?' she said lightly.

'Tell me, tell me,' begged Jofre.

Juan grinned at him, accentuating his drawl. 'It was nothing, little brother. That since you appear to have reached manhood overnight, Sancia must have helped you to grow enormously.'

Everyone laughed but Jofre who, puzzled and unhappy, appealed to Cesare. 'Is it bawdy, Cesare?'

'The best our soldier brother can contrive,' he replied. 'Where did you learn the art of war, Juan? In a Spanish bordello?'

'And you theology, Cesare? From your Spanish cut-throat? Perhaps, Lord Cardinal, you would question our Holy Father's decision?'

For a moment Cesare was caught off balance; he shot an interrogatory glance at Rodrigo. 'He's not infallible . . . What decision?'

There was a pause, then Juan announced with an air of triumph, 'To send me as Captain-General against the Orsinis.'

Rodrigo stared straight ahead, his face impassive. Cesare leapt to his feet again, towering over his father, his voice a hissing whisper. 'Is this true?'

'You are a churchman, Cesare.'

'Then unfrock me!'

But Rodrigo pretended not to have heard him, his eyes once again on Sancia. Cesare saw his father's look. His expression changing from one of anger to a vengeful smile, he left the table and crossed over to stand near Sancia, staring at her. Sancia, still dancing with the Captain, returned the look. Their eyes met, Sancia dropped the Captain's hand and, as if mesmerised, went over to dance with Cesare.

* * *

'You are a strange man, Cesare Borgia,' Sancia said reflectively as she lay in his dishevelled bed that night. 'Who do you love?'

Cesare got up and went to help himself to a cup of wine. 'No one,' he said tersely.

'You are like me ... Come here.' Cesare moved over to the bed. 'You Borgias.' Sancia's eyes were mocking. 'You have to compete in everything, don't you?'

Cesare gripped her wrist hard, so that she winced. 'What do you mean?'

Sancia gave a derisive laugh. 'Such a close family,' she mocked. 'Where the father goes, the sons follow. You cuckold your brother to spite your father, and yet you don't know ...' She drew in her breath in a sharp gasp of pain as Cesare twisted her arm cruelly.

'Don't know what?'

But Sancia was not afraid of him. 'If you release me, I'll tell you.' As he did so, she looked up at him with an air of teasing triumph. 'The Holy Father has already passed this way. Before his unholy son.'

For a moment, Cesare stared at her angrily. Then he laughed, 'By the bones of Christ! He is invincible.' He flung the cup into the corner of the room, and made as if to get into bed with her.

Sancia warded him off, still taunting. 'A pity I had to marry the only Borgia man who is not a man ...' she said, 'What do you think your brother Juan is like in bed?'

* * *

Juan was invested by his father with the regalia of Captain-General of the Armies of the Church in a splendid ceremony in St Peter's on 26th October 1496, attended by all the Cardinals, the ambassadors and the Roman nobility. Clad in a superb suit of armour inlaid with gold and silver (a placatory gift sent from Milan by Ludovico Sforza), Juan received from his father the traditional cap of crimson velvet, to which Rodrigo had taken care to pin a large diamond with his own hands, and the great standard bearing the papal arms. Juan swaggered in the limelight, while Rodrigo's face beamed with paternal pride, but the expressions of most of those present revealed their ill-concealed disgust at such a blatant act of nepotism. Among them were a contingent of war-hardened Spanish troops, sent by Ferdinand and Isabella of Spain to support their friend and fellow countryman Rodrigo Borgia in his campaign against the Orsinis. Notable among them was the lean, sunburnt figure of Queen Isabella's favourite captain, Gonsalvo Cordoba, who was already winning a great reputation as a military leader, and who could hardly conceal his mortification at having to take second place to this popinjay, the Pope's young son.

The Borgia women happily watched the scene from a balcony in the choir, where they were supposed to remain unseen, but the laughter and chatter of Sancia and Lucrezia could be clearly heard at solemn moments during the Mass, causing further scandal to the onlookers, among them, of course, Johann Burchard, who took mental notes of the proceedings in order to record them later in his diary. Alone among the Borgias, Cesare's face was a frozen mask as he stood among his fellow Cardinals in the stalls ranged beside the high altar, his feelings a turmoil of frustration, envy, and contempt for his brother.

Cesare's silent predictions of a dismal debut for Juan as a General were soon fulfilled. Disaster followed upon disaster for the papal troops under their inept leader. The defiant Orsinis made sallies up to the very walls of Rome to insult the Pope, and sent a donkey into the papal camp with a placard saying, 'I am the Ambassador of the Duke of Gandia', round its neck, and a rude letter addressed to Juan under its tail. Worse was to come: the Orsinis defeated Juan's army at Soriano on 24th January 1497, 'heavily and with great dishonour', as Burchard wrote in his diary. Juan himself was brought back to Rome, gravely wounded.

* * *

'Will my brother truly die?' Cesare drew the Jewish physician aside, at the same time never taking his eyes from the unconscious figure on the bed, beside which Lucrezia sat, her brother's limp hand held to her lips. As Cesare watched her, she rose and kissed her brother's pale cheek. Cesare's eyes narrowed. 'Will he die?' he asked the man again.

'Your Eminence may have confidence in my skills,' the physician assured him.

'I did not speak of your skills. Answer my question. Will he die?'

'Does Your Eminence ask whether I can save him?'

'If you can, by the same token you cannot. Or may not. Do you understand me, Jew?' The menacing words were spoken almost soundlessly, but the physician understood and gave Cesare a glance of horror. Fortunately for him, their conversation was interrupted by the arrival of Perotto, bearing a dispatch in his hands, and of Burchard, summoned by a grief-stricken Rodrigo to discuss funeral arrangements in the event of Juan's death.

Rodrigo's thoughts were only for his wounded son. Ignoring the scroll which Perotto thrust urgently into his hands, he addressed Burchard. 'Messer Burchard ... our son ... this brave and valiant soul ... is close to death ...' His voice broke, and he stopped to wipe the tears from his eyes.

'No! He must not die!' Lucrezia burst out, holding Juan's hand to her tear-wet cheek. Cesare watched this expression of love and grief from beneath lowered brows. His face grim, he walked quickly over to his father, took the scroll and read it.

Rodrigo regained control of himself. 'Despite our grief, you must prepare for our consideration a funeral ceremony

66

worthy of the name of Borgia and of him who so nobly bore it. A Solemn Requiem...'

'Will Your Holiness declare a Te Deum of thanksgiving before the Requiem Mass?' Cesare broke in.

Lucrezia's voice was shocked, 'Brother...!'

Cesare held up the paper and, with a note of derision in his voice, intended for his father, said loudly, 'This brings news that the Spanish have driven the Orsinis from the field and into their rat-hole castles.'

'O, Merciful God!' Rodrigo's voice rang out melo-dramatically as he sank to his knees, arms outstretched and eyes heavenwards, 'that has brought us joy in this hour of sorrow, the glory of our son who was the architect of this victory!'

Cesare was stupefied. 'Architect! What architect?'

Lucrezia rose and went over to Cesare to restrain him. 'Cesare! Do not abuse him!' she spoke sharply in defence of her wounded brother, only angering Cesare the more.

'A fool could've seen that Juan would be defeated. Am I to be told that the triumph of greater Captains was his design?' Lucrezia put her finger on his lips to silence him. He seized her hand roughly and stared hard into her face. 'Your hand stinks of his sweat,' he said, flinging it away from him, and strode towards the door, screwing up the paper and tossing it towards the kneeling Pope in a gesture of disgust.

*   *   *

'Cesare hates me! He plots to kill me. That's why I'm going, if you want to know.' Giovanni Sforza, dressed in travelling clothes, faced Lucrezia with the guilty defiance of the weak.

'You dream of plots, Giovanni. Even the slightest sound at night, and you jump out of your skin. Rest assured that Cesare does not think enough of you to hate you – unless you cross his path. I told you to be careful not to displease him.' Lucrezia's tone was calm, non-committal as if the imminent flight of her husband was a matter of indifference to her.

'It is enough for him that I live and breathe,' Giovanni screamed at her, stung by her coolness. 'He wants to kill me to rid your family of our marriage.'

'Killing you would not be necessary, Giovanni, you must know that. You know the law ...' Lucrezia looked steadfastly at him.

Giovanni dropped his eyes before her accusing stare. 'You know I've tried,' he said wretchedly. 'You know! In Pesaro...'

'On my father's orders.' Lucrezia was inexorable.

'Please, Lucrezia, can you not love me, even so?'

'Why, even so?'

'That we may be happy ...' his voice trailed away.

'Under cold sheets,' her voice accused him.

'Lucrezia,' Giovanni pleaded. 'Would you have me dead, and marry again?'

'I would have a man!'

The insult was too much for Giovanni to bear; he turned on her viciously. 'A Borgia! In a Borgia bed!' Then, horrified at what he had said, he fell at her feet, clutching her skirt, 'Lucrezia, Lucrezia ... forgive me ... forgive!'

Lucrezia pulled her gown from his hand, looking down at him expressionlessly, feeling no emotion, neither pity nor contempt. 'Had I married a man,' she said, 'I would have taken his hand and gone with him gladly wherever he wished. Defying God and my family, whatever he wished.' She turned away from him and walked towards the door, 'You had better go, Giovanni. Run to your Uncle Ludovico in Milan. I will not keep you here.'

'Lucrezia ... !' Giovanni wailed, stretching out his hands towards her in supplication, but she had already turned her back on him, and walked out of the room without a backward glance.

* * *

Sancia sat naked before the glass in her bedchamber, her olive-skinned body glowing in the candlelight which caught the flame tint in her titian hair. She pretended to be absorbed in the task of combing it with an ivory comb set in silver, but in reality she was watching Cesare's face reflected in the glass, as he watched her in return, like the two wary animals they were. 'Lucrezia's husband has left her. Run away to his uncle in Milan.'

Cesare shrugged indifferently. 'I thought he might. If he were frightened enough...'

'Of you or by you?'

Cesare did not answer. Instead he took a strand of her hair and began to play with it, twisting it round his fingers. 'You know what I want,' he said. 'Tell me. You are her confidante.'

'Why should she tell me anything she keeps from her loving brother?' Sancia mocked him.

'Women trust each other.'

'Does she not trust you?'

Cesare was becoming angry at Sancia's verbal fencing. 'I am beginning to tire of you. Each time I visit you I lighten my purse to divert your husband's silly attention from us. Today it was a white Arab, with silver harness. A thousand ducats for the pleasure of riding his wife.'

'Should you find me too expensive, Your Eminence,' Sancia retorted, 'I shall not miss you. I'll not lack for Borgia men. There's your father – and your other brother. The thought of my bed will soon restore Juan to health ...' She smiled tauntingly at him. 'How does that please you?'

Cesare shrugged. 'Tell me what I asked you.'

Stung by his indifference, Sancia resolved to wound him. 'What's the matter, Cesare?' she said silkily. 'Are you offended because Lucrezia's not jealous of me?'

'Whore.' Cesare locked his hand in her hair, twisting it to turn her face towards him. Despite the pain, Sancia continued to smile at him unafraid. 'I would joyfully whip you,' he said between clenched teeth.

'If that pleases Your Eminence.' She placed her hand on his fist, caressing it. 'I can please all you Borgia men. Play nursemaid for my husband. Hold up a mirror to Juan's vanity. And cry "Amen" when your Holy Father pants above me and prays for God's understanding.' She dug her nails suddenly into his flesh. 'So whip me, Eminence, if that's your desire.'

Cesare shook his hand free, releasing her. 'Has their marriage been consummated? Answer me!'

'Would Giovanni leave Rome otherwise?'

'He runs from shadows.' His voice became urgent. 'Sancia, please, I must know. Did she tell you it was done? Was it done?'

*　　*　　*

'No,' Lucrezia said. 'Not once. Not once in four years.' She was sitting on the edge of Rodrigo's bed, the only light coming from a flickering silver hanging lamp filled with olive oil, casting strange shadows on the dark chamber beyond the bedhangings, where only the golden Borgia bull stood out. Rodrigo sat upright, supported by embroidered pillows, his eyes fixed upon his beautiful daughter, whose hand he caressed.

'Then Cesare was right,' was all he said.

Lucrezia was reproachful. 'You set him to discover what I would have willingly told you, had you asked before.'

'The idea was Cesare's, not mine,' Rodrigo said apologetically.

'I believe you.'

'Dear child,' Rodrigo's voice took on a pathetic note, asking for sympathy. 'I was wrong to marry you to Sforza ... Can you forgive a father's foolish error? My only hope was that this marriage would please you.'

'No. That it would serve you.'

Rodrigo feigned surprise at such an idea. 'How so? It has brought me nothing but pain.'

'It brought you Sforza votes and won you the papal crown.'

Rodrigo sighed, pained. 'You wish to wound me.'

Lucrezia was unmoved. 'If you ask me to believe childish lies, *you* wound *me*.'

Rodrigo puller her closer towards him, kissing her hand in apparent contrition. Then he closed his mouth about her little finger. Lucrezia trembled perceptibly, but went on as if nothing had happened. 'You will dissolve my marriage?'

Her reaction to his caress had not escaped Rodrigo; it excited him. 'If you so desire.'

'As you desire to be free of an alliance which binds the independence of your office.'

'You speak with a woman's voice, but these are a man's thoughts. Do I hear Cesare talking?'

'No. I too am a Borgia.'

Rodrigo tried, but could not overcome his rising sensuality. His hand moved to her head, casually loosening her hair so that it fell to her shoulders. He managed to keep his voice calm. 'Would you wed again, Lucia?'

'If Your Holiness did not require that, you'd not be so ready to rid me of Giovanni Sforza.'

Rodrigo said admiringly, 'You are a Borgia!'

Lucrezia's voice was firm and uncompromising as she said, 'But this time, father, let it be a man. He may serve you as you wish, only let it be a man who will satisfy me!'

Rodrigo was moved, 'Lucrezia ... Lucia ... beloved daughter ... I believe I love nothing in this life as much as I love you ...'

In an excess of confused emotion, he pulled her to him, her proximity overwhelming his self-control. Lucrezia made only the slightest effort to resist, 'It's late, father...'

'Dearest Lucia ... do I weary you? Lucia ... I love you ... embrace me to show me that you love me, embrace me!' He put his arms around her, enfolding her, resting his head upon hers in a loving and paternal attitude. Then his lips touched her hair, moved to her eyes, her lips, gentle no longer but greedy with desire as he kissed her throat, then moved downwards. Lucrezia too was aroused, her eyes closed, the blood throbbing in her as she felt her father's hands uncover her breasts, felt his lips wildly demanding them, heard his half-crazed prayers, 'Merciful God ... have compassion on my frailty ... Merciful God ... forgive this poor sinner...'

*　　*　　*

Lucrezia sat in the Belvedere garden, holding up a glass for Juan, who, now fully recovered from his wound, was absorbed in his favourite occupation, choosing a new wardrobe. At the moment, he was trying on a scarlet velvet cap adorned with drop pearls, frowning at his image in the glass. Behind them, Sancia lounged on a carved stone bench, indolently eating grapes from a rock-crystal bowl. Jofre fed doves while Rodrigo sat in a canopied chair to protect himself from the spring sun, observing the idyllic family scene, content. His happy smile became less broad as he observed Cesare striding towards them, and his cordiality somewhat forced as he pressed Cesare to share his happiness. 'Cesare! See God is good to us. Your brother is well again.'

Cesare replied tersely, 'And has been these two weeks.'

'No, Lucia, no . . .' Juan's voice was exasperated. 'Hold it thus. That I may see the great pearl that hangs above my ear . . .' His sister laughed good-naturedly, and kissed her brother's ear.

Cesare made an impatient gesture. 'Was I called from my duties to witness this?' he said.

'We are a family again,' Rodrigo soothed him; 'without your presence we would be incomplete. Take joy in that.'

'I take joy. Now will Your Holiness permit me to leave?'

Juan's voice drawled, 'Holy Father . . . have you soothed my intemperate brother?'

Rodrigo said, quickly and firmly, 'He has no dispute with you.'

Juan was in a good mood and inclined to be generous. 'And I wish none with him. Take my hand, Cesare!' When his brother ignored his outstretched hand, he shrugged with a good-humoured smile, and turned to the servant who was holding out a new doublet for his inspection. 'That I will take, but with more gems on the sleeves . . . And tell the rogue if he sends it to me again like that, he'll lose an ear!'

Cesare appealed to Rodrigo. 'Must we waste time on this mummery? You know we're not yet done with the Orsinis.

The father may be dead, but you still hold his two cubs in a cage...'

'I'm faint from this excitement,' Juan interrupted. 'Sister, cool my forehead with your hand...' Lucrezia gently stroked his brow, a gesture which Cesare observed with a black look.

Rodrigo rose, his concern for his son taking precedence over all other considerations. 'Enough,' he said. 'We've tired him. He must rest. Come, my dear son, we will see you to your chamber, where Lucrezia shall sing for you...'

Cesare turned on his heel. 'Very well,' he muttered under his breath, '*I* will deal with the Orsinis...'

* * *

Paolo Orsini looked up apprehensively as the door of his cell in Castel Sant'Angelo swung open, and blinked in the sudden light of the torch which Michelotto carried. Cesare came through the door behind him, and nodded to Michelotto with dismissive gesture. Michelotto placed the torch in a sconce and left them. Paolo rose weakly from the filthy straw on which he had been lying, attempting to put a brave face on his condition. 'My Lord Cesare...' he said, then anxiously, 'my brother Giovanni?'

'He lives.'

Paolo's face lit up with relief. 'May God be thanked!'

His joy was short-lived, as Cesare added, 'But must shortly hang.'

'Then grant me that mercy too.' Paolo's voice was anguished. 'First my father...'

'Yes, your father,' Cesare cut in. 'As he can no longer speak, perhaps you will tell us. What letters did your father receive from Giovanni Sforza?'

Paolo was puzzled. 'Letters? What letters... I saw none.'

'Do not prevaricate with me, Paolo Orsini. You know they were written.'

'Since I saw none, I cannot say.'

Cesare changed his tactics. His expression softened into a smile, as he extended his arms to enfold Orsini in a friendly

73

embrace, his voice emotional as he addressed him, 'Paolo
... Paolo ... old friend. You were ever honest with me. How
can we be enemies? Will you believe that your life is as dear
to me as your brother's is to you?'

The ingenuous Paolo was moved. 'Indeed, My Lord, I
hope I may...'

'Believe it, Paolo. I've interceded with His Holiness. He
has spared you.'

'No, My Lord, while Giovanni ...'

'Paolo, Paolo ... Always your honour ... Don't be a fool.
Dead you cannot help your brother, alive you may save
him.'

'My Lord?'

'He will live. If you'll be of service to His Holiness.'

'But I know nothing of letters from your sister's husband...'

'That!' Cesare clapped him on the shoulder. 'That
matter's of no consequence to His Holiness. Now come with
me.'

*   *   *

Paolo Orsini was despatched by Rodrigo to treat of peace
with his kinsmen who were still holding out in their castles
in the Campagna, despite their defeat at the hands of
Gonsalvo de Cordoba and his Spaniards. Peace was agreed
at Easter 1497, when the Orsinis surrendered their prisoners in return for an indemnity, and were confirmed in their
rights to their castles. It was an uneasy end to a war which
neither side had won and which had left so much bad blood
between Borgias and Orsinis that no sensible man could
doubt that sooner or later hostilities between them must be
resumed. For the moment, however, Rodrigo affected to
receive the Orsinis with the most cordial friendship, celebrating a Mass of thanksgiving for the peace, and going
through the ceremonies of Holy Week with a benign countenance. One such ceremony was the traditional washing of
the feet of twelve paupers of the city, an occasion attended
by the whole papal court and, of course, the Borgia family.

Cesare, dressed in his Cardinal's robes, stood beside Ascanio Sforza as they watched Rodrigo go through the perfunctory motions of washing the pauper's feet, an awkward task for one of his bulk, since it involved edging on his knees along the row of selected poor.

'My sister's cheeks are pale.' Cesare nodded towards Lucrezia who sat, white and still, in a chair, her hand entwined with Juan's, as Sancia whispered in her ear. Cesare frowned as he saw Juan and Lucrezia exchange a meaningful look, but he continued with what he had to say to Sforza. 'Does Your Eminence think she may be ill?'

Ascanio's thoughts were elsewhere. 'The air is close,' he replied abstractedly.

'Or she's unhappy, perhaps,' Cesare went on, 'at the absence of her husband. What does Your Eminence hear from your nephew?'

Ascanio became suddenly alert. 'Nothing,' he said cautiously.

'The boy was gone from Rome too soon.'

'Too soon?' Ascanio replied, puzzled.

Cesare's voice was bland, but with a hint of menace. 'To answer the charge by Paolo Orsini . . .' He paused. 'Forgive me, I thought Your Eminence must know.'

Ascanio was by now uneasy. 'Know what?' he asked.

'That your foolish nephew sent letters to the Orsinis . . . His Holiness would confer with you on that – and related matters . . .' With a slight inclination of his head, Cesare moved away, leaving Ascanio a prey to apprehensive thoughts: what devilry was in the wind, now?

* * *

He had not long to wait to discover what the Borgias wanted of him. Early in June, he was summoned to a curious ceremony in the Vatican in the presence of the Pope, attended by Cesare, two other Cardinals, and Juan and Jofre. Lucrezia sat, stiff and pale, at a small desk, while Perotto, standing beside her, read out the contents of an imposing-looking document.

75

'The Lady Lucrezia Borgia,' he intoned, 'does further affirm, testify and complain that her husband, the Lord Giovanni Sforza, did not keep her company, fittingly, as a husband should, in that manner required under the sacrament of marriage for the procreation of children, and that she is therefore a virgin still as God made her. And further, for this and other reasons heretofore set down, she does ask that her marriage be set aside, dissolved and made null and void.' As Perotto finished reading, he placed the document before Lucrezia, offering her a pen with which to sign it. After a slight hesitation, she did so.

At the other side of the room, Rodrigo beckoned to Ascanio Sforza, his voice lowered so that others should not hear him. 'Your nephew must sign a like paper.'

Ascanio was definitely nervous, 'Your Holiness . . . I may not be able to persuade him that . . .'

'Ascanio,' Rodrigo's voice held a warning note, 'we've been pleased to forget the letters which that foolish youth sent to the Orsinis . . .'

'Holiness, he does assure me that . . .'

Rodrigo continued inexorably, 'And that . . . according to the confession of Paolo Orsini, made under oath to our son, the Cardinal of Valencia, those letters were written at your prompting. All this, Ascanio, for the love we bear you, we have been pleased to forget.'

Ascanio was powerless. 'It shall be as Your Holiness wishes.'

'Good.' Rodrigo smiled at him. 'And remember that the boy must swear that because of his impotence the Lady Lucrezia is still *virgo intacta* . . .'

*   *   *

'An untouched virgin!' Sancia threw back her head in an ugly laugh that was full of meaning.

'Why does that amuse you so? Envy, perhaps? It's not a state that would suit you, Sancia,' Cesare drawled from the bed across which he was lounging, fully clothed.

'You don't know?' Sancia grinned at him cruelly.

Cesare leapt up and seized her threateningly by the wrist, giving it a slight twist as he did so. 'Tell me why?' he ordered her.

'Ask her,' Sancia snapped at him, then, as he twisted her arm up behind her back, she gave a scream of pain, drew back her lips from her teeth like a she-wolf, and spat out, 'Your virgin sister is with child!'

Reeling with shock, Cesare released her. A split second later, he hit her across the face with the back of his hand, sending her flying against the wall. Pinning her against it, his face close to hers, he hissed: 'You lie!'

'Why should I?'

'Who is the man? Who?'

'Who else but a Borgia!'

Cesare stepped back, stunned with horror. Sancia, frightened but still defiant, saw that she had wounded him almost beyond endurance.

'Juan . . . Juan!' Cesare's voice was almost inaudible, but Sancia heard what he said and looked surprised. Then she smiled a triumphant smile. What if he had mistaken her meaning? Why should she care? It was enough to hurt him and to twist the knife in the wound.

'She'd not tell you . . .' Cesare was grasping at straws.

'But he would!'

Cesare's horror-stricken face showed her that he believed it.

'It's true!' she screamed at him, 'It's true, your beloved sister and . . .'

But Cesare could bear it no longer; turning from her he stumbled towards the door, unable to restrain a shout of agony and rage, 'Juan . . . Lucrezia . . . !'

* * *

'Lucrezia – I must see her! Where has she gone?' Cesare burst into Rodrigo's bedchamber the following morning, as the Pope was making his toilette.

Rodrigo carefully wiped his hands dry on a linen cloth

offered him by a servant before replying. He did not look at Cesare. 'Your sister is gone from Rome.'

'Gone? Without a farewell to me? Gone where?'

'To the convent of San Sisto.'

Cesare was surprised and suspicious. 'Why?'

'Leave us,' Rodrigo ordered the servant. Then, still avoiding Cesare's eye and choosing his words with care, he said, 'It was her wish to retire from public life until her divorce is concluded . . .'

Cesare broke in savagely, 'And her child born.'

There was guilt and sadness in Rodrigo's voice. 'Cesare . . .'

'You thought I'd not know of it?' Cesare's voice was bitter.

'Not yet.'

'And the father? When was I to learn his name?'

Rodrigo said tonelessly, 'The child will be born in darkness and forgotten in ignorance. You need not know its father's name.'

'I do know it.'

There was a long silence. Then Rodrigo, protective guile making him non-committal, said slowly, 'Then let God guide your conscience . . .'

'And yours.'

Rodrigo nodded gravely, 'And mine.'

'Amen.' Cesare's voice was sarcastic.

'Cesare . . .' Rodrigo held out his hand in appeal for compassion, finding none.

'That's all you'll say?' Cesare's tone was fiercely unforgiving. Then he turned to mockery. 'Nothing of God's great anger against us?'

Rodrigo sought refuge in obscurity. 'Church and family are his rock, Cesare. Upon them we seek his salvation and understanding. All else is shifting sand.'

'Jesu!' Cesare muttered under his breath. 'May I see my sister?' he demanded.

'She is content.'

'But *I* am not.'

Rodrigo was unyielding. 'You will not see her.' As Cesare

gave him a brief angry bow and turned to go, he called him back. 'Your Eminence!' His tone became redolent of papal authority distancing himself from his son. 'You too will leave Rome. As our Legate to crown the new King in Naples.'

'To keep me away from brother Juan?'

At the bitterness with which Cesare referred to his brother, Rodrigo faltered, a father again. 'He goes with you as our Captain-General ... My son ... remember ... I love him no less than you all...'

'I always remember that, father,' Cesare said meaningly. 'I'll also remember he's my sister's brother...'

Returning to his apartments, he summoned Michelotto.

*   *   *

'My cousin, Lord,' Michelotto announced. 'Don Ramiro de Lorqua.' Cesare leaned back in his chair, surveying the man who was bowing before him. He saw a man of small but muscular build, the family hardness of expression which he shared with Michelotto being the dominating feature of his dark face. 'Yes,' Cesare thought to himself, 'he'll do. A man who would shrink at nothing.' Aloud he said, 'You serve my brother Juan?'

'I have that honour, Your Eminence,' Ramiro answered.

'In what capacity?'

'However he may desire, Your Eminence.' Ramiro was respectful but unabashed.

'How specific?'

'Specific discreet, Your Eminence.'

Cesare looked at Michelotto. 'Your cousin's a man of few words, my friend.'

Michelotto spoke for him. 'He's the Duke's pimp, My Lord.'

Ramiro smiled proudly, 'I can find a pleasing lady blindfold in the dark. If Your Eminence pleases, I can...'

'No,' Cesare cut him short. 'If you're to serve me, what other skills have you?'

'My Lord,' Ramiro spoke slowly so as to give his words more effect, 'I have a hand with a garrotte that can snap a man's neck as quickly and easily as you would a twig. And open up a stubborn backbone with the point of a knife...'

'A talented family yours,' Cesare nodded to Michelotto. 'I thank you, Don Ramiro, I shall soon send you word by your cousin how you may be of service to me...'

Ramiro bowed low and withdrew.

'He could betray me to my brother,' Cesare said to Michelotto.

'Not while he fears I'd slit his throat,' Michelotto replied calmly, 'and besides, he would be Your Eminence's man. He has ambitions beyond procuring wenches for the Duke's pleasure. He loves not the Duke...'

'Loves him so little that he would encompass his death? It may not come to that. The threat of death may serve as well as the deed itself.'

'Not so, My Lord. A dead man cannot take revenge.'

'But others may.'

'My Lord, a powerful Prince ...' Michelotto hesitated. 'Are we speaking of such?' he asked delicately.

'In hypothesis.'

'A powerful Prince knows that rather than lose his favour, grieving kinsmen will soon forget their dead...'

Cesare nodded. Their eyes met in understanding.

*   *   *

Rodrigo received Vannozza in his privy chamber, raising her graciously from her knees, and kissing her courteously. He was clearly surprised by her visit, and not a little uneasy as to its purpose, though he concealed his unease under an urbane manner. 'Vannozza,' he said, 'we see you too rarely...'

'Holiness,' she said timidly, 'I would see our daughter.'

'She is in retreat at San Sisto, and cannot be visited.'

'But Rodrigo,' in her anxiety Vannozza forgot the formal mode of address, 'she'll be afraid.'

'Afraid?' he feigned astonishment. 'Our daughter? Of what?'

'The pain ... the loneliness ...'

'She's not ill.' Rodrigo's tone was brisk. 'And she has the good sisters for company.'

'But when the child comes ...'

'Child?' Rodrigo blustered. 'What child? There's no child.' He got up from his chair and pretended to search for some papers on his desk to hide his face from her.

Vannozza, aware how great the distance between them now was, pleaded with him, her voice full of sadness, 'I asked little of your love, Rodrigo, and wanted little beyond that. Is it too much now ... must you deny me this one small kindness?'

Rodrigo turned towards her again, changing the subject with a disarming smile. 'Of course! You shame me, Vannozza. I've not yet done what I promised when the French left, a new house ...'

'I'm content with my villa on the Esquiline.'

'Good.' Rodrigo was jovial, feigning interest. 'And does its vineyard flourish? And your worthy husband, is he in good health?'

Vannozza nodded, barely able to hide her disappointment.

'Excellent. Excellent.' Rodrigo took her hand and kissed it. 'I'm indeed glad you came, Vannozza. I'm in grievous need of your help. May I rely upon it?'

'Your Holiness knows you may.'

Again Rodrigo turned away from her, he paced the room, a tone of genuine distress in his voice, as he told her, 'Our sons perplex my heart. I'm torn between severity and indulgence with them. Juan ... for example, Juan wishes me to hang a poor wretch who he says insulted him. And Cesare ... you know how difficult he is. Now they go to Naples together, and their hostile natures give me some cause to fear ... Vannozza, I beg you, ask them to sup together with you before they go. Persuade them to travel as friends, as loving brothers ...'

* * *

81

Cesare, Juan and Jofre sat round their mother's table under the vine-covered trellis at her country villa on the Esquiline. The sky still glowed with the light of midsummer over the Eternal City, crickets whirred in the vineyards round the house, and the young grapes hung in gleaming bunches over the brothers' heads. Light played on their faces from olive-oil lights placed among the bowls of peaches, the trenchers of country bread and white hunks of pecorino cheese on the wooden table. Juan had drunk deeply from the flagon of wine which he kept near him, his face was sweating and flushed with triumph as he gloated over the death of the young man who had insulted him, hanged at Rodrigo's orders. 'And when I rode over Sant'Angelo bridge, there he was. Forty feet above me at the end of a rope. Biting the foul tongue that called me bastard...'

Vannozza looked pained, and her husband Canale frowned, but they said nothing. Juan would not have listened anyway. Jofre, however, was intrigued. 'Does it take long to die, Cesare?' he turned to his eldest brother, 'To hang and to die...?'

Cesare smiled. 'As long as vengeance desires, and the hangman's skill may contrive, little brother.'

'Do your eyes come out, like grapes on stalks?'

Vannozza tried to stop the conversation. 'Jofre ...' she began, but Juan was still interested in his experience. 'I saw his. On his cheeks, it seemed. Looking down at me.'

'In envy, no doubt,' Cesare said quietly, 'of so noble a man.'

'With so rich a doublet!' Jofre chimed in.

'So fine a cape.' Cesare's face was mock serious.

'So gay a plume!' Jofre echoed.

'So long a sword...'

Juan, sublimely unaware that his brothers were not in earnest, could not resist adding to this paean of praise, 'So rare a horse!'

'And so splendid a saddle,' Cesare went on, delightedly.

At this point even Juan's overweening vanity was penetrated by suspicion. 'Yes,' he said. 'Your gift surprised me, brother.'

'An impulse, brother,' Cesare replied.

But Juan was still suspicious. 'You do nothing by impulse,' he said.

'Gratitude, then,' Cesare replied. 'That fool who called you a bastard, by the same token insulted me.'

'So you sent me a silver saddle? No.'

'We are all Borgias. Touch one, touch all,' Cesare reminded him.

Juan was not mollified. 'I know what you really mean. I should've challenged him and killed him.'

Cesare sighed. 'I told you it was impossible,' he said to Vannozza.

Juan rose abruptly from the table, petulant anger in his face. 'He's involved you in his tricks!' he said to Vannozza. 'I'm returning to Rome. Now.'

'Juan...!' Vannozza's voice was soothing. 'My son, I asked him to be gentle with you, in love and friendship. Am I wrong to wish that?'

Cesare, for once, was conciliatory. 'Let the matter pass,' he said.

Vannozza took a firm tone. '... you shall not leave my house in anger. I've grieved too long over your quarrelling to endure it further. Juan!'

But Juan was not to be persuaded. He did not leave but stood there, looking stonily out over the hills. Cesare moved over to Vannozza, took her hand, kissed it and held it in his. His manner was unusually gentle, and when he spoke to Juan his voice was persuasive. 'Brother ... are you afraid to face me?' Then, as Juan turned slowly towards him, 'To have no love for you would be unnatural ...'

'You've shown little evidence of it,' Juan said drily.

'I'll not deny it's been clouded with envy,' Cesare admitted.

Juan raised his eyebrows ironically. 'And now that's gone! Like that!' he snapped his fingers. 'By what miracle?'

In answer Cesare lifted his mother's hand expressively, 'This lady's love for us both.' He kissed her hand again before releasing it and approaching Juan, pleading with him, 'Must we be ingrate sons and cause her more sorrow? Our father too has commanded me to cherish you.'

Juan still refused to be persuaded. 'Not for the first time,' he said.

'To my shame,' Cesare admitted. 'But this time I've given him my word. Will you believe it ... and take my hand?'

'You laughed at my wounds,' Juan said resentfully.

'May God forgive me that, brother. I was jealous of them.'

'You mocked my campaign against the Orsi...'

'Again jealousy ... a weakness in me. Forgive it now, brother.'

'Juan ...' Vannozza pleaded.

'Take my hand, brother,' Cesare said, holding out his hand to Juan with a disarming smile. Juan hesitated, looking from his mother to Cesare, then he relented and reluctantly put out his own hand. Cesare grasped it, pulling Juan to him in a warm embrace.

Vannozza smiled with relief and joy, her hand in her husband's. 'My sons,' she said, 'it is late. You must return.' Then her eyes widened in surprise and alarm, as she glimpsed a dark masked figure standing just beyond the reach of the lamplight. 'Who is that?'

Juan had evidently been expecting someone. 'My servant, Ramiro,' he explained, and strode towards him, his face full of pleasurable anticipation. They whispered together briefly, then Ramiro, at a gesture from Juan, leapt up to ride pillion behind him.

Juan was in high spirits as the three brothers rode back to Rome, his previous sullen mood having given way to one of excitement. When they reached the narrow winding streets of the Ghetto opening off the Piazza Judea before crossing the Tiber, he reined in his horse. 'Here I leave you, brothers,' he told them.

Jofre was worried. 'It's dangerous to ride alone. Take my groom.'

Cesare's voice was reassuring. 'That rogue behind him looks sturdy enough,' he nodded towards Ramiro. 'Besides, you waste your breath, Jofre. When a lady calls, nothing will keep my brother at home.'

Juan smiled delightedly. 'My own groom meets me in the Piazza Judea, with my night-armour,' he said.

'Three of you, in one pleasure-bed?' Cesare jested.

Juan laughed, then with a wave of his hand he wheeled his horse and disappeared into the mouth of a dark alley, the silent Ramiro riding behind him.

* * *

The waning moon glinted on the silken surface of the river, coiling round a barge, laden with timber, anchored to the bank, and on the sleeping figure of the watchman who guarded it. He awoke with a start to the sound of hooves and, raising his head cautiously, for it was a dangerous hour of night when all sensible men should be in their beds, he saw two men emerge from the mouth of the nearby alley opening onto the wharf. They looked around, as if to check that no one was there, then disappeared back into the alley. A rider on a white horse emerged with the body of a man slung across its crupper, supported at the head and legs by the first two men so that it should not fall off. The horseman wheeled his mount so that the hindquarters faced the river, then, at a muttered command, the two men took the body and slung it into the water. When the strange men had disappeared silently back by the way they came, the watchman plucked up courage to peer over the side of his boat. The body was that of a young man, richly dressed. For a moment it floated on the surface of the water, the pale face turned up to the moon. Horrified, the watchman saw that the eyes were fixed with an expression of terror, the lips drawn back in agony. Whoever it was had not died a pleasant death. Then the corpse vanished beneath the water.

* * *

'Dead? My son dead?' Rodrigo's voice rose to a scream. 'How mean you dead?'

'From many wounds, Your Holiness. They found the body of the Duke in the river ...' The Spanish Captain, unwilling bearer of evil tidings, was afraid to look at the Pope.

Rodrigo leaned back in his chair as if he were going to faint, his face grey with shock, knuckles gripping the arms of the chair, his eyes, rolling round the room in search of comfort, rested upon Cesare, appealing to him. 'Cesare ... Cesare ... Tell me it is not true.'

Swiftly, Cesare crossed the room to kneel before his father, taking his hand and kissing it in a gesture of filial devotion, his face a mask of simulated grief. 'My father, I fear it is ... I have seen him ...' He turned away his head, as though unable to bear the memory. 'But he shall be revenged, his murderers shall not go unpunished ...' Raising his hand, his features grieved but composed, he called the Captain.

The man stepped forward, 'Eminence!'

'The woodseller ... you were to put him to the question. What did he say ...?'

'Nothing, Your Eminence. At least he has no more to say ...'

'What do you mean? Do not trifle with me,' Cesare menaced him.

'He died, Eminence. Your man Michelotto questioned him too hard. He was old ... the last turn killed him.'

'Bunglers! I should have you whipped!' Cesare shouted at him. 'Now get out of my sight!' As the man backed out of the room, frightened, Cesare turned to Rodrigo, who was lying back in his chair, staring at the ceiling, as if stunned. His voice became gentle. 'Come, Father,' he said. 'Come and see Juan. Burchard has arranged a magnificent lying in state for him. He looks as handsome now in death as he did in life.' Moving like an automaton, Rodrigo rose from his chair to take Cesare's arm, his steps faltering like those of an old man.

Juan lay in state in a side chapel of the basilica of St Peter's next to the Vatican, the chapel in which his great-uncle, Pope Calixtus, founder of the family fortunes, was interred. The papal embalmers had done their job well, his eyes were closed and his features composed as if he were but sleeping. Burchard had seen to it that he was dressed in his finest clothes, the great candles beside the bier were reflected in the rubies of his crimson velvet doublet (which concealed the nine stab wounds he had received), and his blonde hair, cleansed now of the Tiber mud, gleamed silken on a pillow of cloth of gold; upon his breast lay the sword and insignia of Captain-General of the Church.

Cesare fell to his knees beside the body, his blood-red Cardinal's robes spread about him. He bowed his head in prayer for several minutes, then rose to kiss his dead brother's cheek. As he did so, he heard his father's voice raised to heaven in a long cry of agony and grief, 'Juan . . . my beloved son . . . Juan!' There was the muffled sound of a heavy body falling. Cesare turned to see Rodrigo lying apparently lifeless on the floor.

*   *   *

'The Pope', Burchard wrote in his diary, 'when he heard that the Duke had been killed and flung into the river like dung, was thrown into a paroxysm of grief, and for the pain and bitterness of his heart shut himself in his room and wept most bitterly . . . His Holiness neither ate nor drank anything from the Wednesday evening until the following Saturday, nor from the morning of Thursday to the following Sunday did he know a moment's peace . . . The Cardinal of Valencia went to the door of his room, persuading him to open it . . .'

'Your Holiness!' Cesare placed his ear against the panelling of the door, listening for his father's voice. A low animal moaning could distinctly be heard, but otherwise there was no response to his call. He stepped back from the door, nodding to two waiting guards with pikes to break it down. The heavy wood soon splintered under their attack, and Cesare stepped through the shattered panels into the dark chamber beyond.

'Father?' He could see nothing in the darkness. The stench in the room choked his nostrils. Quickly crossing to where chinks of light showed from behind shuttered windows, he flung them open. Light and noise from the city below flooded into the room, the bright June sun falling upon the huddled figure of Rodrigo, crouched in a foetal position in a corner of the room, his face unshaven and grey with sleeplessness, his hands shaking. He stared at Cesare, his bloodshot eyes blank, unrecognising, shrinking back in terror. Gently Cesare lifted him to a chair, and knelt humbly to kiss his feet.

'Your Holiness has grieved enough,' he admonished, dismissing the guards with a gesture of his hand. Then, when they had gone, he shouted at his father, 'Three days are enough of this!'

He was surprised by the strength and ferocity of Rodrigo's reply, '"Where is Abel, thy brother?"'

Cesare pretended not to understand his meaning, but replied, 'Where is my father, Rodrigo Borgia?'

But Rodrigo continued in his biblical strain, bitterly accusing, '"The voice of thy brother's blood crieth unto me from the ground!"'

'Father!' Cesare's voice was shocked. 'That night we embraced! In love. And left our mother's house in friendship. Comfort *my* grief!'

Rodrigo's eyes filled with tears. He reached forward to touch Cesare's cheek with his hand. 'In friendship, Cesare?' he said hesitantly, the longing to believe patent in his voice.

Cesare grasped his father's hand firmly, willing him to do so, 'I swear it. As you are Pope.'

'Juan ...' Rodrigo said pathetically. 'If I had ten Papacies, I'd give them all to bring him back.'

'He's with God,' Cesare said. 'And I with you.' He rose, still holding Rodrigo's hand, and stood beside his chair, strength emanating from him, dominating the older man in his weakness. 'Fear nothing,' Cesare said fiercely, bending over his father, 'you are Pope. I am your son. Together we may bestride the world...'

As if hypnotised by his son's power, slowly Rodrigo responded, raising Cesare's hand to his lips.

* * *

Confident that he had mastered his father, who, in an agony of remorse, promised to reform both himself and the Church, Cesare rode south to Naples later that month as Papal Legate, his head full of plans for himself and his family. Now that Juan was dead, the task of founding a Borgia dynasty in Italy must lie with him. He was going to Naples ostensibly to crown the new King Federigo, but actually to browbeat the King into providing a new husband for Lucrezia and a bride for himself – when he should cease to be a churchman. His heart lifted within him as he dreamed of the worldly glory that must await him once he had put off the hated churchman's robes. He felt sure of himself, confident of his power to plot his own destiny and to fight for it. He would take Juan's place as his father's General, but he would go beyond that. Under his father's suzerainty lay the Papal States, the lands of the Church, straddling the centre of Italy, from the borders of the kingdom of Naples in the South to the confines of Florence, Milan, Ferrara and Mantua to the North. Rich lands, ruled by unruly Princes, many of them contemptuous of the Church's authority; prizes there for the taking by a man bold enough to fight for them. 'A man may do anything if he wills . . .' Cesare repeated to himself, mindful of the phrase which represented everything, indeed all, that he believed in. For Cesare, God and chance had no part in the scheme of things.

4

Il Valentino

LUCREZIA SAT ALONE on a bench in the vaulted cloister of the Convent of San Sisto. The air was heavy with the sultry heat of late summer, matching her own sombre mood. She was dressed in the black of mourning for Juan, the curve of her belly now clearly visible beneath the gathered folds of her gown, for she was five months pregnant. This pregnancy brought her no joy, rather she regarded it as a shameful secret she carried within her, the reminder of a terrible sin for which, if she were to die in childbirth, she would burn in hell, her soul unshriven, because there was no confessor to whom she could entrust her guilt. She felt terribly alone. In the three months she had been in the convent none of her family had visited her. Cesare was in Naples with Sancia, and her father . . . Lucrezia shuddered. Juan was dead now three months, but terrible rumours still circulated about his death. Lucrezia had several times caught the sisters whispering about the murder of the Duke of Gandia, and in her own subconscious mind a dark suspicion was circulating which she could not and would not admit.

The sound of hasty footsteps interrupted her gloomy reverie. She looked up to see one of the nuns running towards her, habit and veil flying. 'Madonna Lucrezia,' the sister gasped, out of breath, 'there is someone to speak with you. A man. Come quickly.'

Lucrezia rose wearily and somewhat crossly from her bench. Probably, she thought, yet another message from her father which she would refuse to answer. 'It may be someone I don't wish to speak to,' she said petulantly, as the nun hurried her into the visitor's room, drawing up a chair beside the shutter which concealed the grille behind which her unseen visitor waited. She opened the grille and withdrew hastily as if fearing male contamination. The light in the room was dim and Lucrezia's eyes accustomed to the strong sun outside; she could just distinguish a dark masked figure behind the bars.

'Lucia...'

At the sound of Cesare's voice, Lucrezia ran to the grille, pressing herself against the bars, her hand searching for his, her lips touching his face as he removed the mask. 'Cesare ... What are you doing here? Did your father ...? Did our father send you?'

'I left Naples yesterday at dawn and have come straight here.'

'So quickly!'

'I bought some fine new horses. A splendid barbary mare.'

'And was it beautiful? You crowned King Federigo. Sancia is always telling me how beautiful Naples is ...' She drew back a little, looking at him uncertainly. 'We haven't spoken since Juan died ...' Then she leaned forward again, hands grasping the bars, eyes searching her brother's face beseechingly. 'The Orsinis killed him. It must have been them. No one else could have wanted...'

'No one,' he soothed her. 'While he was alive I envied him. But I would not have killed him because of that.' His voice took on a lighter note as if he were cajoling a child. 'Lucia, you must hear what I have come to tell you. What I have found for you in Naples.'

'For me?'

'I found a husband.' Lucrezia's face fell, she turned away her head. He gripped her wrist, willing her to listen to him. 'Hear me, Lucrezia. It's Sancia's brother, Alfonso of Aragon. He's seventeen and handsome and full of spirit. I showed him the miniature I have of you and he is burning to marry you. And the King has agreed.'

'I can't marry him.'

'You say that because you are married to Giovanni. But he has run away.'

Still Lucrezia refused to look at him. 'I cannot marry anyone,' she whispered.

'Of course you must marry,' Cesare said with some impatience. 'And first you will meet Alfonso.'

'Cesare, I can't!'

'Of course,' he said soothingly. 'You are going to have a child. Everything can be arranged. No one knows of this except the family. And we shall force Giovanni to agree to a divorce on grounds of non-consummation.'

'It's not for myself you want me to marry Alfonso,' Lucrezia said resentfully. 'It is for your own ambition.'

Cesare's voice was stern, commanding her to obey him. 'It is for the future of the family. That is what I think of. Now Juan is dead I have to make new plans – for *all* of us.'

Lucrezia stared at the ground; her voice was strained when she spoke. 'Then you must help me.'

'How? How must I help you.'

'There's no one I can tell . . . I have to make a confession – and I can't. Not to the priest who comes here. Cesare,' her voice became frightened, pleading. 'Suppose I die and go to hell? Let me confess to you.'

'I am not a priest.'

'You are a Cardinal.'

'I am not a true priest,' Cesare said, irritated.

'Cesare, *please*. You must hear me. There is no one else. Don't let me go to hell unshriven . . .' Then, as he nodded reluctantly, 'I have sinned . . . I must tell you . . . Ask me what I have done.'

'How have you sinned?' Cesare's voice held a note of bitterness. He did not want to hear this confession.

Lucrezia knelt at his feet in the attitude of the confessional, her head bowed, her right hand beating her breast. 'Father . . . *Mea culpa, mea culpa, mea maxima culpa*. The child . . . the father of my child will be someone close to me by blood. I was persuaded to commit this sin . . .'

'I knew,' Cesare said quietly. 'Sancia told me. It was Juan . . .'

Lucrezia looked up sharply, surprise and suspicion in her face. 'Sancia? When did she tell you that? Cesare!' As he hesitated, '*When* did she tell you?'

'In Naples. When I was ill. Juan was dead. Perhaps she thought it didn't matter...'

'But it wasn't Juan... She said that to make you jealous, to play with you. You know how she is.'

Cesare said, very slowly, 'It was not Juan?'

Lucrezia shook her head, unable to look at him. 'So you see why ... there was no one I could confess to. For the family...'

Cesare's voice shook with a cold fury. 'Our father. Who art in hell...'

*   *   *

Rodrigo looked up from his prayers and spoke reprovingly. 'You were too rash, Cesare. You let your desires carry you away. We have warned you of this before.'

'Father. A family failing, perhaps.'

Rodrigo appeared not to notice the strange note in his son's voice. 'Not with us,' he said briskly. 'Not in negotiation. Never reveal your aims. Don Federigo needs our support. Had you been cool with him, he might have *offered* you his daughter's hand. But you demanded it.' He rose from the *prie-dieu* and seated himself in a chair. 'Perhaps he would refuse in any case,' he said reflectively. 'He needs the backing of Ferdinand of Spain more than he fears ourselves. Ferdinand and that pious Queen of his would never allow a Cardinal to marry...'

'He said, "Show me a Cardinal who can marry and put off the hat – and *then* I will give him my Carlotta,"' Cesare told him angrily.

'The voice of Spain,' Rodrigo said. Then he continued in a serious tone, 'And we ourselves are not persuaded. We have our grief ... Perhaps it is too early for you to step into Juan's shoes.'

'I never wanted to be a priest. You know that!' Cesare said fiercely. 'And I can serve you as Juan never did.' He began to pace up and down the room. 'How can I be a priest? I don't believe in God.'

'Of course you believe in God!' Rodrigo was dismissive. 'You believe in Him as we do. God is the Creator. God is Life . . .'

'And Juan is dead.'

Rodrigo's voice trembled as he replied, 'It is the sins of men that spoil God's handiwork . . . Our sins as well. We promised to reform the Curia after Juan was killed . . .'

'And have you?' Cesare's tone was ironical.

'The Commission we appointed hasn't reported yet . . .' He paused. 'But what is that to you?'

Cesare did not reply. There was a silence between them. Then Rodrigo said hesitantly, 'Cesare, come here that I may look at you. There is something in your voice which tells me all is not well. What happened to you in Naples?'

Cesare did not answer his question. Then he said, 'I saw Lucrezia.'

'When?'

'On my way here this afternoon.'

Rodrigo leapt to his feet, his voice eager. 'Did she speak of us? We have sent messages begging for her return, but she refuses. Time and time again . . .' Cesare did not answer, staring fixedly at his father. 'Why don't you answer?' There was a long pause as Rodrigo saw the answer in Cesare's eyes. Then he turned away, raising his hand to his breast in a gesture of contrition. '*Miserere nobis* . . .' he whispered, 'can she forgive?'

'I think she has.'

'God knows how we have suffered – thinking of her. But if she forgave us – God may forgive us too. And you . . . ?' He turned to face his son.

Cesare's voice was ice-cold, deadly. 'You have no need of my forgiveness. But I have need of yours.'

Rodrigo gripped his arms with both hands, in an agony of fear. 'Don't speak. We absolve you without confession – for every sin you have committed! There are things between us that should not be spoken. For the love of God, Cesare! For the love we bear you ... tell us no more.'

But Cesare was inexorable. 'I thought *he* would have been the father of her child.'

Rodrigo dropped his hands and turned his face away, his voice ineffably sad, defeated. 'We knew ... You always hated him ... He stood in your way, but it was our sin for which he died. And we are justly punished – losing our dearest son ...' He looked at Cesare for a long while, then he said wearily, 'So. What is it you want?'

'What I have always wanted. The glory of this world. Not of the next.'

'It shall be done. We shall release you from your vows. Now go, Cesare, we shall receive you formally tomorrow.' He made the sign of the cross, then, as Cesare turned to leave, he called him back. 'We have not spoken of Lucrezia's marriage. There is the question of the divorce. The paper to be signed by Giovanni Sforza.'

'He has signed it,' Cesare grinned savagely, 'whining upon his knees before his uncles in Milan. Ludovico told him that if he wasn't impotent he had better prove it, there and then, publicly, on the body of a whore. He preferred to sign ...' His voice became grim. 'They tell me he said other things, detrimental to Your Holiness and to my sister's honour.'

'What things?' Rodrigo's voice was anxious.

'He declared that he had known her an infinity of times. That she was a whore. That ... that Your Holiness had taken her from him to enjoy her yourself...'

Rodrigo said dully, 'He will be believed. There is the child.'

'Yes,' Cesare reflected, 'the child ... who else knows of it besides ourselves?'

'No one. Well ... There is one...'

'Perotto?'

Slowly, almost reluctantly, Rodrigo nodded.

Cesare smiled to himself. It was not a pleasant smile. 'It may be useful,' he said, moving towards the door.

'Cesare! What do you mean by that? We ... we demand

to know!' Rodrigo's voice was anxious, fearful, but Cesare had gone without giving him an answer.

* * *

Perotto knocked at the door of the Pope's bedchamber, his face beaded with sweat from the urgency of his mission. The hour was late, well after midnight, and the Pope, he knew, would not be alone, but the message he held in his hand would not wait. It was from the Reverend Mother of the Convent of San Sisto, a message for which he himself had waited for long hours in the cold winter night outside the convent gate, the Lady Lucrezia's childbirth screams ringing in his ears.

Rodrigo had been awaiting him anxiously. 'Enter!' The noise disturbed the girl sleeping at his side, who turned on her back, revealing shapely breasts. Rodrigo sat up eagerly as Perotto entered, seizing the message from the Chamberlain's hand. A strange expression crossed his face, a mingling of relief, guilt and anxiety, even disappointment. 'It is well,' he said simply.

'Holy Father,' Perotto bowed to take his leave.

'Don Pedro ...'

Perotto paused at the door and turned to look at his master enquiringly, puzzled by the note of apprehension in his voice. 'Your Holiness wishes?'

'Nothing, my son ... May God in his mercy protect us both ...'

* * *

Briefly, before he fell asleep snuggled close to the body of his mistress, Pantasilea, Perotto wondered at the anxiety, even terror he had detected in the Pope's voice. Fear of God, perhaps, on account of the Lady Lucrezia. A Pope could fear no man ... Drowsiness overcame him, and he slept.

There was the faintest creak as the door of the bedchamber opened, and two dark figures slipped into the room. A shaft of light from the corridor outside showed up the two sleeping forms on the bed.

'Take the girl!' Michelotto shouted to Ramiro as he fell upon Perotto. Pantasilea had time for one terrified scream before Ramiro's hand covered her mouth. Irritated, Michelotto turned for a moment and, with a deft movement, slit her throat with his knife. Perotto slipped from his grasp and ran to the door, crying for help. As he came out into the corridor, Michelotto close behind him, Cesare stepped from the shadows, a drawn sword in his hand.

'My Lord,' Perotto screamed. 'Help ...' His cry was cut off in a strangled, choking sound as Cesare ran him through. Blood spurted up into Cesare's face, which he wiped off with a gesture of distaste, looking down at the young Spaniard's body. Then he looked up into the watching faces of Michelotto and Ramiro, and said with great emphasis, 'He knew my sister, Michelotto.'

'She is avenged, My Lord. Her honour's saved,' Michelotto replied solemnly.

'Ramiro,' Cesare questioned him, 'you understand the cause?'

'Yes, My Lord.'

'See that it's known. And throw the bodies into the Tiber where they'll be found ...'

*　　*　　*

'They say the Pope's favourite chamberlain, one Perotto, has been found dead – fished up out of the Tiber with a stone around his neck,' Ascanio Sforza's neighbour whispered as the Cardinals waited for the Pope to appear to conduct Lauds in St Peter's.

'So I have heard. From the German clerk, Burchard, who knows everything,' Ascanio replied cautiously.

'They say too that His Holiness was sorely distressed at this death. That it was ordered by the Cardinal of Valencia – to avenge his sister's honour.'

'Surely, such a step was unnecessary,' Ascanio said

97

dryly. 'The Pope's commission has declared her *virgo intacta*, my nephew having failed to consummate the marriage...'

'They say ...' the Cardinal began, then, surprised, 'Ah! There comes the Lady Lucrezia. It is many months since we last saw her here. Her figure seems somewhat altered, one would almost say ... what think you, Eminence?'

'A miracle...'

They fell silent as Rodrigo entered from the vestibule, dressed in his pontifical robes. He stopped as if frozen when he saw Lucrezia, who came forward to kneel and kiss his foot, then he recovered his composure and bent down to raise her. For a long moment they looked at each other, then Rodrigo murmured, 'Let him who is without sin cast the first stone ...' and, lifting his hand, he blessed her before passing on to the high altar.

'A scene of repentance and a pardon? Strange ...' Ascanio murmured. 'Mary Magdalene and Christ's Vicar upon earth. We lack only the son to complete the Trinity . ∴. Where is the Cardinal of Valencia?'

'He comes rarely to these ceremonies,' said the other. 'It is said he finds the cloth each day more irksome. But here he comes, and in haste it would seem...'

Regardless of the outraged protests of Burchard, Cesare mounted the altar steps to where his father stood solemnly incensing the altar, and knelt beside him in the attitude of an acolyte. 'Holiness,' he whispered urgently, 'Charles of France is dead ... He hit his head against a door-lintel at Amboise...'

'God have mercy,' Rodrigo said piously. 'He was always clumsy — and never fortunate...'

'His misfortune will be fortunate for me, I think,' Cesare whispered.

Rodrigo smiled and nodded.

As Cesare rose and backed down the steps, Rodrigo's strong voice broke out in a chant of exultation, '*Gloria in Excelsis Deo ...*'

* * *

Charles of France died childless in the spring of 1498, and was succeeded by his cousin, Louis of Orléans, with the title of Louis XII. Louis was older and shrewder than his unfortunate cousin, but he too had his eyes turned towards Italy and he too had need of Rodrigo Borgia for the success of the two projects dearest to his heart. His first object was domestic, to divorce his wife, Jeanne de France, a good woman but deformed in body and childless, in order to marry his predecessor's widow, Anne of Brittany, who was not only graceful and accomplished but the heiress to the great feudal appanage of Brittany, an important accession to the crown of France. This was the first step, and one in which the Pope's agreement was essential firstly to a divorce and secondly to a dispensation allowing him to marry his cousin's widow. The second object was the fulfilment of a dream of conquest which had taken possession even of Louis' practical mind. Not only had he inherited Charles's rights to the kingdom of Naples, but he himself, through a grandmother of the former ruling house of Milan, had a dynastic claim on that dukedom whose wealth and desirability he had experienced at first hand when campaigning in Italy with Charles in 1494. Papal approval would be necessary if such conquests were to be considered legitimate in the eyes of the world. And so, soon after his accession, Louis despatched an emissary, the Bishop of Orléans, to sound out Rodrigo Borgia.

'King Charles was like a son to us,' Rodrigo said gravely. 'Most bitterly do we lament his loss. We should be pleased, Lord Bishop, if you would convey to Her gracious Majesty, his widow, our profound condolences...'

The Bishop of Orléans glanced uneasily from Rodrigo to Cesare. He was perfectly aware, as they all were, of the nature of the relations between the Pope and his son and the late King of France. That was no longer of interest to any of them. All three knew that King Louis had sent the Bishop to ask a favour of the Pope, only Orléans did not know how much the Borgias would make him pay. He bowed, 'I shall, of course.' Then he hesitated, glancing at Cesare. 'Your Holiness, it was on the subject of the late King's widow that

His Majesty, King Louis, has begged me to consult with you. The affair is somewhat delicate ...'

Rodrigo waved his hand encouragingly. 'You may speak in the presence of the Cardinal of Valencia as to ourselves.'

Orléans bowed again, this time in Cesare's direction. 'Eminence.' Then he drew closer, as if afraid of being overheard. 'Your Holiness. My Lord King Louis contracted an agreement at the time of his marriage that if King Charles should predecease him without issue – then he should put aside his present wife and marry in her place King Charles's widow. This arrangement, Your Holiness, was entered into for reasons of state alone. It is true ...'

'That King Louis' present wife is hideous,' Cesare broke in mischievously.

'Your Eminence is pleased to jest. Your Holiness, I swear that no such carnal matter ...'

'No such matter would influence our judgement,' Rodrigo said loftily. 'Nonetheless, to allow His Majesty to fulfil his pledge, a double dispensation would be necessary. Both for the annulment of his present marriage ...'

'Which is no marriage, Your Holiness, either in the eyes of God or man,' Orléans said stoutly.

Rodrigo ignored the interruption, '... and to allow a second marriage to his kinsman's widow. These questions will greatly exercise the Curia. Those of the Spanish persuasion we are convinced will be opposed.' He paused to let his point sink in. 'And we are bound to Spain – both by blood and by the interests of our holy office.'

The Bishop's face fell. 'Then my cause is lost,' he said, glancing at Cesare, who echoed him.

'And mine as well.'

Orléans coughed and tried a different tack. 'Your Holiness may be aware,' he said innocently, 'that the Cardinal of Valencia entreated the late King's support in some business of his own. Without success.'

Rodrigo nodded. 'We know of it.'

Very deliberately Orléans said, 'His Majesty King Louis now advises me he would give support for the return of the Cardinal to the secular state, and for his marriage to the daughter of the King of Naples. He is also prepared to grant him the duchy of Valence with a revenue of twenty thousand gold francs. Together with a personal subsidy of twenty thousand gold francs per annum.' He stopped, well pleased with himself and his negotiation.

'It is not enough,' Rodrigo said coldly. The Bishop looked crestfallen.

'You see, My Lord Bishop, how I am opposed?' Cesare said plaintively.

Orléans was not yet prepared to give up. 'What more is needed, Holiness? His Majesty is determined on this course and I believe he would agree...'

But Rodrigo was non-committal. 'Time, My Lord Bishop. Give us a little time. We shall speak again.' Orléans bowed, accepting his dismissal, and withdrew.

Cesare and Rodrigo looked at each other. Cesare smiled. 'I shall have my army,' he said.

'Yes.'

'And you will see what I shall do.'

'Yes,' Rodrigo said again, foreboding in his voice. 'I fear it...'

*　　*　　*

'So you'll marry Alfonso to please Cesare?' Sancia teased Lucrezia as they played at shuttlecock in the Belvedere garden.

'To please Cesare, yes, I suppose so. He wants it so much. I do not think I ever want to marry again...'

'Not even Alfonso?'

Lucrezia smiled. 'Just because he's your brother...'

'Lucrezia, he's *very* good-looking. It's possible for a sister to appreciate a brother's looks,' she added slyly. 'Like you and Cesare.'

'Quite innocently.'

'Oh, yes, of course. Although ...' She stopped playing, frowning a little.

'What?'

Sancia picked up the shuttlecock, saying nothing.

'Are you not going to tell me?' Lucrezia was offended.

Sancia relented. 'I think I *shall* be jealous. Just a little. And I never was before. Not of you.'

'That was easy,' Lucrezia said seriously. 'You never had a cause. As I did.'

'Because of Cesare?' Sancia asked. Lucrezia did not answer, twirling the racquet between her fingers, her eyes fixed on the ground. 'Lucrezia, Cesare cares nothing for me. He doesn't even like me much. I'm just his whore. It's you he loves.' Still Lucrezia said nothing. Irritated, Sancia attempted a wounding little jest. 'I really see no reason for you Borgias to marry anyone. Except each other...'

Lucrezia paid no attention, she was intent on something else. 'Sancia,' she said, 'when you were in Naples with Cesare ... what did you tell him?'

Sancia stared at her, surprised. 'Cesare? In Naples? He thought he had the pox. We went to bed together and it cured him. Why? What did he tell you?'

'Nothing.' Lucrezia shook her head, forcing a smile, her face strained.

Sancia was solicitous. 'Of course, the child.' She put her arm protectively round Lucrezia. 'How slender your waist is, just as it was before. Was it very terrible?' Lucrezia nodded. Sancia gave her a sisterly hug. 'You'll forget all about that when Alfonso takes you to bed. You'll forget that ninny of a Sforza with his empty codpiece – and that other one – Wait ... till you see Alfonso ...'

*   *   *

Lucrezia was radiant as she joined hands with her bridegroom Alfonso of Aragon under the naked sword traditionally held over the heads of newly-married couples, in this case by the Spanish Captain of the papal guard, Juan Cervillon. Alfonso was everything that Sancia had said he was, tall, fair and handsome, with a winning smile and a gentle but spirited manner. It was a June wedding, as had been her marriage with Giovanni Sforza just five years before, and held, as that had been, in the Vatican. But

Lucrezia felt a rising excitement within her that erased the memory of her sulky, inadequate first husband from her mind. At the pressure of Alfonso's hand she felt a thrill run through her, and glanced, half-guiltily, at Cesare standing back by the wall, a pale, dark figure in his flame-coloured robes, his face set as if he were attending an execution.

Rodrigo, on the other hand, showed every sign of delight at his daughter's second wedding. King Federigo, anxious to avoid a rift with the Pope over his continuing refusal to give his legitimate daughter, Carlotta, as a bride for Cesare, had given Rodrigo everything he asked. The Dukedom of Biselli had been bestowed on his nephew, Alfonso, so that the Pope's daughter would be a Duchess, and the King had even agreed to Rodrigo's condition that the young couple should live with him in Rome after their marriage.

Rodrigo sat at the wedding feast following the ceremony with Vannozza at his left hand, his face wreathed in smiles. Vannozza, her expression distant, appeared not to be sharing his joy. 'Are you not proud to see your daughter, the Duchess?' he asked.

'Now her lover's dead,' Vannozza replied dryly, 'where is the child?'

Rodrigo frowned slightly. 'With a wet nurse. One of our choosing.'

'How was it named?'

'We call it Giovanni.'

'Why Giovanni?' Vannozza refused to drop the subject of her grandchild, despite Rodrigo's terse responses.

'Why? What else? It was her husband's name!' Then, taking her hand, he smiled. 'Come, Vannozza. Rejoice at your daughter's wedding. See she is dancing with Cesare – your son has a strange sense of humour,' he added critically, 'he's wearing the mask of a unicorn, the symbol of chastity...'

Lucrezia and Cesare danced together, the slow graceful movements of a pavane, their bodies moving together as one. Lucrezia could not see the expression in her brother's eyes behind the horned white mask, but she could sense the strength of the feelings emanating from him. The old feelings of terror and love for him flooded through her, momentarily quenching her gaiety. 'Cesare ...' she breathed, 'why the unicorn? ... It ... it means chastity ...'

Cesare bent his head towards her, his words an urgent whisper in her ear. 'Fidelity. Till death ...'

Alfonso approached and took her from him, Sancia slipping into Lucrezia's place. Rodrigo watched the bridal pair. Tears of pride in his eyes, he turned to Ascanio Sforza seated at his right. 'Mark them, Ascanio ...'

'A handsome couple, Holiness.'

'And this time,' Rodrigo said with more enthusiasm than tact, 'there will be a coupling. Look! He can scarcely wait.'

Ascanio smiled urbanely. 'I'm sure he has ...'

Rodrigo laughed delightedly. 'We shall see!'

*　　*　　*

Rodrigo stood beside the nuptial bed in the bridal chamber, his hands gripping the heavy curtains concealing the couple within. The family and wedding guests crowded round the door, jostling each other in their anxiety to witness the bedding. Cesare was nowhere to be seen. With a shout, Rodrigo flung the curtains apart to reveal Alfonso and Lucrezia naked in each other's arms. 'A bedding!' Rodrigo cried. Then he dropped the curtains back, and swayed as if he were about to faint. 'Out!' he murmured. 'It is done ...'

*　　*　　*

Within weeks of Lucrezia's wedding, Cesare's negotiations with the King of France were complete. Early in August he received news that King Louis was sending an envoy, Monsieur de Trans, to Rome with the patents investing him with the counties of Valence and Diois, and ships to escort him to France. For Cesare, the die was cast. The time had come to put off the hated robes of a churchman. On Friday 17th August 1498, Burchard, shocked, recorded in his diary,

'There was a secret Consistory, in which the Cardinal

Valentino declared that from his early years he was always, with all his spirit, inclined to the secular condition; but that the Holy Father had wished absolutely that he should give himself to the ecclesiastical state, and he had not believed he should oppose his will. But since his mind and his desire were still for the secular life, he besought His Holiness, that he should condescend, with special clemency, to give him a dispensation, so that, having put off the robe and ecclesiastical dignity, he might be permitted to return to the secular estate and contract matrimony; and that he now prayed the most reverend Lord Cardinals to willingly give their consent to such a dispensation...'

On the same day, 17th August, the King's envoy, de Trans, arrived in Rome bearing the letters patent that would entitle the former Cardinal of Valencia to call himself Duke of Valentinois. For Italians, the two foreign titles sounded much the same; he began to be known by the name by which he was to become famous – and dreaded – 'il Valentino'.

*   *   *

Cesare, dressed in a leather jerkin and hose, was practising equestrian exercises in the park of the Belvedere. As the day of his departure for France approached, he devoted more and more time to perfecting his considerable physical skills to prepare for his new role as a military vassal of the King of France.

Lucrezia, Sancia, Alfonso and Jofre stood watching him, Lucrezia's eyes shining with pride as she watched her handsome brother leaping from the back of one horse to another as they galloped side by side. 'Bravo, il Valentino!' she called to him, clapping her hands in admiration. 'Did you see that?' she said enthusiastically, turning to Alfonso.

Alfonso smiled faintly. 'Yes, I saw.'

'Il Valentino!' Lucrezia went on excitedly. 'Cesare will be so splendid when he goes to France. He's ordered a new sword – the most magnificent you've ever seen. And yesterday he killed eight bulls at a bull-fight in Cardinal Ascanio's park...'

Sancia said dismissively, 'In Naples I saw Miguel Alvarez kill fourteen bulls in a single afternoon.'

'Oh, Naples!' Lucrezia said. 'You and Alfonso are always talking about Naples...'

She broke off in horror as Cesare lost his balance and fell heavily, rolling among the flailing hooves. 'Cesare!' In anguish for his safety she ran to him, followed by the others, but Cesare was already sitting up by the time they reached him. 'Cesare,' Lucrezia said anxiously, clutching his shoulders, 'dearest Cesare, are you hurt?'

Cesare, winded, gasped for breath. 'In the shoulder...'

'In Naples I once saw a hundred riders fall off two hundred horses in a single afternoon,' Sancia said maliciously.

Alfonso laughed. Cesare looked up at him coldly. 'It's funny? Forgive me. I missed the joke.'

Alfonso replied innocently, 'Yes, you were falling off a horse. You would.'

Cesare rose and dusted himself. 'It is better to fall from a horse than to be gored by a bull ...' he said ominously, looking straight at Alfonso.

*   *   *

As the day of his departure for France drew near, Cesare spent wildly in his desire to impress the court of King Louis, so much so that supplies of luxury goods in Rome were exhausted and additional items of jewellery, silks, gold and silverware had to be imported from Venice. Cesare even wrote to his old racing rival, the Marquis of Gonzaga, to ask for coursers; when they arrived, he had them shod in silver. He ordered an entire harness in gold for the day of his formal reception at court, wedding gifts of rock crystal, gold and silver for his bride-to-be, and even, it was said, a princely travelling privy covered with gold brocade without and scarlet damask within, with silver vessels within the silver urinals. The gentlemen of his suite, which included

106

Michelotto and Ramiro, now promoted to be Master of his Household, were clad in cloth of silver and gold, but the magnificence of Cesare's costume on the day of his departure outshone them all.

When he came to take leave of his father, he was dressed in white brocade with a black velvet mantle thrown over his shoulder, on his head a black velvet cap blazing with large rubies, while his boots were sewn with gold chains and pearls. In his hand glittered the great parade sword which he had had specially wrought for him by the Jewish master, Ercole of Ferrara, with scenes representing the life of his hero and namesake, Caesar.

'Such a blaze of splendour! And at such a cost! The court of France will be compelled to greet you as a great Prince.' Rodrigo stretched out his hand for the sword. 'Let me look at it ... beautiful ... The work on this is exquisite...'

'The scenes represent the triumphs of Caesar,' Cesare explained. 'Look,' he said, pointing with his finger to a scene which showed Caesar riding in a chariot inscribed 'D. Cesar', 'you see the name on the chariot?'

'Caesar! Don Cesar – your Spanish name ...' Rodrigo was delighted. 'And here you cross the Rubicon, "*Jacta est Alea*" – the die is cast ...' He looked up at his son, his face suddenly serious, even apprehensive. 'Caesar was murdered – since he began to think himself a god. You should remember that.'

'I have no wish to be a god,' Cesare said impatiently, 'It is enough for me to be a man. God made the world, but man can master it – if he wills.' He took the sword and held it before him, as if he were swearing a solemn vow to himself. 'Like Caesar I shall conquer. My will is set against the fates. And one day I will die – by the knife or by His grace – it makes no matter. All else is dust. For me – and Caesar.' He raised his eyes from the sword and looked straight ahead of him, as if he were gazing into the future. His voice rang out with a fierce ambitious passion, 'I shall be Caesar ... or nothing!'

Rodrigo studied his son with a worried expression, then he put a hand on his shoulder as though to bring him back to earth. 'God will go with you, my son, whether you choose or not . . . But be careful of the French. Louis is not a fool as Charles was. It suits him now to favour us, but it may not be so when we have served his need.' He crossed the room to his desk upon which lay two scrolls. 'Here is the Bull of dispensation which allows Louis' marriage to the Queen Dowager, Anne of Brittany. And my letter commending you to him . . .' He stared down at the scrolls, hesitating. 'Perhaps we should have waited. He promised to obtain for you King Federigo's consent to offer you his daughter's hand. As yet we have heard nothing . . .'

'I have crossed my Rubicon,' Cesare said with decision. 'I cannot wait now.'

Rodrigo sighed. 'You never could.' Then he added wryly, 'When you see Federigo's daughter at the French court, see that you inspire her with the same impatience . . .'

He handed the scrolls to Cesare, who bent to kiss his ring. 'Goodbye, Holy Father.'

'My son. *Benedicat.* The future of the house of Borgia is in your hands. So remember. I have a Spanish heart still. I cannot trust the French.'

'We need trust no one . . .' Cesare replied confidently. 'Once I have my army. No one but ourselves.'

Rodrigo smiled at him, reassured. 'It shall be as you say. Farewell, Don Cesare!'

Tears stood in Lucrezia's eyes as she said farewell to her adored brother. 'Dearest Cesare,' she whispered, embracing him, 'may you find happiness in France . . .'

'You talk like a woman, Lucia,' he answered. 'For a man there is no happiness, only fame . . . or nothingness . . .' He held her fiercely against him. 'Be true to me, whatever happens. Remember the bond we swore in Montegiordano.' He kissed her, then abruptly turned away, walking out of the room without a backward glance.

The whole papal court watched the departure of the Pope's son for France, many of them filled with foreboding as to what this new alliance would mean for Italy. Among the apprehensive ones was Ascanio Sforza, whose brother stood to lose his ducal crown to Louis. 'The ruin of Italy is confirmed,' he said despondently to the Milanese envoy who stood beside him, 'given the plans which Father and Son have made ... It is to be feared the Holy Spirit has no part in them...'

* * *

Four months later, the glittering procession of the Duke of Valentinois wound its way through the streets of the little town of Chinon beside the River Loire towards the great castle on the hill where King Louis waited to receive his new vassal. The townfolk, accustomed to the plainer ways of the French court, gaped as the Italians passed, staring dumbfounded at the rich display. First came twenty-four mules bearing the Duke's coffers and chests covered with cloths embroidered with the ducal arms; then twenty-four more with their trappings halved in red and yellow, the King's colours, twelve with coverings of yellow-striped satin and six with cloth of gold; behind them came sixteen great chargers in cloth of gold, crimson and yellow satin; then eighteen pages in crimson velvet and cloth of gold. Six more mules followed with saddles, bridles and trappings of crimson velvet, and two all covered in cloth of gold and carrying coffers. The onlookers murmured and nudged each other; some said these must be jewels for the Duke's mistress, others that they could be Bulls or fine Indulgences from the Pope in Rome, or perhaps some holy relics. The Duke's retinue of thirty gentlemen clad in lavish suits of gold and silver followed; then came the musicians, also in cloth of gold, bearing their tambours, gold-stringed rebecs, their trumpets and clarions of silver; then twenty-four lackeys liveried in crimson velvet halved with yellow silk. Lastly, mounted on a tall Gonzaga courser with trappings of red satin halved with cloth of gold, came Cesare himself. He outdazzled them all, his cap blazing with rubies, and round his neck a collar with a huge pendant diamond, which onlookers estimated to be worth thirty thousand ducats.

King Louis, a tall, wiry man of thirty-six, some thirteen

years older than his new vassal, watched the brilliant display from a window of the great hall of the castle, where once Joan of Arc had harangued his predecessor Charles VI. Louis was dressed in a plain suit of black velvet, his customary apparel; his lips curled slightly as he took in the peacock spectacle below him. 'A great show for a Duke of Valentinois,' he remarked ironically to Giuliano Rovere who stood beside him.

'Your Majesty, the Duke Valentino is Spanish but his habits are Italian,' Rovere replied apologetically. 'Too often we make display of our importance with an outward show. In France Your Majesty's example is rightly followed. It is the man you measure – and not his clothes.'

Louis smiled. 'And they say he has brought a privy for his personal use for which the chambers are finest silver. I suppose – when he makes water – it is pure gold!'

As a fanfare of trumpets and clarions announced Cesare's approach, Louis turned from the window and crossed the hall to mount his throne, flanked by Rovere and groups of smiling, whispering courtiers, mocking the Italians' extravagant display. Cesare entered, making a low bow at the door and almost sweeping the floor with his jewel-encrusted bonnet.

'Welcome, Duke of Valentinois. You may approach.'

Cesare came forward to the steps of the throne, bowed deeply and thus made as if to kneel to kiss the King's foot. Louis stood up and, taking him by the shoulders, raised him to his feet. 'Welcome to our court at Chinon.' Cesare kissed his hand. 'You know His Eminence.'

'Of course,' Cesare said, looking at Rovere coolly. He bowed, 'Your Eminence.'

'Excellence,' Rovere replied cordially. 'You have lost your tonsure but none of the respect I held for you.'

'I am sure.' There was a note of sarcasm in Cesare's voice.

'His Eminence has been most diligent as an Ambassador of the Holy Father,' Louis said as he seated himself on his throne. He leaned forward, his chin resting on his hand, looking closely at Cesare. 'I trust, My Lord Duke, you have brought with you the dispensation that we seek. Our eyes are eager for it.'

'As the Holy Father is eager to have news from Your Majesty ... of Naples,' Cesare replied.

'Your marriage to Don Federigo's daughter. We have urged it strongly. But His Holiness will understand. Fair ladies cannot always be persuaded by the counsel of others. The appearance of a suitor may do much more.'

'Duke Valentino's appearance is certainly eloquent,' Rovere interposed.

Cesare looked directly at him, as he said evenly, 'But appearances may deceive, Eminence. As His Majesty knows ...'

Louis smiled, affecting a hearty manner. 'My Lord Duke,' he said, clapping his new vassal on the shoulder, 'there must be no deception between us.'

But that night Cesare, well aware of the hostility that surrounded him at the French court, slept with Ramiro and Michelotto guarding his door. The pitfalls of this enterprise loomed large before him as he lay sleepless in the darkness. He knew he could not trust Giuliano Rovere, but could he trust the King? And more, could he rely on his father in Rome to hold out against the pressure that would be put upon him?

*   *   *

'Deception!' Rodrigo bellowed at Ascanio Sforza. 'You accuse *us* of turning two faces to the world!' He turned to point at Alfonso, his son-in-law. 'And look at him! Oh, I know very well what has been going on. You've been reminding him that his mother was a Sforza. Or rather would have been a Sforza if his dear father, who was without doubt the most cruel, most vicious, and above all the most vulgar personage who has ever lived ...' He stopped briefly as the attendant prelates passed the cope over his head, then he re-emerged. 'If he had not chosen, as I say, to propagate this fine young man – my son-in-law – not from the Sforza stock, but on the body of a whore! The Sforzas of

Milan and the Aragonese of Naples! Brigands and whores!'
he shouted. Burchard and the attendant Bishops who were
robing the Pope appeared to be deaf to this extraordinary
tirade, but Alfonso, his face angry, turned away in disgust.

Ascanio Sforza, as usual, was diplomatic. 'I'm sorry,
Holy Father, if I have offended you ...'

Rodrigo was not to be placated. 'It is fortunate for you,
Sforza, and you Alfonso,' he said unpleasantly, 'that Cesare
is far away in France. You know him well.'

'It is true that the Duke Valentino is a most vigorous
young man,' Ascanio replied, 'well practised in the use of
arms, horses, leaping – all athletics ...' He moved closer to
Rodrigo, speaking in a low warning tone, 'But believe me,
Holy Father, Louis of France wants him simply for his own
designs. And you should warn Cesare not to aim so high –
as he may do this time – that in his falling he will break too
many of *your* bones ...' Rodrigo stared at him silently;
Ascanio had touched a nerve. Sforza continued, this time
adopting a persuasive tone, 'You should place your trust
not in barbarians but in those whom in your inmost heart I
believe you would prefer. In Spain. And in Milan.'

'Then you should offer something more than threats,'
Rodrigo said harshly. 'And we have been threatened. The
envoys of Spain and Portugal accused us of having pur-
chased the Papacy! They threaten to call a Council to have
us deposed. Do you know what more? They dared to tell us
that the death of Juan was a divine chastisement for our sins
...' He laughed, then went on venomously, 'Very well! But
God has given us another son to bear our name, while the
Spanish sovereigns are without a direct successor. To us
God gives and takes away. But from the good Catholic King
he takes and gives nothing in return!'

He sat down triumphantly, while Burchard knelt to place
the white satin slippers embroidered with the papal arms
upon his feet. Then he rounded on Alfonso. 'Let me give
you some advice in your turn, Alfonso, since you and your
ally of Milan have been so prodigal with yours. Tell your
uncle, Don Federigo, that our patience is at an end. Let him
send word to France and instruct his daughter, Carlotta –

that tender virgin – that we shall wait no more. She shall have one last chance to yield to Cesare. And if she will not ...' his voice changed, a note of uncertainty crept in, '... then we are cheated. I warned him of this ... *Virgo Maria* ...' He got up and placed a hand on Ascanio's arm in a gesture of conciliation. 'It is true, Ascanio, the French are barbarians. He should not yield too much ... I warned him ... He will not be able to escape from Louis as he did from Charles ...'

*   *   *

Cesare stared hard down the length of the King's table at the dark head of Carlotta of Naples, bent in an attitude which was meant to appear submissive but which he knew to be obstinate. His brows knit together in an expression of angry frustration. He well knew what was behind the Princess's obdurate rejection of him – the intrigues of the Sforzas and the family of Aragon to prevent the marriage and thus break up the alliance between the Borgias and the King of France which they knew, or rather suspected, boded ill for both their houses. Cesare was furious; angry with himself for having handed over his trump card, the papal dispensation, to the King and receiving nothing in return, angry with Louis, who had taken that trump, married Anne of Brittany, and yet failed to provide Cesare in return with the Neapolitan bride he had asked for. He was also disquieted; he had staked his all on this French throw, and now it looked as if he had crossed his Rubicon for nothing, that he would return from the French court empty-handed, to be the laughing stock of Italy.

Louis, labouring to keep the conversation going, saw Cesare's look and sighed. Borgia's patience, he well knew, was at an end; he had been three months at the French court without result. Louis had heard that Cesare had been making preparations for departure – whether this might be bluff he did not know, but he was not prepared for a rift with the Papacy, and he still needed the Borgias. He had arranged this uncomfortable meeting between Cesare and

Carlotta, disguised as an informal dinner with himself and Queen Anne, in a last bid to persuade the Princess to accept Cesare's suit. But it was proving to be even heavier going than he had feared, and the omens were not favourable. Would Cesare, he wondered, be prepared to accept the alternative he had in mind?

Aloud he said pleasantly to Cesare, 'Excellence. You wish for anything?'

Cesare continued to frown as he stared unblinkingly at Carlotta. 'Yes,' he said meaningly, 'my answer. You promised it would be tonight.' There was a silence.

'My dear,' Louis began gently, addressing Carlotta, his voice embarrassed. The girl raised her head, stared help-lessly for a moment at the King and Queen, then flushed, bit her lip, and got up from her place to run from the room, hardly pausing to drop a quick curtsey to Their Majesties. Louis became still more embarrassed. 'Madam,' he appealed to the Queen, 'she seems upset...'

Anne rose from the table. 'I shall go to her,' she inclined her head towards Cesare, 'if His Excellence will allow ...' She followed Carlotta from the room.

Deprived of his consort's moral support, Louis glanced uneasily at Cesare who sat, stony-faced, staring before him as if nothing had happened. 'Ah, well,' Louis sighed, 'no change.'

'Your Majesty is mistaken,' Cesare said evenly.

'How so?'

'There has been a change. Since I came to Chinon three months ago, Your Majesty has married the Queen. Which you could not have done...'

'Of course, of course.'

'... without the dispensation from His Holiness, which I delivered to you. And for which I have had nothing in return. Nothing but my shame.'

Louis looked at the ceiling, as if seeking inspiration from his emblem, the porcupine, glittering gold on the bosses of the vaults. 'It is ... unfortunate ...' His voice took on a firmer tone. 'It may be you were wrong to think only of Naples. In my own case, I think only of Milan. I am so determined to take Milan that other things seem less important. But in the long run,' here he reverted to the use of the royal 'we', 'we cannot forget that Naples belongs to us through our house of Anjou...'

There was a long pause as Cesare considered the prospects of this new alignment, then he said slowly, 'And for me?'

'You must have considered the papal cities, the Romagna, Bologna, Forli, Rimini, Pesaro...'

'For the walls of cities such as these I should need more than an army. I should need artillery.'

'Which we have...'

'And the cost of enlisting the services of *condottieri*...'

'Which could be met.' He leaned forward and laid his hand on Cesare's arm, 'You see... we have not forgotten. We made a promise to His Holiness.'

'To secure a Princess.'

A hint of a smile passed over Louis' bony features. 'If it would not insult you to consider – someone else instead...'

'A Princess?'

'The daughter of a great and noble Duke.'

'Do I know her?'

'Come and see.'

Rising, Louis led Cesare through the adjoining chamber to a small curtained balcony, overlooking the Queen's apartments. Louis drew back the curtain, and the two men looked down to see Anne of Brittany seated at her embroidery, surrounded by her ladies, all of them young and many of them beautiful. A dancing lesson was in progress, for Anne was a cultured woman and her court a finishing school for the daughters of the French nobility whose parents wished them to learn the new accomplishments.

'There.' Louis pointed to a beautiful fair-haired girl, dressed in green silk. 'That is Charlotte d'Albret, daughter of Alain le Grand, Duke of Guyenne, Count of Dreux, Penthièvre and Perigord, Viscount of Tartas and Limoges, Lord of Avesnes. Is that enough for you? And her mother is kinswoman to the Queen... you would be of our family.'

Cesare was silent watching the slim figure of the girl as she danced. Her grace and her long blonde hair reminded him of Lucrezia, although she must be a few years younger. Barely sixteen, he thought. In looks she far excelled Carlotta of Naples, and there were other considerations in her favour...

'She is called the loveliest daughter of France ...' Louis said in his ear. 'I believe matters could be arranged ...'

'I should want an army of three hundred lances, twenty thousand heavy cavalry,' Cesare said flatly.

'You would take Milan in my company.'

'After which Your Majesty would invest me with the Lordship of Asti.'

'And you would obtain free passage through the Papal States for our forces to enter Naples and assist us in its reconquest.'

There was a pause, before Cesare, never taking his eyes off Charlotte, said slowly, 'Naples. And Milan. For the Papal States...'

'And Charlotte is beautiful...'

Cesare smiled, his face lighting up. 'Sire,' he said, 'it is enough.'

*　　*　　*

Cesare, according to a French chronicler, married Charlotte d'Albret *'de grand cœur'*, his enthusiasm for the match kindled by Louis' promises, increased by the beauty, gentleness and goodness of his bride. He lavished upon her all the carefully-chosen gifts he had brought from Rome intended for Carlotta — brocades, silks and jewels worth twenty thousand ducats, the jewels including a great pear-shaped pearl, a ruby clasp and five emeralds all set in gold, a pendant of rubies, a collar of twenty rubies and eight pearls, a diadem for her hair made of twelve rose diamonds and thirty pearls, and a cascade of unset pearls, diamonds and other gemstones. Apart from jewels there were table services — salt cellars, plates, spoons, forks, dishes, jugs, basins, sauceboats, flagons and other vessels, vases for spices and for wine – richly wrought in gold, silver gilt, enamels and rock crystal. There were fine damask table-cloths and elaborate table centres – miniature warships in mother of pearl, a citadel with four towers in silver, and a fountain worked in silver gilt and enamel in the form of a bell tower which issued forth jets of rose-water.

The marriage was celebrated in the Queen's private chapel at Blois on the River Loire, and was followed by a magnificent wedding feast held in great silken tents set up in the meadows below the castle. There were jousts and tournaments, Louis invested Cesare as a knight of the Order of St Michael, the highest order of chivalry in France, and the Queen gave him her ring. No one was to be in any doubt as to the reasons of state which lay behind the ceremonial, for Charlotte's marriage contract, witnessed by the King and Queen, declared that Louis gave his consent to the match for 'the great and commendable services which the high and powerful Prince Don Caesar de Borgia, Duke of Valentinois, has rendered to him and to his crown, and hoping that the aforesaid Duke, his relatives, friends and allies will render them unto him in the future, and likewise for the conquest of his kingdom of Naples and of his duchy of Milan . . .'

The following day, Cesare gave his father an account of his wedding night prowess to reassure him that this mar-riage, at least, could not be annulled on the grounds of non-consummation. He signed the letter proudly with all his French titles, 'Cesare Borgia of France, Duke of Valen-tinois, Count of Diois, Lord of Issoudun, Captain of a hundred lances of the Kings ordinance . . .'

*   *   *

'Alfonso,' Lucrezia said happily as they lay in bed, 'my father has heard from Cesare, about his wedding night. And King Louis wrote to him too, and sent him a hundred bottles of claret . . .'

'I, too, heard from *my* friends about your brother's wed-ding night,' Alfonso said coldly. He lay on his back staring

117

at the ceiling, and Lucrezia, snuggled beside him in the bed, could not see his expression. 'He says that the ladies who watched through the keyhole said he was much inconvenienced because the pharmacist had given him laxative pills in mistake for an aphrodisiac.'

Lucrezia giggled. 'But it didn't matter,' she said. 'The King told my father in his letter that Cesare had performed even better than he had when he married the Queen. He made love to Charlotte twice before supper and six times at night. He's so strong – nothing would matter to him. And they say ... they say she is very pretty, and very much in love with Cesare ...' Alfonso made no response. Lucrezia stroked his arm placatingly. 'Am I always talking about Cesare? That is what Giovanni said.'

Alfonso's tone was unfriendly. 'Now you are talking about Giovanni!'

Lucrezia shrugged. '... Twice before supper. And six times at night ... Has my belly grown too big? Is that why?'

Alfonso said, his voice serious, 'Lucrezia. My uncle, Ascanio Sforza, has left Rome. To go hunting.'

'Has he run away? Your uncle, the Cardinal, has run away, hasn't he? He is afraid because of Cesare and the French ... Has he gone to Milan?'

'No. He has gone hunting.'

'You don't trust me either, do you? Because of Cesare. Because I am a Borgia.' She buried her face in his chest, her voice breaking. 'Please, Alfonso, don't run away too. Giovanni ran away, but I didn't mind that because I didn't love him. I didn't mean to talk again of Giovanni. Or of Cesare. Alfonso!'

He turned to her and crushed her in his arms, his chin resting on her golden head, his expression grave.

*   *   *

'My Lord!' Charlotte's anxious cry cut through the fresh morning air. 'My Lord ...' She reached Cesare's horse, out of breath, and looked up at him questioningly. 'You rose without telling me. Where are you going?'

Cesare smiled, indicating the falcon on his wrist, 'You see. We shall take some herons.'

Charlotte was only partly reassured. 'And come home again ... I trust you have good sport.' Then she seized Cesare's hand and kissed it.

He turned quickly to his men, 'Come.'

Charlotte backed slowly away, her eyes never leaving Cesare. 'Farewell, My Lord,' she said.

Cesare inclined his head towards her and moved off, with Michelotto at his side. Michelotto looked at his impassive face. 'My Lord,' he said. Cesare did not reply. 'My Lord, she knows that all your goods have been sent to Lyons where you will meet the King.' Still Cesare did not answer but rode on looking straight ahead of him. Michelotto continued, 'You keep yourself a man apart, My Lord. Even from your wife.'

'It is the mercy of God, Michelotto.'

'The mercy of God?'

'One day I shall see your face no more. I shall not know that day.'

'You did not wish to see her tears ...'

'If I die for Milan – she may cry then. It will be time enough.'

Michelotto gave a backward glance over his shoulder. 'She watches you still,' he said.

Cesare did not turn his head. 'I am as merciful as God, Michelotto. And as cruel.'

'You will not teach men to love you as they love God.'

'No. But as they fear him.'

He spurred his horse forward suddenly into a gallop, the past already forgotten, thinking only of the future which lay ahead of him.

*   *   *

Even as Cesare rode away from Blois and Charlotte, his bride of two months, without a backward glance, Alfonso slipped out of Rome, without a word to his pregnant wife.

Lucrezia was distraught. Weeping, she ran through the

corridors of the Vatican to fling herself before her father as he knelt at his early morning prayers. 'Father!' the desperate Lucrezia tugged at the sleeve of his robe, 'Father! Help me! Alfonso's gone. He's run away. Because of Cesare. Please, Father, get him back! Get him back!'

'My child, my child.' Rodrigo enveloped her in his arms, rocking her like a baby. 'You shall have him back. Never fear. No harm shall come to him. He is the father of your child ...'

Suddenly, the door of the chamber burst open to reveal an angry Sancia, and beside her a man whose clothes were torn and spattered with blood.

'What means this interruption?' Rodrigo asked angrily.

'Your son, my beloved husband, has been wounded in a street brawl. This, his servant, has just returned with the news.'

Overawed, the man stuttered, 'Your Holiness ... My Lord, your son ...'

'The patrol took him,' Sancia interrupted, 'and put him under lock and key in Sant'Angelo.'

The servant appeared to have collected himself. 'Holy Father. We had gone by the Calimala Francesca – under the Tetto de Pisani ...'

'To pick up boys,' Sancia said scornfully.

'Is he badly wounded?' Roderigo asked, not over-concerned.

'In the flesh, Holy Father, some blood was drawn. He begs Your Holiness to order his release ...'

'He can do no harm there. He is no son of mine,' Roderigo said shortly.

Sancia's attention was distracted by Lucrezia sobbing at Rodrigo's side. 'What's the matter?'

'Alfonso has run away. Left her with child,' Rodrigo told her.

Sancia did not seem surprised, but merely nodded. 'And I too must take my leave of you,' she said. 'It seems Rome will soon not be safe for anyone of my blood. I shall go to join Alfonso, and leave you Borgias to welcome Cesare home.' Her voice was bitter.

'Sancia!' Lucrezia cried, running to her, 'Take me with you. Take me to Alfonso.'

'Lucrezia!' Rodrigo too rose to his feet, his voice agonised. 'Do not go with her! She is a whore ... Listen to me! I will give you Nepi ... Ascanio Sforza's castle. I will order Alfonso to come back to you there. He will obey me ... He must ... Cesare will make him do so...'

'Cesare!' Sancia spat out the name, as she snarled at Rodrigo. 'Cesare will destroy you. And not just you, you monstrous old man! Not you alone! But all Italy!' She turned and swung out of the room, with Lucrezia running after her.

Rodrigo seemed powerless to stop them. He sank down on the *prie-dieu*, his head in his hands, mumbling, 'Cesare ... Cesare must come home...'

5

Father and Son

CESARE RODE BESIDE King Louis into Ludovico Sforza's capital, Milan, from which Ludovico had prudently fled a few days before. The Milanese greeted the French coolly, but stared with interest at the Pope's son riding in the place of honour at the French King's side, dressed in the King's colours of crimson and yellow which signified that he now belonged to the royal house, and followed by three thousand heavy cavalry, the lances of his command. Baldassare Castiglione, who was to write a famous book on etiquette, noted that Cesare held himself 'gallantly', but others interested in more serious matters, the envoys of the Italian states such as Venice, Mantua and Ferrara, saw the favour with which he was treated by Louis and feared what this might portend for Italy.

Rodrigo received the news of Cesare's arrival with delight – and relief – as he rode towards the castle of Nepi in the first week of October. He had never liked the French marriage, and had feared that Cesare's flirtations with Louis would lead him into a trap from which he might not escape, held hostage by the King for his father's good behaviour. But Cesare's letters and the reports of his own agents at Milan had reassured him, and he was in high good humour as he rode into the courtyard of the castle which had once been his and which he had given to Ascanio Sforza in exchange for his vote. Ascanio, he thought, eyeing the Sforza arms above the gateway, had been stirring up trouble in his, Rodrigo's, family, putting Alfonso and Lucrezia against Cesare, making them afraid of what Cesare and Louis might do. He would soon put a stop to that, reassuring them with his paternal authority, just as he had succeeded in persuading that foolish boy Alfonso to forget his fears and return to Lucrezia.

His face lit up with joy as he caught sight of his daughter, now heavy with child, waiting to greet him. He dismounted from his mule to enfold her in his arms. 'Our daughter ... And you are well! How great your belly is! It will be a boy ... we know!'

Alfonso stepped forward to kiss Rodrigo's ring. 'Don Alfonso ... *Benedicat*.'

Jofre, who had been quickly released from prison, followed, also to receive an amicable blessing. 'Jofre, our son.'

Rodrigo stood with his arm about Lucrezia, but his eyes were upon Alfonso. 'You fled Rome,' he said sternly.

'Holy Father, I obeyed your summons to return from Naples,' Alfonso replied defensively.

'Our letter was to the King, your uncle. It was the light of these eyes,' he hugged Lucrezia to him, 'that should have drawn you here, not my messenger.'

'I am assured, Your Holiness, that I need never fear you ...'

'If you remain a faithful husband, what should you fear from us?' Then, opening his arms in an expansive gesture, he addressed them all, beaming with pride, 'I bring you news! Cesare and King Louis ride into Milan in triumph! It is the Duke and Cardinal Sforza who must flee in terror. Whilst *we* disport ourselves in Nepi – Ascanio's castle – our gift to you, dearest Lucrezia. Come, let us go within ...'

Sweeping them all with him, he entered the great hall of the castle, where refreshments were laid out on a long table of chestnut wood, while Jofre's musician and latest favourite, Tommasino, gently plucked at the strings of his lute. Juan Cervillon, Captain of the papal guard, stood at attention behind Rodrigo as he sat eating heartily and recounting news of the French entry into Milan.

'There was no treasure in the Castello Sforzesco when Louis entered,' he said, biting into a ripe purple fig with evident satisfaction, at the same time eyeing a very pretty girl waiting upon Lucrezia. 'Cesare tells me that the Duke had oaken jewel chests with special locks made by da Vinci – but they were found open and empty. Ludovico had taken with him two hundred and forty thousand ducats in gold . . . all his jewels and pearls – a fortune . . .' He whispered something in Lucrezia's ear, indicating the girl with a gesture.

'Angelina,' she replied smiling.

'Ah!' Rodrigo nodded in high good humour. 'Where was I? Yes. Cesare also writes that the French are making themselves as hated in Milan as they were here in Charles's days. Their soldiers spit on the floors of rooms – when they do not do worse – and outrage women in the streets. They have ruined da Vinci's great statue of Ludovico's father, Francesco Sforza, by using it as target practice for their arrows. The statue was of clay – like the dynasty of the Sforzas. We Borgias will make ours of bronze.' He smiled triumphantly round the table.

'The French are barbarians . . .' Jofre said nervously. 'They may do to us what they have done to the Sforzas – and Alfonso's family before,' he added tactlessly.

Rodrigo frowned, but glossed over his son's gaffe. 'Oh yes, we know them for what they are. And we have thus warned Cesare. He understands. But he must have an army. We desire above all else to make him a great Lord in Italy, as he is now in France. They hailed him in Milan as Duke Valentino – the people shouted in the streets.'

'But Lord of where?' Lucrezia interrupted him. 'What state can Cesare win for himself here in Italy?'

Rodrigo smiled tenderly at her. 'Does our little bird begin to sing of politics?' he said fondly. 'You thought Cesare would make himself the King of Naples.' He looked from face to face. 'And so did you, Jofre. And you, Alfonso. So did the King . . .' He smiled broadly, and took a handful of sweetmeats from a dish, before continuing, 'You see how little you understand us. Are we not Spanish by blood like the house of Aragon? The Borgia bull and the arms of Aragon are united in *both* your marriages. The Borgias do not want Naples. We do not threaten you. That was the message Captain Cervillon here took to the King. That's why he ordered you to come to Nepi.' He turned to look up at Cervillon standing erect behind him. 'Is it not so, Captain?'

'It was so, Holy Father,' Cervillon replied.

'You see?' Rodrigo smiled again, a happy, reassuring smile, as he looked round their anxious faces.

There was a pause, then Alfonso ventured, 'And yet, Holy Father, you have not answered...'

Rodrigo nodded. 'Lucrezia's question. Yes ... very well.' He leaned forward, his hands clasped before him on the table. 'On our return to Rome, we intend to issue a papal Bull – against the Lords of Rimini, Pesaro and Faenza, depriving those Lords of their cities as unworthy Vicars of Holy Church.' He paused to pop a sweetmeat into his mouth, before continuing, 'And against Caterina Sforza, the Lady of Forlì...'

The musician Tommasino looked up suddenly, his hand faltering on the lute strings, then he bent again to his music.

'These are our cities,' Rodrigo went on, 'the lands of Holy Mother Church. Tyrants have wrested them from our protection, despoiled their people with taxation and refused to us the payment of the census which is our due. Now it will be too late for them to send their bags of gold to our treasury. We shall refuse it. So their lands shall be forfeit. Cesare will restore them to our care. And we shall declare him their overlord – Lord of the Romagna!' He looked round the table. 'Who can object to that?'

Nobody said a word. Then Jofre said timidly, 'To do this Cesare will need the arms of France.'

'Louis had promised them.'

'Then Cesare has offered something in return.' Alfonso's voice was hesitant. 'They said in Naples ...' He stopped, giving a quick glance at Cervillon.

Rodrigo's voice was suddenly sharp as he followed Alfonso's glance. 'What?'

Alfonso went on bravely, 'France would have Naples if she could, Holy Father. That is all I mean.'

Rodrigo relaxed, refusing to take notice of the

implication of Alfonso's words. He beckoned the girl Angelina to him, slipping his hand to her waist. 'Alfonso,' he said patiently, 'we are as one That's what I came to tell you. You must return to Rome. Lucrezia's son will be born there. Jofre must come as well And Sancia. I miss her pretty, whorish face.'

'Sancia remains in Naples, Holy Father.' Jofre's voice was complaining.

Rodrigo reassured him. 'Captain Cervillon will bring her back,' he said firmly. 'He is a Spaniard and the King trusts him well. You shall *all* come back to Rome.'

*   *   *

Cesare rode hard through the Porta Viridaria next to the Vatican, Michelotto a dark shadow behind him. Torches flared in St Peter's Square outside the Palace of Santa Maria in Portico as they reined up their horses. 'First I will see Madonna Lucrezia,' Cesare said briefly to Michelotto, 'then to Sant'Angelo.'

Michelotto nodded as Cesare threw him the reins of his horse and strode through the portal, the guards saluting him as he passed.

Lucrezia, pale and exhausted after the birth of her son, lay half-awake and propped up by pillows as Cesare came into the room. At the sight of him Angelina, who was sitting beside the bed, rose up in terror. Lucrezia's eyes opened wide. 'Cesare.'

He stood looking down at her, a dark figure in the sombre black velvet which he had now adopted as his habitual dress, symbolic of his single-minded ambition. 'So. You had a son,' he said.

She nodded. Then, 'Leave us, Angelina,' she commanded. The girl curtsied and hurried out of the room. 'Why have you come to Rome? I thought . . . I thought you were in the Romagna . . .'

'I was summoned by our father.' He took her hand lying on the coverlet and kissed it; she held his fingers. 'There has been a plot against His Holiness so I was summoned.'

'Against our father? Is it grave?'

'It is nothing.'

'Cesare,' her voice was full of relief and love, 'I am glad you came to see me.'

'Why?'

'Because I love you. And because I feared ...'

'What did you fear, Lucrezia?'

Lucrezia turned her face away from him against the pillows. 'I fear for us. For me and for Alfonso. And for our son.' She turned again to look directly at him. 'I fear the French,' she said deliberately.

Cesare squeezed her hand reassuringly. 'You should not fear them,' he said smiling. 'We have taken Imola for the Holy See. Now I shall take Forlì from Caterina Sforza. The people do not love her, they gave the town to us while she cursed them from the castle walls for yielding to us like whores. Soon we shall take the castle too from that beautiful and valiant lady so like a whore herself – who pays her Captains between the pillars of her thighs.' In spite of herself, Lucrezia smiled. Cesare went on, 'I have an army from King Louis at my command. Why should you fear the French? You are not Caterina Sforza. You are my sister.'

'... And Alfonso's wife,' Lucrezia said meaningly.

'You should not listen to what Alfonso tells you. Alfonso hates me.' Then, as he saw her turn her face away from him, he said more fiercely, 'I know he plots against me and seeks to make our father turn away ...'

Lucrezia pulled her hand away from his. 'No?' she said, then accusingly, 'it's *you* who betrayed us? *You* promised Naples to the French. It's not Alfonso who told me. It was Captain Cervillon who said ...'

Cesare got up abruptly, as if wearied by the conversation.

'Cesare!' There was fear in her voice. 'Cesare, where are you going? I didn't mean to speak about Alfonso. He has done nothing against you. Nothing. Please, you know I love you. There is so much I want to say to you. Why do you go?'

Cesare was already halfway across the room. 'I must,' he said over his shoulder, 'to Castel Sant'Angelo.' He went on to open the door. 'They hold a prisoner who was party to the conspiracy to kill the Pope. He was a servant to Caterina Sforza named Tommasino ...' Lucrezia stared at him petrified as he went on, 'He was also Jofre's musician. So you see, Lucia, it's a dangerous world. Be careful whom you trust ...'

*   *   *

In the dungeons beneath Sant'Angelo, Cesare and Michelotto looked down at the half-naked figure of Tommasino, lying semiconscious on the filthy straw. He was unmarked, save for his hands which were a bleeding, shapeless mass.

'The castellan's men have spoiled him.' Michelotto gave his professional opinion. 'You must deal gently with him, My Lord,' he warned.

Cesare knelt beside the straw pallet, a pomander held to his nostrils to counteract the stink of the dungeons. 'Tommasino.' His voice was gentle. 'Tommasino ... I am the Duke Valentino ... I can help you.'

The young man's face twitched with pain, he moaned, trying to touch Cesare with his mangled hands. Cesare took his arms carefully. 'You played the lute ... Had I been there I should not have let them harm your fingers.'

'My Lord ...' Tommasino mumbled faintly.

'They shall torture you no more,' Cesare's voice was kind, soothing, 'if you will tell me what you know.'

'I will tell you ...'

Cesare interrupted him. 'Gently, Tommasino, there is nothing to fear now. Tell me. It was Battista da Mendola, was it not? He came to you in Rome ...'

Weakly, Tommasino followed his lead. 'He was sent ... By the Madonna ...'

'The Madonna of Forlì, Caterina Sforza,' Cesare prompted.

Tommasino moved his head in assent. 'Battista told me – he would win back her favour towards me – if I would help him. He had a message from the citizens of Forlì to deliver into the hands of His Holiness the Pope ...'

128

'And you agreed to help him. As my brother's servant within the Vatican...'

'If I had known ...' Tommasino shuddered. 'The Chamberlain wanted to take the message away from Battista. It was rolled up and sealed in a cane. Battista became alarmed that the Chamberlain would open it, and so he protested. They arrested us.'

'It was a poisoned message,' Cesare told him. 'The Madonna of Forlì had deceived you. Did Battista say ...?'

Tomassino shook his head. 'I know nothing, My Lord.'

Cesare paused, then, 'You do not wish me to hand you back to the castellan's men?' he said suavely. Tommasino shook his head again, trembling. Cesare went on, 'The message was sealed in a cane. It purported to be a document of surrender from the citizens of Forlì ...'

'Yes, My Lord.'

'... but truly it was from Madonna Caterina – and poisoned to kill the Pope. How was it poisoned, Tommasino?'

'Battista said ... there was plague in the town ... the Madonna laid the paper on the body of one who died ...'

'The Pope is a god on earth, Tommasino,' Cesare said sternly. 'You were foolish to try to kill him.'

'My Lord ... I swore to die. For our Madonna.'

'Verily you were a troubadour,' Cesare said sarcastically. 'You believed your own songs of chivalry. But your Madonna is no gentle name ...' He got up and turned to Michelotto. 'See that they hold him safe. He will be needed.'

He went to the door. From the pallet, Tommasino's feeble voice called to him, 'My Lord!'

'Yes, Tommasino?' Cesare was impatient.

'There is one in the Pope's guard who mocks you. He is the lover of the Princess Sancia who hates you. You should beware.'

'Don Juan Cervillon,' Cesare said grimly. 'Yes, I know.'

*   *   *

'Cervillon?' Rodrigo's voice held apparent horror and disbelief. 'Who has said this?' Four faces looked at him in damning confirmation, those of Lucrezia, Alfonso, Sancia and Jofre. Rodrigo shook his head. 'I'll not believe it.'

'Everyone knows!' Sancia exclaimed.

'Ask Lucrezia's maids. Or Sancia's. They've all heard the stories ...' Alfonso added.

Rodrigo held up his head. 'We shall not listen to slanders,' he said defiantly.

'They are not slanders, Holy Father,' Alfonso insisted. He broke off as the door opened and Cesare came in, again dressed in black velvet and wearing a black cloak and a sword.

Rodrigo's voice was relieved. 'But here *is* Cesare. He shall answer for himself ...' He looked straight at his son, his voice questioning. 'Cesare. Have you heard? The body of Captain Cervillon has been found lying in the street. Close by the door of his nephew's house. He was murdered. His head almost cut off by a sword's blow, they say ...'

'No, Holy Father.' Cesare's voice was politely surprised. 'I had not heard it.'

'You gave the order,' Alfonso accused him.

Cesare turned towards him calmly, raising his eyebrows. 'If it is true that he was murdered I am surprised, Don Alfonso, that you do not claim the deed yourself ...' He looked deliberately at Sancia. 'I cannot believe it, but I am told Captain Cervillon boasted he had lain with your sister. And that she doted on him.'

Sancia laughed harshly, shrugging her shoulders. 'Alfonso wouldn't be so foolish – or he would need a stiletto for every second man in Rome! There is nothing to be gained from talking to Cesare. Come, Jofre,' she commanded, as if calling a lapdog, and turned to leave the room.

Jofre, however, faced up to his elder brother, challenging him. 'I know why you killed him,' his voice rose in shrill defiance, 'because of what he said in Naples. That you had made a secret treaty with the French and that you promised ...'

Rodrigo broke in, 'But is this true? Cesare, tell me the truth. Had Captain Cervillon spoken of such things in Naples?'

'I believe he did,' Cesare responded nonchalantly.

Rodrigo appeared to be genuinely appalled. 'We are much distressed to learn this. He was our envoy.'

Alfonso burst out, 'But, Holy Father, what Cervillon said was true!'

'Hold your tongue!' Rodrigo thundered. 'You will leave our presence. All of you but Cesare – we will speak with him alone ...' Then, as Lucrezia kissed his hand, he lowered his tone, but his voice was still commanding. 'Such disputes between the members of our family distress us deeply. But we shall permit no treaty with the French that gives them Naples. Alfonso, Joſre! You understand?' They bowed reluctantly and left the room, followed by Sancia, whose reverence towards Rodrigo was defiantly contemptuous. None of them looked at Cesare as they went out.

Only Lucrezia, her face a mixture of love and horror, paused to speak to him. 'At our wedding Captain Cervillon held the sword over our heads, and he carried our son to the font at his christening. Did you know that?'

Cesare said tonelessly, 'Then I am sorry for it.'

'But for what?' Lucrezia cried passionately. 'May God have mercy upon you, Cesare!' She ran out of the room, leaving Rodrigo and Cesare alone.

Cesare spoke to his father as if nothing had happened. 'The artillery is drawn up before the castle of Forlì, and I must be there for the assault. I came to say farewell. And, when we have taken the fortress, we have the evidence to blacken the Madonna Caterina in the eyes of all Italy. It is prepared. With the witness.'

Rodrigo nodded, pleased. 'Excellent. Excellent. We shall catch the Madonna in the trap she prepared for us – or so it will appear.' He shook his head. 'What a foolish man was Cervillon! He was a soldier. They are less guarded than women with their tongues. You must be more careful. Promise Louis what you want – but sign no treaty that gives him Naples. We do not like these dealings with the French. You know that.'

Cesare inclined his head, as he knelt for the Pope's blessing. 'I think, Holy Father, all will go well . . .'

Rodrigo made the sign of the cross over his son's head automatically, his mind on other things. 'See that it does. *Benedicat*, Cesare. Bring Caterina Sforza back to Rome in triumph like the great Caesar at your chariot wheels . . . She was so beautiful when last we saw her. A brave Madonna! For old times' sake we shall be sorry if she prefers to die . . .'

* * *

Caterina Sforza stood at the window of her castle of Forlì, waiting for her captor. Below her the great walls of the Rocca Ravaldino, in its time the strongest fortress in Italy, gaped in ruins where Cesare's French artillery had breached them. Smoke and flames billowed across the inner courtyard where the magazine had exploded, flickering with a lurid light over the heaps of bodies lying half-submerged in the moat round the inner keep. It lit up too the fine strong features of Caterina, still a beautiful woman though now in her forties, her strong sensual mouth – she had had nine children, three husbands and countless lovers – the auburn hair and white skin of which she was so proud and took so much care, and the full curve of her breast under the steel corselet specially fashioned for her. A remarkable woman, Caterina Sforza; as skilful with a sword as with an embroidery needle, she kept a private book in which receipts for beauty potions were mixed with others for abortifacients and slow-working poisons.

Steps sounded in the corridor outside the room. Caterina turned as Cesare entered, his clothing muddy and wet to the knees. 'Il Valentino,' she said with ironical courtesy.

The French commander, Yves d'Alègre, who had been guarding Caterina until Cesare should arrive, bowed to him. 'My lord . . . the Lady Caterina has surrendered herself to me . . .'

'Thank you, d'Alègre. You may leave us.'

'My Lord.' D'Alègre made as though to leave, then stopped as if something was concerning him. '... I regret that I must make the matter plain. The Lady of Forlì has given herself into the hands of France. On this understanding and with respect, My Lord, I take my leave ...'

He bowed and withdrew, leaving Caterina and Cesare staring at each other warily. The last time they had met to parley for the surrender of the castle, Caterina had attempted to trap Cesare by pulling up the drawbridge unexpectedly. Now they were at close quarters, but as captor and captive, young man and older woman, the sexual possibilities latent. A handsome man, Caterina thought, in other circumstances she might have found him attractive ...

Cesare offered her a chair. She shook her head. 'Very well,' he said, sitting down himself. He looked at her arrogantly, head thrown back. 'You were unwise to refuse to surrender the fort. It cost you many lives.'

'I have heard how your soldiers behaved in the town. I could not in honour surrender my people here.'

Cesare shrugged. 'No man of mine has abused your people. It was done by the French, to whom you have chosen to surrender yourself.'

Caterina looked at him but did not reply.

'... You believe what you have heard,' Cesare said, 'that the French will hold no woman prisoner.' He smiled cruelly, as again she made no response, and went on, 'It may not be so. You offered your services to the Duke of Milan. The French will remember that – Duke Ludovico is the King's capital enemy, and now he is taken and on his way to a French dungeon, and cannot help you. You would have been wiser to treat with me.' He paused, enjoying himself, then he shrugged. 'It makes no difference, after all. The French will sell you to me. We have only to agree the sum.'

Caterina looked at him for a long while, running her eyes deliberately over his body. Then she said, smiling, 'I trust then it will be a large one!' She moved over to him. 'I am not accustomed to be bought and sold, My Lord. But if it must be so . . .' She knelt suddenly at his feet, her white hand on his leg, caressingly. Her voice was silky. 'These boots are wet. Should you not take them off?'

Cesare looked down at her, non-commital. 'If you choose.'

She began to unlace his boots, her hair falling over his thighs. Cesare sat motionless, watching her until she stopped unlacing the boots, her hand moving from the laces up his leg. Then he bent swiftly forward and grasped her hand. She looked up at him, her face close to his. 'Where is your son?' Cesare said coldly.

Caterina's face, which had been soft and beguiling, froze. 'Ottaviano? You think I would be so foolish as to let him fall into *your* hands?' Her voice was contemptuous, her eyes full of hatred for him who had humiliated her. 'You are a cold man, Cesare Borgia. Well fitted to be an unfrocked priest. The bastard of a Pope!' She tried to pull away from him, but he still held her fast.

'And you,' he said coolly, 'the bastard daughter of Milan. Did you think I would risk dipping in a well where so many greasy pitchers have been before me?'

With her free hand, Caterina struck him across the face. He smiled and released her. She backed away from him across the room, as he bent to lace up his boots again. 'I shall conduct you to my quarters in the town,' he said. 'And rest assured you shall sleep a virgin sleep tonight. My officers will guard you from the French. Whether you will or not.' He stood up. 'Are you ready?'

Caterina stood quiet and proud. 'Yes, I am ready.'

Cesare opened the door for her to pass through into the corridor. 'I regret, Madonna,' he said courteously, 'that you will have to tread on the bodies of the dead. There is no other way.'

'Duke Valentino,' Caterina said loftily, 'in my time I have seen many deaths. It is useless to weep for the dead. For them it is finished. Death has the only triumph, my lord. One day you too will find it so.'

Cesare inclined his head. 'Indeed so, Madonna. But that day may be closer for you than for me. For you, your reign is

134

over, for me it has only just begun. And I intend to enjoy my triumph like Caesar. Alive and in Rome. And you shall accompany me.'

*　　*　　*

Rome. The last week of February 1500. It was carnival time when, as a puzzled envoy of the Sultan reported to his master, 'all Christians go mad'. Courtesans dressed as boys roamed the streets throwing gilded eggs filled with rose water at men whom they fancied. There were races for donkeys, wild boars, prostitutes and Jews up the long Via Lata from the Porta del Popolo. On this day, 26th February, the Via Lata was particularly crowded; not only was it carnival time but also Jubilee Year, and the city was overflowing with pilgrims eager to ease their way to heaven with the Pope's special Indulgences; on this day the street was crowded above all with Romans, who had turned out to see the Roman-style triumph of the Pope's son, Duke Valentino, who was to enter the city through the Porta del Popolo, with the Lady of Forlì, Madonna Caterina Sforza, in his train.

Outside the Porta del Popolo, Burchard was in despair. Despatched there by Rodrigo to organise the procession in a manner befitting the occasion, he was driven to distraction by the behaviour of Cesare's Swiss and Gascon mercenaries, who refused to recognise his authority and took up positions in the procession which did not properly belong to them. Worse still were the hordes of gypsies, yokels, small boys and camp followers who had joined Cesare's progress through the villages along the Via Flaminia, and who were quite beyond Burchard's power to control. Even those who should have known better behaved badly, the envoys of England and Naples picking a quarrel over precedence with the representatives of Cesare's brother-in-law, Charlotte's brother, Jean d'Albret, King of Navarre. It was, Burchard reflected in despair, even worse than the day of King Charles's entrance into Rome.

Only Cesare remained calm, a dignified and dramatic

figure in a plain black velvet robe, his only ornament the gold collar of the Order of St Michael. It was his first public appearance in Rome since his gorgeous departure for France eighteen months before. Everyone noticed the change in him, the stark simplicity of his costume in comparison with the peacock splendours of 1498, the quiet confidence with which he sat his horse at the head of his column of armed men. He was only twenty-four, but while the women exclaimed over his handsome looks, the men could not fail to note the parallels with Caesar, which were underlined by an allegorical procession celebrating his triumphs in the Piazza Navona next day. Most predicted a great future for him, and those that did were troubled by feelings of disquiet.

Rodrigo's sentiments, however, were of extravagant joy. Ambassadors noted that he alternated between tears and laughter as he craned over the balcony of the loggia before St Peter's to catch a glimpse of Cesare's procession as it wound its way to the Vatican. Then he hurried to the Sala del Pappagallo to receive Cesare formally; even then he could scarcely keep still on his throne, as he waited for the doors to open to admit his son.

Finally, with a blare of clarions, the great doors swung open, and Cesare walked in, passing through the ranks of the papal guard to kneel at his father's feet. 'Most Holy Father,' he declared in ringing tones, 'in this year of jubilee I deliver into your hands the city and people of Forlì which I have taken for the Holy See.'

Rodrigo could contain himself no longer. Crying 'Rise up! Rise up, my beloved son!' he embraced Cesare, tears of paternal pride staring in his eyes. 'Don Caesar! In triumph! You shall be Lord of the Romagna. We shall create you Captain-General of our army – Gonfalonier of Holy Mother Church. You shall be invested with the Golden Rose – in token of our esteem and our great love, *Gloria Patria et Filio* ...' As he hugged Cesare to him, he whispered in Spanish in his ear, 'So, where is Caterina ...?'

* * *

Rodrigo received Caterina Sforza, his prisoner, in the same Sala del Pappagallo which had witnessed Cesare's triumphal entry the previous day. This time the room was empty but for Rodrigo, with Cesare standing beside him and Lucrezia seated on a cushion at his feet. Rodrigo remembered Caterina as the lissom young virago in her twenties, who with sword in hand had defended Castel Sant'Angelo against the Roman mob in the days of Pope Sixtus. His face fell slightly in disappointment as she knelt before him, head bowed in reverence. 'Ah ... she was younger ...' he murmured to himself as he made the sign of the cross above her in blessing. '*In nomine Patris, et Filii, et Spiritus Sancti, Amen,*' he intoned. Then in his normal voice he said cordially, 'When last we saw you, Caterina, we carried your son at his christening.'

'It is fifteen years, Your Holiness,' Caterina replied, smiling.

'And you defended Castel Sant'Angelo, striding the battlements with a hawk on one hand, a sword in the other ...' He turned to Lucrezia, 'Do you remember Lucrezia, you were just five years old – how we heard the guns?'

'Yes, Holy Father.'

Rodrigo addressed Caterina again, his voice still friendly, 'But you're well lodged in the Belvedere? We intend to treat you as our guest not as our prisoner.'

Cesare followed up his father. 'All that is needed is that you sign a declaration renouncing your rights and those of your children to the cities of Imola and Forlì – which *I* hold.'

'And I should have my freedom?' Caterina questioned him.

'You would remain in Rome,' he replied.

'Then you offer me nothing, My lord Duke. I am here. As you see.'

Rodrigo spoke, asserting his authority. 'You are not humble, Caterina, though you kneel. What do you seek?'

'I do most humbly beseech Your Holiness to let me depart. For Florence ...'

'... Where you will join your son.' Rodrigo's voice was

stern. 'It is wilful of you to refuse what the Duke has asked. You have no friends. Your uncle, Duke Ludovico, has been taken. Together with your uncle, Ascanio. They are both prisoners of the French.'

Lucrezia's face displayed her unhappiness at being witness to this scene. She rose from her cushion. 'Holy Father. You will excuse me?'

Rodrigo motioned to her to go, intent on the business at hand, but Cesare's eyes followed her intently as she left the room. 'What do you say?' Rodrigo thundered at Caterina.

'I shall never renounce my cities, Holiness. For my children's sake.'

'Then you remain in prison like all the family of Sforza!' Cesare told her with an air of finality, turning on his heel to follow Lucrezia.

'Cesare!' Rodrigo was annoyed.

'Forgive me, Holy Father, but there is a matter I must attend to,' he replied, and continued on his way towards the door.

'What shall we do then?' Rodrigo said somewhat plaintively, 'with the Madonna?'

'Put her in chains and let her hang – until her tongue is sweeter!' Cesare replied savagely, and went out.

'Lucrezia ...! Stay!' his voice rang out down the long corridor. Lucrezia paused reluctantly and turned, waiting for him to come up with her. 'Why did you run away?' Cesare said, looking down at her, searching her face for a guide to her feelings. He grasped her hand.

'To tell Alfonso ... that his uncles have been taken by the French.' She tried to pull away from him. 'You hold too close, Cesare. Please let me go.'

Cesare said earnestly, his voice tender, 'Our father spoke of when you were a child ... at Montegiordano. When we were taken from our mother and you were frightened by the guns ... You remember? I promised that I would be a soldier – and you were comforted. Lucrezia. I have been loyal. To you alone ...'

'You have a wife in France. And now you have a daughter,' Lucrezia said distantly.

'I care nothing for them. It was always so ... only you and me ... since we were children.' He pulled her close to him, his voice fierce, demanding. 'Choose, you will have to choose now.'

'Choose...?'

'To keep faith with me. Or with Alfonso.'

Lucrezia's face closed. 'Alfonso is my husband, Cesare. Let go my hands,' she commanded him.

'I shall not let you go. Till you have sworn,' he blazed.

'You are mad. And it isn't true. You were not faithful. It was the Spanish tongue we spoke under the bedclothes at Montegiordano. And the Moresca that we danced. It's France that you have married, Cesare. And it is you who have to choose now.' With a supreme effort she pulled herself free of him. 'Do you not see?' she said, almost despairingly, 'I love Alfonso!' Then deliberately, 'I ... love ... Alfonso.'

She turned from him and ran down the corridor. Cesare stared after her, his face sombre and his eyes dark.

*   *   *

Cesare sat in his apartment idly playing dice with Michelotto. Outside a violent summer storm raged, gusts of wind and hailstones shaking the windows, while claps of thunder exploded overhead. Suddenly there was a violent thunderclap louder than the rest, and the building seemed to shudder. There followed a dead silence, then the sound of distant shouting and of running feet. The two men looked at each other questioningly, Michelotto instinctively crossing himself. Cesare stood up and moved towards the door. As he did so, it burst open unceremoniously to reveal Burchard, breathless and powdered with dust.

'Lord Duke! The Pope ... an accident ...' Behind him, through the open door voices could be heard shouting in panic, 'The Pope is dead! The Pope is dead!'

Cesare stood as if transfixed, his face white. For an instant he saw his world in ruins, before he had even had time to grasp it. Then he pushed Burchard aside and ran towards his father's rooms, followed by Michelotto. Burchard trotted after them, explaining breathlessly, 'The Holy Father . . . he was with the banker, Messer Chigi . . . they were discussing the Gaetani castles . . . the chimney fell in. Gaspare and I escaped. They were buried . . .'

But Rodrigo had been saved. The great beam which had fallen across the papal chair as he sat upon it, killing Lorenzo Chigi with whom he was conversing, had protected him from the weight of the fallen masonry. By the time Cesare reached the scene, Rodrigo's chamberlain, Gaspare Poto, with the help of some of the guards, had succeeded in extracting Rodrigo from the ruins. He was bleeding from a superficial head wound, feeble but conscious.

'Father!' Cesare fell upon his knees, catching his father's hand and bringing it to his lips. In that moment he felt as if he too had escaped death. In that moment he realised not only how much depended upon Rodrigo's life, but how easily that life could be cut off, and thus how swiftly he himself must move to ensure that he gained everything that he wanted and could protect what he won. The beam that hung perilously above the Pope's head could so easily have cut off his own future. This realisation added an urgency to his plans which had not been there before. He could be so easily Caesar or nothing.

*   *   *

Rodrigo lay in bed, propped up on pillows, attended by his new favourite, Angelina. Cesare and Alfonso stood near his bed, Lucrezia knelt beside it, kissing her father's bandaged hand. Giulia Farnese too was there, hastily despatched by her family to the Pope's bedside to plead for her uncle, Giacomo Gaetani, who lay in prison in Sant'Angelo, his estates confiscated by the Borgias. Rodrigo looked at her sardonically for a moment, then he smiled, putting out a hand to fondle her face. 'We loved you once . . .' he said reminiscently.

Emboldened, Giulia began, 'Holiness, my uncle, Giacomo Gaetani ...'

Rodrigo made a weary gesture with his hand, 'He shall be released ...' He looked round at the anxious faces hovering about the bed. 'So ...' he said, smiling, but the undertone in his voice was grave, 'You thought we would be worms' meat, did you? What would you have done then? What of your quarrels, Cesare ... Alfonso?' Neither of them answered him, nor met each other's eyes. 'Learn to live together,' Rodrigo admonished them earnestly. 'Life is so sweet ... One day you'll know ... Life is sweet ...' Then he made a gesture of weariness, dismissing them. 'Lucrezia, I want only you – and Angelina.'

'I would speak with you later, Holy Father, Giacomo Gaetani ...' Cesare said urgently.

'Yes.' Rodrigo's voice was drowsy, self-indulgent, 'Later ... Our head is painful to us. Angelina shall wring a towel in water and bind it close ...' He lay back, closing his eyes. The two women remained by his bedside as Cesare and Alfonso withdrew, still without a word to each other.

* * *

Alfonso stared down at Lucrezia as she sat at her mirror twisting a string of pearls into her hair. She caught his expression in the glass, and turned to him, startled, 'Alfonso! What is it?'

'Giacomo Gaetani is dead.'

'Dead? When did he die?'

'He was poisoned.' He turned and walked over to the window. 'The castellan summoned Giacomo's wife and sisters to Sant'Angelo last night. They were told he had been taken ill. But he was dead.'

Lucrezia was silent for a moment, than said anxiously, 'But why should they think he was poisoned?'

'Giacomo suspected it before because of the pains he had from taking food. After that his mother brought everything to the prison herself. For the past three days the guards have prevented her.' He paused and turned to look directly at her. 'Lucrezia, everyone knows he was poisoned.'

Lucrezia said emphatically, 'It was not my father. Is that what they say?' She rose from her seat and went to Alfonso, taking his hand. 'I was there when he agreed to set Giacomo free,' she said earnestly. 'Why should he poison him?'

Alfonso took her by both arms, holding her in front of him, willing her to face what he believed to be the truth. 'I do not think it was done by the Pope,' he said slowly. 'I think it was ordered by Cesare.'

'He had no reason ...'

'Yes,' Alfonso said bitterly. 'He had no reason – so no one will suspect.' As he turned her face away from him, he released her arms.

Lucrezia stood apart from him, angry now. 'That is absurd,' she said fiercely. 'Cesare is right to say you hate him. Whenever something terrible occurs you think he is the cause.'

'Other people think likewise.'

Angrily, Lucrezia turned from him and went to sit before her mirror again, nervously twisting her hair round her fingers. 'I care nothing for other people or for their opinions ...'

But Alfonso went on, inexorable, arms folded, watching her. 'They'll say it was done for you.'

Amazed, Lucrezia swivelled on her seat, 'For me?'

'Your father gave you Sermoneta – Giacomo's estates. If your father had released him, he could have claimed them back one day. But dead men can do nothing. I believe Cesare had him poisoned for you.'

'But Cesare knows that I would not allow it ...' Lucrezia was horrified but still unwilling to believe Alfonso.

'Whether you would or not, it touches you – because you owe your gain to him. It is a debt in blood which you cannot disclaim. So people will say ... you are a true Borgia ...' A fit of rage and disgust seemed to overtake him, and he turned away from her. 'Cesare is a thing of darkness. He will drag us all into the pit. You and the Pope.'

Lucrezia pleaded, 'Alfonso, it isn't true. Let me speak to Cesare.'

But Alfonso was not listening to her. Something or someone in the garden below had caught his attention. 'I wish he was dead,' he said between his teeth, his eyes narrowing as if an idea had occurred to him and he was considering it. Then he turned and swung purposefully out of the room.

'Alfonso! Come back!' Lucrezia screamed after him. Then she flung herself face downward on the bed, sobbing, 'Alfonso ... Cesare ...'

*　　*　　*

Stars shimmered in the glowing night sky of summer above St Peter's, the square before the steps to the church was unnaturally still and silent. Although it was a hot July night, Alfonso shivered slightly, drawing his light cloak about him, as he made his way home towards the door of the Palazzo of Santa Maria in Portico. Suddenly, from a pool of shadow at the base of the colonnade, a group of men emerged, wrapped in dark capes, moving towards him. Alfonso quickened his pace, hoping to reach the door of his house in safety, but in a moment they were upon him.

'Help! Guard!' Alfonso shouted, as he felt steel pierce his thigh. Another sword-thrust penetrated his right arm, then he fell, half unconscious from a blow on the head. As he did so, he heard footsteps running to his aid, the papal guard, alerted by his cry. His assailants abandoned the attack and fled across the steps of St Peter's, vanishing into the darkness. There was the clatter of hooves and they were gone. The terrified guards, recognising Alfonso, half carried, half dragged him to the safety of the Vatican, leaving a trail of blood dark across the steps.

Lucrezia's first instinct when she saw her husband unconscious and bleeding was to run to her father for help and protection. 'Father!' she cried as she burst into his bedchamber, where he was dictating a letter to his Chamberlain, Gaspare Poto. 'Father!' She was hysterical. 'Alfonso ... he's dying ... dying!' She flung herself into

Rodrigo's arms. 'He was attacked . . . just now in the piazza. He's wounded . . . save him . . . please save him.'

'Be still, my child,' Rodrigo comforted her, then to Poto, 'See what the matter is!' he commanded. The Chamberlain nodded and left the room.

'Father!' Lucrezia's voice was desperate, 'He's bleeding to death . . .'

'Is a doctor with him?'

'Sancia is with him. I came to tell you. Oh, Father, I can't believe it. Who could have wanted to harm Alfonso? He was so good . . .' She stopped, and turned her head to follow Rodrigo's eyes. Cesare came into the room, his face expressing shock.

'It's true?' Rodrigo asked him.

Cesare nodded. 'He was attacked on the steps of the basilica by a group of men who rode away.' He addressed Lucrezia, his voice solicitous. 'I have seen his wounds and they are being dressed. I think that he will live.'

'He will live!' Lucrezia got up and ran to the door. 'I must go to him, and watch him. No one shall ever try to harm him again!'

Rodrigo looked at his son questioningly. 'You say . . . they were armed men . . .' Then, when Cesare did not answer, he said hesitantly, 'Cesare. You did not try to kill the Duke?'

Cesare had his back to him, looking out of the window. 'No,' he said, 'but if I had, it would have been no more than he deserved.'

Rodrigo sank back in relief, but his suspicions were not totally allayed. 'The King of Naples would not forgive it,' he warned. 'Pray God, he will be saved. I shall put a guard upon his room. You understand?'

Still Cesare remained looking out of the window. Then he said slowly, 'One thing I do understand. Now – if he lives – he must kill *me* . . .'

* * *

Alfonso lived, he was young and strong and the papal physicians skilful. Within a month he was well enough to

144

get up and sit in a chair in his room in the new Torre Borgia, the tower Rodrigo had had built overlooking the Vatican gardens. The bright sun of the August morning streamed into the room, not yet shuttered against the heat of midday. Sancia and Lucrezia sat with Alfonso idly chatting, Sancia's favourite hunchback playing a lute at their feet. 'Did you know ...' Sancia said, looking speculatively at the hunchback, 'that men with humps are supposed to be abnormally virile ... like dwarfs ...?'

Lucrezia laughed. 'Sancia ... you talk of nothing but that.'

Alfonso smiled. 'There's nothing else she knows of ...' He held out his hand fondly to Lucrezia. They were interrupted by a knock at the door. 'Enter!' Alfonso cried.

A sudden silence fell as Michelotto stepped into the room, Ramiro at his heels. The hunchback dropped his lute and huddled behind Sancia, seeking protection. 'What is it? Why have you come?' Lucrezia asked, a note of anxiety in her voice.

Michelotto bowed, his face bland and his voice suave. 'From my master, My Lady. He requests the Duke of Biselli to go with us.'

'No!' Lucrezia turned to Alfonso. 'You shall not go with them!'

Alfonso looked at her meaningly, but said only, 'It will be well. Go to your father and tell him that Cesare's men are here.' Then, as she rose to go, he urged her, 'And go quickly.'

Sancia rose to follow Lucrezia, the frightened hunchback at her skirts. 'And I will go to Cesare,' she said. 'If he wants to see you, he should come himself.' Then, before she went out, she looked warningly at Michelotto. 'My brother is under the protection of the King of Naples and of the Holy Father. Do not forget that.'

Michelotto bowed at her retreating back. 'I am aware of it, My Lady,' he said, then he smiled and said under his breath, 'but I am in the service of the son ...'

Alfonso heard him and tried to get up from his chair, as Michelotto and Ramiro moved towards him. 'My Lord,'

Michelotto said in mock solicitude, 'you are weary. You should rest ... in peace ...' Swiftly the two men seized Alfonso and carried him to the bed. There was a brief struggle, then stillness broken by a choking cry, quickly stifled.

As Lucrezia ran frantically towards her father's apartments, she rounded a corner straight into Cesare's arms. He held her as she pounded against his chest with her hands, struggling to be free of him. 'No! Let me go ... I must ...'

'Lucrezia,' Cesare said gravely, 'he meant to kill me. I saw him at the window ...'

'No!' Lucrezia screamed at him, then, with the realisation of what Cesare meant, a look of terror came over her face. 'Alfonso ...'

Her body went limp in Cesare's arms. He cradled her as if she were a child. 'You have seen nothing. And it is done.' Then he picked her up and strode with her along the corridor towards the Torre Borgia.

'There is no mark on the body?' Cesare spoke from the doorway, the unconscious Lucrezia in his arms. Michelotto nodded. 'Then it was well done.' He looked down at his sister. 'She must not see it,' he said, indicating the body on the bed. 'Take it to the chapel of Santa Maria in the basilica. The Duke of Biselli shall lie where the Duke of Gandia lay,' he said with the ghost of a smile. 'But my brother-in-law does not merit the honours done my brother. See to it that he is interred with expedition – and in silence.'

Michelotto inclined his head. 'It shall be so done, My Lord,' he said. He and Ramiro wrapped Alfonso's body quickly and expertly in the coverlet and carried it out of the room. Cesare laid Lucrezia gently on the bed, and stood for a moment looking down at her, then he bent and touched her cheek.

*   *   *

'Lucrezia?' Rodrigo's voice sounded hopeless, despairing as he sat with his head in his hands, before the implacable

146

figure of Cesare, his face impassive in the flickering lamp-light. 'How is she? How did they answer you? The two of them ...'

'They have barred the door. Sancia is with Lucrezia and will not let us speak. She should be sent to Naples.'

'Naples ...' Rodrigo sighed. 'What is to be done? How shall we inform the King?'

'Tell him his son meant to kill me. I saw him at the window with a crossbow in his hand.'

'And you think that King Federigo will believe *that*?'

'I think others who mean to kill me will remember it.'

Rodrigo gazed at him with something like horror. 'Caesar ... Or nothing,' he said.

'I choose my way,' Cesare said evenly; 'there is no other course.'

'And if we do not choose to follow ...'

'Then, Holy Father, you must do what you will.'

Rodrigo leaned back wearily, closing his eyes. 'What *I* will!' he said ironically. 'I have not done that since I was a boy, playing among the olive groves of Valencia. Spain ... my heart is still in Spain ...' he mused. Then, with an effort, he recalled himself to the present, and opened his eyes, looking hard at Cesare. 'What have you promised Louis? You must tell me, Cesare. Tell me now.'

Cesare's voice was expressionless as he replied, 'I promised Naples to France. For Louis' support in winning the Romagna.'

'So it was true ...'

'Yes.'

'You had no right to make such a treaty.' Rodrigo rose, with angry dignity. 'Go your way, Cesare. But go alone.' He motioned Cesare from the room, but Cesare did not move. 'We shall write to Federigo and tell him what you have done. To your own house and family!'

'You will then charge me publicly? With the murder?'

'Yes! With the murder.'

There was a pause. Then Cesare said, slowly and distinctly, 'Then I will answer you. For it was not the first. I will answer not only for Alfonso's death – but for my brother's.' His voice was cruel. 'You have not forgotten the reason why Juan died?' Rodrigo sank slowly down into his chair. Cesare moved to stand over him. 'The nuns of San Sisto care for an infant who is now two years old. Giovanni ... I have committed crimes I will confess. But there is one that I have not committed ...'

Rodrigo seemed unable to speak, staring up at Cesare as if hypnotised.

'I would protect the honour of this house – and make the name of Borgia great long after we are dust. It is you, Holy Father, who must now decide if we shall bow to fate. Or bend it to our will.'

For a long moment, Rodrigo stared at Cesare without speaking. Then he got up, his shoulders bowed, his voice toneless. 'I must go to Lucrezia,' he said, 'they tell me she is half-dead from weeping.' At the door he paused, but did not look at his son. 'You saw Alfonso at the window ... with a crossbow in his hand ... aimed at your heart.'

Cesare inclined his head. 'Yes, Holy Father.'

'I will write so to the King. But there can be nothing between us and Naples from this day forth. And that is why you killed him.' He went out, staring expressionlessly before him like a blind man. Cesare watched him, a smile of triumph on his face.

*　　*　　*

Rodrigo, his face sad and anxious, sat beside Lucrezia's bed, holding both her hands in his in a vain attempt to comfort her. Sancia stood, a fierce, vengeful figure on the other side of the bed, staring venomously at Rodrigo. Lucrezia's feeble voice came from the bed. 'The men who did it ...?'

'Three men have been arrested,' Rodrigo replied. 'The hunchback. And the doctors who attended Alfonso. They will be put to the torture.'

'Michelotto? Ramiro?' Lucrezia was puzzled.

'And Cesare,' Sancia put in savagely. 'Well, Holy Father. Tell her what you have done with Cesare.'

148

Rodrigo would not look at her. 'Leave this chamber. We command you!' he shouted.

'Now you shall hear the truth . . .' Sancia's voice was full of hatred and contempt.

'We banish you to Naples! Leave on this instant – or you'll be flogged!'

Her head high, Sancia moved to the door. 'I would not stay in Rome now if all the College Cardinals went on their knees!' As she went out she threw back over her shoulder, 'Ask him, Lucrezia, ask him what he has promised Cesare. And you will know how evil a man can be! Only a man. Ask him . . . what he has done.' She went out, slamming the door behind her.

'Lucrezia.' Rodrigo's voice was pleading as he stroked his daughter's hair. 'You are so young . . . tomorrow it will be nothing. You think another day will never come. But you will see – tomorrow the sun will rise just the same . . .' Then, as Lucrezia turned her head away, 'Think of the family. Think of us. Cesare too . . . He wants the highest fame – not only for himself – but for the house of Borgia. And for you . . .' He kissed her hand. 'Alfonso wanted to kill him. We believe that. Well, he is gone. But one day – one day soon – another man will come. Quite as handsome – and much more splendid . . .'

'No!'

'You will see . . .'

'I shall never see him again! And I shall never see Cesare – or if I do, I'll tear his eyes out!'

'Be careful what you say . . .' Rodrigo began nervously.

'I hate you! You can do nothing for me! I want him back, I want him back, I want him back! I want Alfonso back again . . .' She turned over onto her pillows, weeping bitterly.

Rodrigo rose and stood for a moment, looking down at her. 'You must go to Nepi,' he said gravely. 'When you are strong. And the child, Rodrigo, too. You have had fever. It is dangerous for you to remain in Rome at this time of year.' Then, as Lucrezia said nothing, a look of helplessness came over his face. 'I can do nothing . . . Forgive me.'

A muffled voice came from the pillows. 'Yes. I know. I must go to Nepi.'

'It will be best.' Rodrigo turned and walked heavily from the room, his steps slow and faltering as if he had suddenly become an old man.

*   *   *

'The Pope has sent away his daughter and his daughter-in-law and everyone except Valentino ...' Burchard wrote wonderingly in his diary. 'All Rome trembles at this Duke, that he may not have them killed. And many say that the cause of the death of Alfonso was the supreme lust for dominion of Cesare Valentino Borgia who now reigns in the Vatican ...'

6

The Widowed Bride

CESARE, MASKED AND accompanied by Paolo Orsini and a French gentleman, left the Vatican and rode out of Rome to a long-awaited rendezvous. He was about to receive the reward for which he had pledged Alfonso Biselli's life. Turning his horse into the courtyard of a country tavern, he dismounted and went in, flinging the reins to an ostler. A man rose to greet him as he strode in followed by Paolo Orsini; it was Yves d'Alègre.

'Captain d'Alègre!' Cesare embraced him warmly. Then, indicating his companion, 'Paolo Orsini. Captain Yves d'Alègre in the service of His Majesty, King Louis of France.'

'The Duke has told me of your valour in the capture of Forlì,' Paolo Orsini said politely.

D'Alègre bowed. 'The Duke is gracious ...'

Cesare shouted to the landlord for wine, and motioned them to be seated. 'What is your news from Paris?' he asked d'Alègre. 'I have four thousand men here under my command – my own troops and those of My Lord Paolo and his brother Giulo, who are engaged to serve me. But I shall not move from Rome until I have your promise from the King.'

D'Alègre smiled, taking a scroll from under his cloak and handing it to Cesare. 'I have it here, My Lord Duke, under his seal ... His Majesty has consented to despatch two thousand infantry and three hundred men-at-arms.'

Cesare raised his eyebrows. 'The lancers impress the country people, but they cannot break down the walls of cities. What artillery?'

'Sakers and falconets ...'

'Great cannon?'

'His Majesty has given no precise undertaking. But I will convey to him your needs.'

'Siege cannon,' Cesare said firmly. 'As much as he can spare – and a bombard. With full ammunition.'

He paused as the landlord brought a tray loaded with flagons of wine and goblets and set it on the table. Then Paolo Orsini spoke. 'And for our part ... what have we undertaken to the King?' he asked.

'You mean what have I undertaken on your behalf,' Cesare said half humorously. 'Tell My Lord Paolo, Captain, what I have promised.'

D'Alègre's voice was solemn, as if he were reading out the terms of a contract. 'The Duke of Valentinois has engaged himself to secure free passage for the armies of France to reconquer the state of Naples. For which he will contribute a force under his own command, and secure the recognition of His Holiness the Pope for the King's conquest.'

'You see?' Cesare spoke to Paolo reassuring him. 'There's nothing here to injure the Orsinis. It is your enemies the Colonnas, who are bound to Naples, who must beware. Captain d'Alègre knows nothing of our Roman family quarrels – but he can tell you what I say is true.'

'My Lord,' Paolo said earnestly, 'I need no assurance but from yourself ...'

Cesare gave him a quick look, concealing his contempt for such gullibility. 'Trust no one who has a reason to deceive you,' he said shortly. 'Captain d'Alègre has none.' Then he turned to the Frenchman. 'D'Alègre, when you return to France, I would have you take with you some gifts for my wife. They are not weighty – simply spices and sweetmeats from Venice such as she has asked me for ...'

D'Alègre looked penitent. 'My Lord, I had forgot ... The Duchess of Valentinois gave me messages. For you and for your sister, the Lady Lucrezia ...'

Cesare got suddenly to his feet, the interview ended. 'She is not in Rome,' he said shortly and strode out of the room.

* * *

Rodrigo received Lucrezia's letter as he prepared to meet the Venetian Ambassador with Cesare. He was surprised to see her characteristically untidy writing on the scroll, since hitherto, in her anger and distress, she had maintained silence as far as her family in Rome were concerned. He read it, frowning, putting it away when Cesare, for whom he had been waiting for the past hour, finally appeared. He spoke to him in a tone of understandable exasperation. 'So there you are. It is impossible to do business with you now – no one can reach you until after noon. You turn night into day, and day into night. The envoy of Venice has been waiting these two hours. We told him we must speak first with you and sent him away. Had you been here in time we could have done business before Prime ...'

'I admire your vigour, Holy Father,' Cesare smiled. 'After the ladies entertained us last night ...'

A look of pleasurable reminiscence crossed Rodrigo's face. 'Ah yes, the dancers ...' he said, then, with some asperity, 'but *I* rose at six o'clock ...' Cesare bowed in homage. Rodrigo, annoyed, continued, 'Age makes no difference to me. But *you* are young! How do you manage on compaign? You cannot sleep all day.'

Cesare became serious. 'It's the campaign I came to speak about. The papal treasury is making difficulties over the sums that have been authorised ...'

Rodrigo was surprised and incensed. 'Difficulties? How dare they? For four years we have kept the holy office free of debts – a thing they never saw before. It was not done by penny-pinching. It is the *income* we have increased. Only this year we have negotiated a contract for the alum mines with Messer Chigi which will increase the revenue by many times the sum – how much will you need to maintain the army? What sum each day?'

Cesare considered, then replied, 'A thousand ducats.'

'You may need more,' Rodrigo told him, his voice businesslike. He understood money and was irritated by Cesare's vagueness and prodigality in this respect. 'We shall create new Cardinals, that is the easiest way to raise it. The College will accept ten – or a dozen – more. We shall tell them they must come to you to pay the first fruits . . .' He meditated for a moment, making mental calculations. 'And some will pay as much as twenty thousand for a Cardinal's hat . . . We could elect Marco Cornaro – to please Venice. And we must have some Spaniards loyal to ourselves . . .'

Cesare nodded. 'Yes, Holy Father, but there are other considerations besides money for the campaign. There is our security. There is Venice. I cannot undertake the campaign unless her friendship is assured . . .'

'There is something else,' added Rodrigo, and his voice held a peculiar note. 'It is not Venice we have been thinking of since we rose this morning . . .' He moved to a table on which a map was lying unrolled. 'Come here, Cesare,' he said, his finger on the map. Cesare moved over and stood looking down at it. 'Here,' Rodrigo said, pointing to the Marches and the Romagna, 'here are the cities you will take, Pesaro, Faenza, Imola. We have assured the friendship of Venice with promises of help against the Turks who are attacking her empire, but there is another neighbour on the northern frontier who will eye your advance with suspicion, and perhaps hostility – Ferrara. Have you considered that?'

'I wrote to Duke Ercole of Ferrara on my last campaign assuring him of my friendly intentions towards his family and his state . . .'

Rodrigo clasped his hands together and looked up at the ceiling, as if invoking God's assistance. 'If there were only some way we could be sure of the Duke, make a firm alliance with him.' He sighed and cast down his eyes, his voice demure. 'His son has lost his wife. A fine young soldier – only twenty-four and handsome.'

'A marriage?' Cesare said quickly. 'Between Alfonso d'Este . . .' Rodrigo nodded. 'And Lucrezia?' Cesare shook his head. 'Impossible. She refused even to return to Rome.'

Rodrigo held up Lucrezia's letter. 'She has written to us, signing herself – "the most unhappy lady". But she will not return while you are here, that's true.'

'And it's a match that could never be arranged. Alfonso d'Este of Ferrara . . .'

'*Lacrime Christi!*' Rodrigo exclaimed. 'Why must it be Alfonso – the very name she must forget? They could have called the boy by any other! But think, Cesare,' he said, pointing with the letter to the map, 'think of the advantage it would bring us. The territory between Venice and the Romagna always secure. And Lucrezia – the Duchess of Ferrara!'

'Holy Father,' Cesare said doubtfully, 'Alfonso d'Este is the hereditary Prince – the legitimate Prince, legitimate son of the proudest family in Italy ...'

'And we had thought that you were proud!' Rodrigo reproved him. 'She is *our* daughter! Cesare, the Duke can be bought like any other man. It is Lucrezia who must be persuaded. You can persuade her.'

'But she would never see me.'

'No, she would not agree if we approach her first. But she is lonely – her letter tells us that. And you must travel with your army to Pesaro. It is not far to turn aside – as if on impulse ... You are the brother she loved the best ...' he added persuasively.

Cesare stared down at the map thoughtfully. It was obvious that the plan appealed to him. Then he raised his head and smiled at Rodrigo. 'They say it's rough – the road to Nepi,' he said.

* * *

Lucrezia knelt at her *prie-dieu*, trying to pray, but she was distracted by the bright stare of the little monkey which sat beside her, picking its fleas and watching her. More than that, she was distracted by her thoughts. The emotional numbness which had followed the first shock of grief and bereavement had now passed, and disturbing memories of love and passion crowded her thoughts, tormenting her nights and even her moments of prayer. She was truly lonely now, and starved of male companionship, with the dry prospect of a long life as a widow stretching drearily in front of her. 'Take Cicero away,' she said crossly to Angelina. 'How can I pray to the Virgin when he is watching me, and scratching?'

155

Angelina picked up the little creature which clung to her, its large eyes still fixed upon Lucrezia. 'He means no harm, My Lady,' she said.

Lucrezia smiled. 'But he is not a good confessor. He looks into my eyes and I'm ashamed ... Angelina,' she said abruptly, 'have you a lover?' The girl was confused, not knowing what to answer, but Lucrezia went on, almost musing to herself, 'sometimes I think that I'm cursed because I can't forget ...' She was interrupted by shouts and the clatter of hooves in the courtyard.

Angelina ran to the window. 'My Lady!' she cried in surprise, 'it is the Duke Valentino – with a party of horsemen!'

Lucrezia got up and ran to the window. 'Cesare!' she exclaimed to herself. 'Now why has he come?'

*　　*　　*

Lucrezia stood at the head of the long stone stair leading up to the great hall of the castle. Below her at the foot, she saw Cesare, handsome as ever, dressed in black, a suite of gentlemen, among whom she recognised Paolo and Giulio Orsini, behind him, flanked by his personal guard wearing his livery of red and yellow with the name 'Cesar' embroidered on their chests. This sudden eruption of colour and masculinity into the quiet female world of Nepi came as a shock. Lucrezia herself was dressed entirely in black, a widow's veil over her face, white from long days and nights of self-imposed isolation in her rooms. Momentarily, however, at the sight of Cesare, she forgot her widow's dignity and began to run down the steps towards him, but stopped as she saw him draw his sword. Then he knelt, head bowed, holding the sword with its hilt towards her in a gesture of submission. Lucrezia found she could scarcely speak. 'Rise, Duke Valentino,' she whispered, 'and approach me ...'

He rose and came up the steps towards her, but did not touch her, nor did she extend her hand for him to kiss. Instead she turned with all the cool dignity she could muster, and led the way up the stairs into the great hall.

156

Cesare and Lucrezia sat alone together at the long table in the hall that night, the other diners having been dismissed. 'Well?' she said interrogatively, 'why have you come here?'

Her manner towards him was stiff and cold; in return his voice was gentle, persuasive. 'I came to tell you . . . that you have won.' He leaned towards her, but still he did not touch her. 'You may go back to Rome on your own terms. A respected widow in your own right. That is what you asked. That is what our Holy Father promises to give.'

Lucrezia was still wary. 'He sent you to tell me that?' Cesare nodded. 'And you,' she went on, 'what do you say, Cesare?'

He shrugged. 'Your letter was to him. You asked me for nothing.'

'What could I have asked of you?' Lucrezia said in a passionate whisper. 'I remembered how my husband died – on your orders.'

'You could have asked for my life.' Cesare's voice was equally intense. 'I would have given it.'

'I didn't want your life.'

'Life . . .' Cesare said. 'Here, you have no life. You dress in black. Eat off earthenware – like a good Spanish widow. But you drink good wine – and your eyes sparkled when you saw me . . . and my gentlemen, though you tried to hide their light. I know you well, Lucia. As you know me. And I know that you are burning to live again.' He watched her face as she looked back at him, her expression betraying nothing. 'Our father is an old man, Lucia. Soon he'll be dead. But you and I – we can take the world. And I shall take it. I shall be Caesar or nothing. I shall be King of all Italy. You will see . . .'

'And what will you make me?' Lucrezia enquired coolly.

'What do you want to be?'

'Myself.'

'Then we shall be faithful to each other. And to ourselves.' He stood up. 'You will go back to Rome. And I march on Pesaro.'

Lucrezia was surprised. 'You will take Pesaro?'

'But not your Giovannino. He has run away from me again. I shall have the city without even drawing my sword.'

'Giovanni was never brave.'

'No, never. Not on the battlefield. Nor ... in bed.'

There was a silence. Then Lucrezia looked up at him, a strange expression in her eyes. Suddenly he reached down and took her in his arms, pulling her to him. She yielded passionately, her head back, his lips on her throat. She took his head in her hands and pressed it to her breasts. 'Lucia!' For one brief moment, Cesare's voice was a cry of despair. Then they pulled apart and stood staring at each other, breathing quickly. 'Lucia,' Cesare said with a passionate intensity, 'we must and shall be ourselves. Goodnight.' He turned quickly away and went out.

Lucrezia was still breathing hard, her eyes closed, she reached out to the table for support, leaning against it. '*Virgo Maria*,' she gasped, 'I shall go back to Rome.'

*   *   *

Rain poured down on the piazza of St Peter's as Lucrezia's bedraggled suite drew up at the door of the Vatican. Lucrezia could not repress a shudder at the sight of those steps which less than a year ago had been stained with Alfonso's blood.

'You are cold, My Lady?' Angelina asked anxiously. But Lucrezia did not answer her; her thoughts were on the past as she looked up at the walls of the Vatican and across the piazza at the Palazzo of Santa Maria, her home as a young girl, then as a bride, with Giovanni – and with Alfonso. For a moment she felt afraid to enter those walls that had seen so much, to put herself once again into the power of her father and her brother, a pawn in their grandiose plans.

'Lucia, my child! It is as though you had risen from the dead!' Rodrigo's voice was joyous as he folded her in an exuberant embrace. 'Now that you are here these terrible storms will cease. The sun will shine again. Flowers will appear. The birds will sing ...' He held her away from him, looking at her closely. 'You look well. A little pale, perhaps. But beautiful as ever. Lucia, my child, we have great plans for you, Cesare and I. Such a future.'

Lucrezia freed herself from his embrace. 'Yes. Cesare told me. But it is impossible.'

'Why do you say impossible?'

'Father,' Lucrezia's voice was sad, hesitant, 'just now, as I crossed the piazza, I thought of Alfonso . . . and Giovanni. How can I marry again? It is better to remain single – if you bring only misfortune to your husbands.'

'If you believe in evil stars – which we do not,' Rodrigo reproved her. Then he took her hands, smiling expansively. 'And our star, the Borgia star, is rising in the Romagna. Cesare has taken Pesaro. He has taken Rimini. Only Faenza holds out against him – and he will take Faenza too when the rains have ceased . . . The Prince Alfonso d'Este is there to witness Cesare's bombardment – to be the wife of an Este! Duchess of Ferrara! And Cesare, Lord of the Romagna . . . and why should he stop there? There is such a glorious future for you, my children – and it will not be long delayed . . .'

* * *

Cesare and Alfonso d'Este were watching the bombardment of Faenza by the Borgia artillery. Cesare had personally supervised the setting up of the batteries armed with his new French guns. He had a passion for the new science of artillery, which was shared by his aristocratic guest, although Alfonso, with a deliberate policy of keeping his distance, took pains to conceal his interest. His voice when he spoke to Cesare was aloof. 'The ball fell short again. The walls of Faenza seem to be holding out against your French guns.' Cesare said nothing, and Alfonso went on, 'How long they have defied you. Of course the people of Faenza have always been strangely loyal to the Manfredis. It must annoy you to be defied by a lad who's not yet seventeen.'

'He's as brave as he is young,' Cesare replied. 'I intend to make him a captain in my army when this is over.'

159

'Astorre Manfredi? No doubt he will be happy with any future outside the walls of Castel Sant'Angelo.' Alfonso said ironically.

There was an awkward pause, then Cesare said, 'You're thinking of Caterina Sforza ... I will promise you, Prince Alfonso, that I will release the Madonna of Forlì as soon as she is ready to resign her cities to the Holy See.'

'She is an obstinate woman. I am not surprised you find her difficult. My first wife, of course, was a Sforza.'

'Yes, I know.'

There was a pause, as both men watched the bombardment. 'This time, the gunner has the right trajectory,' Alfonso commented. 'A few more hits like that, and the wall may yet be breached.'

'Yes,' Cesare said shortly. Then, adopting a deliberately casual tone, 'I think the Duke your father recently received a letter from His Holiness the Pope.'

'Yes.' Alfonso was non-committal, and the tone of his voice was definitely not encouraging.

'About the future of our two families ...' Cesare went on, undeterred.

'Do you know my sister Isabella?' Alfonso asked him. 'The Marchesa d'Este Gonzaga?'

'We have not met.'

Alfonso continued in his high drawl, 'She has a passion for antiquities. Nothing less than four hundred years old is of any interest to her at all. One can understand that, I suppose ... Ah! another hit ... The past is easily destroyed. And so much of the present one would prefer not to exist ...'

'The house of Borgia is of the present,' Cesare said evenly. 'The house of Este has a noble past. But which, My Prince, is of the future?'

'Fortune determines that ...'

'Fortune determines nothing,' Cesare said firmly. 'It is up to us. I am of the future. And a passion for antiquities may leave the house of Este to crumble into dust.' Alfonso turned to stare at him, his face betraying nothing. 'I have an alliance with the King of France,' Cesare went on. 'Where will you look for your defence – if you are threatened by

160

Venice or by myself? Your father is Duke of Ferrara, but mine is the Pope of all Christendom, and his weapons are spiritual as well as temporal.' Alfonso continued to look at him steadily, his expression unchanging as Cesare spoke. '... An alliance with the house of Borgia may be distasteful to your sister the Marchesa. But it may be wise.'

Alfonso raised his eyebrows. 'What a strange discovery ...' he began.

'What is?'

'That you and I have something in common after all.' He turned to stare into the distance, again watching the guns. 'However repellent is our duty, we shall each do what we must. You to secure the future. And I to save the past ...'

'But you will do your duty – as the Duke your father tells you? Cesare said meaningly.

'Oh yes, of course.'

'My sister, the Lady Lucrezia, is a very beautiful woman.' Cesare's voice held a note of exultation.

'So I have heard.' Alfonso's voice was cold.

*   *   *

Several leagues to the south of Faenza, Michelotto and Ramiro waited, with four other mounted men, under cover of some trees; in the distance a small party of armed guards could be seen making their way northwards up the road towards them. As they approached, Michelotto spurred his horse forward, followed by Ramiro and the others. 'Remember!' he warned, 'Duke Valentino has ordered – strike only if you must. Ramiro and I will take the ladies.'

It was a fine, bright day, the sun sparkling on the corselets of the guards, and on the colourful travelling cloaks of the two women riding in their midst. Of the two, one was the more richly dressed: she was Dorotea Malatesta, soon to be called Caracciolo. The illegitimate daughter of one of the signorial family of Malatesta of Rimini, she was travelling from the court of Urbino, where she had been living under the protection of the gentle and cultivated Duke and Duchess, to Venice where she was to join the husband to whom she had just been married by proxy, Gianbattista Caracciolo, a Neapolitan gentleman in the service of Venice who was many years her senior. Dorotea was twenty-three and a beauty; she had had many admirers at the court of Urbino, among whom there had been one she could not forget. She sighed as she remembered the last carnival at Urbino.

Her thoughts were interrupted by the sudden clash of swords and angry shouting. She looked round to see Michelotto, arms outstretched to seize her. There was a cry as one of the men of her escort fell from his horse, wounded; the other three turned tail and fled down the road, ignoring Dorotea's cries for help and those of her maid who was struggling in Ramiro's arms. The next moment Dorotea found herself uncomfortably seated before Michelotto on his horse, his arms about her were like steel; she struggled hopelessly. 'Gently, My Lady,' Michelotto warned. 'If the horse should bolt . . .'

'Who are you? Where are you taking me?' Dorotea demanded, frightened.

Michelotto smiled. 'Don't be concerned to know,' he said. 'You are in good hands. And will soon be in the hands of someone better – who waits for you with high desire . . .'

Dorotea shuddered as they passed through the gate of a fortress. 'Where are we?' she asked timidly. She was afraid of this fierce man who had not scrupled to tie her hands roughly behind her back. He did not reply, but swung her down off the horse and half led, half dragged her through the vaulted portal of the keep, up flights of steps and along corridors into a small, richly furnished chamber. Realising that at least she was not in a dungeon, Dorotea recovered some of her composure. 'You will pay for this,' she told Michelotto haughtily. 'The Duke and Duchess of Urbino will have you punished, and all Venice will be in arms. My husband . . .'

She stopped as Michelotto knocked at a door leading to an inner chamber, signalling her to be quiet. The door opened and Cesare came in to stand before Dorotea. She stared at him in silence. Neither of them spoke. 'It is done,

My Lord,' said Michelotto, 'as you required. The birds are netted safe. Only one falconer was gored.' He bowed and left the room.

Cesare smiled at Dorotea as she continued to stare at him dumbfounded. 'I knew that you were on the road to Cervia,' he said.

Dorotea felt herself trembling. Il Valentino ... she had never thought that she would see him again after Urbino. She had been wildly attracted to him, but there she had been protected, surrounded by courtiers. Now she was in his power, unsure of herself, and more than a little afraid of him. All she could say was, 'You should have warned me. I never thought ...'

'It would have been unwise. Your mother knew too much already – and your maid I didn't trust. And yet I couldn't let you go to Venice – if the marriage was against your will ...'

Dorotea attempted to smile, but her lips trembled and her voice was almost inaudible as she said, 'And will you hold me here ... against my will?' Then, as Cesare took her in his arms, she went on, her voice stronger but shaking with emotion, 'I cannot defend myself. You see that ... Oh, My Lord. Promise that you will hold me.'

Cesare bent to kiss her lips. 'Dorotea ... I promise I shall hold you. Against Venice and against the world ...'

*   *   *

The face of the Cardinal of Venice, Marco Cornaro, was stern as he complained publicly and bitterly to the Pope of the Duke Valentino's conduct. Rodrigo's astonishment was plain for all to see. 'We shall not believe it,' he told Cornaro. 'If the Duke has done this, he is mad! You say the lady was taken on the road by armed men?'

But Cornaro was implacable. 'It is impossible to conceive, Your Holiness,' he thundered, 'in what part of hell such a crime could be committed. The lady had been recently married in Urbino, under the protection of Duke Guidobaldo. Her husband, Gianbattista Caracciolo, is a

Captain of infantry in the army of Venice, and thus to offend him is to insult our Serene Republic.'

'You say – recently married?' Rodrigo queried.

'By proxy, Your Holiness,' Cornaro replied.

'Forgive me, Your Eminence,' Rodrigo asked with an air of innocence, 'but how old is the Lady Dorotea?'

'I know only that she is young – and most beautiful.'

'And her gallant husband?'

'I believe, Your Holiness, he is a nobleman of some fifty years.'

Rodrigo raised his eyebrows. 'The matter is quite beyond our understanding,' he said. 'But you say the Council of Venice have sent their Secretary to question the Duke on the affair?'

'Holiness, the Duke informed our Secretary that he knew nothing of the lady's whereabouts. I fear, Holy Father, he added that he did not lack for women.'

'Well, that is true.' Rodrigo could not repress a smile.

'But he also admitted, Holiness, that one of his officers, a Spaniard, had made her acquaintance in Urbino during carnival. And that she had presented this Spaniard with some embroidered shirts. The Duke has ordered this officer's arrest – but he has disappeared.'

'Then,' Rodrigo said urbanely, 'it appears the Duke has done all that is possible.' He straightened himself in his chair, now sure of his ground. 'Cardinal Cornaro,' he commanded, 'we shall be grateful if you will convey to Their Excellencies in Venice our profoundest sympathies in this scandalous affair. The Duke, we are sure, is as distressed as ourselves – for to give offence to Venice at this time especially is contrary to his interest and, we believe, to his desire . . .'

Cardinal Cornaro bowed and withdrew, his face a mask of anger and disbelief.

*   *   *

'He did not believe us!' Rodrigo shouted at Cesare, who stood before him impassive, as his father paced up and down the room, raging. 'You have offended Venice in order to satisfy your lust. Now, as if that were not enough, you have turned your armies against Florence, a city which is under the protection of France, knowing that this would displease King Louis! Have you gone mad?'

Cesare was unmoved by Rodrigo's anger. He shrugged. 'I frightened Florence to please my Captains,' he said, 'the Orsinis in particular. It is of no consequence.'

'You risked too much to content men of little importance,' Rodrigo berated him. 'I needed you in Rome. In a few days the French army will be here themselves. And *you* should be here with them.'

'I *am* here,' Cesare said shortly. 'And now that I am, what of Duke Ercole's letter?' He indicated the paper which Rodrigo held in his hand. 'And Lucrezia's marriage to his son?'

Rodrigo calmed down and handed Cesare the letter. 'Duke Ercole bargains like a tradesman,' he said. 'He demands two hundred thousand ducats for Lucrezia's dowry. And remission of Ferrara's dues to the Holy See. He can name any price – so long as he sees no necessity to force his son to the marraige.' He sat down, his face clouding with annoyance. 'Do you know what Alfonso said when the marriage was proposed to him? He told his father that if he wanted whores he could find them in the brothels of Ferrara – without bringing them into the palace.'

'He will not find one as gracious as Lucrezia,' Cesare said calmly.

'Then you accept this gross insult to your sister?' Rodrigo was surprised.

Cesare shrugged. 'If he marries her, the insult is no more. That is his use to me. One by one the proud families of Italy bow to the name of Borgia ...'

'And we shall make him bow,' Rodrigo agreed. 'Louis can do it. We will give no recognition to Louis' rights in Naples until Duke Ercole signs the marriage contract. He must submit to France.'

Cesare nodded, handing back the letter. 'What does Lucrezia say?' he asked.

'She wouldn't talk of it at first. Now it is strange . . . the more the Duke demands for her dowry, the more it seems to please her.'

'The more she will take with her – to Ferrara.'

'Yes,' Rodrigo said angrily. 'Women are all whores. We believe that.' His voice changed. 'But there is something else . . . it seems to please her to make us pay to let her go. Why should that be?'

'It may be her revenge,' Cesare said slowly.

Rodrigo looked at him sharply. 'Revenge?'

Cesare returned his look, then he said meaningly, 'There is a child in Rome . . .'

A look of infinite pain and horror crossed Rodrigo's face. 'God have mercy! I didn't think of it.' He sank back, closing his eyes. 'We shall lose her. Is that not enough?'

'Not yet, Father,' Cesare said acidly. 'First we must content the French . . . with Naples. D'Alègre arrives tomorrow with the advance guard.'

*   *   *

A flourish of trumpets announced the arrival of Captain Yves d'Alègre for his official reception by the Pope. Rodrigo, who still at heart disliked and distrusted the French, concealed his true feelings beneath a majestic exterior, receiving Cesare's companion-in-arms with every appearance of cordiality, smiling broadly as Burchard introduced the Frenchman, who was accompanied by Paolo Orsini and his brother Giulio. 'Your Holiness,' Burchard intoned, 'Captain Yves d'Alègre, commanding the armies of His Majesty of France.'

D'Alègre knelt to kiss the Pope's foot. Rodrigo made the sign of the cross over him. *'Benedicat te . . .'*

As d'Alègre rose and stepped back, the Orsinis came forward to be formally introduced by the Master of Ceremonies. 'Captain Paolo Orsini. And Captain Giulio Orsini. Commanders of their forces in the service of the Duke Valentino.'

Rodrigo blessed them, beaming. 'Our sons Paolo and

166

Giulio ... the triumph of your arms in restoring to us the cities of the Romagna has placed you high in our esteem. God will reward you.'

'We humbly thank Your Holiness,' Giulio replied. 'We desire only to be of your service.'

'And you shall serve us now,' Rodrigo told him. 'Against the state of Naples, whose infidel King has dared to make alliance against us with the Turks. We have already taken steps against your enemies, the Colonnas, who serve the faithless King. You shall go to Naples with our blessing.' He turned to Burchard: 'Master of Ceremonies. We trust that the arrangements for the quartering of the French armies are well in hand.'

'Yes, Holy Father,' Burchard replied with a satisfied air. 'Shelters have been provided beyond the Ponte Milvio. We have sent Captain d'Alègre one hundred and fifty butts of wine, bread, meat, fruit, eggs and other necessaries.'

He handed a list to Rodrigo, who glanced down it. He raised his eyebrows, 'And fourteen prostitutes?' He looked at d'Alègre. 'What is the size of the force under your command?' he enquired.

'Fourteen thousand men, Your Holiness.'

A faint smile passed over Rodrigo's face. 'Well ... they are Roman women. They must serve,' he said as he handed the list back to Burchard. He continued, addressing d'Alègre, 'You have a request, I understand?'

'Your Holiness,' d'Alègre replied, 'His Majesty King Louis desires your clemency towards a prisoner – the Madonna Caterina Sforza whom Your Holiness has detained in Castel Sant' Angelo. His Majesty instructed me to make this request to Your Holiness, since it was to me the Madonna of Forlì surrendered her person.'

'Caterina was an evil daughter to us,' Rodrigo replied coldly. 'She plotted against our life and she is charged with this offence. But if His Majesty requests it, we shall extend our mercy to her – when she has surrendered to the Holy See the charters of her cities.'

Yves d'Alègre inclined his head in a gesture of

167

submission. 'I am instructed, Holy Father, that the Madonna now yields to this demand.'

'Then,' Rodrigo said graciously, 'you make take her – with our blessing.'

*   *   *

Caterina Sforza blinked as unaccustomed light flooded into her cell. For a moment she could not see d'Alègre, who, for his own part, hardly recognised her as the same woman he had seen in the fortress of Forlì just over a year before. Her time as a pampered prisoner in the gilded cage of the Belvedere had been short, Cesare having soon ordered her to the dreaded dungeons below ground in Sant'Angelo, on the pretext that she had plotted an escape. Her hair had been turned white by her ordeal, and her appearance was so changed that d'Alègre was moved to pity. He kissed the hands of which she had once been so proud, boasting that they were 'soft as sable'; they were now filthy, engrained with jail dirt. 'Madonna,' was all he could bring himself to say.

Caterina's voice was hoarse and shaking. 'Captain d'Alègre ... then it is true? I am to be released?' She sounded disbelieving.

'Yes, Madonna,' he reassured her gently. 'I am to conduct you to the house of the Cardinal of San Clemente – where the deeds of your release must be signed. You understand what is agreed?'

Caterina nodded and attempted to rise from the filthy pallet on which she had been lying. D'Alègre hastened to help her. She gave him the ghost of a smile. 'My body is a little weak, for I have been in irons ... but they have not broken my spirit. Through you I surrender my person to the King of France. But never to him ... to that devil.' Gathering some strength, she spat ...

'To His Holiness?' d'Alègre enquired, shocked.

Caterina shook her head. 'No ... that Prince of hell ... Cesare Borgia!'

D'Alègre gave her his arm and, leaning on him heavily,

she limped down the corridor towards the light. 'Farewell, My Lord, may God save you!' she called out to the darkness.

There was a clank of chains and a white face appeared at a grille. 'Madonna,' a young voice whispered.

'Astorre Manfredi, Lord of Faenza,' Caterina replied to d'Alègre's enquiring look. 'They have just brought him here. He was foolish enough to trust il Valentino, and this is his reward. Imola, Forlì, Rimini, Pesaro, Faenza ... where will these Borgias end?'

*   *   *

'... Ferrara,' Rodrigo ended, then he said to his Chamberlain, Gaspare Poto, to whom he had been dictating, 'You will see that this letter goes to the Duke Valentino by special courier? Then you will bring me in Messer Bellingeri, Secretary to Duke Ercole, that we may speak with him.'

Poto nodded and withdrew, returning with a small, stout man who immediately sank to his knees before the Pope, kissing his ring. 'Messer Bellingeri!' Rodrigo's voice was jovial, 'the news you bring us is most joyful.'

'Duke Ercole asked me to convey to Your Holiness that Prince Alfonso has agreed to his betrothal to Madonna Lucrezia with a full heart.'

Rodrigo nodded benignly, then, assuming a business-like tone, he said sharply, 'And to the terms? One hundred thousand ducats in gold bars ...'

'And one hundred thousand in jewellery and precious things. The Duke accepts the dowry.'

'Then he may sign the marriage contract in Ferrara without more delay,' Rodrigo replied with finality.

'There are of course, Your Holiness, some matters still to be arranged ...' Bellingeri said with an apologetic air.

'I see none,' Rodrigo replied coldly. 'Duke Valentino has taken Capua. The fall of Naples we expect within the month. Once the contract is signed, we shall invest King Louis with the kingdom. What else must be agreed?'

Bellingeri was hesitant. 'Nothing, Your Holiness, of substance ...'

'Two hundred thousand ducats is substance enough!' Rodrigo interrupted dryly.

'It is a matter of some delicacy ... there is a child ...'

There was a silence, then Rodrigo said hurriedly, 'The son of the Duke of Biselli, the little Rodrigo. Rest assured, Messer Bellingeri, he shall be well provided for. And he shall stay with us in Rome.'

Bellingeri bowed, relieved, but only up to a point. 'Your Holiness is gracious. The son of the Duke of Biselli is, I think, the only child to be considered ...'

'The only one,' Rodrigo said firmly.

'Your Holiness will forgive me,' the envoy's tone was once again apologetic, 'but one hears so many things ...'

'What things? Be plain, Messer Bellingeri, with your meaning. If it affects the marriage ...'

'Some three years ago, Your Holiness, the Duke received a report concerning the birth of a child in Rome. It came from Venice and was not therefore to be believed. But it was said ...'

'A child was born.' Rodrigo's voice was calm. 'What the Duke heard was true.'

Bellingeri was surprised at this frank admission, his voice curious. 'Your Holiness?'

'It was the child of an unmarried lady – and one of my family,' Rodrigo said dismissively. 'We shall issue a Bull to place the matter beyond dispute.' He rose to indicate that the interview was at an end, then, as Bellingeri bowed and turned to leave, he added deliberately, 'On the day the marriage is announced.' Then, to Poto, who was waiting to see the Secretary out, 'We will speak with Madonna Lucrezia. Send word to her of our arrival ...'

* * *

'Holy Father!' Lucrezia knelt before Rodrigo, dismissing Angelina with a gesture of her hand. 'Nothing is wrong?'

'Is it my custom to bear ill-tidings?' Rodrigo smiled,

raising her and holding her hands. 'God is kind ... Louis and Cesare have entered Naples. I have a letter from Duke Ercole that would set your cheeks aflame with pride. He tells us that God must have illuminated the heart of His Holiness in allowing him to condescend to mingle his blood with that of the Este family!' He touched her cheek. 'And when I see such beauty – I know that it is true.'

Gently Lucrezia disengaged her hands. 'It is not true,' she said. 'In truth they despise me. But I shall change them when I am Duchess of Ferrara. I shall be gentle in every-thing I do – and go to Mass every day.' She turned to look at her image in a glass, touching her hair. 'And I shall make them love me.'

'And you will dance no more?' Rodrigo chided her affec-tionately.

'I am tired of dancing,' Lucrezia answered shortly.

Rodrigo's voice was hurt. 'But we should never tire of seeing you. Nonetheless you will leave us – since you are tired of Rome.' He was appealing to her for comfort, words of affection, but she gave him none. He turned away, his face sad. 'I came to tell you,' he said, 'that I must leave Rome tomorrow, to visit the castles of the Gaetanis and also the Colonnas, which we have taken for their treachery. Sermoneta we shall bestow upon your child Rodrigo. But there are also your lands and the castle at Nepi ... You will take a splendid dowry to Ferrara – but you cannot take your lands. We must bequeath them to someone of the house of Borgia – one who is near to us. And we have determined who it shall be.' He turned back to her, his expression pleading. 'One whom you have not seen since he was born – but who will come to us when you have gone away. And one we pray whom you will not despise.' He paused, fearing some hostile reaction. 'He is here and waiting. Shall we bring him in?'

Lucrezia nodded, saying nothing. Rodrigo went to the door and opened it, calling 'Come, child.'

A nun entered the room, leading a small boy by the hand. He was about four years old, a bright, dark child with a lively expression. Rodrigo took him by the hand and led him over to Lucrezia. 'Giovanni,' he said, 'this lady is your dear sister, Madonna Lucrezia. You may kiss her hand.'

As Giovanni came forward, shyly formal, to kiss her hand, Lucrezia bent down and took him in her arms. 'Giovanni,' she said. When she looked up at her father, her eyes were full of tears. 'I thank you, Holy Father.' Then she hugged the child again. 'We shall be together for a little time . . .'

Satisfied, Rodrigo began, 'Whilst I am away . . .'

Lucrezia's voice was anxious. 'But, Holy Father. How can you go? Cesare is in Naples. Who will have charge of your affairs whilst you are gone?'

'We have appointed you, Lucrezia.'

'I?' Lucrezia stared at him in amazement, tinged with concern. 'Holy Father, I am not worthy . . .'

* * *

'His Holiness committed the Chamber and Palace with all their business into the hands of his daughter Donna Lucrezia . . .' Burchard wrote in his journal, his pen scratching with indignation at this unheard-of usurpation. 'During his absence she occupied the papal apartments and had the authority to open all letters sent to His Holiness . . .'

'A bad business, Poto,' Burchard commented as he stood stiffly at the back of the audience chamber, beside the papal Chamberlain. Both men watched incredulously as Lucrezia, seated on the papal throne, conferred with the senior Cardinals, opened papal commissions and dictated answers. 'No such thing ever happened in the reign of Pope Sixtus, nor of Pope Innocent, even though he had eight children.' Poto, a faithful servant of Rodrigo, thought it best not to comment himself, but merely nodded. Burchard, carried away by his outraged feelings, continued, 'They say it is because the Duke Valentino is away in Naples, and His Holiness cannot trust anyone who is not of his family. Still . . . that the sacred College of Cardinals should be ruled by a woman . . .'

'Do not forget, Messer Burchard,' Poto said primly, interrupting his colleague before he should go too far, 'that Madonna Lucrezia is a great lady and will shortly be Duchess of Ferrara.'

'In order to make the Duke Valentino even greater ...' Burchard replied.

* * *

On the day that her betrothal to Alfonso d'Este was publicly announced, Lucrezia rode in procession through the streets of Rome to give thanks at the church of Santa Maria del Popolo. She was dressed in brocaded cloth of gold which, it was rumoured, had cost three hundred ducats, and was escorted by four Bishops and three hundred horsemen. A continual cannonade sounded from Castel Sant'Angelo, the great bell of the Capitol tolled and, to add to the din, the streets were crowded with people shouting, 'Long live the most illustrious Duchess of Ferrara!' That night, many bonfires were lit on Sant'Angelo and throughout the city, all the buildings were brightly illuminated with torches and, as Burchard noted, 'the people became wildly excited, causing some anxiety ...'

Cesare and Michelotto, having ridden hard to Rome after the bloody capture of Capua, pushed through the cheering crowds to the door of Lucrezia's palace. As they dismounted and started to climb the stair, Lucrezia's Fool came running down, wearing the rich golden dress his mistress had discarded that day. Furious, Cesare caught him by the throat. 'Fool ... what do you here?'

The Fool was terror-stricken, recognising Cesare. 'My Lord Duke,' he stuttered.

'In your lady's clothes."

'Lord Duke ... it is the custom ... We heard from Ferrara – our lady is betrothed. The Holy Father ordered it. All Rome is celebrating. Madonna gave the dress to me – which she wore this morning to give her thanks at Santa Maria. And I must show the people ...'

Cesare cast him aside and continued his way up the

staircase. The Fool for his part made his escape, shouting, 'Long live Our Lady! Long live the Duchess of Ferrara!'

'Listen to the crowd, My Lady,' Angelina said, as she and other ladies dressed Lucrezia in another new gown, this time of mulberry silk brocaded with gold. 'My Lady, you must let them see you.'

'They are cheering the fool,' Lucrezia said, reaching out her hand. 'Show me the headdress.' As she did so, the door opened unexpectedly and Cesare came in. The ladies dressing Lucrezia froze as they saw him, holding their breath. Lucrezia was as surprised as they were. 'Cesare ...' she said, 'you came from Naples ...'

'Yes, from Naples!' he said as the ladies slipped quietly out of the room behind him. 'I see that Rome is in festival. But not for me.'

'The word reached us only yesterday that I shall be Duchess of Ferrara.'

'And our Holy Father has ordered these celebrations.'

'Are you not glad?' Lucrezia moved forward to embrace him. 'It was your wish that I should marry Alfonso d'Este. And you have taken Capua. And Naples. We have cause for celebration surely?' She looked at him questioningly. 'Cesare? Why do you look so stern?'

'The Holy Father issued a Bull five days ago,' he said bitterly, 'to legitimise your son Giovanni. It names me as the father. "The son of Cesare Borgia – and an unmarried woman".'

Lucrezia said in a conciliatory tone. 'It was done as it was done for you – and all his children. There is a secret Bull which shows the truth.' She held his arms, looking up into his face, searching for a clue to his reaction. 'He admits there that he himself is father to Giovanni. So there shall be no stain ...'

'You named me as the father of your child. Yours ... and his,' Cesare said in a low voice, and he turned away from her and stood at the window, his back to her.

'For Giovanni!' Lucrezia appealed to him. 'So he should remain a Borgia. If the marriage was to be announced – provision had to be made ...' She went over to him at the

174

window. 'Cesare ... if you had been here I would have asked you, but you were not. So it was done. How else could I be Duchess of Ferrara?'

He seemed not to hear her as he stood staring down at the cheering crowds in the piazza below. 'When we took Capua ...' he said slowly, 'the town was sacked. The Gascon infantry looted a wine shop and ran wild in the streets. They killed everyone they saw. They raped the women. They raped the children. And they slit the bellies ...'

Lucrezia's voice was full of horror as she touched his arm, willing him to look at her. 'Cesare ...'

Suddenly he turned and held her to him, looking down at her with a strange expression. 'Lucrezia. It was done for you.'

'For me?'

'So our names shall be remembered. They died for nothing else. God didn't hear them – they'll be dust and nothing more. But not you or I ...' He paused, and for a long moment they stared into each other's eyes. 'Cesare Borgia. And Lucrezia. We shall be remembered. Be faithful only to me ... not to him – our unholy father who prays to a nameless god ... You shall have the world – not the hereafter. And your name eternal ... Is it enough?'

'I shall be Duchess of Ferrara. It is enough for me,' Lucrezia said expressionlessly.

'In name ... but nothing more. Say it!'

'In name ... and nothing more ...' she said slowly, as if the promise were dragged out of her. Her eyes held by his, she was mesmerised as ever by his power over her.

Cesare threw back his head in triumph. 'I shall give a party in celebration,' he said. 'On All Saints' Eve! Angels and demons both shall be welcome to the feast – *sancti in gloria*! And we shall dance!'

* * *

The candles were guttering in the elaborate bronze holders as Cesare and Lucrezia danced, their bodies moving as one. It was almost dawn and Lucrezia, her eyes closed, was virtually asleep on her feet. Round them, Cesare's Spanish and Italian officers, including Ramiro, Michelotto and the Orsinis, danced with the courtesans who had been brought in for their entertainment. Some of the girls were half naked, their bodices pushed down by lascivious hands. At the long table, Rodrigo watched the dancers; beside him Dorotea Caracciolo, her hair hanging loose, had clearly taken too much wine. Her eyes followed Cesare adoringly, perhaps even a little sadly – he had been dancing with Lucrezia all night and seemed reluctant ever to let her go.

Rodrigo indicated his son and daughter proudly. 'It is their Spanish blood, Dorotea,' he said. 'You saw nothing like this at carnival in Urbino, did you?'

'They never saw him,' Dorotea mumbled, her eyes never leaving her lover. 'He wore a mask. So my mother wouldn't know.' She swayed against Rodrigo. 'Holy Father ... he would do anything for me – perform such feats ... He can bend a horseshoe. I've seen him do it ... with his hands ...'

Rodrigo was interested. 'Cesare? Bend a horseshoe?' He beckoned to the servant standing behind him. 'Bring us a horseshoe! Bring it to us now! Let us see if Cesare can do it ...'

Cesare was by now supporting Lucrezia in his arms; she was exhausted, clinging to him. 'Cesare ... I must rest ... It's almost day ...'

But his vitality was unabated, indeed night was the time that he felt most alive. 'The sport has not yet begun! Wait! You shall see.' Releasing his sister, he seized one of the dancing courtesans. 'Angelica,' he ordered, 'take off your clothes.' Then, as she hesitated, he added roughly, 'Why do you wait? You were all paid for it! I paid you well! You will do as I desire.' Then he shouted to the other dancers, 'The sport will now begin.'

As the girl began to take off her dress, Cesare picked up a candlestick, motioning for Ramiro and Michelotto to do the same. 'What is the game, My Lord?' Ramiro asked.

'There shall be races. And the fastest whore shall win! Set out the course ...' He set down the candles, beginning to

176

mark a track of flame before the table. 'Come, Michelotto! Ramiro! Set down the candles – but not too wide ...'

Michelotto grinned. 'Do we race for the Palio?'

'They shall be timed. One by one – so there shall be no jostling. No unseating of jockeys. And as they go ...' He took a dish of chestnuts from the table and scattered them along the track. 'There,' he ordered the girls who were crowding round him, 'you will pick up the chestnuts in your teeth ... every one of them.'

Rodrigo shouted excitedly, 'Surely they should be mounted? Each whore should have a mount!'

Michelotto joined in. 'There'll be prizes for the riders too!'

While Giuli Orsini cried, 'We'll use our sticks!'

Cesare seized Angelica by the wrist and threw her to the ground at one end of the row of candles. 'The start is here,' he told her. 'You go between the candles – on your hands and knees.' Then, as she began to crawl along the track, he stopped her. 'Wait! We shall call the count together. Are you ready to the mark? Go!' He clapped his hands, calling on everyone to keep time with him as the girl crawled between the candles, her heavy breasts swinging, her dark hair hanging to the ground, as she bent her head to pick up the chestnuts with her teeth, then flung them aside. The men crowded each side of the track, shouting out the time as Cesare called it, 'Four! five! six! seven!...'

Rodrigo got to his feet to join them, dragging Dorotea with him. 'Eight!' he shouted, 'Nine! She should be mounted! We said they should be mounted...'

Lucrezia, by now utterly exhausted and finally wearied by her family's enjoyment of this entertainment, walked towards the door. Cesare, who had been watching her all the time, saw her go and followed to catch her arm. 'You do not stay to see the race,' he said harshly.

'I have seen enough.'

His hand gripped her arm fiercely so that she winced. 'Remember ...' he said, 'this.' He turned her to face the room, where Rodrigo was now playing a leading part in urging on the participants.

'Ramiro rides the mare!' Rodrigo shouted. 'Ah! She's fallen...'

Cesare's face as he watched his father was heavy with contempt. 'Remember our Holy Father when you are in Ferrara,' he told Lucrezia. 'Remember him in Rome...' He swung her to face him. 'And remember me. Alfonso will be as cold as ice. You are a Borgia. It is to me that you belong ... When you kneel to pray – or lie in his bed ... remember ... Have I your promise? Now – and for ever...'

Their eyes were locked together for a long moment, then Lucrezia whispered, 'As it was in the beginning ... is now ... and ever shall be...'

'Time without end. Amen.'

Cesare's voice rang in Lucrezia's ears as she turned and ran from the room. Drunken shouts from the men watching the race echoed after her down the corridor, her father's recognisable amongst them. Cesare's face was alive with a strange exultation as he seized Dorotea, and pressed her roughly to him, crushing her against the wall.

* * *

Alone in her room, Lucrezia leant against the window niche, staring out over the silent city. Dawn was beginning to break at the edges of the sky. A new day, Lucrezia thought bitterly – would there ever be a new beginning for her, a new life which would be simple and uncomplicated – an escape into pure air from the overheated atmosphere of her family, their passions, jealousies and ambitions – and their crimes? She closed her eyes, unable to fight off the vision of her father's face, flushed and sweating, his eyes alight with sensuality as he urged on the naked whores in the chestnut race – and of Cesare, who had deliberately intended that she should bear this degrading image of her father indelibly stamped upon her memory in order that he alone should control her for ever.

She was now twenty-one, and old beyond her years from her experiences at the hands of her father and brother. She had lived so long in their shadow that she had been unable to see the light beyond. Now, at long last, the revulsion she felt at the scenes of that night had brought to the surface her subconscious desire to escape from the passionate thraldom in which she had lived. As she opened her eyes and looked out over the city in which she had been born and which perhaps soon she might never see again, Lucrezia realised that this Este marriage, however distasteful it might be, offered her only chance of a new life away from her family. Away, above all, from Cesare, that dark star who until now had controlled her destiny, and whose power over her would never, she knew, entirely be broken. Even now, as she tried to conjure up the memory of Alfonso, the husband she had loved, dead only just over a year, it was Cesare's face that she saw, Cesare's voice that rang in her ears. Lucrezia shivered. As if to exorcise an evil spell, she flung herself on her knees before the image of the Virgin above her *prie-dieu*. '*Virgo Maria*,' she prayed, 'I *shall* go to Ferrara. Please, let it be soon . . .'

7

The Great Game

IT WAS NOT, however, until late December of the year 1501 that the reluctant Duke Ercole finally sent his sons to Rome to fetch Lucrezia. Cesare, mounted on a superb Gonzaga horse, greeted the Este brothers at the gates of the city. Alfonso was not among them; the party was headed by his three younger brothers, Sigismondo, Ferrante and Cardinal Ippolito, who were to finalise the negotiations, to attend the marriage which was to take place by proxy, and to bring the bride back to Ferrara. As Cesare welcomed them, he watched them closely, sizing them up. Sigismondo, a grave-faced young man in sober travelling dress, would, he thought, be the hardest bargainer of the three; Ferrante, slim, languid and elegant, he discounted as a lightweight to whom nobody would pay any heed; but the Cardinal Ippolito ... he might be the man for the Pope to work his wiles upon.

Ippolito d'Este, an athletic giant with a hooded falcon at his wrist, bestrode his great charger proudly, his only concession to his ecclesiastic status being a red cloak over his fine clothes and a red skull cap on his abundant dark curls. He had an open, honest, merry face – the sort of man, Cesare considered, whom his father would be able to twist round his papal finger. After all, the Estes were not in a position to bargain much; King Louis had pressed Duke Ercole to the match, and the Duke, menaced by France and the Borgias, had had no alternative but to agree. But Rodrigo had still not definitely promised Louis what he really wanted, recognition of his right to Naples, and thus he had the Estes more or less where he wanted them. Cesare smiled to himself. They called his father a Catalan – well, everyone knew that there was nothing like a Catalan to drive a hard bargain. He smiled again, this time openly. 'Welcome to Rome, My Lords,' he said, bowing with a flourish. 'His Holiness the Pope desires me to greet you in his name. And to conduct you to the Vatican where he will receive you.'

The young Estes returned his bow coldly. They were unhappy at their brother's forced betrothal to the Pope's bastard daughter, and they had heard enough of Cesare Borgia to feel extremely wary of him. 'My Lord Duke,' Sigismondo said, 'we thank His Holiness, and are anxious to kiss his holy foot.'

He spurred his horse forward to follow Cesare through the city gate, to the sound of Borgia clarions, escorted by the halberdiers of Cesare's personal guard, liveried in red and yellow with 'Cesar' emblazoned across their chests. Cannon thundered from Sant'Angelo as the procession crossed the bridge over the Tiber leading to the Vatican, as if to underline this display of Borgia force.

At the door of the Vatican, Cesare took leave of them, pleading urgent business, instructing Burchard to keep them waiting as he conferred with the Pope. The young Estes kicked their heels impatiently in an antechamber, as Burchard nervously assured them that the delay in their being received would be short, that His Holiness was presently at prayer. Shouts of laughter from behind the closed doors of the Sala del Pappagallo, however, gave the lie to his words. Burchard looked unhappy, the Estes exchanged glances. 'The Almighty must be in a jesting humour today,' Ippolito grinned.

'Eminence ... Excellencies ... forgive me ... a moment only ...' The embarrassed Burchard made his escape, scuttling thankfully out of the room.

Ferrante frowned. 'This is insufferable,' he said. 'That murderer ...'

'Softly ...' Sigismondo warned.

'That braggart murderer welcomes us with an army, and now we're kept ...'

181

'We shall behave as our father directed. It's agreed I speak for us all?'

Ferrante glanced contemptuously at Ippolito. 'No doubt Cardinals take precedence here,' he said sarcastically.

'Brother, you wish to speak for us?' Sigismondo said courteously to Ippolito.

The Cardinal crossed himself. 'God forbid that I should do so!'

Sigismondo continued, 'So. We debate not the marriage but some of its terms. And remember ... France or Borgia could swallow us as a lizard does a gnat ...' He broke off as gusts of hearty laughter once again came from behind closed doors. The brothers looked at each other, eyebrows raised.

Rodrigo sat roaring with laughter, while the Chamberlain Poto read aloud from a paper which he held in his hand. Beside him Cesare sat grim-faced, while a shocked Burchard and an expressionless Captain of the Guard stood beside the door. 'Continue, Gaspare,' Rodrigo said.

'I've heard enough,' Cesare snapped.

'Yet there's more.'

Burchard interrupted anxiously, 'Your Holiness...'

Rodrigo nodded. 'Yes, yes, Johann. We'll receive them shortly. Continue, Gaspare.'

Poto held up the letter, reading it with some embarrassment. ' "It is difficult to know which of these two is the more execrable. The father favours the son because of his own perversity and cruelty ..." ' He stopped, shocked. 'Holiness...!'

'Go on.'

' "The Cardinals see all and say nothing because they are bought. They flatter the Pope because all live in terror of his fratricidal son ..." '

Cesare got up angrily. 'Enough!'

Rodrigo motioned him to be still. 'It's not enough. Continue, Gaspare.' He smiled, watching Cesare's face as if he were taking some bitter satisfaction from Cesare's rage, a small revenge for the humiliations his son had inflicted upon him.

Gaspare read on, ' "His . . . his . . . fratricidal son . . . who was once a Cardinal but has now become an assassin. He lives in splendour like the Great Turk, surrounded by whores and guarded by soldiers. Upon his order any man may be killed, his body thrown into the Tiber, and his property become forfeit to this monster who . . ." '

Cesare snatched the letter from Poto, ripping it apart. 'I'll fill the wretch's gullet with lead from his own press!' he swore.

Rodrigo rose, still enjoying the scene. 'Do nothing about it,' he advised Cesare as he moved towards the door. 'A lie ignored is a truth maintained.' Then as he reached the portal he turned, a faint sardonic smile on his lips, 'Yet a lie maintained may reveal a truth . . .'

As his father went out to greet the Estes, Cesare stared furiously after him, then he turned to the Captain of the guard, shaking the paper in his face. 'You said you knew who spewed this vomit?'

'Yes, My Lord. A Neapolitan. Girolamo Manciani.'

'Find him.'

'But, My Lord . . . His Holiness said . . .'

'Do as I order! His Holiness is occupied with the Este Princes.' Seeing the look upon Cesare's face, the Captain nodded silently and went out. Cesare moved to the door to hear what was being said in the next room.

Rodrigo greeted the Estes warmly as they knelt before him. Motioning for them to rise to their feet, he seated himself on the papal throne, his face beaming. 'Your Eminence . . . Excellencies . . . God gives us joy to see you here! A splendid carnival has been arranged in the city in honour of this marriage.' He rubbed his hands jovially.

Sigismondo stepped forward. 'Holiness, our father require me to ask . . .'

Rodrigo appeared not to have heard him. 'A race of wild boars from the Campo di Fiori to St Peter's steps . . .'

'If I may remind Your Holiness that . . .'

'Followed by a race of naked whores from the Borgo.'

Ippolito's face brightened. 'Indeed, Your Holiness?'

Rodrigo watched him closely. Cesare had told him that

this ingenuous fellow would be the easiest to bend to his will. He shook his head as if Ippolito had been shocked at such proceedings. 'Indeed, but the people expect such things. More to your taste, perhaps, the Lord Cesare is to stage a pastoral dialogue in his palace.'

Ippolito's face fell. 'Indeed,' he said dully.

Sigismondo again attempted to speak. 'May I ask Your Holiness when we may con...'

But Rodrigo addressed Ippolito, 'And the Lord Cesare's Spanish gentlemen are to assault a mock fortress in the piazza before his house. Armed with sharp swords.'

'Bravo!' beamed Ippolito.

They all looked round as Cesare entered the room; Rodrigo merely nodded to acknowledge his presence, then he addressed the brothers, 'Who is to act as proxy for the Prince Alfonso?'

Ferrante bowed. 'I am, Your Holiness.'

'Holiness, may we now consider ...' Sigismondo persisted.

Cesare broke in, smiling, 'Have you brought a horse to race?'

'A dozen I'll match against any of yours,' Ferrante smiled proudly.

'Forgive me, Your Holiness ...' Sigismondo tried again.

Cesare addressed Ferrante, 'Three thousand ducats.'

'Agreed.'

Rodrigo intervened. 'Why are we wasting time with such idle things!'

Sigismondo was grateful. 'Thank you, Your Holiness. Our father requires me to raise certain matters which he...'

Rodrigo made a dismissive gesture. 'No, no ... Tomorrow, tomorrow! We'll talk with His Eminence tomorrow.'

Ippolito looked helplessly at Sigismondo. 'With me, Your Holiness?'

'Of course, Eminence.'

Ippolito was appalled. 'But...'

184

Rodrigo smiled reassuringly then, turning to Cesare, 'Cesare! Take these Lords to your sister!'

*　　*　　*

Lucrezia stood, pale and erect in the candlelight, facing Cesare defiantly. She was dressed in black, her widow's mourning. Cesare eyed it with distaste. 'I shall receive them here,' she said coldly, 'dressed in black as I am. A widow, remember.'

Cesare gripped her wrist, pulling her face close to his. 'No, sister,' he said evenly, 'you're a joyous bride ...'

'Widow and bride. You've made both of me.'

'Our father commands it.'

'What's he now? An old man. And afraid of you.'

'We need this alliance with Ferrara,' Cesare reminded her.

'The Estes hate us. To them we're *parvenus*.'

Cesare smiled contemptuously. 'They swallow their hate. When I met those fools with my four thousand horsemen, the youngest chewed through a finger of his glove in envy.'

Lucrezia could not maintain her stand against him. 'Cesare ... I'm tired ... grief exhausts me ...' she pleaded.

He embraced her, stroking her shoulders and her hair soothingly. 'Sweet sister ... gentle Lucia ... last night, I remembered ... long ago when you were five ... I brought you a horse, black as night ...'

'With a Spanish saddle of red leather.'

'You remember.'

'And would rather forget.'

Cesare's voice was gentle, persuasive. 'If I could turn the world on its course, I'd direct it wherever you desired. As in my heart I truly wish I were no more than a simple knight of St John, a poor soldier of Christ. Will you believe that?'

'Gladly,' Lucrezia's voice was still obstinate, 'When I know that you believe it yourself.'

'Will you believe I can make you do as I wish?'

185

As always, Lucrezia yielded to the force of his will. 'That I believe,' she said dully.

Cesare released her, smiling. 'Then go down to them. Show them what you are. A Borgia. In gold and jewels. The brightest gem in our father's crown.'

*   *   *

Lucrezia appeared at the head of the stairs, a radiant figure in white brocade, her hair, red-gold in the torchlight, bound with a fine gold fillet and two rows of pearls, her face covered by a veil of fine gauze. For greater contrast with her youth and beauty, she was escorted by an elderly Spanish gentleman of her household, tall, white-haired and dressed in black. As she descended the staircase, the Este brothers, despite themselves, could not restrain their admiration. Ferrante gasped, even Sigismondo's cold eyes lightened, while Ippolito was open-mouthed. 'A most beautiful and gracious lady your sister, Lord Duke,' he said to Cesare as he moved forward to greet her.

Cesare sensed Michelotto beside him, heard his voice in his ear. 'Lord, they have found him. The Neapolitan scribbler. He is in Sant'Angelo...'

Cesare nodded briefly. 'You know what to do.'

'My Lord, another matter...'

'What is it?'

'Vitelli is in Rome. With Baglioni and Paolo Orsini. They ask when they may see you.'

'Let them wait.' He indicated the Estes with his eyes. 'Those fools over there say they have horses to outrun any in my stables. Is it true?'

'My Lord. The Marchesa, their sister, is wife to Gonzaga. They say she has persuaded the Marquis to send them some of his best coursers for this occasion...'

'So the proud Isabella would try to fall with me... I have beaten the Gonzaga stable before, and will again. See to it, Michelotto.'

*   *   *

'Cesare,' Rodrigo enquired, as late that night he sat in his chamber eating a frugal supper of bread and fruit, 'where is she now?'

Cesare paced the room impatiently, a grotesque carnival mask dangling from one hand. 'Lucrezia? On her knees beside her husband's tomb.' Then, smiling at Rodrigo's look of alarm, 'A valediction only. She'll forget him in another man's bed.'

'And how will you?'

Cesare shrugged. 'I've forgotten him already. And I'll see many more dead faces before midsummer.'

'You'll take Urbino?'

'All cities whose revenues you would recover. All that still dispute my title as Lord of Romagna.'

'But, Cesare, the Duchess of Urbino will be linked to Lucrezia by ties of kinship; she is sister-in-law to the Marchesa Isabella.'

'Easily broken. With a sword.'

Rodrigo was irritated. 'It's not presumption in us, we hope, to remind you that the lands you take and those you hold will be under us?'

'If you remember, they could not be held at all without me.'

'They'll appeal to Venice...'

'Which will do nothing. At the wish of France.'

'The campaign will be costly.'

'Let the vanquished pay.'

'You move too rashly.'

Cesare shrugged. 'As time obliges me.' He turned to go. 'Your Holiness keeps me from our guests.'

'Cesare!' Rodrigo's voice was sharp with anxiety tinged with anger. 'What? After Urbino?'

There was a long pause, then Cesare said, 'Florence.'

Rodrigo rose in fury, his hands trembling with anger as he moved over to grasp Cesare's arm. 'No! It's madness!'

Cesare shook him off. 'A Borgia dynasty in the Romagna ... remember your own words ... requires the subjection of that Tuscan republic of stall-holders.'

Rodrigo clutched the edge of a table for support, still shaking with anger. 'Not yet!'

'Now!' Cesare told him. 'So finger your beads, Holiness. Leave campaigning to me.'

'Fool! Imbecile!' Rodrigo screamed at him. 'France has promised them twelve thousand men if you march against them. Remember the last time...'

'I shall not offend King Louis,' Cesare said calmly.

Rodrigo raised his hand as if he would strike his son. 'I forbid it. Cesare ... we are Pope! We forbid it!'

'Then I must promise Your Holiness that your Captain-General will not set foot in Tuscany,' Cesare replied urbanely. 'Now, if Your Holiness will give me leave, I must keep my appointment to take the reverend Cardinal Este whoring. You can talk to him in the morning...'

Rodrigo groped for his chair and sank back into it, staring after his son in helpless frustration.

*   *   *

Ippolito d'Este's head swam with tiredness as he faced a brisk Rodrigo the following morning, trying desperately to remember the instructions his father had given Sigismondo. 'Holiness, a dowry of two hundred thousand ducats,' he said.

Rodrigo shook his head. 'Eminence. The figure was agreed with your father's envoy. One hundred thousand.'

Ippolito looked confused. 'Holiness, may we not call my brother Sigismondo? He'll be able to tell Your...'

Rodrigo's voice was solicitous. 'You appear tired, Ippolito. We were thoughtless to summon you so early. When no doubt you spent the night upon your knees...'

'My knees, Holiness?' Ippolito said cautiously.

'Asking for guidance.' Rodrigo's voice was bland.

Relieved, Ippolito replied with a nod, 'Indeed, Holiness.'

'Devotions lift the spirit but exhaust the mind.' Rodrigo smiled. 'Rest easy, my son, we shall help you. The remission of your father's dues to the Holy See, for how long was it to be, you remember?'

'Ten years, Your Holiness.'

Rodrigo shook his head sadly. 'Five, Ippolito, five...'

Ippolito looked wildly round the room, seeking help, but there was none.

Rodrigo went on inexorably: 'You have brought the jewels for Madonna Lucrezia to wear?'

'Your Holiness, my brother Sigismondo advises me that ...' Ippolito rolled his eyes, he was now sweating with confusion.

'As an earnest of your family's good faith,' Rodrigo interrupted him.

'Holiness,' Ippolito said desperately, 'they are only *displayed* at weddings and may not...'

'Do you not trust us to return them, Ippolito?'

'No, Holiness ... Yes, of course! Holiness, our father wished my brother Sigismondo to speak of these...'

'You are a Prince of the Church, Eminence. We are Pope. Is it improper of us to prefer your counsel?' He leaned forward to touch Ippolito's arm in a sympathetic gesture. 'We know. We know how much haggling must pain you. So we must be brief. There is the question of the child...'

Ippolito looked more unhappy than ever. 'Holiness ... My father ... My brother Alfonso ... Holiness, the child's presence in Ferrara would be an unhappy embarrassment...'

'Ippolito!' Rodrigo was grieved. 'Would you deprive a mother of her son?'

'But, Holiness ... my father's Ambassador assured him you were agreed the Lady's sons ... the Lady's son should remain in Rome.'

'Were he not a grievous burden on our purse.'

Ippolito struggled on, 'Holiness, he has a revenue of fifteen thousand...'

Rodrigo's voice was definite. 'The castles and lands now held by the Lady Lucrezia must pass to him.'

Ippolito said nothing, dumbfounded.

Rodrigo rose from his chair to signify the end of the interview. 'You see how easy it is for honest men to reach agreement?' he said affably. 'All is satisfactory. We congratulate you, Eminence. Now go, my son, and convey the happy news to your brothers. I have other business to attend to.' Then, as the unhappy Ippolito prepared to leave, he asked innocently, 'My son, the Duke Valentino, is treating you well?'

*　　*　　*

The tortured body of the Neapolitan, Manciani, hung lifeless in chains against the wall of the dungeon under Sant'Angelo. 'He'll speak no more, Lord Duke,' Michelotto said, as Cesare entered the room, still wearing a carnival mask. Cesare took the dangling head by the beard and raised it, glancing briefly and contemptuously at the agonised face.

'You should have cut out his tongue,' he said shortly, 'as a warning to the next man who dares . . .' He dropped his hand. 'The Lord of Faenza, you say?' he said meaningly.

'His friends, Lord. They paid him. To slander Your Excellency . . .'

'So that the people of Faenza might rise up against me calling for Manfredi. Is that not so, Michelotto?'

Michelotto nodded, grinning. 'If you say so, My Lord.'

Cesare took off his mask and threw it on the floor; he smiled, a cruel smile. 'The Lord of Faenza must pay the penalty of his treachery, Michelotto. Did you not once, when first we met, tell me that I must always strike first?'

'My Lord, it is the only way – for a Prince who would survive.'

Cesare turned and went to the cell door. 'His Holiness shall know of this,' he said.

*　　*　　*

'Never, Cesare!' Rodrigo was horrified, but firm.

'His friends paid the scribbler. They must be punished, or he must – in their place. They have conspired against you.'

Rodrigo shook his head. 'It was nothing . . . nothing . . .'

Cesare leaned forward, both hands on the desk at which Rodrigo was working, speaking slowly and distinctly as if to an imbecile. 'Faenza is in the heart of the Romagna. If it revolts in favour of Manfredi it could undo all the work we have done. Men will cease to fear us, cease to think that we are invincible. Duke Ercole of Ferrara will have second thoughts about your alliance.' He paused to let his meaning sink in, then he continued, 'This boy, Astorre, was the heart and mind of Faenza's resistance in the past – and we must think of the future. Am I making myself plain to Your Holiness?' Rodrigo did not answer, but his eyes showed that he understood. 'They could make his release a rallying cry. I cannot open my campaign with that knife at my back,' Cesare went on.

Rodrigo's voice when he spoke was curiously equivocal, despite the firmness of his words. 'Sant'Angelo is a papal fortress. I have authority there. You'll not touch him.'

Cesare rose. 'So be it,' he said mildly. 'I'll do nothing to spoil my sister's joy in her wedding.'

*   *   *

On 28th December 1501, to the sound of trumpets, clarions, lutes and rebecs, Lucrezia, her head held high, walked for the last time from the Palazzo of Santa Maria in Portico across the piazza of St Peter's to the Vatican. She wore a dress of rich golden brocade, with a train borne by Angelina and others of her ladies, her hair covered with a veil of golden gauze, her neck and ears bare of jewels. Ferrante and Sigismondo d'Este walked on either side of her, and behind her fifty Roman noblewomen, richly attired, followed in procession. The party mounted the steps to the Sala Paolina above the doors of the palace, where the ceremony, conducted by the Bishop of Adria, took place.

The Bishop initiated the proceedings with a long, rambling sermon, but Rodrigo cut him short with an impatient gesture. 'My Lord Bishop, to the ceremony!' he said curtly.

At a signal from Burchard, a long table was brought forward and placed before Rodrigo. Ferrante d'Este, as proxy for his brother, led Lucrezia forward and presented her with a golden ring. Then it was the turn of the Cardinal Ippolito who, somewhat apprehensively, placed on the table a small coffer containing the Este jewels. 'Most gracious Lady,' he said to Lucrezia, 'I pray you do not despise these paltry trinkets. I promise that when you reach Ferrara, the Duke my father will lavish upon you others far more worthy of your beauty...'

As he opened the coffer, Rodrigo dipped in his hand and drew out a glittering array of head ornaments, necklaces, bracelets and pendants of diamonds, pearls and rubies, all intricately set. He placed a cap studded with fourteen large diamonds, as many rubies and a hundred and fifty pearls, upon his daughter's head. 'We thank the Duke,' he said, beaming. 'We thank Your Eminence, in your father's stead ...' Then he took Lucrezia in his arms, enfolding her in an exuberant embrace. 'Come, Lucrezia,' he said, 'we will celebrate your wedding...'

Lucrezia's face as Rodrigo led her to the banquet table in the adjoining room was a mask of resignation, her hand was cold and unresponsive to his eager clasp. As she sat down, the musicians began to play and Rodrigo motioned the company to the dance. Lucrezia remained sitting bolt upright in her stiff golden robe. Her eyes met Cesare's in a long look of passion mingled with defiance.

*   *   *

Lucrezia knelt before her father to take her final leave of him, her face calm and drained of all emotion.

'You will remember all I've told you,' Rodrigo said anxiously.

'I shall remember everything,' she said tonelessly.

'And you'll write to me – often?'

'As you desire.'

Rodrigo smiled, coaxing her to do the same. 'I'll come to

Ferrara in the spring ... You'll surely be with child then. I'll come ... and all will be well.'

'I know we may never see each other again.' Lucrezia refused to respond.

'Lucia,' Rodrigo pleaded, 'all I've done ... all I've wished ... is to be the good servant of my Church and my family.'

'You've made both serve you,' she said dryly.

'As I serve God,' Rodrigo reproved her.

'May he forgive you.'

'Lucia,' Rodrigo wheedled, 'will you write to Cesare? On my behalf. Urge him to ... to ...'

'It's too late,' she interrupted him coldly. 'He no longer needs you. He no longer needs God.'

Rodrigo was suddenly enraged by her contemptuous attitude. 'And *I* have no further need of you!' he cried.

Lucrezia got up from her knees and faced him; she was shaking with repressed emotion. 'At last we're honest!' she told him. 'Now listen to me well – if my husband is an ape, I shall love him! Hunchbacked and wall-eyed, I shall cleave to him! Because I'm glad to be gone from you all!' She began to weep, her shoulders trembling in anguish. Rodrigo, his face twisted in an expression of terrible pain, moved forward to embrace her for the last time. She pushed him away and ran to the door, going out without looking back. In the courtyard below, the first flakes of snow of the new year were falling, spotting her scarlet cape and resting invisible on her ermine hood. Smiling graciously to Ferrante and Sigismondo Este who were to escort her, Lucrezia rode out through the gate on her way to Ferrara.

A mile outside the city, a horseman waited by the Via Flaminia, dressed in black velvet, covered by a long fur mantle. Lucrezia reined in her horse, recognising him instantly: 'Cesare,' she breathed. He wheeled his horse beside her.

'Lucia,' he said, his lips warm on her cold hand, 'this is the beginning – for both of us.' He raised his head and stared into her eyes for a long moment. 'Remember,' he said, 'you and I. Now – and for ever.'

Then he turned his horse and galloped back down the road towards Rome, a dark figure against the falling snow.

*   *   *

Cesare looked out of the arched window of his new palace in Trastevere, the same palace of San Clemente in which Caterina Sforza had finally signed away her rights to her cities. He stared northwards over the white meadows outside the city, towards Ferrara – and the Romagna. The Romagna – it was time to plan a new campaign. 'Michelotto!' he called over his shoulder without turning round. 'The Orsinis and the others, have they arrived?'

'They wait below, My Lord.'

'Then let them wait. It'll show them who's master.'

In another room of Cesare's palace, the Captains waited their summons. Vitellozzo Vitelli, a grizzled, bearded, sunburned figure, leaned against the window niche, apparently listening to the sound of the bells tolling Lucrezia's departure for Ferrara; Cesare's old friend, Gian Paolo Baglioni, and Paolo Orsini, sprawled in chairs, were looking at Vitelli. 'So,' Vitelli turned towards them, 'the cat is married to another mouse. But they will find that Este is more dangerous game than the others . . .' He moved into the room and stood facing them, leaning on a great two-handed sword. 'I wonder . . . when Our Lord Cesare is sucked into hell, will the bells toll for him? And will those cheering fools out there say a prayer for him?'

Gian Paolo answered him, 'And will you, Vitellozzo? You serve him as his *condottiere* as we do.'

'As my own master,' Vitelli replied scornfully. 'My ancestors were masters of Città di Castello when his were herding goats.'

Paolo Orsini said, 'And now you take his pay.'

'For sixteen guns and a *condotta* of three thousand men. A soldier's pay. Honest pay. I do not . . . *serve* him.'

'Fine logic, Vitellozzo,' Paolo said dryly.

'Orsini and Borgia in harness. That's fine logic. Gian Paolo?'

'He is my friend.'

'And therefore should be watched.'

'He'll not betray us,' Gian Paolo said loyally.

'Not again. Not twice,' Vitelli said evenly. 'Isn't that why we're here?'

Orsini and Baglioni looked at each other uneasily, aware of the dangerous direction in which Vitelli's words were tending. 'It was agreed ...' Paolo said, 'You'll take his word?'

'Upon the Holy Cross only,' Vitelli riposted grimly. He half drew his cross-hilted sword from its scabbard. 'In Christ's name only! And may still ...' He thrust it back into its sheath.

The door-hangings parted without warning and Cesare strode into the room. Apparently overjoyed at seeing his Captains, he embraced each in turn. 'Vitellozzo ... old friend!'

'My Lord.' Vitellozzo bowed.

'Paolo ... Paolo Orsini!'

Orsini smiled. 'Lord Duke.'

'And Gian Paolo Baglioni. It's good to see you here. Yesterday ... yesterday His Holiness told me how much he regretted his harshness in banishing you.'

'My Lord.' Baglioni inclined his head.

'So.' Cesare's manner was expansive. 'Now we all campaign together again!'

Vitelli was cautious. 'Times are at a change, My Lord ...'

Cesare ignored him. 'With your help, I'll have the finest army in Italy.'

But Vitelli would not be deterred. 'For France or Spain, My Lord?' he questioned Cesare.

'You serve me, Lord of the Romagna,' Cesare replied.

'It's not wholly yours,' Vitelli reminded him.

'A castle here, a town there. Before midsummer I shall hold it all ...'

'For France or Spain, My Lord?'

'Let each knock,' Cesare told him cheerfully. 'Cap in hand.' The *condottieri* looked at each other doubtfully. In the high game of international politics it mattered a good deal which side you were on. Choosing the losing side could mean you lost your lands, like the Colonna – or your life, like Virginio Orsini. Cesare watched them. Then he smiled exuberantly and put a hand on Vitelli's shoulder. 'Vitellozzo!'

'My Lord?'

'Times *are* at a change. In the spring the people of Arezzo and Pisa will rise against Florence.'

'Florence.' Vitelli's voice was disbelieving. 'Again!'

'Again.'

'What does Your Excellency propose?'

'You, Vitellozzo, march to the aid of Arezzo. You, Paolo, to Pisa.'

Vitellozzo smiled cynically. 'And where will you be?'

Cesare dropped his hand and turned away for a moment. Then he swung round, a smile of triumph on his face. 'In the ducal palace of Urbino. Where France, Spain and Florence can shortly kneel at my feet.'

Baglioni's eyes lit up in admiration. 'My Lord ...!' he reached to grasp Cesare's hand.

'No.' Vitelli's voice was stubborn.

'No?' Cesare was surprised. 'Have you forgiven the Florentines for hanging your brother?'

'I forget nothing,' Vitelli replied meaningly. 'I forgive nothing.'

Cesare looked at Orsini. 'Paolo? The Orsinis are pledged to restore their Medici Kinsmen to the Lordship of Florence.'

'France now stands behind Tuscany,' Vitelli interposed.

'A King preserve a republic?' Cesare riposted. 'Vitellozzo!'

Paolo Orsini said hesitantly, 'My Lord, nine months since, after Faenza fell, we offered you Florence on the point of a lance ...'

'And can again.'

'You refused it,' Vitelli accused him. 'You deserted us.'

Putting on a show of anger, Cesare shouted, 'That was the Pope's work! Not mine!' He held out his arms to grasp

196

Vitelli's. 'Vitellozzo ... old friend ... Do you not truly believe that I don't choke on that betrayal?'

Vitelli stepped backward, freeing himself from Cesare's hand, his face enigmatic. Then he drew his sword and, holding the cross of its hilt out to Cesare, he said, 'In Christ's name and upon His Holy Cross I shall keep faith with you ...' Cesare took the sword, and held the hilt to his lips. 'In Christ's name,' he repeated, 'I shall keep faith with you, as I believe you will with me ...' As his eyes watched his captains, an imperceptible smile played about his lips.

* * *

By the late spring of the year 1502, Cesare's plans for a daring pounce northward were well advanced. He intended to make a lightning strike against Urbino, on the southern borders of his own lordship of the Romagna, to dislodge Duke Guidobaldo and his Duchess. It was an audacious plan, for Duke Guidobaldo was well loved and apparently firmly established in his mountain duchy; he was also connected to the ruling families of Italy through his Duchess, who was sister to the Marquis of Mantua, and thus sister-in-law to the proud Marchesa Isabella d'Este Gonzaga. Simultaneously with his conquest of Urbino, Cesare planned to strike once more against Florence, by fomenting revolt in the Florentine subject cities of Arezzo and Pisa by means of his *condottieri*, and then menacing the beleaguered Florentines with the threat of his army on their borders. It would be a gamble, for Florence was under the protection of France, and would certainly appeal to Louis for help. Moreover, Louis would soon be in Italy, mustering his army at Milan before marching southwards to contest the kingdom of Naples with Spain. Like all successful gamblers, however, Cesare had weighed the odds carefully, and was not afraid to make a high throw while secretly keeping his options open.

And so every day was spent in preparation, filling the campaign chest, recruiting men, buying arms and interviewing agents who would provide the groundwork for the fifth column within the threatened cities which was to act in conjunction with Cesare's forces outside. Cesare had a remarkable grasp of military matters; he was interested in every new technique and invention, particularly in the field of artillery and fortifications. Above all he was interested in plotting the logistics of the complicated strategy he had in mind.

On this spring day, Cesare sat at a table in his palace. It was late morning and he had just arisen. The remains of his breakfast of bread, fruit and wine could be seen among scattered piles of papers. Michelotto and Ramiro, the latter now obviously prosperous and richly dressed, stood in attendance. 'Ramiro,' Cesare said, 'that Florentine engineer, the one who used to serve Ludovico of Milan. Did you bring him with you as I asked?'

'Da Vinci, My Lord. He is in the antechamber, working on his papers. If Your Excellency would care to inspect them? . . . They say he has a marvellous skill as a draughtsman.'

'Ludovico Sforza, for all his faults, had excellent judgement,' Cesare replied, chewing on a crust of bread. 'And he was wise enough always to employ the best. Let us see this man . . .' He rose from the table, biting at the tough crust of the loaf with his strong white teeth, and went into the antechamber, where a man was bent over a desk, working on the head of an old man in crayon. He was so absorbed in his work that he did not notice Cesare's arrival, and Cesare did not speak to him, bending to rifle through the papers that lay scattered on the floor about the desk. Many were portrait studies, anatomical drawings of men and horses; these he discarded, looking with particular interest at those which illustrated siege-works and war machines. 'You know the outworks and fortifications of Florence?' he asked the artist abruptly.

Da Vinci raised his head, stood up respectfully and bowed. He was middle-aged, about fifty years old, and bearded, with remote dreaming eyes. At his belt hung a clutch of notebooks, and his hands were stained with crayon and charcoal. He was simply, even poorly, dressed. 'My Lord. Your Excellency proposes to besiege the city?' His voice betrayed his surprise.

Cesare did not answer his question. 'Guile may be more effective than any of your engines,' he said. 'But what of Urbino?'

'Your Excellency will see I've devised a system of trench-works, advancing by stages, and slowly...'

'I'm not a leisurely man,' Cesare cut in. He held up a drawing, puzzled. 'What's this?'

'A plan for a flying machine, Your Excellency, whereby a man ... standing upright within it, as you see ... raising and lowering his arms...'

Ramiro laughed, a harsh bark of contempt, but Cesare, though incredulous, was interested. 'A flying man?'

'Indeed, Excellency. It was the fanciful notion of winged angels that perplexed my mind...'

'As they might any sensible man. Birds fly, Leonardo. Men walk.'

'A bird is but an instrument working to certain mathe-matical laws, and it should be within the capacity of man ... with the aid of machinery ... to produce such move-ments as may lift...'

But Cesare was no longer listening, his attention once again turned to his military projects. 'I need maps of Urbino...' he said peremptorily, '... as you did for Arezzo. Plans for siegeworks close to walls, where guns may be well placed.'

Da Vinci bowed. 'Your Excellency will engage me as your engineer?'

Cesare nodded. 'You'll be well paid.' He glanced at da Vinci's threadbare clothes. 'Knowledge must be a nig-gardly employer ... You'll find me a generous one – if you do well. Now. Bring me the plans I want within five days ... I march in seven.'

'Excellency, may I accompany your army? To study the attitudes of men in combat ... examine cadavers ... the working of bone and muscle...'

'Leonardo,' Cesare said with some exasperation, 'a

sword smith may not direct the blade he makes, or a groom tell his master where to ride. Ramiro! You will accompany Messer da Vinci to the Romagna. Let it be known that on my orders he is to have the facilities he needs. After he has given me the plans I asked for.' Ramiro bowed and accompanied da Vinci out.

Cesare turned to Michelotto. 'You'll stay in Rome when I leave.'

'I may not ride with you to Urbino?'

'Wait for letters Vitelli is to send from Arezzo. And join me when the Pope has left Rome for the summer ...' He went to the door, pausing on the threshold. 'You understand me, Michelotto?'

'My Lord?'

'When the Pope has gone ... light a candle for the young Lord of Faenza.'

* * *

Astorre Manfredi rose uncertainly from the straw upon which he had been lying as the door to his cell swung open. Two men came in bearing torches, which they set in holders against the wall. Manfredi peered at them uneasily; their faces were unfamiliar and not reassuring. 'Who are you?'

Michelotto spoke first, 'Good friends, My Lord.'

'Friends?'

Michelotto pulled a paper from the cuff of his gauntlet. 'To bring Your Excellency relief.'

Manfredi stared at him incredulously, hope dawning in his eyes. 'Relief ...? I am to be released ...?'

Michelotto smiled at him, holding out the paper, 'Indeed, my lord. Your sufferings are about to end.'

Manfredi fell upon his knees in joyful relief, crossing himself. Behind him Ramiro moved swiftly. Taking a silk noose from his sleeve he slipped it over the Lord of Faenza's bowed head, and twisted it. There was a desperate struggle before Manfredi's writhing body fell still and slumped lifeless to the ground. Michelotto shook his head disapprovingly. 'Ill executed, Ramiro,' he said. 'The soft living of your Romagna governorship is spoiling your old skills.'

The two men lifted the torches from their holders and went out, without taking any further notice of their victim. 'Now,' said Michelotto as they walked up the dark passage towards the light, 'You are to return to the Romagna, and I to join the Duke at Urbino.'

*   *   *

The Florentine envoys, Bishop Soderini and Secretary Niccolò Machiavelli, rode into the courtyard of the great ducal palace at Urbino. The leading envoy, Soderini, was distinctly apprehensive; they had been summoned by Duke Valentino, in the most peremptory manner and without notice of the matter of which they were to treat; he foresaw a disagreeable interview with the man who had so recently and so easily dislodged Duke Guidobaldo from his duchy of Urbino. Machiavelli, on the other hand, was looking forward to meeting this man of whom he had heard so much, who had threatened his city the previous year, and expelled so many established Lords from their territories. This Duke Valentino, Machiavelli reflected, could be a man after his own heart, who worked the rules of statecraft out for himself and bent them to his will.

The courtyard was filled with armed men bearing Cesare's colours. Amongst them Machiavelli noted a group of dejected prisoners in chains and, beside them, the dark figure of a man who he knew by reputation as Valentino's executioner, Michelotto.

Michelotto stepped forward to greet them, his hands on his hips, his attitude mocking rather than respectful. 'Welcome to Urbino, my masters,' he said. 'The Duke is already waiting for you.'

'If we might first rest ...' Soderini began.

'No, My Lord Bishop.'

'But ... but ... we've been two days on the road from Florence. I ... I insist!'

Michelotto paid him no further heed, merely turning to

hammer with the hilt of his sword upon the heavy studded doors behind. The door being opened by a heavily-armed guard, Michelotto motioned the envoys inside. Before following them, he beckoned to the Captain in charge of the six prisoners, and whispered something in his ear, pointing to a window high in the wall above. The Captain looked surprised, then smiled and nodded. Michelotto turned and went in, the bolts of the great doors crashing behind him.

Cesare received the envoys in a heavily-guarded chamber high above the entrance hall. He was dressed in black as usual, but wore half-armour with a sword at his belt for security. The atmosphere was one of tension and unease, and Cesare's manner as he received the two Florentines was menacing rather than welcoming. He motioned them to be seated and, as soon as they had complied, he began to pace up and down the room, delivering a violent harangue: 'I know the city of Florence is ill disposed towards me!' he said angrily. 'I know what you Florentines think of me! I do not want to hear the hypocritical vapourings of your Council. *You* have not kept the promises you made to me last year when I withdrew my forces from your territory. *You* have conspired with France against me!'

Soderini shifted uncomfortably in his chair – it was all as he had feared, and worse. He glanced nervously at the two armed guards by the door, the two crossbowmen at the window, and Gian Paolo Baglioni, whom he knew to be Valentino's *condottiere*, standing, arms crossed, against the wall. His colleague sat impassive at his side, chin resting on his hand, watching Cesare intently, as he continued to pace the room.

'You must give me some security of your good faith,' Cesare went on, 'then Florence will find me as staunch a friend as I can be an implacable enemy. I am Lord of Romagna and I do not fall on my knees to beg favours of a republic of coin-clippers. I owe you nothing, but you are in my debt for the tolerance I've always shown your city. Last year I spared you, but now you have exhausted my forbearance, and I – not you – shall say what may and may not be done!'

A faint smile crossed Machiavelli's face as he watched this exhibition, formulating his thoughts. 'Why,' he reflected, 'should this magnificent Prince honour his word? No prudent ruler should do that when times change the circumstances in which it was given. If all men were good, all Princes might be honest, but since most men are wretched animals who would deceive a Prince if they could, he would be foolish to honour his word. And no Prince need lack for good reasons to justify his bad faith . . .'

'Messer Machiavelli?' Cesare's voice cut sharply across the envoy's musings.

'My Lord Duke?'

'You are amused?'

'Forgive me, My Lord Duke . . . a cautionary thought, no more.'

'Since it thus occupies your mind, perhaps I should hear it.'

'A Prince who gives his word, My Lord, may argue that when times change the circumstances in which it was given, it need no longer be honoured . . .'

'I've not so argued.'

'Thus, when our Government asks you to remember your assurance of last year that you would commit no hostile act against it . . .'

'I have not done so. I am in Urbino. I've not set foot in Tuscany. Does that not show my good faith?'

Machiavelli paused, then with a faint smile he said, 'Yet Vitelli is in Arezzo.'

'Am I accountable for that?'

'Is he not your man?'

'He is my man. But I swear to you that I knew nothing of this business of Arezzo . . .'

Soderini felt it was time that he took some part in the conversation. 'Then Your Excellency will recall him?' he asked.

Cesare's face darkened, his voice rose threateningly as he turned upon the Bishop. 'Don't expect any favours from me! I don't regret the injury Vitelli has done your city. He has suffered too much from its cruelty – as I have from its insolence! As far as I am concerned, the further he takes things, the better I shall be pleased!'

Soderini, taken in by Cesare's show of anger, attempted to soothe him. 'My Lord Duke, these accusations are unjust. Our Government wishes only to have Your Excellency's assurance...'

'Understand me, My Lord Bishop!' Cesare said fiercely. 'I don't like your Government! I do not trust your Government! You'd do well to change it. I'm not the man to play tyrant, but before God I'll destroy any who think to play tyrant over me!' He swung away from the envoys, as if attempting to control his anger.

'Lord Duke.' Soderini was hesitant but persisting. 'You ask for our good faith. May we not ask that of...'

Machiavelli put out a hand to restrain him; he cleared his throat. 'My Lord,' he said humbly, 'What do you require of us?'

For a moment Cesare said nothing, but beckoned to one of the crossbowmen and took his weapon from him. He appeared to be absorbed in taking his aim at something below in the courtyard. Then he said, without turning his head, his eyes narrowed as he looked down the bolt at the target, 'Florence must decide what it wishes me to be. A good friend. Or a relentless enemy.'

He released the bolt. From the courtyard below rose an agonised cry. Cesare straightened and turned towards them with a charming smile, his anger gone as if it had never existed. He beckoned the envoys to the window. Sprawled face down in the centre of the courtyard lay the body of one of the prisoners, the bolt of the crossbow protruding from his back. Cesare calmly put out his hand to the other guard for his weapon, handing him the used bow in return, which the man began to reload. Without a word, Cesare took aim again; another man fell, grasping his throat.

The other prisoners were now aware of their danger and sought to escape from the trap, two of them hammering on the door of the castle in useless supplication, a third attempting to hide himself among the tethered horses, while the fourth sank to his knees in prayer. Since he was the obvious target, Cesare shot him without further ado, then aimed at the prisoner hiding behind the horses. The terrified animals reared, pulling at their tethering ropes and revealing the man to Cesare's bow-shot. He too fell a victim.

'My Lord Duke ...' Machiavelli addressed Cesare, who turned to look at him, raising his eyebrows, as he automatically stretched out his hand to take a recharged bow. 'My Lord Duke!' he repeated, his voice holding a tinge of dry amusement, 'four is a point well made. Would five, or six, not labour it?'

Cesare smiled and shrugged then, turning back to the window, he took aim again. Two more bolts were enough to dispose of the remaining prisoners. 'Friend or enemy, Messer Machiavelli. Florence has a week to decide...'

*　　*　　*

'A month, and still Florence has not answered you,' Rodrigo said. 'Did you truly believe they'd be so easily frightened?' He was walking with Cesare in the Vatican garden, having summoned his wayward son home for consultation. There was an atmosphere of tension between the two men. Rodrigo disapproved of Cesare's ways and methods, was suspicious of his intentions, and uneasily aware that he could no longer control his son. Cesare kept his own counsel, but beneath an impassive exterior he in turn was irritated by what he regarded as Rodrigo's pusillanimity.

'The game's not yet done,' he replied.

'It has a new player.' Rodrigo scattered a handful of grain to the white doves who flocked about him. 'King Louis has arrived in Milan.'

'I sent you word of that myself.'

'The King has asked me to restrain you...'

'And can you?'

Rodrigo did not answer, loth to expose his powerlessness. Instead he tried another tack in the game of domination which he and his son were playing, a game Rodrigo knew he could not win. 'The taking of Urbino has outraged the world ...' he said spitefully.

'You had no objection when I proposed it.'

Rodrigo continued, seeking to undermine that armoured self-confidence, 'You've blundered. Kings and Princes will turn against you.'

Cesare's voice was silky as he riposted, 'That pleases you? If I fall, so will you. Giuliano Rovere is with Louis, as eager to wear your crown as he was ten years ago.'

Rodrigo drew himself up. 'I am still Pope...'

'Whose crown rests on the point of my sword.'

'And whose feet are stained with the blood it sheds,' Rodrigo said bitterly.

Cesare's voice was ironical. 'When it profits you, you dip your fingers in blood and call it Holy Water...'

'May God forgive you.' Rodrigo was becoming angry now.

Cesare smiled, goading him. 'And the Devil take us both if I falter now.'

Rodrigo fought back, still seeking to touch him on a weak point. 'You challenge disaster,' he said. 'Louis is angered by your treatment of Florence ... by what your *condottieri* have done in Tuscany...'

Cesare shrugged. 'Declare for him against Spain in Naples, and he will embrace me.'

'You know I may not.'

'The Spanish Pope!' Cesare jeered.

Rodrigo said with dignity, 'For neither or for both. But not for one against the other.'

'Then I shall. I'll ride to Milan.'

'No...!'

'And if my *condottieri* still trouble him, I'll throw him a bone to gnaw upon.'

'No! I forbid you to go! I shall prevent it!'

'How?' Cesare laughed, mocking him.

For a moment Rodrigo could not speak, staring at his son with a look in which horror, terror and humiliation were mingled. For him, it was the moment of truth. When he found his voice it shook with rising emotion. 'All you've ever done has been with intent to diminish me and raise yourself. You've bought the loyalty of the Cardinals with false promises, with boys and women. You've destroyed the Lords of the Romagna so that neither I, nor my successors, may use them against you. You ... you murdered your brother and countless other men who stood in your way. You killed your sister's husband ... you would have corrupted your sister ...'

'Had not you done so first.'

Rodrigo almost choked. Tears sprang to his eyes. 'God ... Church ... and family ... You'd leave me with nothing.'

Cesare took his father's hand and kissed the papal ring with a mocking gesture, almost throwing Rodrigo's hand from him. 'You still have that.'

Rodrigo drew himself up to his full height in a final, desperate attempt at command. 'You will not go to Louis!'

'Ask. Don't order me.' Cesare's voice was cold as ice.

There was a long pause as the two men stared at each other. Then Rodrigo dropped his eyes in surrender. 'I ask it.'

Cesare smiled. 'Then I'll go to my camp at Fermignano and hunt boar instead,' he said lightly, turning to go.

Rodrigo stopped him. 'Your sister is with child!'

Cesare turned back, surprised. 'So? It's the way with women.'

'I miss her sweet presence, Cesare ...'

'What now?' Cesare's voice was bored.

Rodrigo was apologetic. 'Am I wrong? I've told your brother to recall his wife to Rome. She should never have been banished ... Am I wrong? Sancia's smile will cheer my loneliness.'

'Bed whom you please,' Cesare said brutally, 'but you can no longer expect them to smile – especially Sancia.'

Stung beyond endurance in the last citadel of his manhood, Rodrigo screamed at him, 'When I'm gone the wolves will tear you to pieces!'

'When you're gone, Holy Father, I'll look into the face of the sun.' Cesare bowed ironically and turned on his heel.

'Remember Icarus!' Rodrigo shouted at his departing back. 'He flew too close to the sun and fell to earth...'

* * *

It was still early morning, but the July sun was beginning to make itself felt, as Cesare rode into camp at Fermignano, after hunting boar in the brakes of the hills since dawn. He was dressed in green, and as usual superbly mounted; beside him two cheetahs strained at their handler's leashes, and behind two dead boar, blood trickling from their sides and snouts, swung between two pairs of mules. Cesare appeared to be in excellent spirits as he swung off his horse outside his tent where Michelotto was awaiting him. 'He's here?' Cesare asked him. Michelotto nodded towards the tent. 'He came alone?'

'With twenty horsemen, but no other Captain.'

Cesare nodded, smiling, and strode in. Inside, Ramiro and Vitellozzo were standing close together, talking in low voices as though they feared to be overheard. Cesare stood at the entrance for a moment watching them unobserved. 'Good-day,' he said.

Ramiro started guiltily; bowing somewhat nervously to Cesare, he edged past him out of the tent. Cesare's eyes followed him coldly, then he turned back to Vitelli. His smile held no warmth, nor did he offer the *condottiere* his hand. 'You came with speed, Vitellozzo,' he said.

'I met your messenger on the road. I was coming at my own prompting.'

Cesare said nothing for a few minutes as he moved over to the table, poured himself a goblet of wine without offering any to Vitelli, and began to strip off his clothes. Then he said flatly, 'Why?'

'I smelt betrayal.'

Cesare took up a cloth and began towelling his body vigorously. He frowned. 'Again? You've too sensitive a nose.'

'I took Arezzo in your name,' Vitelli reproached him.

'And proclaimed it publicly,' Cesare replied coldly.

'You didn't forbid it.'

'I didn't command it.'

'Must I play with words?' Vitelli asked angrily.

'When you've learned how to use them, my friend.' Cesare's voice was contemptuous.

'I've used one here that begs an answer,' Vitelli said deliberately.

Cesare looked up angrily, working up to a mock show of rage. 'Betrayal? You doubt *my* good faith?'

'I doubt everything that doesn't come within the reach of my arm and sword.'

'That would encompass all your wits.' Cesare's voice was insulting.

'You've told the Florentines you knew nothing of Arezzo,' Vitelli charged him.

'What did I know?'

'You swore upon the Cross to keep faith with us...'

'So long as you kept faith with me.'

'That I've done!' Vitelli exclaimed, exasperated.

'By displaying my badge and shouting my name in Arezzo,' Cesare said, a note of deadly rage rising in his voice.

'As your *condottiere*!' Vitelli burst out.

'You had leave from my service to avenge your brother. By what ... by what right do you involve me in that?'

Vitelli now realised that Cesare had outwitted him, manœuvred him into some trap which he was about to spring. He tried to leave. 'We're too much at odds,' he muttered, 'I'll return later.'

But Cesare was not prepared to let him go until he had finished with him. 'Stay!' he commanded, 'and answer! By what right?'

'If you're set on provoking me, My Lord, remember I'm not without power...'

'Your guns make little noise, Vitellozzo,' Cesare said contemptuously.

'Loud enough to be heard in Rome!' Vitelli shouted, grim faced.

'You threaten me? You ...?' Cesare gave a fine exhibition of towering rage, throwing the towel in Vitelli's face. 'I've done with you! Withdraw from Arezzo!'

'Since I'm not there at your ...' Vitelli began, but Cesare, furious, gave him no time to finish.

'Withdraw!' he shouted at him, 'or I'll march on your towns and lordship and reduce them stone by stone. I'll leave nothing but dust and grieving women!'

His face set, Vitelli swung out of the tent without a word. As the curtain closed behind him, Cesare's face broke into a smile of satisfaction. As if in celebration, he poured another goblet of wine and downed it in a gulp. 'Michelotto ...!' he shouted. Then, as Michelotto entered, 'Prepare the horses for Milan,' he said. 'And yours for Rome. Let us hope the Holy Father will give you indulgence for the news you will bear him ...'

*　　*　　*

'Madness!' Rodrigo shouted. 'Madness! He went alone?'

Michelotto stood before the enraged Pope, head bent. He was not enjoying his mission. 'No, Your Holiness. With two gentlemen, dressed as Knights of St John ... He advised the King of his coming ...'

Rodrigo was aghast. 'Blundering fool,' he muttered, almost to himself. 'This could mean the end ... Once in Milan they'll never let him go. And Giuliano Rovere is with Louis ...' Then he pounded his fists on the desk in front of him in frustration and rage. 'Get out!' he shouted at Michelotto, 'before I have you thrown into Sant'Angelo!'

Michelotto did not move. 'Holiness ...' he began unhappily, 'Holiness, I am to tell you – he'd not write it – that he'll give the King your promise of five hundred men-at-arms ... and free passage for the French army in its advance upon Naples ...'

Rodrigo sat motionless, his face empty of all expression. Wearily he raised his hand in a gesture of dismissal. Michelotto willingly seized the opportunity to withdraw.

As he backed out of the room, he heard the Pope mutter to himself one word – 'Naples...'

*   *   *

Rodrigo was still sitting at his desk staring at the painted wall, although it was now dark and the candles had been lit, when Gaspare Poto opened the door hesitantly. 'Holiness?' he said uncertainly.

Rodrigo turned his head to see Jofre and Sancia come in. His face lit up with an expression of great joy as he rose to embrace them, 'Sancia...! Sweet child...! How we have longed to see your face again.'

'And I yours. Just once more.' She drew back to avoid Rodrigo's embrace. 'No!'

Rodrigo was taken aback. 'No! I may not embrace you?' he asked surprised.

'I'd rather swallow a toad,' Sancia spat at him.

Bewildered, Rodrigo turned to Jofre. 'What...? Is she ill?'

'Yes!' Sancia screamed at him. 'Sick. Tainted by your accursed family. You are the Vicar of Hell. Anti-Christ and...'

'No. Sancia. No!' Rodrigo was horrified, shaken. 'Stop her, Jofre!'

But Sancia raved on. '... Beast. Man of blood! It's done.' She turned to Jofre. 'Take me away.'

Jofre did not move, looking foolishly at his father, who had recovered some of his composure. 'Sancia!' Rodrigo pulled her to him. 'Tell us. What is it?'

She was not sobbing hysterically. 'Murderer ... my brother's murderer...'

Foolishly, Rodrigo tried to soothe her with an embrace. 'No ... no, child ... not I...'

Sancia screamed at him, fighting him away from her. 'Cesare! In your name.'

Rodrigo was becoming angry. 'Be silent, girl!'

'Christ curse you! All of you!' She spat suddenly in Rodrigo's face.

'Guard ...!' he shouted in a fury. 'Guard ...!' Then, as the men came running, he pointed a shaking finger at Sancia. 'Take that bitch away ... that Neapolitan whore ... Bury her ... bury her in Sant'Angelo!'

Sancia, frightened now as the guards seized her, appealed frantically to Jofre for help. but Jofre had something of the Borgia guile if not the courage and, turning his back on her, he knelt to kiss the hem of Rodrigo's robe, as she was dragged out screaming, 'Murderers! Accursed murderers! You will be betrayed as you have betrayed us ...'

Her voice died away in the distance. Rodrigo sat motionless. 'Betrayal ...' he whispered, 'we will be betrayed ... as we have betrayed them.'

8

The Wheel of Fortune

VITELLOZZO VITELLI LAY sweating and grunting with pain in the bedchamber of his stronghold at Città di Castello. He could not rise from his bed to receive Gian Paolo Baglioni, who was concerned to see him in this condition. 'You're ill...'

'It's nothing. Get out, you rogue!' Vitelli yelled at the servant standing by the door. He shifted painfully to raise himself on the pillows. 'Nothing. The French disease. And the slut wasn't worth it.'

'You'll recover soon?' There was a note of anxiety in Baglioni's voice.

'If I survive hot plasters of arsenic and rose-water. Yes! God willing, I'll sit a horse again before autumn.' His voice strengthened. 'But you've come, Baglioni. You're with us!'

'Yes. I've come, but...' His face expressed his concern as Vitelli, attempting to embrace him, gave a sharp grunt of pain. 'Vitellozzo ... old friend...'

'No,' Vitelli gasped, 'I'm unmanned, that's all, where I should be best manned. There's bread and wine over there ...' Baglioni crossed to the table and began to eat hungrily. 'Where is Cesare?' Vitelli asked.

'Gone to Milan. To face Louis of France alone.'

Vitelli gave a laugh of satisfaction. 'The French will do our work for us!'

'He could offer them help against Spain,' Baglioni said uncertainly.

Vitelli grunted derisively, 'Without *condottieri*, without us, he's nothing to offer.'

213

'Michelotto is raising militia from the people of the Romagna.'

'Rabble!'

'... who believe he protects them from tyranny.'

'As a wolf does a herd of sheep.'

'It seems he no longer trusts us and ...'

'Too late,' Vitelli said shortly.

But Baglioni was still uncertain. '... and with French help he may ...'

'Too late!' Vitelli said definitively. Then, 'Do you weaken?'

Baglioni shook his head. 'I may not. And yet ...'

Vitelli pointed to papers strewn across his bed. 'Letters,' he said, 'from the Orsinis ... Oliverotto and others ... We meet at La Magione to form a league. Gianbattista Orsini will sit at our head.'

'A blind old man!' Baglioni interjected.

'With less bone and sinew than you'd find in an egg-white. But he's still an Orsini, and a Cardinal, and if he rallies what's left of honesty in the College of Cardinals we may justly remove that bastard. And the father of bastards.'

'The Pope too?' Baglioni was horrified.

Vitelli put out his hand. 'Listen, Gian Paolo. Cardinal Rovere would thank us for emptying a chair he hopes to fill ...' He grinned savagely. 'And Cardinal Rovere is in Milan with the French. Our Duke will find them close as ticks in a harlot's hair. Take my hand, Gian Paolo,' he said fiercely. 'Do you weaken?'

Baglioni took Vitelli's outstretched hand. 'No,' he said slowly, shaking his head. 'I once loved Duke Cesare as a brother. But his treachery ... his infamy ... Christ forgive me – but now I wish him dead.'

Vitelli looked up at him, smiling. 'As God's my maker, Gian Paolo, I swear we'll tear him from his high saddle and walk upon his face!'

*   *   *

Head bowed in submission and clad only in the simple robes of a humble Knight of St John, Cesare stood before

King Louis in the great hall of the Castello Sforzesco at Milan. It was August, and despite the thick walls and great vaulted ceiling of Ludovico Sforza's palace, the air was heavy, stifling. With Cesare's entrance, however, the atmosphere had become electric. Eager anticipation showed on the faces of Cesare's enemies who surrounded the King – Giuliano Rovere, with Ascanio Sforza released on Rovere's surety, the deposed Duke of Urbino with his brother-in-law, Francesco Gonzaga, Marquis of Mantua, burning to avenge the wrong thus done his sister the Duchess, Guidobaldo's wife.

Louis' face was haughty as he looked at Cesare, his voice cold as he addressed him. 'Your Grace is an unexpected visitor.'

Cesare raised his head, his expression one of calm confidence. 'No doubt Your Majesty has been too busy to read the letter I sent in advance,' he said.

'And unnaturally dressed,' Louis said disapprovingly.

'That I might travel quickly and unmolested.'

'With no escort?'

'None but these two gentlemen, Your Majesty.'

'And no baggage.'

'I required none, Sire.'

'So I'd take you for a poor medicant . . .' What might have been the ghost of a smile crossed Louis' face.

'I've not come to beg, Majesty.'

Louis resumed a haughty tone. 'You may regret you came at all. We've good reason to be displeased with you.'

'And I to reassure you, if that's so.'

'When it was known you'd reached Milan,' Louis continued with a brief glance at Rovere, 'we were advised . . . to relieve Italy of your troublesome presence by carrying you back to France.'

Rovere and Sforza exchanged quick, satisfied smiles. Cesare looked at them coldly, then his face broke into a smile of winning charm. 'How could I resist such an invitation? Your Majesty's hospitality is justly renowned.'

Louis stared at him for a moment, then he laughed and,

rising from his throne, he moved towards Cesare, his arms wide to embrace him. 'Cousin ... dear cousin!' he said, shaking his head, 'we have lacked for your wit to enliven us for too long!' Then, turning to the astounded courtiers, he ordered, 'A chamber ...! Prepare a chamber next to my own. And food ... food and drink for this weary traveller!'

* * *

Cesare sat in the magnificent salon of his suite of apartments next the King's, dining heartily on a variety of dishes which had been set before him. He grinned to himself as he remembered the look on his enemies' faces when Louis had embraced him. They had all been hoping to witness his downfall, these proud lords ... his smile grew broader as he thought of Rovere, out-manœuvred for the second time ...

The hangings at the door parted to a rustle of silk robes. Cesare looked up to see Rovere and Ascanio Sforza enter. He raised his eyebrows, smiling. 'I expected to see Your Eminences before this.'

Ascanio was surprised. 'You knew we'd come?'

'Of course he did.' Rovere's voice was sharp.

'But your own expectation has disappointed you, Rovere?' Cesare said silkily.

Rovere inclined his head in acknowledgement. 'It's true I believed the King would receive you less warmly.'

Cesare grinned again. 'Do you hope to disarm me with candour?'

Rovere shrugged. 'It's sometimes more effective than duplicity.'

'And sometimes indistinguishable.'

There was a pause, then Rovere said, 'May we be seated?' Then, as Cesare motioned them to sit at the table, he went on, 'Since Your Grace expected us, you no doubt know the reason for our visit.'

'You wished to hear what service you might do me.' There was a teasing note in Cesare's voice. He got up,

216

carelessly taking a leg of chicken which he proceeded to eat as he paced up and down the room, not looking at the two Cardinals.

'The King's humour is subject to sudden changes. His cordiality may not be constant.' Rovere's voice was expressionless, but he watched Cesare like a hawk.

'I can understand you've found that so,' Cesare said, chewing.

'In my case, he's always listened graciously to my counsel.'

'Which I may be wise to employ?'

'It could be of advantage to you.'

Cesare paused, his back to them. 'How so?'

Ascanio Sforza, less subtle than his companion, broke in, 'Milan is full of your enemies...'

Cesare wheeled to face him. 'Including your Sforza kinsmen!'

Ascanio was indignant. '... Who've suffered greatly from your ...'

Rovere stopped him hastily. 'Ascanio!' He smiled placatingly at Cesare. 'His Eminence wished to say that my counsel could secure the King's protection from their hostility.'

'In return for my gratitude alone?' Cesare's voice was ironical.

Rovere paused, then he said blandly, 'How is His Holiness?'

'In excellent health for a man of his years.'

Rovere inclined his head, making a spreading gesture with his hands. 'I'm truly pleased to hear it.'

Cesare threw the chicken bone into a corner, and appeared to be examining closely the grotesque decorations on the ceiling. 'Age and infirmity must eventually triumph ...' he said musing.

'Indeed. I pray the Holy Chair will be as wisely filled when he departs.'

Cesare looked at him directly. 'May I leap-frog part of the way for Your Eminence? When His Holiness is dead, I shall still be Prince of the Romagna.'

'And Captain-General of the Church, I hope,' Rovere interposed. 'Our interests need not conflict.'

'If the King is advised to banish my enemies from his court...'

'And I may be assured the Holy Chair will be suitably occupied...'

'To your satisfaction.'

Rovere bowed. 'As you say.'

Cesare resumed his pacing of the room. 'The King's great friend, the Cardinal d'Amboise, thinks himself qualified,' he said.

'So I believe,' Rovere replied. 'But His Majesty might be persuaded against it...'

'In favour of another.'

'... If he were assured d'Amboise would not be accepted by the College of Cardinals...'

'Whom I influence and instruct.'

Rovere smiled. 'I'm pleased Your Grace has such understanding.'

Cesare turned with a little bow. 'Your Eminence may count upon it.'

Rovere's smile became warm. 'Then we'll not keep you longer from your bed,' he said, rising, and, followed by the silent Ascanio, he made his way majestically out of the room.

A few moments later, a door at the other end of the chamber opened, and Louis' head appeared. 'I heard voices ... who was it, cousin?'

'No one of consequence, Your Majesty,' Cesare replied.

The King came into the room smiling. 'Come,' he said impatiently over his shoulder; then, as two servants entered, their arms heaped with rich clothes, 'See – I have brought you clothes for your stay with us. From my own wardrobe.'

Cesare bowed. 'Your Majesty is too gracious.'

'I'll not have you shambling about my court like a beggar.'

Cesare assumed an expression of mock piety, 'A poor Knight of St John...'

Louis gave a shout of laughter and, clapping Cesare on the shoulder, he sat down at the table, pulling him down beside him. 'Come, cousin, we'll take wine together. We'll enjoy ourselves in Milan. Ludovico Sforza, the rogue, knew how to live – there's this palace and a great park for hunting at Pavia. We've missed you – these Italian Princes with their long faces make sad companions.'

* * *

Ascanio Sforza's expression was troubled as he and Rovere made their way back from Cesare's apartments. 'Giuliano,' he said, 'he believed nothing of that . . .'

'Nor I, of what he said.' He smiled grimly. 'But it will trouble his sleep.'

'Then how have we discredited him here?' Ascanio asked, feeling himself out of his depth amidst such tried intriguers.

'Do you think we could visit him without the King hearing of it?' Rovere asked.

Ascanio was even more perturbed. 'I said as much when you proposed it,' he said petulantly.

'You said little else,' Rovere told him dryly. Then, seeing the other's offended expression, he laid a conciliatory hand upon his arm. 'No. Ascanio . . . hear me. Lies flourish better upon half-truths. Tomorrow morning, at the King's *levée*, we tell him that Cesare summoned us, that he spoke of a time when the Pope must die, and offered me the votes of the College against d'Amboise in return for my support of the Spanish cause in Naples. The King will credit it, I assure you . . .'

* * *

'. . . Speaking of Italian Princes . . .' Louis continued, as he helped himself to the ample remains on Cesare's table, 'the Marquis of Mantua has asked my leave to challenge you. Sword and dagger.'

'Does Your Majesty wish me to oblige him?' Cesare asked, pouring the King a fresh goblet of wine.

Louis grinned. 'The Duke of Urbino would be content to hang you.'

'On the highest gibbet, I hope,' Cesare smiled.

'But the Florentines make less clamour against you now.'

'Republics are by nature fickle in purpose,' Cesare replied scornfully.

Louis drank a deep draught. 'I restrained them – with difficulty. It seems your savage Vitelli declared he'd make you King of Tuscany.' He gave Cesare a long look.

'He acted without my authority,' Cesare said earnestly. 'Florence knows I ordered him from Arezzo.'

Louis continued to look at him. 'You'd not come before me otherwise,' he said levelly. 'That Florentine, Machiavelli, Secretary to their Council ... he says you may not be measured against other Lords of Italy. That you're a new power.'

Cesare shrugged, as if it were a matter of indifference what other men said of him. 'I'm what God made me.'

Louis smiled at this. 'You believe in God?'

Cesare smiled back. 'When he favours me.'

'And you believe he favours you now? Is that what you've come to tell me?'

'God has instructed me to confirm what I've already written to Your Majesty ...'

'You have the Pope's word?'

Cesare nodded. 'His offer of men and arms in your campaign against Spain. Free passage through the Papal States to Naples. My own sword as his Captain-General, if you've need of it.'

Louis impulsively put out his hand to touch Cesare's arm in a gesture of gratitude – then a thought seemed to occur to him, and he paused. 'In return for what?' he said suspiciously.

'Your continuing love and protection,' Cesare answered simply.

'From whom?' Louis was puzzled, wary. 'Mantua and Urbino bluster no more. Florence will do as I say.' He looked at Cesare for a minute thoughtfully, then, 'Are you afraid of your own *condottieri*?'

'Not while I have good friends like Your Majesty.' Cesare's voice was confident.

'I see ...' Louis appeared to be studying the design of the goblet he held in his hand. Then he asked, 'Is His Holiness in good health?'

'As his years permit. But age and infirmity must eventually triumph.'

Louis shook his head sadly. 'Alas. And his successor must be thought of. My good friend and wise counsellor ... Cardinal d'Amboise...'

'An excellent choice.'

'You'll agree to it?'

'Before all men,' Cesare replied. 'As I told Cardinal Rovere a while ago, when he was here with Cardinal Sforza...'

Louis was again suspicious. 'But you deceived me. You said they were of no consequence.'

Cesare shrugged. 'Nor are they.'

Louis asked sharply, 'Why were they here?'

Cesare looked directly into the King's eyes. 'To enlist my support,' he said, 'and that of the Cardinals for Rovere against d'Amboise.'

Louis got up from the table in a fury, spilling the wine as he did so. 'The rogues ...! Italian rogues! They slander you and then betray me! I'll banish them from Milan!' Then he glanced at Cesare, his face lightening. He came back to the table and gripped him by the shoulders, looking into his eyes for assurance and trust. 'Cesare ... when we meet ... in public council ... it should not seem we're already in accord.'

'Your Majesty may rely upon my discretion,' Cesare said lightly.

'You'll bargain hard?'

'But submit.' Cesare grinned.

Louis laughed, clapped Cesare on the shoulder, and turned to leave. 'Sleep well, cousin.' Then, at the door he stopped as if he had just remembered something. 'Yes,' he said, 'the Duke of Ferrara sent word. Your sister has been brought to bed of a still-born child. Did you know?'

Cesare got up, shocked out of his usual composure. 'No!'

Louis was almost amused to see this real display of emotion in him. 'She's gravely ill,' he said, 'do you wish to go to her?'

Cesare bowed gratefully. 'If Your Majesty permits.'

Louis smiled, a little spitefully. 'No. Not yet. Your impudence deserves some punishment. You will need our safe-conduct to go to Ferrara ...'

*　　*　　*

Cesare stood beside the bed in the darkened chamber, looking down at Lucrezia's unconscious figure. Her face was waxen against the pillows, her blonde hair lank and dark with sweat. The surgeon at his side said nervously, 'She's asked for you many times, My Lord Duke ... these past ten days ...'

'How is she?' Cesare's voice was anxious.

'Very weak, My Lord, she must be bled ...'

'Where's her husband?' Cesare asked curtly. Then seeing the surgeon hesitate, he said, 'No matter.' Bending, he took Lucrezia's limp hand in his. 'Lucia ...?' he said urgently, 'Lucia ...'

'My Lord,' the surgeon interrupted him gently, 'She must be bled. There is no other remedy.'

'Then do so. Forthwith.'

The surgeon's assistant approached the bed, holding cupping bowl and knives. The surgeon sat beside Lucrezia and pulled up the covers to reveal her leg. He looked questioningly at Cesare. 'My Lord. You would rather retire ...?'

'No,' Cesare said impatiently.

As the surgeon took hold of her foot, Lucrezia suddenly moved, moaning and drawing her leg away. The surgeon, knife poised, looked at Cesare for help. 'My Lord, if you would hold her foot ...?'

Cesare bent and grasped Lucrezia's leg below the knee, holding it down. 'Now,' he ordered. 'Be quick!'

*　　*　　*

Cesare knelt in lonely vigil beside Lucrezia's bed. There was real anguish in his face as he wiped the sweat tenderly from her face with a fine cloth. 'Lucrezia,' he whispered, 'Lucia ... Forgive me ... All will be well if you forgive me ... But you must live ... Live, sweet sister, live! We are Borgia ... one blood, one heart, one spirit ... Dear Christ, we're life itself!' He shook her gently. 'Lucrezia, do you hear me. We're life triumphant!'

Lucrezia stirred, her lips moved. 'Cesare?' she said drowsily.

'Sister?' His voice was eager.

'Love me ...' she whispered.

He brought her hand to his lips, kissing her fingers.

'Cesare ...' she repeated feebly, 'Cesare ... love me.'

His rare tears fell upon her fingers. 'For all eternity,' he said.

*   *   *

'He's only a man like any here!' Vitelli's voice rang fiercely through the rafters of the great hall of the castle of La Magione, brooding over Lake Trasimene. Nine pairs of eyes stared at him, some unconvinced, while one, those of the half-blind Cardinal Orsini who presided at the long table, merely turned, unseeing, in his direction. Paolo Orsini stood at the Cardinal's right hand, flanked by Gian Paolo Baglioni. Six other men, discontented Captains of Cesare's, sat round the table. Vitelli, still sick of the pox, lay on a litter, haranguing them in the powerful voice which had urged on many a man of war to his death. He lifted the long sword lying by his side. 'And can die like any man!'

The conspirators exchanged looks, muttering amongst each other. Above the confused murmuring, the feeble voice of the Cardinal Orsini could be distinguished, in a quavering call for silence, 'Hear me ... hear me!'

'You old fool!' Vitelli said savagely, 'you waste our time!'

Paolo Orsini, shocked, defended his kinsman. 'Vitelli!'

Vitelli paid him no heed. 'Play with your beads and leave this to us!' he barked at the Cardinal.

This time, Paolo's voice was sharper. 'Vitelli!' he warned.

Vitelli turned on him too. 'Yes, My Lady Paolo?' he mocked.

Paolo Orsini took a step towards him, hand on his sword, but Baglioni restrained him, turning to the Cardinal and saying respectfully, 'Yes, Eminence?'

The Cardinal peered in the direction of his voice. 'Baglioni? Is it you?'

'Yes, Eminence. Please continue.'

Encouraged, the Cardinal quavered, 'This isn't a defensive league ... It's not what your letter suggested, Baglioni. You're proposing a war against ...'

Vitelli interrupted him brutally. 'We'll have a war, propose it or not.'

Baglioni interposed, explaining in a gentle tone, 'Eminence, this matter is no longer secret. The Pope intends to seize us all and charge us upon our lives with ...'

The Cardinal was incredulous. 'How do you know this?'

'We've seen the papal letter,' Vitelli told him.

'Then show it to me. I would see it.'

Vitelli laughed harshly. 'He would *see* it!'

Paolo Orsini said warningly, 'Take care, Vitelli!'

Baglioni motioned to Vitelli to be still, at the same time laying a restraining hand on Paolo's sleeve. 'Eminence,' he addressed the Cardinal, 'we can no longer delay. We have ten thousand foot, a thousand horsemen ...'

'Against Cesare's rabble of peasants,' Vitelli interjected.

Baglioni went on, 'And we may expect the help of Venice and Florence.'

The Cardinal shook his head. 'No,' he said, 'France holds them in leash.'

'We have their word to aid us,' Vitelli told him.

There was a note of sarcasm in the Cardinal's voice as he replied, 'What value has that in this game of betrayal?'

'If that's the game we play, why should we trust the Orsinis?' Vitelli snarled at him.

The Cardinal said with dignity, 'The Orsinis have

suffered the Borgias beyond endurance – they have shed our blood. And you meet here in my house. By that we are committed to your enterprise.' He had now succeeded in establishing his role as chairman. He turned to Gian Paolo. 'Speak, Baglioni. What is proposed?'

Baglioni stepped forward, a scroll of parchment in his hand, raising his voice as he addressed the conspirators. 'Cesare has called upon us for his campaign against Bologna. But it's a ruse to test us. In a week the people of Urbino rise for their Duke against Michelotto's garrison. We give them aid and defy ...'

'Enough!' Vitelli barked, 'we know all this.' He gestured to the scroll in Baglioni's hand. 'Do we sign?'

There was a general cry of 'Sign ... sign!'

Vitelli held out his hand, 'Give me the bond!' Baglioni handed him the scroll with a quill pen hastily dipped in ink. Vitelli scrawled his name upon it and thrust it towards the Cardinal, his lips curled in a snarling grin. 'Here's a quick end to Borgia and Borgia bastard. Sign!'

Slowly, carefully, almost reluctant, the Cardinal complied, followed by the other conspirators who added their names to the bond. As they did so, Vitelli let out a shout of triumph, thrusting his huge sword towards the ceiling. 'This is for you, Cesare Borgia!'

*   *   *

Cesare stood over his father, forcing Rodrigo to countersign papers to finance his campaign. He had just arrived from camp at Imola, and his black armour and thigh boots were splashed with mud.

Rodrigo, his face a mask of helpless rage, was shouting at Cesare who paid him absolutely no heed, 'You fool ... you imbecile ... you'll destroy everything. You madman ... I renounce you! Cesare! I renounce you!'

'Your Holiness is displeased with me?' Cesare asked innocently.

'Am I dis ... you miserable ingrate ... you son of a whore!'

Cesare merely raised his eyebrows and pushed another paper in front of him. 'Three thousand ducats will not buy a month's fodder for two thousand horse.'

Rodrigo raged on, 'You call here as if it were a tavern-stop ... and casually tell me you've committed me to the French cause!'

Cesare shrugged. 'Small reason for so much choler. I want ten thousand ducats for ...'

'For what?' Rodrigo interrupted him angrily. 'You have no army! Your *condottieri* are now at La Magione ... plotting against me!'

'Against us,' Cesare corrected him. 'There are French horsemen coming from Lombardy. Their forage-master will require three thou ...'

Rodrigo struggled from his chair, almost choking with anger. 'I don't want the French here!' he shouted. 'The world falls upon us and you threaten Bologna!'

Cesare's voice was calm. 'The threat was enough. They've offered me horse and foot. And a *condotta* for eight years.'

'How did I beget such a fool!'

Cesare had had enough of insults. His voice took on a hard tone as he said evenly, 'Your Holiness has explained that. I'm the son of a whore.'

Rodrigo became subdued, aware that he had gone too far; his voice took on a gentle, almost pleading note. 'Cesare ... you've aroused a nest of sleeping wasps.'

'The Orsinis? We shall see ...'

*   *   *

Paolo Orsini and the Cardinal were alone in the hall at La Magione, standing at the top of the great staircase, having bid farewell to their fellow conspirators. The Cardinal peered myopically down the stair. 'Have they gone, Paolo?' he asked.

'We're alone, Eminence,' Paolo told him.

The Cardinal leant heavily on Paolo's arm. 'Guide me to my chair ...' Then, when he had seated himself laboriously again before the table, he said, 'Paolo, the soldiers of your *condotta* ... Who has been their paymaster?'

'Duke Cesare,' Paolo answered.

'And were they regularly paid?'

'Yes, Eminence.'

'Then, can we now trust them to turn against him?'

Paolo Orsini shifted uncomfortably on his feet. 'Eminence ... we signed the bond.'

The Cardinal made a dismissive gesture. 'It would've been foolish not to – with Vitelli rattling his sword.'

'Even so,' Paolo argued, 'honour us to keep ...'

The Cardinal silenced him with a wave of his frail hand. 'Honour does not make good sense out of bad judgement, Paolo. However, it must be considered that those loud-mouths may succeed in bringing Duke Cesare down ...'

'As we desire.'

'Perhaps,' The Cardinal nodded, musing. 'But I've no wish to make Giuliano Rovere Pope. Would you have Vitelli as Captain-General?' He smiled reminiscently. 'When I was a boy, Paolo, I'd wait until others had shaken the peach tree before I gathered the fruit ...'

'Eminence ...' Paolo said hesitantly, 'Eminence, Cesare Borgia has written to me.'

The Cardinal nodded again. 'And to me,' he said.

*　　*　　*

'Written to the Orsinis? But why, in the name of God?' Rodrigo was puzzled.

'To assure them we believe they intend us no mischief,' Cesare told him.

'They'll not believe it!'

Cesare smiled, picking up his cape and sword from a chair. 'When a man with the flux is eager to relieve his bowels, he'll leave by any door that's opened to him ...' He moved to the door. 'I told the Cardinal Wasp to bring his conscience to you.'

'Cesare ...' Rodrigo called after him, 'Lucrezia sent no word to me?'

Cesare's response was equivocal. 'No. Yes, her love and duty, I suppose.'

Rodrigo asked anxiously, 'The Estes are pleased with her?'

'They're thankful her dead child was a girl and not a boy.'

'But her husband is kind to her?'

'He is,' Cesare's voice was ironical. 'He spends most of his time in taverns.'

Rodrigo was anguished. 'Lucia ...!'

'May I now leave for Imola?'

'Should you not go to Urbino ... it is closer to Rome?' Rodrigo's voice betrayed a different anxiety.

Cesare smiled. 'You are afraid, Father? There is no need – the danger is not here in Rome. And Michelotto will hold Urbino ...'

*   *   *

Michelotto rode dispiritedly through Cesare's camp at Imola, the bedraggled remnants of his Urbino garrison straggling behind him, defeat written all too plainly on their faces. He grimaced as he dismounted in the courtyard of the castle, not relishing the prospect of telling the Duke that he had been beaten out of Urbino by a mob of mere townsfolk, and, to add insult to injury, ambushed on the road by a rabble of peasants.

The Florentine Secretary, Machiavelli, who was waiting to be received by Cesare, observed Michelotto's arrival with interest, and drew his own conclusions. As soon as Michelotto had disappeared, Machiavelli went to question his weary followers. It would be useful to know the truth before talking to the Duke ...

Cesare was serene, his face betraying neither anxiety nor disappointment, as he received Machiavelli. He was occupied in selecting maps and plans which lay on a table before him, and passing them to an armed servant to be packed in a leather travelling bag.

Machiavelli bowed, his eyes on Cesare's face. 'Such ill

fortune was not to be expected, My Lord Duke,' he said. 'At Urbino in June the fates seemed to smile upon Your Excellency . . .'

'The constellations this month do seem favourable to rebels, Messer Niccolò,' Cesare replied.

'Your Excellency's composure is admirable . . .'

Cesare smiled. 'It may be that I trust no astrologer who's not within reach of my arm.'

'Or perhaps the King of France is sending you five hundred Gascons . . .'

Cesare raised his eyebrows. 'You are well informed, Secretary,' he said, then his smile grew broader. '. . . And two thousand Swiss,' he added.

'You've raised eight hundred foot from the Val di Lamone.'

'Six thousand from the Romagna,' Cesare corrected him. 'You return to Florence?'

'This day.'

'When you give your Council so exact an account of my forces, tell it also that I expect it to heed the King of France and mind its own affairs.' He nodded to the servant and moved to the door, motioning Machiavelli to follow him.

The Secretary paused. 'May I inform the Council that you'll now put those forces into the field?'

Cesare turned at the door, his voice bland as he asked, 'Against men who write to me of their friendship? To whom I respond as warmly? Come, Master Secretary, I must take my leave of you.'

Cesare took the envoy's arm in a confidential manner as they walked down to the courtyard. 'I'm opposed by fools, Messer Machiavelli. You're a wise man. Why are they fools, do you think?'

'Because they trust each other . . .'

'And write to me?'

'Because they have no trust.'

Cesare smiled. 'Try again, Master Secretary,' he said.

They had reached the courtyard. Machiavelli looked at Cesare levelly. 'They would rather trust you than each other,' he said.

Cesare laughed and swung himself into the saddle. 'Travel safely, Messer Niccolò,' he said, and spurring his horse he galloped out of the courtyard with his escort, leaving the Secretary staring after him thoughtfully. A formidable man, this Duke Valentino, he reflected. Personally, he would not like to be counted among the ranks of his enemies.

*　　*　　*

Cesare's rebel Captains were gathered in the ducal palace at Urbino, which they had recently won back for its former ruler, Duke Guidobaldo, who was still in exile. The atmosphere was one of angry discord, with Vitellozzo Vitelli glaring at Cardinal Orsini across the table round which they all sat. 'What does all that word-spinning mean?' he asked savagely.

The Cardinal Orsini's face was expressionless. 'We may no longer hope for success,' he told them, 'now that the King of France has told Venice and Florence that if they support our enterprise he'll treat them as enemies.'

'Then what has Rovere done for us in Milan?' Vitelli asked angrily.

'I fear the King has banished him from court ...'

Vitelli struck a great blow with his fist on the table. 'The devil take you, Cesare Borgia!' he bellowed in fury.

Gian Paolo Baglioni addressed the Cardinal, recrimination in his voice, 'Eminence, you counselled delay.'

The Cardinal shook his head. 'No. Caution.'

'Delay!' Baglioni accused him, 'while you scribbled letters to Valentino!'

'You too have written to him, Baglioni,' the Cardinal retorted.

Vitelli looked wildly up and down the table at the faces of the men sitting round it. 'Written? To whom?'

But the Cardinal did not hear him, eager as he was to make counter-accusations. 'As others here have done. And received letters from him. You too, Vitelli. We know you've had letters from Duke Cesare.'

'And wiped my backside with them!'

'Perhaps,' The Cardinal's voice was cold, he was now in command and determined to have his way. 'Now, hear me, all of you. We stand alone. Friendliness – except, perhaps, for the man we declared our enemy.'

'You treacherous priest,' Vitelli hissed at him.

Gian Paolo interposed. 'Vitelli!'

The Cardinal turned his almost sightless eyes towards him. 'You do understand me, Baglioni?'

Slowly, Baglioni responded. 'He's offered an end to all past grievances ... remission for injuries done ...'

The Cardinal took up the theme. 'The defence of your interests and lordships in perpetual alliance. Has he so written to others here?'

There was a general chorus of voices in affirmation. Only Vitelli remained silent. He hobbled away from the table and went to the window, staring out over the bare hills, tawny with autumn, northwards towards Imola, where Cesare waited. Behind him, Cesare's Captains carried on the debate.

Paolo Orsini continued, 'He has sworn to do so – in return for our loyalty and service.'

The Cardinal spoke again. 'Is it not plain, therefore, that we have shaken his self-confidence? May we not profit from that?'

Vitelli swung back from the window and stood, quivering with rage, beside the table. 'Am I among madmen?' he shouted.

The others ignored him. 'Are we then all agreed?' the Cardinal asked them. They nodded.

The blind Cardinal turned to his kinsman with a questioning look. 'They consent, Eminence,' Paolo said.

'Not I!' Vitelli said bitterly, but the Cardinal continued as if he had not heard him. 'Then we shall meet with the Duke Cesare. Who shall go to Imola. You, Paolo?'

'My Lady Paolo goes to meet her master,' Vitelli mocked, mincing.

Paolo turned red with anger but, managing to control

231

himself, he said, 'Yes, I will speak to Cesare – to arrange a meeting for us all.'

Vitelli cried, now despairing, 'You'd abandon me!'

'If you would have it so,' Paolo replied coldly.

'I'll meet him,' Vitelli said between his teeth, 'with my sword!' He turned and hobbled furiously from the room.

'So,' the Cardinal Orsini continued, as if nothing had happened, 'Paolo will go to Imola, and I to Rome – to speak with His Holiness. We'll have the Pope's security for his son's word.'

*   *   *

With the idle, destructive grace of a cat teasing a victim, Cesare's gloved hand swept the chess pieces off the board. 'Bully!' Jofre screamed at his brother, while his favourite, a young boy, cowered, staring at Cesare with frightened eyes. 'They said you were at Imola.'

'I'm where men find me,' Cesare replied, a teasing smile on his face. 'Now I'm in Rome, little brother. Would you rather I were still at Imola – so you can play . . .' He glanced contemptuously at the boy who was now grovelling anxiously on the floor, gathering up the scattered chess pieces. 'And how is your delightful wife – the Princess Sancia?'

Jofre looked up at him through long lashes, his expression sullen. 'Still in prison – the whore!' he said viciously.

'Which, I doubt not, she has already turned into a brothel, as she does every other place in which she resides,' Cesare replied. 'Now, where is our Holy Father? I must speak with him.'

'In there.' Jofre motioned with his head towards an inner chamber. 'Working. With Gaspare Poto.' Then, as Cesare turned his back to enter his father's room, Jofre kicked at the chess pieces the boy had painstakingly reassembled, scattering them again across the room. The boy looked up at him with tears in his eyes, and Jofre's expression, at first spitefully cruel, softened into one of tender remorse. He knelt down to embrace the lad.

Cesare entered his father's room without knocking. Rodrigo, by now accustomed to these lightning apparitions, looked up without surprise. In a corner of the room, Gaspare Poto nervously scratched away with his pen, pretending to be wholly absorbed in his work. 'Well?' Rodrigo questioned. 'You're certain he's coming?'

'More certain of that than I am sure you'll play your part as you should ...'

Rodrigo gave an embarrassed glance in the direction of his Chamberlain. 'Do not address us so imp ...' he said in a low, warning voice.

'I've no time for niceties,' Cesare told him. 'I must return to Imola within the hour.'

'If Cardinal Orsini comes to Rome, I shall ...'

'I've told you – he's coming.'

'... I shall receive him,' Rodrigo said with as much dignity as he could muster in the face of his son's dominant arrogance.

Cesare smiled coldly. 'As a brother, if you wish. Then hold him fast by the neck like a serpent.'

Rodrigo's eyes dropped to his hands folded upon the desk in front of him. 'When will you meet the others?' he asked wearily.

'At the close of the year.'

A faint smile of malicious satisfaction slid across Rodrigo's face. 'Your French cavalry return to Lombardy before Christmas.'

'They'll not know that,' Cesare replied calmly.

Rodrigo's malice was gone, his voice betrayed genuine anxiety. 'Take care, Cesare ...'

'Send my brother Jofre to me,' Cesare commanded.

'No ...!'

'He means nothing to you. You always say he is not your son.'

'He's all I ...'

'He's diverted himself with boys long enough. It's time for him to be a man,' Cesare said with an air of finality. Then he bowed to take his leave with a perfunctory, 'Holiness', and left the room. Rodrigo lifted his hand in a gesture of benediction, then let it fall as his son turned his back on him. Then he called after him helplessly, 'Send me word ... You keep me in darkness ... Send word!'

Cesare heard him as he strode away down the passage. 'No, Father,' he said to himself under his breath, 'Your tongue is too loose. This is my high game ...'

*　　*　　*

Paolo Orsini stood in the antechamber of Cesare's suite of apartments in the castle at Imola. He felt ill at ease and watched Cesare closely, trying to fathom his reactions. He was conscious too of the dark eyes of Ramiro and Michelotto upon him, as he said, 'My Lord?'

Cesare, apparently supremely unconcerned with Paolo's mission, was trying on a new set of armour in the centre of the room. His face and voice gave nothing away as he said, 'Honour, Paolo Orsini, was always a word that slipped easily from your mouth.'

'I endeavour to live by it, My Lord.'

Cesare fidgeted to get the correct fit of the corselet. 'Too tight,' he told the armourer, 'loosen that strap ...' Then he smiled at Paolo. 'And your companions?' he asked.

'You have their word also.'

'So I have.' Cesare's curious smile grew broader. 'Old friends who have stabbed me in the back ...' Then, to the armourer, 'No. Unstrap me now and bring another pair of plates tomorrow.' He looked straight at Paolo again. 'Such friends would now heal my sounds with words?'

'They respond to your own offer of good faith,' Paolo said with dignity.

'Even Vitelli?'

'Even he.'

Cesare's voice was bland. 'Whose only wish was to make me King of Tuscany.' Paolo frowned, made still more uneasy by Cesare's humour. Cesare saw it and, pushing the armourer aside, came forward to embrace him. 'Paolo, old friend. I bear you no ill will,' he said, 'but I must be sure of the others. And know what they offer.' He motioned Paolo

234

to sit down with him at the table. Ramiro and Michelotto remained standing, two dark presences at the back of the room. Cesare looked across the table at Paolo, his eyebrows raised. 'They'll restore Urbino to me?'

Paolo said steadily, 'If Your Grace honours the offers made in your letters to us.'

'Honour again, Paolo,' Cesare said quizzically.

Paolo refused to be provoked. 'Will you meet us?' he said stubbornly.

Cesare looked directly into his eyes, his face serious. 'At Sinigallia,' he said simply.

'When, My Lord?'

'On the last day of the year.' He paused. 'But mark this, Paolo ... You must come ... all of you ... with no more than an escort. As I shall. No bowmen on rooftops. No swords-men in ambush. If I suspect treachery, I shall turn about, summon my army and destroy you. It is agreed?'

Paolo nodded solemnly. 'It's agreed.'

Cesare smiled gently. 'Upon your honour?'

'Upon my honour, My Lord.'

Cesare rose from the table and, as Paolo followed suit, embraced him. 'Then go with God, my friend,' he said.

As the door closed behind Paolo Orsini, Ramiro gave a short, barking laugh. Cesare turned on him, his voice deadly. 'I sometimes forget you're there, Ramiro. You walk so much in my shadow I forget you're there.'

'Always, My Lord,' Ramiro replied respectfully.

'No, I think not.'

'My Lord?'

Deliberately, Cesare took a small stiletto of exquisite workmanship from a sheath at his belt and began to play with it, balancing it between his fingers. 'The King of France advises me to be rid of you ...' he said musingly, looking down at the blade, apparently absorbed in tracing the patterns on its surface. 'And others, my friends, tell me you are corrupt in your governorship ... that you traffic in grain – and grow fat on revenues that should be mine ...' Idly he put the point of the dagger on Ramiro's stomach, bulging above a rich silver belt. Then he looked sharply into Ramiro's worried face. 'Do you plot against me, Ramiro?'

Ramiro stuttered, 'I ...? No, My Lord!'

'Perhaps not. Not yet ...' Cesare said levelly. 'But I remember that when Vitelli came to camp at Fermignano, you and he were thick as flies on carrion. Have a care, Ramiro. The complaints against you are many.' Ramiro stared at him, unable to conceal his terror. Very lightly, Cesare raised the knife and traced a line round Ramiro's throat. 'Do not look to your friend Vitelli to save you,' he said, 'or the Orsini. Put not your trust in treacherous dogs – like yourself!' He sheathed the dagger and turned his back on the terrified man. 'Michelotto!' Cesare said meaningly before striding out of the room.

Michelotto moved swiftly to pinion Ramiro's arms.

*   *   *

The Cardinal Orsini smiled happily across the supper table at Rodrigo. 'Holiness, you give a blind old man great joy,' he said.

Rodrigo reached over and patted the Cardinal's hand. 'You've been a good servant of Holy Church, Gianbattista,' he said in a friendly tone.

The Cardinal struggled to contain his emotion, tears started in his pale eyes. 'So many years wasted in enmity between our families ...' he said, his voice trembling.

'All past, Gianbattista,' Rodrigo reassured him. 'And when Cesare returns to Rome, he'll give you his hand on that.'

'He returns to Rome?' the Cardinal said doubtfully.

Rodrigo smiled broadly. 'For carnival at Epiphany. No one, Eminence ... no one knows how to celebrate carnival without him. He'll devise a thousand follies ... spend ten thousand ducats ... So prodigal is his generosity to his friends. Among whom I include yourself, Eminence, and all your kin.'

The Cardinal nodded his head gratefully. 'Your Holiness

is too gracious to an old man,' he said, moved. 'I hope to live to embrace His Excellency again in friendship ...'

'That is as God wills, Gianbattista,' Rodrigo said, rising and moving from the room. As he did so, three papal guards came in and seized the old man, lifting him bodily from his chair.

'Holiness! Save me!' the Cardinal cried in terror. But it was to no avail. He was taken to the dungeons of Castel Sant'Angelo, where Cesare's minions saw to it that he did not long survive.

*　　*　　*

At Imola, Machiavelli watched the comings and goings of Paolo Orsini with bewilderment. All his enquiries failed to elicit the exact nature of the negotiations – as he wrote to his masters of the Council of Florence, Cesare's secretiveness made it impossible to gauge what he would do next. Machiavelli was weary of his mission, which ostensibly was to drag out negotiations between Cesare and Florence, while in reality the Council intended him to act merely as a spy on Cesare's movements. As far as intelligence was concerned, Machiavelli was reduced to pure speculation, being unable to glean any hard information. He was sick with cold and short of food, Cesare's army having picked the countryside clean as a bone. And, as Christmas approached, he was filled with a sense of impending doom as he observed Cesare's negotiations with his *condottieri*.

'As to the suggested understanding,' he wrote to the Council, 'respecting the terms of which I am still in ignorance, I do not augur well of it. For when I see the two parties concerned, I see on the one hand Duke Cesare, vigorous, confident in his future, blessed with exceptional fortune and backed by the favour of the Pope and the King of France. Confronting him we have a group of Lords who, even whilst they were his friends, were in anxiety for their possessions, and fearful of his growing power; and now, having thus injured him, naturally more apprehensive still. So that I fail to understand how, on the one part, such injury can be expected to find forgiveness, and how on the other, such fears are to be assuaged ...'

*   *   *

Ramiro was led out to execution at dawn on the morning of Christmas Day 1502 in the public square at Cesena. He had dressed himself with care and richly, as had now become his custom; he wore fine leather gloves against the cold, and his brocade cloak was lined with sables. 'Lord Governor,' Michelotto mocked him as he removed the garment, 'you will soon have no need of this. It will not be cold where you are going ...'

Ramiro looked at his rich cloak regretfully. 'It was a good life ... Devil take Cesare Borgia!'

'As well he may ... But he'll take you first, Ramiro. You and your friend Vitellozzo.'

Ramiro shrugged. 'It's a sharp wind. Come, let's make a swift end to it.' He knelt down before the executioner. The long sword gleamed dully in the grey light, as it rose, paused for a moment and then fell with a thud. Blood spurted over the steel as Ramiro's body slumped forward, the head slowly separating from the trunk.

For a brief second Michelotto stood looking down on his cousin and former colleague, then he too shrugged and turned away. 'Leave the body where it is,' he commanded the guards, 'that the people may see it. And fear the Duke's will ...'

*   *   *

'I told you we could not trust Cesare Borgia!' Vitelli shouted at Paolo Orsini across the hall of the ducal palace at Urbino where the *condottieri* were assembled in uneasy conference. 'Now that old fool of an uncle of yours has put his imbecile head straight into the noose...'

Paolo Orsini was white with anxiety, staring at the sweating courier as if he could not believe his ears. 'Imprisoned ...? The Cardinal ... in Rome?'

'Yes, My Lord,' the messenger said.

'Paolo,' Gian Paolo Baglioni said urgently, 'you must believe it. They've had it put about publicly that His Eminence is confined by the plague. So we'd expect no treachery...'

'The man lies!' Paolo Orsini said desperately.

Vitelli hobbled across the room towards him. 'No,' he told Paolo, 'his brother serves the Vatican. Pay him well.' He grinned, a wolfish grin. 'God is good to us, my friends.'

'What!' Paolo exclaimed. 'Good!'

'Listen.' Vitelli struck his hand lightly on the table. 'That old fool of a Pope moved too soon – unfortunately for His Eminence but fortunately for us. Now we know what to expect from his bull-calf. Is it to be done my way?' Paolo Orsini hesitated. 'Come, Paolo,' Vitelli urged, 'there's no other choice. We must strike first before the bull-calf has us on his horns.'

Reluctantly, Paolo put out his hand to grasp Vitelli's. Vitelli looked towards Gian Paolo Baglioni, who came forward to put his hand on theirs, but with some hesitation. As he did so, another messenger came bursting into the room, haste overcoming courtesy. He knelt before Vitelli. 'My Lord,' he gasped, 'a message from Lord Cesare's camp. Today, at dawn, Messer Ramiro was executed in the public square. No reason was given for his death ...'

A look of anxiety crossed Vitelli's face. 'Ramiro ... dead ...' he said. Then he asked the messenger, 'Duke Cesare – has he yet moved?'

'Yes, Lord. He marches south. To Sinigallia.'

*   *   *

In the cold light of a winter afternoon on the last day of the year 1502, Cesare rode out of his town of Fano south down the Via Emilia towards Sinigallia. He was wearing full armour and accompanied by Jofre and a party of armed men. The sad, grey Adriatic shore stretched drearily to

239

the horizon to his left, while to his right the bare hills concealed a considerable body of his men. 'So?' Cesare greeted Michelotto, waiting for him on the road. 'All is prepared?'

'Lord Duke, my thousand Swiss hid themselves in Sinigallia a week ago. Your horse and foot wait between the town and Vitelli's forces to the south . . .'

'He's come then?'

Michelotto nodded. 'Last night. At dusk. With Orsini and four others. And twenty riders like yourself. Baglioni I met on his way to Perugia; he said he had the flux . . .'

'You should have taken him there and then, Michelotto. I would have him kennelled like the treacherous dog that he is . . .'.

'My Lord, I could not. Without arousing the suspicions of the others.'

Cesare nodded. 'It is well. And the others?'.

'They're in a house in Sinigallia . . . the one of which I told Your Excellency . . . thinking themselves secure. They have men in the town, but they'll be no use to them by nightfall . . .'

*   *   *

Paolo Orsini peered out of the double-arched window, straining his eyes in the failing light. His evident nervousness irritated Vitelli who was sitting at a table about to begin eating. 'Be still, Paolo – you're spoiling my supper,' he said exasperatedly. 'You saw the signal when we arrived.'

'I saw *a* siganl. Who gave it?'

'My man. I know his cap and beard.'

'His cap and beard.' Paolo's voice was sarcastic. 'Jesu!' He turned away from the window to look uneasily at Vitelli. 'And where's Baglioni?'

'He'll be here shortly,' Vitelli said impatiently. 'Now. May I have your permission to eat?'

Paolo nodded slowly and went over to the table to sit

down, the other *condottieri* moving to make place for him. But while the others ate heartily, Paolo seemed to have little appetite for food. Vitelli good-naturedly attempted to allay his doubts. 'Cry Orsini,' he said, chewing and waving his knife in Paolo's direction, 'or Vitelli ... from that window and the street will fill with men.'

But Paolo remained jumpy. 'This house is a trap,' he said.

'To be well sprung ...' Vitelli grinned, spearing a hare's leg from the platter with the point of his knife.

'Upon whom?' Paolo said nervously, rising from the table. 'I'm going to find Baglioni.'

As Paolo reached the door, it opened to reveal Cesare on the threshold, smiling expansively. 'Old friends!' he exclaimed, coming into the room. 'Your hand, Paolo,' he said, grasping the stupefied Orsini's hand as he passed and drawing him after him into the room, then releasing him.

'There's much we should debate, My Lord,' Paolo said uncertainly as the others gaped at Cesare, momentarily taken aback.

'Why else should I have come?' Cesare said pleasantly, walking over to the window and glancing out.

'We debate nothing!' Vitelli said fiercely.

Cesare appeared not to have heard him; he gave an apparently involuntary grimace. 'Jesu!' he exclaimed as if hard pressed. Then, as they all stared at him, he said in explanation, 'Cold nights in the saddle are hard on the bladder. Before we talk ... give me leave for a moment.' He gave a little nod, walked casually towards the door and went out.

The *condottieri* stared at each other uneasily for a moment, then Vitelli, quicker to recover than the others, cried, 'Treachery!' Half drawing his sword, he limped swiftly towards the door, but as he did so it burst open to reveal Michelotto, sword in hand. Armed men wearing the Borgia colours poured into the room, seizing the *condottieri* and disarming them. Paolo Orsini only had time to run to the window and shout 'Orsini' before he, too, was overpowered.

Michelotto smiled at him coldly. 'Save your breath, Lord Paolo, you have not long to enjoy it ...'

*   *   *

'A most beautiful deception, My Lord,' Machiavelli said, smiling, as he came to offer the official congratulations of his Government to the Duke of Romagna on overcoming his treacherous enemies. 'An act worthy of a Roman, as King Louis, I hear, has described it.'

Cesare's face was alight with exhilaration. 'I thank you and your Government, Master Secretary,' he said with a slight bow. 'It was well, was it not, to deceive those men who had shown themselves masters of deception? And Vitelli, sworn enemy of your city ...' With a gesture of his hand, he invited the envoy to observe the scene in the square below the window.

'Cesare! Cesare Borgia!' a hoarse cry rose up from below. 'Absolution ... I've not confessed!'

Machiavelli looked down into the square below. Paolo Orsini and Vitellozzo Vitelli were seated back to back on a scaffold, bound together. Beside them two executioners were preparing the cords and sticks of the garrotte under the expert direction of Michelotto. While Paolo Orsini sat bolt upright, motionless, staring straight ahead of him, Vitelli writhed in his bonds, crying out to Cesare, 'Cesare! Promise me the Pope's indulgence ...!'

Machiavelli's face expressed distaste. 'Hardly a Roman way to face death,' he commented, 'crying for indulgence. Or does he mean compassion?'

Cesare made a signal with his hand. The executioners, at a sign from Michelotto, took up the cords of their garrottes, looped them expertly over their victims' necks, and gave them a swift twist round the sticks provided, choking off a last appealing cry from Vitelli, 'Ces ...'

'Compassion, Messer Machiavelli?' Cesare asked him, turning his back on the two contorted figures on the scaffold below. 'Compassion is no part of ruling, it cannot bring unity. Order and obedience are imposed by fear.'

Machiavelli bowed, but added, 'If those who fear a Prince do not also hate him ...'

With genuine interest, Cesare asked, 'Are fear and hatred indivisible?'

'With respect, Excellency, no,' Machiavelli replied seriously. 'Do we not fear God? Also, men love and hate upon their own prompting, and none other. But they can be made to fear those who wish to be feared.'

'Therefore?' Cesare asked.

'Therefore,' Machiavelli repeated, 'a wise Prince, if he cannot be loved, should make himself feared without being hated. And may thus govern without fear himself.'

Cesare looked at the Florentine for a long moment, considering what he had said. Then, finally, he spoke, 'Maybe so, Master Secretary. But was it not my great namesake Caesar who said he would rather be feared than loved ...?'

Machiavelli inclined his head. 'Your Excellency recalls the end of the story?' he asked innocently.

A strange expression crossed Cesare's face. 'Yes,' he said distinctly, 'I remember it, but still I challenge fortune. Who knows what the end will be?'

* * *

'The Duke,' Machiavelli wrote later in his report to the Council of Florence of the year 1503, 'throughout that year until late summer, having, in his own words, relieved the country of a swarm of troublesome insects, enjoyed such power as no Prince of Italy had known before. Those Lords of the Romagna whom he had not killed were silenced by fear. His government was now so sound that he was able to treat with France and Spain as an equal, holding each apart and waiting upon his decision. Truly he had become an example to all Princes who, in the future, may seek absolute power and unquestioned authority. And if men did not believe him when he said he merely held that power in the name of the Church ... if such men argued that he had made a servant of his father the Pope, no one was bold enough to say so, for the thought of his anger was now a terror to all ...'

*   *   *

Storm clouds were gathering over Italy in that late summer of 1503. In the north the ponderous forces of Louis of France were moving slowly south from Lombardy, bound for the kingdom of Naples, where they would clash with the army of King Ferdinand of Spain despatched to Italy under Gonsalvo de Cordoba to wrest Naples from the French. In Rome, Cesare waited to see which way the wind of victory would blow. He was now the first Captain in Italy with a fine army at his back. Both sides, he knew, would have need of him, and he could virtually dictate his own terms. Men, envying him, called him 'the son of Fortune' ...

*   *   *

Cesare and Rodrigo sat at dinner in the Vatican. It was a sultry August night and not a breath of air moved the fine gauze which covered the windows as a precaution against the deadly mosquitoes from the swamps of the Roman Campagna. Even the added warmth of the candles guttering in the bronze holders seemed intolerable. Sweat poured off Rodrigo's heavy jowls; he looked old and ill, and his hand shook as he peeled a peach with a silver knife. Cesare's face was burning; he dipped a napkin in the bucket of melting snow in which the wine stood cooling, and pressed it to his forehead, then he took a flagon and filled his father's cup, leaving his own empty. 'You take no wine?' Rodrigo said suspiciously.

'I've no stomach for it tonight.'

Rodrigo gulped down the cool Frascati in one draught, looking maliciously at his son over the rim of the goblet. 'You've the French disease again.' He turned grey, put down the goblet hastily and wiped his sweating face with his lawn sleeve.

'And what ails you?' Cesare asked.

'I'm old, Cesare ...' Rodrigo said pathetically. 'August in Rome is fatal for fat men ...'

Cesare ignored this plea for sympathy. 'Then leave it. Or grow thin.'

'Young men think youth is eternal!' Rodrigo said sadly.

'An old man's lie. We know it's too brief. I've one enemy only now – time.'

'And no friends.'

'When have we needed them?' Cesare asked arrogantly.

Rodrigo looked at him, weariness in every line of his face. 'You will. When I am dead.'

'I told you once. When you're dead, I shall look into the face of the sun.'

'And I warned you.' Rodrigo gave a sudden gasp of pain. '... Too late. All is now darkness ...' He held his stomach, breathing quickly in short pants, 'Cesare ... I ... I ... am ill ...'

But Cesare ignored him. It was as if he were talking to himself, seeing into the future. 'Five years ago,' he said slowly, 'I put aside my Cardinal's hat. I can assume it again.'

'What?' Rodrigo said feebly.

'All things are possible,' Cesare replied.

'You ... you would be Pope?' Incredulity made Rodrigo momentarily forget his pain.

Cesare looked at him, his face hard. 'When you were elected, when you were asked what name you took, you said "I take the name of Alexander the Invincible!" I made that braggart boast a reality. All things are possible.'

Impelled by pain and at the same time horror at Cesare's suggestion, Rodrigo half rose from the table. 'No ... not that ...' he gasped, then he was overcome by an uncontrollable fit of retching. Cesare watched his father's agony, his face expressionless. 'Cesare ...' Rodrigo's eyes were filled with a sudden terrible suspicion. 'Cesare ... you ...?' His hands reached out wildly towards his son, then he fell to his knees, vomiting.

Cesare rose to his feet, but not to help his father. The weakness that he too had been fighting all evening overtook him; he swayed, clutching the table for support. 'Burchard!' he shouted, 'come quickly ... the Holy Father is ill ...'

* * *

Rodrigo lay motionless on his bed, his face ashen, his eyes staring glassily at the ceiling. Beside the bed Burchard stood reproving the surgeon, who had just finished cupping him, for taking too much blood. 'Ten ounces ...' he said disapprovingly, 'is a great deal for a man of seventy-three. You will kill him.'

'It is not I that will kill him ...' the surgeon replied meaningly.

Burchard ignored him, his eyes on the sick man's face. 'Has he asked for his sons?' he enquired.

'For no one. Not once in three days ...'

A croaking sound came from the bed; Burchard moved forward and inclined his ear to the Pope's lips. 'Holiness?' He looked up at the surgeon. 'He is asking again if he has been poisoned ...'

The surgeon shrugged his shoulders wearily, 'I've told him it's the Tertian Fever ... he doesn't seem to understand. And that the Duke has it too ... he won't hear me.'

Again an incoherent sound came from the bed. Rodrigo's eyes were full of fear, his shaking lips mouthing a name. 'Ces ...' he said, 'Ces...'

In another part of the Vatican palace, Cesare too was lying in bed; for security he had not returned to his own house. He was sweating, his eyes bright with fever, but he was fighting to maintain consciousness. Michelotto sat beside his bed, watching the physician who was offering him a draught of dark liquid. Cesare shook his head warily.

'Rest easy, My Lord,' Michelotto told him. 'I made him drink some himself.'

Cesare drank it. When he spoke it was with an effort, his voice a hoarse whisper. 'Where is ... where is the Pope?'

'In his bedchamber, My Lord,' the physician answered.

'Will he die?'

The physician looked confused. 'My colleague, Lord, is attending him ...'

'Michelotto,' Cesare gasped out, '... no one knows of our sickness?'

'No one outside the Vatican,' Michelotto reassured him.

Cesare stared at the surgeon. 'Cure me ... cure me!' he said fiercely. Then, exhausted by the effort, he fell back on the pillows, closing his eyes, his body trembling.

Michelotto grasped the physician by the collar of his robe. 'If he dies,' he said, 'I swear you'll follow him.'

The surgeon looked at him in helpless terror, 'Messer Michelotto ... the fever is too high, it must be reduced ...'

'Then do so. And quickly.'

The surgeon was flustered. 'I need ... I need ...'

'Name it!' Michelotto said impatiently.

'Cold water ... and ice. A great quantity. A large jar ... the largest used for holding oil ...'

An hour later two servants came staggering into the room bearing between them a huge earthenware jar, and behind them came others with buckets of water and frozen snow from the ice-chamber which they emptied into the jar until it was threequarters full. Cesare sat on the bed, naked but for a loin-cloth, his body quivering with fever, his eyes staring eagerly at the jar. Under Michelotto's direction, two of the servants lifted Cesare off the bed. Clumsy in their nervousness, they held him high in the air above the jar, then dropped, rather than lowered him into it. Cesare's mouth gaped in a great cry of shock and pain.

*   *   *

'The Lord Duke will live?' Burchard questioned the physician.

The man shrugged. 'Who can tell, Messer Burchard? He was on the point of death. But the treatment may work. He is young and strong. But His Holiness ...' He looked towards the bed where the Pope lay. 'We can do no more ... It is in God's hands now.'

'Lucrezia!' A cry almost of agony came from the bed,

then a muttered, '*Mea culpa, mea culpa, mea maxima culpa* ...' repeated over and over again until it was cut off in the harsh, choking rattle of death.

The surgeon took a small silver paten from his pocket and held it over Rodrigo's mouth. The surface remained clear and unmisted. He looked at Burchard. 'You had better tell the Duke his father is dead,' he said. 'But tell him gently, or the shock might push him too into eternity ...'

9

The Razor's Edge

CESARE LAY UNCONSCIOUS, a waxen image of death, as Michelotto bent over him, trying to shake him back to life. 'My Lord! Open your eyes!' Then, as Cesare remained apparently lifeless, 'Answer by the blood of God! If you hope to live ...'

Cesare's eyelids fluttered, his lips barely moved. 'Michelotto...'

'Hear what I say, My Lord,' Michelotto said urgently. 'The Pope is dead. His Holiness is dead. Your father.' Still Cesare did not open his eyes. Michelotto was uncertain whether he had heard. 'Your father's dead, Lord. Your brother's here. Tell us what we must do.'

Cesare stirred again. 'My brother ... Juan ...'

Jofre leant over the bed. 'It's Jofre ...' Then, as Cesare opened his eyes, 'What are we to do? His Holiness is dead.'

Cesare stared at them for a long moment. 'I did not think of it,' he said slowly. 'I too ... How long have I been in fever?'

'Six days,' Michelotto told him.

'Six days!' Cesare gripped Michelotto's arm urgently. 'Be quick. Lock the doors to the Pope's chamber. Seize the keys.'

'Yes, My Lord.'

'Behind the bed there is a closet ... his secret treasure. Bring it to me. Now.' Then, as Michelotto turned to go, he ordered him, 'Put a guard on this door.'

'It is already done, Lord.'

He went out, leaving Jofre standing beside his brother's

bed, his face apprehensive. 'Jofre . . .' Jofre bent his head to hear Cesare's hoarse whisper. 'Be loyal. Or I shall slit your belly and draw your guts . . .'

* * *

'Two seconds from eternity, Gaspare,' Michelotto snarled. 'Where are the keys?'

Gaspare Poto's eyes bulged with terror. 'Under his pillow,' he gasped, for Michelotto held a knife at his throat.

Without a glance at the body of the dead Pope lying there, Michelotto searched the pillows and drew out a heavy bunch of keys. 'Throw him out,' he said to his men, indicating Gaspare, 'and bolt the door after him.' He tore down the tapestry behind the bed to reveal a closed door, and hurriedly tried key after key in the lock until he found one which turned. He disappeared into the closet and returned dragging a heavy chest. 'Two more,' he said tersely, nodding towards the cupboard. While the men pulled the coffers out of the recess, Michelotto opened his with an 'Ah!' of satisfaction as the lid went back to reveal the glittering heap of intricately-wrought objects in silver and gold, uncut stones and pearls. 'Search quickly,' he told his men, 'there may be more.'

From the other side of the heavy oaken door came the shouts of the palace servants engaged in their customary plundering. The shouts came nearer as they approached the Pope's private apartments, then there was a hail of blows on the door. Michelotto's lips were drawn back in a wolfish grin. 'The dogs . . . we've left them only the bones. Draw your swords and open the door.'

As they flung open the door, the crowd of men without drew back, suddenly silent, frightened by the sight of the weapons. As Michelotto and his men, dragging the three heavy chests and with their arms laden with silver candlesticks and other objects, disappeared down the corridor in the direction of Cesare's rooms, the crowd grew bold again and poured into the Pope's room, struggling

250

with each other in their greed, stripping walls, furnishings, even the piscatorial ring from the dead man's finger.

*　　*　　*

With a great effort Cesare raised himself on his bed to run his fingers through the jewels in the chest which Michelotto had placed beside him. 'It will buy a Pope. All that I need and more. I have the money. I have an army. The Cardinals lack both ...' He raised his eyes to heaven in mock piety. 'I thank you, Holy Father. Let the Devil keep your soul. I ... have the rest ...' He smiled in contempt as he saw Jofre cross himself. 'You mourn him?' he asked.

'He was our father ...'

'He never owned you,' Cesare told him cruelly. Then, in a kinder tone, 'Don't fear, little brother,' he said. 'You shall have your share of all. Only be loyal to me ...' He fell back on the pillows, the effort had exhausted him, and he fought for breath. 'Michelotto ... Where are the armies of France and Spain? They have heard ...?'

Michelotto nodded. 'Of His Holiness' illness. Yes. Now they are racing each other for Rome. There is little time.'

'Who commands ...'

'The Spanish force is led by Prospero Colonna. He is at Marino – only a few hours' march away. The French will take some days yet to reach the city. They're commanded by Yves d'Alègre.'

'Hold my forces here,' Cesare gasped out. 'See they are paid. Send word to the Romagna to stand firm ... Jofre!'

'Yes, Cesare.'

'Go to Prospero Colonna. Tell him – I will restore his lands. Michelotto will give you the countersigns of his fortresses – my pledge ...' He paused to gather strength again. 'Bring him here so I may treat with him. He must come ...'

Jofre was doubtful. 'You think he'll trust you?'

'No ... but he'll trust you – you have been faithful to the Spanish cause. I need his army – or the Orsinis will tear my heart out. Once it is known the Pope is dead. All of our family. Where is our mother?'

'I have sent word,' Jofre told him. 'She will come.'

*   *   *

Vannozza stood looking down on the body of the man she had loved. It all seemed so long ago now — when he had been a virile young Spanish Cardinal with so much joy in life and such a powerful body. Now he was dead. An old man of seventy-three who had not even died in peace. His once proud eyes stared now in terror, his once fine body was a mere heap of sagging flesh. Vannozza closed her mind to the dead past. 'Yes? Messer Burchard?' she said.

'My Lady, forgive me.' Burchard's shocked eyes indicated the scene of pillage round them. 'The proceedings have been most irregular. Duke Cesare's men ... the servants ... they have taken all ...' With an effort he bent down and picked up a tapestry left behind by the looters on the floor. 'Nothing has been done according to the proper forms,' he complained. 'I could not find a single member of the Sacred College within the Vatican ...' He spread the tapestry carefully over the body. 'The Cardinal Camerlengo should have been here to verify His Holiness' passing. And there is the bell ... I must instruct them to sound La Paterina, so Rome will know the Pope is dead ...' He started towards the door.

Vannozza put out her hand to stop him. 'It will be the signal for insurrection. Murder and pillage.'

Burchard stared at her. 'But it is the custom,' he objected. 'La Paterina is *always* rung.'

'So if it is not rung, then the Pope will not be dead,' she said. 'Give the Duke time,' she pleaded.

Burchard looked at her sadly. 'Madam, I cannot. It is the custom. The bell must be rung to signify the end of the reign of Our Lord Rodrigo Borgia. What must be, must be ...'

*   *   *

La Paterina, the great bell on the Capitol, swung heavily on its bronze supports, tolling the passing of the second Borgia Pope. From her cell in Sant'Angelo, Sancia heard it and knew what it meant. Pushing off the guard who was caressing her, she ran to the window with a wild cry of joy. 'The Pope is dead ... The Borgia bastard's dead! And I shall be freed. Open the doors!' She raised her eyes to the heavens. 'Now we'll have revenge ... Even the ghosts will rise. My brother and all the rest. Not one to shed a tear. Little Lucrezia perhaps ... Yes ... And Cesare.' She smiled, a triumphant smile.

* * *

Cesare, with Vannozza at his bedside, received Lucrezia's two little sons, Rodrigo and Giovanni, led into the room by their tutor, Cardinal Vera. 'Thank you for your care, Eminence,' Cesare said. 'Write to Madonna Lucrezia in Ferrara that they will now be in our mother's charge.' He motioned to the boys to come closer. 'Giovanni, you are a Borgia. And Rodrigo. You fear no man. You understand?'

'Yes, My Lord,' Giovanni replied bravely.

Cesare nodded. 'Say farewell to Cardinal Vera,' he told them, 'and go with the Lady Vannozza.' As Vannozza led the boys out, Cesare beckoned to Cardinal Vera to come closer. 'How is it in the streets?' he asked.

'Some swaggering and shouting,' Vera told him. 'There will be worse.'

'What have you heard?' Then, as Vera hesitated, he said with a trace of impatience, 'Come, Eminence.'

Vera looked grave. 'We passed a party of the Orsinis' men. Armed and crying "Death to the Borgias! Death to the Spanish Jews!"'

Cesare's face betrayed no surprise. 'The Cardinals have met?'

'We are called to the church of Santa Maria in the morning. They dare not come to the Vatican while you are here ...' Vera smiled faintly.

Cesare's voice was suddenly strong. 'I shall stay – till

they have promised what I seek. I have two hundred lances outside the walls . . .' He looked directly at Vera. 'With my supporters in the conclave I shall make you Pope. How many could be sworn to that?'

'You have eight votes certain, My Lord.' Vera bowed in acknowledgement.

'More.'

'Perhaps eleven,' Vera said cautiously.

'Almost a third. If there is only time . . .' He was becoming agitated, the fever rising again. His face was flushed and sweating, and he turned restlessly on the pillows . . . 'I must be bathed . . . Tell them to send the Greek girl Vasia to me . . .' Then, seeing the concern in Vera's eyes, he gasped sharply, 'I am not in fever!'

'No, My Lord,' the Cardinal said soothingly. Then, as he bowed to take his leave, he paused. 'Lord Duke, I much regret His Holiness' passing . . .'

'You will have no cause to regret it, Juan Vera,' Cesare told him. 'I will make you Pope . . .'

*   *   *

Juan Vera stood up to address the small group of Cardinals assembled in the church of Santa Maria sopra Minerva. There were only twelve of them, most having feared to venture forth from their palaces in the city's state of unrest, and fearful of what Duke Valentino's forces might do. Among them were Cardinals d'Amboise and Caraffa, the French and Spanish candidates for the papal throne, both of whom had hastened to the city ahead of their respective armies, and the thin, frail figure of the Cardinal of Siena, Piccolomini, the only Italian present. Vera, flanked by a small knot of Spanish Cardinals who owed their hats, as he did, to the Borgias, acted as their spokesman. 'Eminences,' he said, 'in the absence of Cardinal Riario from Rome, you have elected me to the high office of Cardinal Chamberlain.'

'To speak for us to the Duke of Valentinois,' Louis' friend, the Cardinal d'Amboise, interjected.

'You must persuade the Duke to leave the city with his army,' Caraffa followed him up.

D'Amboise resumed. 'The Vatican is in the hands of armed men. We are all in danger, and no conclave can be properly held.' He paused for greater effect. 'It may be we shall be compelled to call upon the arms of France ...'

'Those of His Spanish Majesty are nearer, d'Amboise,' Caraffa interrupted him. Then, meaningly, 'Of course, we understand your preference.'

'If you bring in your Spanish troops, Cardinal Caraffa,' d'Amboise warned him, 'there will be clashes with the Orsinis ...'

'Your Eminences ...' Vera began.

D'Amboise turned to address him. 'Monsignor Vera, you see the peril in which we stand. All forces must be withdrawn. Without delay. Then, and then only, can we elect a new Pope.'

'Your Eminences then request me to arrange an urgent meeting with the Duke?' Vera asked them. There was a murmur of assent. He continued, 'We must arrange too for the destruction of the papal seals. And the funeral obsequies of the late Pope ...'

But the Cardinals turned away from him, pretending not to hear. Only Piccolomini nodded politely. Caraffa whispered, 'The late Pope – they say his body turned black because of poison ... and that he called upon the devil before he died ... I'll not attend his funeral.'

'Nor I,' his colleague agreed, and there was a general shaking of heads.

*   *   *

Rodrigo's body lay protected by an iron grille behind the high altar of St Peter's, where Gaspare and Burchard had dragged it for security when fighting broke out as it was being solemnly borne into the church, monks and soldiers quarrelling over the valuable candles that accompanied the Pope's cortège while the body lay dishevelled and abandoned. The August heat had hastened the process of decomposition, and the face was black and puffy, the swollen tongue protruding, the surrounding air putrid with the stink of death.

Burchard, perforce, held a pomander to his nose, as he indicated the body to the three carpenters carrying the coffin destined for it. 'His deceased Holiness,' he said.

The head carpenter, Stefano, looked at it in disgust. 'You should have called us earlier, Master Burchard,' he said.

One of his companions, Bartolomeo, wrinkled his nostrils. 'God have mercy! What did he die of?'

'Poison,' Stefano told him with an air of authority. 'I've seen too many of them. We'll nail him down like all the rest.'

'With respect,' Burchard said warningly, 'and proper ...' But the pomander was no longer sufficient to ward off the nausea which now overcame him, and he hurried away with a muttered excuse.

Stefano shook his head, pityingly. 'No stomach for it.'

'He's the worst I've seen, though,' Bartolomeo said. 'Fearful swollen. Look at the belly, Stefano.'

Stefano grinned. 'Holy water, Bartolomeo, holy wind and water. Stick a pin in that – and you'd have enough to baptise the whole of Rome!'

The third man, Pietro, laughed. 'Come on, fellows, let's to it. There's good money to be earned. Let's batten him down.'

'Not with your hands,' Stefano instructed them.

'How else?' Bartolomeo asked.

'Bring that carpet,' Stefano pointed. 'Now, all together, tip him onto it. Hail Mary, full of grace, hold your nose and shut your face! That's it. Now, roll him up so we don't have to look on him. They say he blessed a hundred virgins every night ... Pietro, hold tight onto that corner. Are you ready? Up!'

They bundled Rodrigo's body unceremoniously into the coffin, which proved to be too small for it. 'It won't go in,' Pietro complained.

'Yes it will – with a few hearty shoves, my lads,' Stefano told him, picking up the mitre and stuffing it down beside the body. 'Mustn't forget the hat or St Peter won't let him in.'

The three men pushed and pummelled the body until they had wedged it down into the coffin. 'Phew!' said Bartolomeo with a grimace. 'From the stink of him you'd think it'd be the other place.'

'Well, the devil take him then,' Pietro said, banging down the lid, 'for no one else will ...'

* * *

Michelotto bowed mockingly. 'It's not the devil who'll take you, My Lord Giulio,' he said, 'but Prospero Colonna and all his army. They came by night.'

Giulio Orsini was surprised and alarmed. 'Colonna?' he said uncertainly.

Michelotto grinned, 'At this very moment he treats with the Duke. You'd be best advised to run back to your rat-holes in Montegiordano before they set on you together ...'

'Be careful, Michelotto,' Orsini said furiously. 'The devil's calling for you as well, and there'll be no Borgia Pope to save you ...' But Michelotto merely smiled coolly up into his face, and with an oath Orsini wheeled his horse and galloped off, followed by his horsemen shouting, 'Death to the Borgias! Death to the Spanish Jews!'

* * *

'You've heard the cries in the streets?' Prospero Colonna asked Cesare coldly. 'They're not friendly to you.'

'The Orsinis. They're your enemies, too,' Cesare reminded him. He lay stripped to the waist on a bed, as Vasia, the Greek girl, massaged his wasted muscles with oil. He raised his head and looked calmly at Prospero, a thin, spare, sunburned figure standing aloofly before him. 'What do you say, Prospero? You are in the service of King Ferdinand of Spain. What has he told you?'

Prospero said nothing, his eyes indicating the girl. Cesare shook his head. 'My mistress. Greek. She understands no

Italian,' he said briefly. 'I will be frank, Prospero. I need your army. Tell me what you want.'

Prospero moved over to the bed and stood looking down at Cesare, his eyes unfriendly. 'I remember Capua,' he said.

'Capua?' Cesare asked, puzzled.

'I defended the town against you, remember? Your soldiers were savages. I saw girls after who had had torches thrust between their legs.'

'Not on my orders.'

'I didn't think so. And the sixty virgins you took with you to Rome ...?' he ended on a questioning note.

'I am a monster. Yes?'

'I believe so,' Prospero replied.

Cesare grunted. 'Ferdinand is a fool to trust you. You believe too much.' He took the girl's hand and squeezed it until she cried out in pain. 'My strength is coming back – you hear the proof? Her lips could give you promises of love, if you believed her. But only the cry of pain is true. Believe tears but never smiles. What does it matter how you hate me? I need you, Prospero! So, in the name of torment – tell me what your master wants.'

Prospero looked at him for a moment, a guarded glance. 'How many votes can you command in the election?' he asked.

'Eleven. Enough to make a Spanish Pope. Whom does he choose? Caraffa?'

Prospero nodded. 'You can secure it?'

'If more are needed they can be bought.'

'And for surety?'

'My person.' Cesare sat up, indicating to the girl to help him dress. 'I need three days to bargain with the Cardinals. They want me to withdraw from Rome. If they agree to my demands, I'll join you outside the city. We'll learn together that Caraffa's Pope.'

'You'll give yourself as hostage ... why?'

'Needs must, Prospero. For my own security. Niccolò Orsini is approaching Rome with fifteen hundred men. You know that between myself and the Orsinis there is blood. I

258

need your army in Rome tonight. And your love not at all. What do you say?'

Prospero nodded, convinced. 'It is agreed.' He paused, looking at Jofre who stood silent on the other side of Cesare's bed. 'There is one more condition. The King requests the release of his kinswoman, the Princess Sancia.'

Jofre gave an involuntary start. 'Cesare ...' he said alarmed.

Cesare said mockingly to Prospero, 'You see, her husband too is anxious for her safety. How strong is love!' Then to Jofre, commandingly, 'Go with him, Jofre, to see the Princess Sancia ...'

* * *

Jofre and Prospero stood before Sancia in her comfortable cell in Sant'Angelo. Having greeted her husband with contempt, Sancia let her eyes take in Prospero – lasciviously, for he was a handsome man. Prospero bowed respectfully, 'Princess.'

Sancia's face lit up. 'Why, you are a proper man ...' she said, half to herself, and moved over to stand close to him to let him breathe her perfume. 'It's almost a year since I saw anyone except the guards. And him,' she nodded towards Jofre. 'Have you brought my release?'

'News of it,' Prospero replied. 'It will follow upon the election of a Spanish Pope. Cesare Borgia will be released from his bond to me – and you will have your freedom.'

'I shall be exchanged? For Cesare?' Sancia asked.

'In effect.'

'How curious,' Sancia mused. Then, eagerly, 'And then you'll kill him?'

Prospero smiled savagely. 'That would give me great pleasure ...'

'Pleasure ...!' Sancia reached out to touch his cheek. 'How smooth your skin is ... I had forgotten the feel of skin like yours...' She smiled seductively. 'Prospero ... I am glad that it is you who will release me.' She put her arms round him, rubbing herself against him. Colonna shot an embarrassed glance at Jofre, who turned away. 'It doesn't matter about my husband,' she said scornfully, 'he's often by me. Prospero Colonna, you shall have *me* – in exchange for Cesare Borgia...'

* * *

Cesare, pale and making a great show of weakness, was carried on a litter to have audience of the Cardinals in Conclave. He was escorted by Jofre, who spoke for him. 'Eminences,' Jofre bowed to the assembled Cardinals, 'the Duke is here in response to your request for a meeting. As you see, he is still weak from fever . . . This audience must be brief. His Excellency will do what he can.'

There was a murmur of sympathy from the Cardinals, many of whom were genuinely moved to see the terrible Duke Valentino reduced to such a helpless state. They were, naturally, the Borgia partisans, but included the saintly and soft-hearted Piccolomini who, before Rodrigo's death, had been heard to refer to the Borgias, father and son, as 'wolves'.

Cardinal Vera stood up to address Cesare. 'My Lord Duke. In view of what the Prince Jofre has said, I shall dispense with courtesies. We are anxious to elect a Pope. For this – all armed factions must leave the city. Which means, Lord Duke, that you and your supporters too must withdraw.'

With obvious effort, Cesare raised himself on one elbow, speaking haltingly and with difficulty. 'Eminences . . . I am anxious also to meet your request. Though I am ill, I am willing to make this journey – if you will pledge my safety. Two things you must agree. To confirm my appointment as Captain-General of the Church. And give your support to me as Lord of the Romagna.'

Caraffa spoke. 'I see no objection to these arrangements. Pending the election of the new Pope.'

'Cardinal Caraffa. I am grateful for your support,' Cesare said weakly.

Caraffa gave a confidential smile and turned to Vera. 'Cardinal Vera. It is agreed?'

'There are some details ...'

'More than details, Cardinal Chamberlain!' d'Amboise broke in angrily. 'Is the Duke aware that an army of two thousand Spaniards entered the city overnight? It's an invasion! This may not alarm Cardinal Caraffa,' he said meaningly, 'but it will alarm King Louis of France. And I must insist ...'

Cesare raised a feeble hand. 'Cardinal d'Amboise ...' He sank back as if suddenly overcome, and beckoned the Cardinal to approach him.

D'Amboise was taken aback and moved over to the litter with some concern. 'My Lord Duke ...' he said.

Cesare reached up to take his hands in a pathetic gesture. 'Prospero Colonna will respect my wishes,' he assured him. 'His army leaves at my command.' His voice was so faint that d'Amboise was obliged to bend his ear to Cesare's lips. Cesare whispered to him, 'Come to me in secret ...' then continued aloud, 'I pledge my faith to you. You know that I have been a friend to France.'

D'Amboise bowed in acknowledgement. 'My Lord, I do remember it.' He stepped back into his place before continuing, 'The terms of this agreement must be set down. I hope to be satisfied.'

A weak voice came from the litter, 'I think you will.' There was the briefest exchange of glances between them.

Cardinal Piccolomini of Siena beamed round the assembly. 'Then we are in accord?' he asked happily. '*Deo gratias*! The love of God has brought our hearts together.'

'Doddering old imbecile,' Cesare muttered under his breath.

The Cardinal of Siena turned politely. 'You spoke, Lord Duke?'

'Nothing, Cardinal Piccolomini, but to ask your blessing for a sick man.'

'You have it, my son,' the old man said kindly, making the sign of the cross over the wolf's cub.

*   *   *

Cesare and the Cardinal d'Amboise were conferring together in Cesare's apartments late that night. Cesare's face was pale in the candlelight but he was no longer feigning extreme exhaustion. He and d'Amboise sat each side of a table considering each other. Each knew he needed the other, it was simply a question of whose need was the greater and who would therefore have to yield the more. Here Cesare thought that he had the edge. D'Amboise desperately wanted the papacy and, with France and Spain at each other's throats in Naples, each side would give anything to have a Pope who would favour them. Cesare, it was generally thought, with his bloc of pro-Borgia Cardinals, could swing the vote either way. Cesare intended that his favour should be dearly bought. His price was the Romagna, where his power was crumbling, the Lords his enemies returning to their former cities, and hostile Venice moving in to take her share. Louis' power was strong in the north of Italy, his troops could help Cesare restore his dukedom, and his influence could hold off Venice and the exiled Lords. Cesare gambled that d'Amboise's fear that the Borgia Cardinals' votes would be sold to Spain would obscure his perception of how great was Cesare's need of France. One thing, moreover, united the two men, and that was distrust of Giuliano Rovere and determination not to see him Pope.

'An Italian, possibly Piccolomini,' d'Amboise was saying. 'No, I do not think that needs to be considered. I believe, My Lord Duke, the election must go either to France or Spain. There were some at first who thought you'd favour your old friend – Cardinal Vera.'

Cesare shook his head. 'He lacks support. He is no use to me.'

'Then we have only to consider whom you should most beware of,' d'Amboise went on thoughtfully.

'Rovere,' Cesare said with sudden venom, 'Giuliano Rovere. Who is with Louis at Milan ...'

D'Amboise nodded in agreement. 'And will return to Rome as soon as you're gone. Rovere is without doubt your greatest enemy...'

'And the reason I have held back from France since the Pope's death.'

D'Amboise replied with a small air of triumph, 'That is *exactly* as I thought. I told our Ambassador so.' He edged his chair closer to Cesare's in a confidential manner. 'My Lord Duke, let me assure you that King Louis is as hostile to Rovere as you are yourself. *I* am the candidate His Majesty favours in this election. All the French party will give their vote to me.'

Cesare leaned back in his chair, studying him. 'And the Italians?' he asked innocently.

'Will divide amongst themselves. It is your ten or eleven votes that hold the balance between France and Spain. *You* will decide.'

There was a long silence. Cesare toyed with a silver pomander hung on a chain round his neck. Finally he said, 'So, d'Amboise. What do you offer?'

'What do you seek?'

'Protection for myself and for my family. With all our possessions and all our lands. The support of France to retain the states I hold – and to regain those I have lost.' He looked directly at d'Amboise, a hard stare. 'Will King Louis offer so much?'

D'Amboise said earnestly, 'My Lord, I can show you letters . . .'

'And can I trust him?'

'What in life is certain?' d'Amboise asked suavely. 'Is there a better course, my lord?'

Cesare hesitated, swinging his pomander. 'One thing is sure, Eminence,' he said, 'I must leave Rome. And my course must be set towards him who offers me the most . . .'

*　　*　　*

'Mother, you must leave now,' Cesare said as he embraced Vannozza. Jofre and the two children, Giovanni and Rodrigo, were already mounted, and the family's baggage sacks and chests loaded onto pack mules in readiness for the journey to Nepi. 'You understand the plan?' he

263

asked her. 'I'll not leave the Vatican myself till the last moment ...'

'When Prospero Colonna will be waiting at the Porta del Popolo.'

'I've arranged to meet him there at the hour of Vespers. But he will wait in vain. By then you'll be many miles along the way to Nepi, and I'll have joined the French.'

Vannozza hesitated before entering the litter which was held ready for her. 'I'm unhappy to leave Rome,' she said.

Cesare bent and kissed her. 'We shall return,' he assured her, 'and soon.' Then he took his leave of Jofre and the children. 'Guard our mother well. We make our separate ways, but I'll join you by tomorrow night.'

'God save you, Cesare,' Jofre said. Cesare raised his hand in salute, then turned on his heel and strode back into the Vatican, as the party rode out of the courtyard.

Michelotto met him at the door. 'My Lord, Cardinal Rovere returns this day to Rome. I have his servant here as you commanded.'

Cesare glanced at the man over Michelotto's shoulder. 'He's to be trusted?'

Michelotto nodded. 'Until the Cardinal's exile, this man was his body servant. Since then he's sold much information to me. I've always found him true.'

Cesare beckoned to the man. 'Come here.' Then as he stood, cap in hand, before him, 'What is your name?'

'Giorgio, My Lord.'

'You serve the Cardinal Rovere?' Cesare asked the man, looking him straight in the eye.

Giorgio bowed obsequiously — Cesare had a reputation for generosity. 'I have not seen my master in nine years, since he left for France,' he replied. 'Sometimes, Your Excellency, the money comes. Sometimes it is not paid. They say my master will soon return to Rome. But while I wait, My Lord ...' He spread his empty hands in an expressive gesture.

Cesare took out a pearl from the purse at his belt and held it up for Giorgio's inspection. 'A pearl of great price, Giorgio,' he said, as the man's eyes glittered greedily. 'You may have it now – and one to match it if you return having done what I require of you. Are you afraid to kill?'

Giorgio shook his head, his eyes fixed on the pearl.

'Even your master?' Cesare went on. 'The deed will leave no trace.'

'How can it be done?' Giorgio asked.

Cesare gave him the pearl and took out a glass phial. 'Break this,' he said, 'and spill the powder in his cup when some enemy is by him. He'll taste nothing. Its effect is slow but certain.'

Giorgio put out his hand and took the phial, then he bowed to take his leave. 'Trust me, My Lord. God bless Your Excellency.'

As he disappeared, Cesare looked at Michelotto questioningly. 'An honest scoundrel, My Lord,' he reassured him.

'Good.' Cesare rose from his chair, but as he stood up he swayed as if he were about to faint, his cheeks were flushed and his eyes glittering. Michelotto stepped forward anxiously, as if to offer his arm in support, but Cesare waved him angrily away. 'I lean on no man,' he said between his teeth. Then, with an effort, he resumed his normal tone. 'All is ready?'

With Michelotto riding beside him, Cesare left the Vatican lying in a litter with crimson damask curtains carried by eight halberdiers. He was followed by his great Gonzaga charger with black velvet trappings bearing the ducal coronet and ridden by a page. It was a carefully-staged spectacle designed to excite compassion, and indeed Yves d'Alègre, when they met outside the Porta Viridaria, was moved to see Cesare so reduced. In truth, he was too ill to ride, the exertions of the past days having brought on a relapse, and when he finally reached Nepi, he lay for some weeks utterly exhausted and in high fever, nursed by Vannozza and watched over with anxious loyalty by Jofre.

With the news that Cesare was safely on his way to Nepi under the protection of Yves d'Alègre's troops, Prospero Colonna realised that he had been tricked. He stormed into the Castel Sant'Angelo, determined that, if he could not have Cesare, he would at least have the Princess Sancia. Sancia was radiant with delight, and instructed her maid to pack her possessions, while Prospero strode about her cell, raging against Cesare. 'Damn Cesare Borgia! May his rotten soul roast in the hottest fires of hell! Three hours we waited at the Porta del Popolo. He has betrayed us!'

'But if you have not Cesare, then why am I released? Who is Pope?'

'There is no Pope! No election! I have released you on my own authority. And Cesare Borgia has vanished like the demon that he is!'

Sancia happily attempted to soothe him. 'Then Rome's well rid of him,' she said. 'He has gone and I shall go to Naples and be your mistress. Who cares who's Pope?'

* * *

Giuliano Rovere, who had arrived in Rome to be present at the forthcoming Conclave to elect a new Pope, sat in his palace making calculations from a list which he held in his hand. 'Caraffa ... that will be nine votes ...' A knock on the door interrupted him. He looked up. 'Yes?' he said as his servant Giorgio appeared.

'A reverend monsignor requests an audience, Your Eminence.'

'That is not unusual,' Rovere told him dryly. 'He will make the fourteenth such caller since I returned to Rome. What is his name?'

'Cardinal Sforza, Eminence.'

Rovere was surprised but not pleased. 'Ascanio ...! He has returned as well. We must see.' He nodded to Giorgio. 'I shall see him at once.' Then, as Giorgio turned to go, 'When you have introduced the Cardinal, stay with me till I dismiss you. Is His Eminence alone?'

'Alone, Your Eminence,' Giorgio replied. He left the room, returning to usher in the tall figure of Ascanio Sforza.

Rovere's hard features broke into a wintry smile; he held out his hands, 'Ascanio! My dear friend!'

As the two Cardinals embraced, Giorgio slipped over to

the table where he had laid out a jug of wine and a cup, and broke the phial into the cup. Then he moved away silently and stood at the back of the room, eyes cast respectfully down, as the two men talked, or rather fenced with words.

'When did you reach Rome?' Rovere asked.

'Yesterday evening, Giuliano,' Sforza replied. 'They tell me you have been here three days.'

Rovere nodded. 'Yes.' But it scarcely seems a moment. After nine years I find I have so many friends.'

'You as well ...' Ascanio had seen Giorgio's movements over Giuliano's shoulder and decided to say nothing unless it suited him.

'You were welcomed?' There was more than a note of displeasure in Rovere's voice.

Sforza smiled. 'The enthusiasm was astonishing. As soon as the news was out, the street was filled with cheers. They cried "Sforza! Sforza!" It was quite deafening.'

'Indeed,' Rovere said politely, standing back and motioning Sforza to a chair. They both sat down. 'People are so glad to see Borgia gone,' he continued, 'it's hard to judge the mood ...' He beckoned to Giorgio. 'Bring the Cardinal a cup.' Then, turning back to Sforza, 'You must stay a little, Ascanio. There's urgent business to discuss.'

There was a pause as the two men looked at each other warily. Then Rovere began cautiously, 'You come with some instruction from the King. Concerning the election.'

'Yes,' Sforza replied blandly. 'His Majesty has released me to cast my vote for d'Amboise.'

'And will you?'

'No.'

Rovere smiled. 'Nor I. I have come to look to my own affairs, not other people's ...' Then he added boldly, 'I *knew* that I could count on you.'

Sforza bridled. 'That will, of course, depend.'

'On what?'

'On which of us obtains most votes. At the first ballot.'

'The first ballot. I see. I see ... I had not realised ...' He seemed preoccupied. Giorgio, approaching with the cup of wine ordered for Sforza, noticed this and, as if by accident,

267

placed it near his master's hand. 'Leave us,' Rovere told him as he picked up the cup. 'We drink then to success,' he said to Sforza. 'Either for you . . . or me . . .' He put the cup to his lips.

Ascanio Sforza had come to a quick decision. He put out a hand warningly. 'Not if you hope to live, old friend. That cup is poisoned.'

Rovere was aghast. 'Poisoned?' he said, lowering the cup and staring at it in horror.

'The hand of Cesare Borgia still reaches out to touch you . . . even now.' Rovere glanced towards the door, suspicion on his face. 'It may make a Pope,' Sforza went on, 'but you? Or I . . .?' He shrugged his shoulders in disbelief.

*   *   *

'Before the Conclave which was to elect our new Lord and Master was held,' Burchard wrote in his diary, 'it was generally believed that Duke Valentino would make Pope whom he willed, since he held in his hand the votes of those Cardinals whom his father Pope Alexander had made. And since the Duke went to Nepi under the protection of France, the Cardinal of France entertained high hopes that the Duke would favour him, and the Duke encouraged him in this, feeding him with promises until the day came for the Conclave. But in reality the Duke knew that he could not make all his Cardinals, who were for the most part Spaniards, vote for a Frenchman, for, although they feared the Duke, so also did they fear the King of Spain. Therefore, he instructed them that if they could not make one of their number, the Cardinal Vera, Pope, then they should choose an Italian acceptable to all, in order that neither the Cardinal Rovere nor the Cardinal Sforza should be elected, for they were his sworn enemies. And so the Borgia Cardinals joined with d'Amboise and Sforza against Rovere, who was leading on the first ballot, and they elected as Pope the Cardinal of Siena, Piccolomini, who took the title of Pius III, thus following his uncle, Pope Pius II, who had been the friend and protector of Rodrigo Borgia. Thus Pius II's nephew was greatly obligated to Rodrigo Borgia's son for his crown. And many were displeased with the outcome because the new Pope, though a good man, was old and infirm, and it was generally predicted that his reign would be a short one ...'

*　　*　　*

Pius III hobbled along the Vatican corridor leaning on a stick. He suffered from gout, and his face was weary with pain and also from embarrassment and irritation at being harried by Cardinal Rovere, who pursued him down the corridor, bombarding him with questions and accusations. 'If Your Holiness will only listen to me!' Rovere's voice shook with exasperation as he towered over the frail Pope.

'My dear Rovere,' Pius expostulated, 'it seems to me that since Matins I have been forced to do little else.'

'Yet Your Holiness will not explain ... You have sent papal briefs to the Romagna confirming the lordship of Cesare Borgia. And to Venice, warning them not to attack him ...'

'But I shall do nothing more,' Pius promised. 'What I have done for the Duke was under pressure from the Spanish Cardinals. Giuliano ...'

Rovere interrupted him fiercely. 'Your Holiness is aware that this is the man who tried to kill me. I know him as a murderer and an extortioner ...'

'Surely our love must go out even to sinners,' Pius said timidly. 'It is the duty of a Pope to have compassion for all.'

'You would let Cesare Borgia rule you as he ruled his father?' Rovere asked furiously.

Pius shook his head – he knew Rovere's temper of old. 'Giuliano,' he said soothingly, 'I gave some comfort to the Duke because I knew that by God's judgement he would come to a bad end. The French have left him and taken their army to Naples. His Spanish troops have left him to join their countrymen against the French. He is alone at Nepi with his family. And he is ill.'

'Cesare? Ill?' Rovere's voice was incredulous but hopeful.

'Very ill,' Pius replied. 'He has asked if he may come to Rome to die – and we have given him permission ...'

'Merciful God!' Rovere burst out.

Pius looked at him reprovingly. 'Surely we *should* show mercy towards a dying man. I do not see what harm can come of it ...' He turned and limped on his way down the passage.

Rovere shouted after him in a fury, 'Madness! He is not dying! It is all a lying trick! You will see ...!' As Pius disappeared into the distance, unheeding, Rovere turned away. Striking a nearby bust off its pedestal with a blow of his powerful fist, he roared in frustration, 'Cesare Borgia. In Rome!'

* * *

Pius extended his ring to a fit and confident Cesare to kiss. 'They told me you were dying,' he said, mortified.

'Your Holiness ... my return to Rome has greatly aided my recovery – with the care of my family who accompany me.'

But Pius was still unhappy. 'Well ... I am only a man – and liable to err,' he muttered to himself.

'I am concerned for your well-being as well, Holy Father,' Cesare said cordially.

Pius lifted his shoulders in a despairing gesture. 'The surgeons have done for us what they can ... but we can no longer kneel to God to offer thanks for our election ...'

'I hope *I* had some part in that,' Cesare interjected meaningly.

'Yes, yes. And we are mindful of it. But don't ask for anything more, we beg. The support we have already given you has cost us quite enough,' Pius said repressively, then, beckoning Cesare to come closer, he said in a low voice. 'Cardinal Rovere believes you tried to kill him.'

Cesare feigned surprise. 'On what evidence?'

'That of a servant.'

'Under torture ... I'm sorry Your Holiness does not wish

to listen to my requests. I came to ask . . .' He paused, as if confused. 'But it would embarrass Your Holiness were I to offer . . .'

'Offer?' Pius' voice was wary but eager. 'Offer what?'

'Something of the expenses for Your Holiness' coronation. It seems the treasury is empty . . .'

'Of everything but debts,' Pius said resentfully. 'We found the cupboards bare. Everything had gone.'

Cesare shook his head regretfully. 'My father had many enemies . . .'

'But he was a good friend to my uncle, Pius II, who owed him the tiara . . .' Again he beckoned to Cesare, his voice confidential. 'Cesare . . . we cannot be crowned. What are we to do? We must have a coronation – even of the simplest kind. But the cost is terrible . . .'

Cesare bowed in sympathetic acknowledgement. 'Holiness. If it would not offend you – borrow from me. A hundred thousand ducats. More if you require.'

Pius smiled, greatly relieved. 'You are a good son to us, Cesare – as your father was to our uncle. We will accept your loan. *Deo gratias*.'

Cesare bowed again. 'Holiness, it will give me great pleasure. And so I may not embarrass Your Holiness further with my presence here – I would leave for the Romagna. I must regain the cities my enemies have taken. I need only a safe-conduct – and your confirmation of my appointment as Captain-General of the Church.'

'As Captain-General?' Pius asked, smiling. 'To be announced . . . at my coronation! Go, my son, with our blessing,' he made the sign of the cross as Cesare knelt before him. 'And God deliver us from our enemies.'

* * *

Giulio Orsini and Gian Paolo Baglioni, both heavily armed, thrust their way into Rovere's palace, elbowing the terrified servants aside. It was after midnight, and Rovere was about to retire; he looked up in surprise and consternation as the door burst open, and the two men came in to kneel at his feet. 'Eminence,' Giulio Orsini cried, picking up the hem of Rovere's robe to kiss it.

'Grant us absolution!' Baglioni chorused, bowing his head in a melodramatic manner. 'Judge us, Eminence, for a deed that must be done.'

Rovere put down the candlestick he was carrying and dismissed the servants. 'This is God's work,' he said piously. 'Leave these gentlemen to me.' Then, when the servants had withdrawn, casting uncertain glances at the two armed men, he asked, 'Why have you come?'

Gian Paolo spoke first. 'We must kill Cesare Borgia.'

'Tonight,' Giulio added.

Rovere smiled indulgently. 'That may indeed be God's work,' he said, extending his hands in a pastoral gesture, beckoning them to rise. 'But I can grant no absolution for a deed that is not yet done ... How will it be accomplished?'

'I've come to Rome with armed men,' Baglioni said eagerly.

Giulio chimed in, 'Our Orsini followers and Gian Paolo's together are ...'

'More than a thousand,' Gian Paolo finished for him.

'Cesare is alone,' Giulio said with satisfaction; 'only a handful of his own people are with him.'

'... And Michelotto and his troops have left for the Romagna,' Gian Paolo added.

Rovere laid a hand on each of their shoulders. 'I cannot give my blessing,' he said. 'You must search your souls for reason sufficient in the eyes of God.'

'The murder of my uncle the Cardinal and of my brother Paolo Orsini,' Giulio said savagely.

'And of our comrade Vitelli,' Gian Paolo interjected.

Rovere bowed his head gravely. 'God knows it is enough.' He looked into their eyes. 'This time,' he said sternly, 'see there is no mistake.'

* * *

Yelling 'Death to the Borgias! Death to the Spanish Jews!' Giulio and Gian Paolo spurred their followers on to the

Vatican gates. Behind them a crowd of Roman rabble, scenting blood, echoed their cries, while Gian Paolo called on the Vatican guard to open the gates.

Their shouting woke Jofre who ran to rouse Cesare, lying asleep in bed with the Greek girl, Vasia, by his side. 'Cesare ... don't you hear them? There's a huge crowd calling for your blood at the gates – they're armed.'

Cesare sat up, immediately alert, and, leaping out of bed, pulled on his clothes. 'How many?' he asked quickly.

'It's the Orsinis. Thousands of them ...'

Cesare pulled Vasia awake by her hair. 'Rouse everyone! My mother! The children! You understand?' he commanded her. 'Jofre ...'

'Yes, Cesare.'

'We'll take horses from the stables. There may be fewer of the mob on that side. There's no one to defend us here. We must break out.' He picked up his sword-belt, buckling it on.

'Where shall we go?' Jofre asked him.

'Spoleto. To join Michelotto – if we escape the city.' He moved over to Jofre. 'You're with me? There's no one else.'

Jofre looked at his brother, eyes sparkling and cheeks flushed with excitement and pride. 'You and I alone ...' he said, 'together!'

The roar of the crowd shouting 'Death to the Borgias' was deafening as they mounted their horses in the stable courtyard and moved up to the gates, a small party of Borgia troops following on foot.

'Stay close!' Cesare shouted to Jofre. 'As soon as the gates are opened – ride straight at them. Go like mad dogs and scatter them. You hear?'

'Open up,' Cesare commanded the guard on the gate. The Borgia troops drew back the great iron bolts and pushed back the gates, struggling against the pressure of the crowd without.

'Now!' Cesare shouted.

He and Jofre spurred their horses forward into the angry mob beyond, the Borgia troops following to engage the Orsini men-at-arms.

'Ride on! Ride on!' Cesare yelled at his brother, hacking right and left with his sword. But Jofre's horse was held back in the *mêlée* just outside the gate and Cesare, seeing this, turned back to help his brother. The two Borgias were now locked in the crush, striking desperately at a forest of hands attempting to drag them down, their swords streaming with blood, cries of pain and anger rising around them. On the edge of the crowd a party of Orsini horsemen appeared, distracted from the main gate by the tumult, with Giulio Orsini and Gian Paolo Baglioni at their head.

'He's there! Cesare!' Baglioni yelled, pointing with his sword.

Cesare heard him, looked up for an instant and saw them blocking his way to freedom. 'Back!' he shouted to Jofre. 'To the gates!' He headed for the gates, now closed, and without hesitation leapt from his saddle to the top as Baglioni and Orsini forced their horses through the crowds towards him. Jofre too attempted to jump up onto the gate, but failed and hung by the hands. As Baglioni and Orsini reached the foot of the gate, Cesare managed to pull Jofre up after him and both dropped down to safety on the far side.

Cesare got up, dusting himself. 'You're injured?' he asked Jofre solicitously, picking his brother up. Jofre shook his head. 'No escape now, little brother Borgia,' Cesare said grimly as the mob battered at the gates.

'Sanctuary . . .' Jofre gasped. 'The Holy Father . . .'

'That imbecile,' Cesare said impatiently. Then, shrugging, 'Who else?' He turned, followed by Jofre, and ran through the courtyard towards the palace.

Behind them the crowd roared, certain of their prey, 'Death to the Borgias!'

*   *   *

Pius lay half-conscious attended by a surgeon and his chamberlain. He was exalted by pain and drugs and seemed not to recognise Cesare as he leant over him. In the distance the roar of the mob could be clearly heard.

'Holy Father ...' Cesare said urgently.

'You hear them?' Pius mumbled.

'My enemies are at the gate ...'

'*Dominus illuminatio mea* ... We are surrounded by a cloud of glory ...' the old man muttered, a seraphic smile lighting up his pale face.

Cesare glanced impatiently at the surgeon. 'My Lord ... the infection's spread. I've infused mandragora to relieve the pain,' the man explained.

Cesare turned back to the bed. 'Holy Father!' he insisted.

At last Pius seemed to hear him. 'Yes, my dear son,' he whispered.

'I place myself and my family under your protection. We shall take refuge in Castel Sant'Angelo. The loan is safe – if you save *us*!'

'My trust is in the Lord. Whom shall I fear?' the Pope replied enigmatically.

Cesare looked puzzled. 'I must be certain ...'

'*Quem timebo* ... No fear ... no fear ...' Pius closed his eyes and seemed to drift off as it were on a cloud of his own imagining.

'He's in danger?' Cesare asked the surgeon sharply.

'A little sleep. He needs to rest. All will be well,' the man reassured him, bending over his patient.

Cesare straightened up, relieved, and turned to the chamberlain. 'Go to the gates,' he ordered, 'and tell that mob the Borgia apartments are empty. We'll slip away under their feet – through the catacombs of the basilica ...'

Cesare sent word for all the family to meet round an open sarcophagus in the crypt of St Peter's, from which a flight of steps led to a secret passage. Jofre stepped into the tomb, followed by Vasia and Vannozza carrying the sleeping Rodrigo in her arms. Giovanni went after her, a small monkey clinging to his shoulder. He hesitated as he looked down into the dark passage below. 'Giovanni ... you're not afraid?' Cesare asked him.

The boy shook his head. 'I'm a Borgia,' he said, stroking the monkey. 'And Cicero's not afraid either – as long as he's with me.'

Cesare took his hand, leading the way for him. 'Come. We must be quick,' he said. 'In Sant'Angelo I'll show you the great cannon on the battlements.'

*   *   *

Cesare and Jofre stood on the battlements of Sant'Angelo looking east over the city to where dawn was just beginning to show at the edges of the horizon. The sound of the crowd was fainter now. 'They'll grow tired by morning,' Cesare said. He looked down at the cannon at his feet. 'I held this fortress against the French. Why should I fear a rabble of Orsini braggarts?' Then he glanced at Jofre with a new appreciation. 'You might have made a soldier . . .' he said.

'If you had needed me.'

Cesare looked back towards the Vatican, his voice heartening. 'They'll soon be gone. We'll join Michelotto in Cesena. They've been loyal . . . I have the Holy Father in my pocket – and that's the key to all the rest. As it was. Is now . . . And ever shall be . . .'

A bell boomed harshly in the distance. 'What's that?' Cesare asked sharply.

'I think it's coming from the Capitol,' Jofre said.

'But they need no bell to rouse the city . . .' Cesare said, puzzled.

Then, as the bell continued to toll, a terrible realisation dawned upon them both. Jofre gripped Cesare's arm in sudden panic. 'Cesare! La Paterina!'

Cesare threw back his head and bellowed at the stars, crying in the face of fortune, 'No . . .! That imbecile! Why did he have to die now?'

10

'Caesar or Nothing'

THE SOFT OCTOBER sun bathed the battlements of
Sant'Angelo in its golden light, a blue autumn haze hung
over the quiet city and in the distance a bell tolled.
Giovanni Borgia sat astride a great bronze bombard watching Cesare, who stood at the edge of the battlements, looking down over the city. 'If the Orsinis come again,'
Giovanni asked Cesare, 'may I fire this bombard?' Cesare
did not answer, seeming not to have heard him, but
Giovanni continued his questioning, 'My Lord? Why have
your enemies all gone away?'

'To elect a Pope ...' Cesare turned and looked at his
nephew. 'They fight so fiercely amongst themselves they
have no powder left for me.' He moved over to the gun and
stood looking down at it, his hand caressing the barrel, his
voice musing. 'I heard the guns defend this castle when I
was still a child. Your mother was afraid...'

'My mother?' Giovanni's voice was puzzled. Cesare,
realising that he had revealed more than he intended,
looked up at the boy and merely nodded, saying nothing. 'I
never saw her.' Giovanni said. 'My father, the Holy Father,
told me she was beautiful.'

'Yes,' Cesare said, 'very beautiful.'

He looked down at the gun again. 'And she was afraid,'
Giovanni went on.

Cesare nodded. 'I told her I would become a soldier and
defend her. I told her I would be King of all Italy!' He
looked up and met the child's eyes. 'Giovanni, they shall
not take it away from me,' he said fiercely. 'Now, when I
had almost...!' He brought his fist down hard on the barrel

277

of the gun. 'God is the enemy who cheats us. Death is the game He plays – but I'll defeat Him ... We'll make our name immortal. You'll be a soldier, too.'

Giovanni nodded, a little shocked at Cesare's hostile reference to God. 'Yes. But I don't think God should be our enemy. I don't think my mother would have told you that. I would have been her soldier. I'm sorry I never knew her.'

Cesare's smile held a hint of sadness. 'I shall be sorry if you never do ...' he said. Then, looking up, he saw Jofre who stood at the entrance to the battlements.

'If I never ...?' Giovanni asked him. But Cesare had already turned and was walking towards Jofre at the door. 'Where do you go, My Lord?'

'To meet my enemy,' Cesare told him. 'Not God, Giovanni – if luck goes with me!' He pointed downwards. 'My enemy here below – Cardinal Giuliano Rovere...'

*   *   *

Giuliano Rovere was waiting for Cesare in the Pope's privy chamber. Suspicious of treachery and angry at being kept waiting, he was pacing the room, shouting at Cardinal Vera who stood patient under his verbal assaults. 'You told me he had agreed to meet with me!' Rovere bellowed at him.

'Your Eminence, he did,' Vera replied in a soothing tone.

'An hour since he should have been here! Cesare Borgia shall not trifle with me now. It is an insult and I shall not endure it ...' He broke off as Cesare entered the room, accompanied by Jofre. 'You were not here, My Lord,' he said angrily to Cesare, 'at the time agreed.'

Cesare bowed. 'A mortification of the spirit,' he said with cool mockery. 'I was impatient to see you and compelled myself to wait.'

'And you believe that you can mock me still?' Giuliano said between his teeth.

'Should I have been impatient?' Cesare's voice was calm. 'We have a knife, Giuliano, each at the other's throat!' He held up his hand, palm down, fingers level, 'Keep your hand steady then. As mine is.'

With an effort, Rovere mastered his anger. 'My Lord . . .'
he forced a mirthless smile, 'you put it well. Eleven years
ago your father cheated me of the triple crown. Now I
believe that God has spoken plainly through the death of
Pius. He intends me for the office of St Peter – and this time
it *shall* be mine!'

'Eleven votes,' Cesare said evenly. 'God's will depends
on that.'

'Made manifest through the wills of men . . .'

'Those votes are mine!' Cesare reminded him emphatically. Then, turning to Vera, 'The Spanish Cardinals are
loyal still?'

'To you, My Lord,' Vera answered pointedly.

'Those votes are mine. Why should I give them to you,
Giuliano? Can you tell me that?' he challenged Rovere.

'For the Romagna,' Rovere's voice was urbane. 'The
papal cities that were yours – but are now falling every day.
The rulers you took them from are coming back – to
Urbino, to Rimini. You may not have heard,' he paused for
greater effect, 'even yesterday Giovanni Sforza recaptured
the citadel of Pesaro.'

Cesare's jaw muscles twitched in a momentary spasm
of anger at this humiliation. 'Giovanni Sforza!' he thought
to himself. 'Who couldn't take my sister – naked – as a
bride . . .!' With an effort he controlled himself. He must
show nothing. Not at this moment. Not to Rovere. 'Yes. It is
true. Each of us has a knife, Eminence. Very well . . . Eleven
votes, Lord Cardinal. For the Romagna.'

An expression of ineffable delight suffused Rovere's
imperial features as he realised that now, at last, he had
reached the moment of triumph. 'When . . . I am Pope!' his
voice was almost reverent in his joy.

Cesare allowed him time to savour his triumph, then he
went on to lay down his terms. 'You will confirm me in my
appointment as Captain-General of the Church. You will
confirm me as the Lord of Cesena and Forlì – and of all the
cities my enemies have taken from me.' He opened his arms
wide in a gesture of friendship, looking Rovere full in the
face with a winning smile. 'We have been enemies,

Giuliano. Think now only of what we might do together!'
He unsheathed the knife at his belt and threw it on the table
between them. 'My knife is there. Will you give me your
hand?'

For a moment, Rovere hesitated warily, then he said,
holding out his hand, 'God's will be done.'

Cesare clasped his hand with a shout of triumph. 'And
we shall act together! Against our enemies!'

Giuliano smiled, a frosty smile.

*   *   *

'We have joined hands to seal our agreement, Michelotto,'
Cesare said. 'Why should I not believe him?' His voice was
enthusiastic, excited at the prospect of renewed action, as
he and Michelotto stood at the table spread with maps, in
his old apartments to which he had returned after Giuliano
Rovere's election as Pope Julius ii. Michelotto shrugged,
but said nothing, staring down at the map which Cesare
had just unrolled. 'You'll take the artillery by way of Arezzo
to Cesena,' Cesare said. 'The Rocca of Forlì is secure for the
present. It's the castellans of Cesena who need our help.'

'Then I must pass by Florence,' Michelotto said slowly,
brooding over the map.

'You have the Pope's authority . . .' Then, as Michelotto
looked at him sceptically, he went on vehemently,
'Michelotto, he was *always* a man of honour. Why should he
break his oath to me?'

Michelotto raised his eyebrows. 'Because you tried to kill
him?'

'You tried to kill *me* once!'

'But then, My Lord, it paid me to let you go.'

'And I have paid him!' Cesare moved away from the
table and stood beside Vasia, watching her try on a necklace before the mirror. 'I tell you, Michelotto, he will keep
his bargain. He needs me in the Romagna against the state
of Venice. No one in Italy has the power that I hold, no
one!' He suddenly grabbed the necklace at Vasia's neck to
swing her round to him. It broke, pearls scattering to the

floor. Vasia's eyes widened in dismay as she looked at him
before kneeling to pick them up. Cesare frowned, and said
nothing for a moment. Then he went on, an angry note in
his voice, 'You will pass by Florence and I shall follow you.
It may be I'll go first to my sister's court at Ferrara.
Madonna Lucrezia is sending fifteen hundred men.' He got
up and went over to grip Michelotto by the shoulder. 'His
Holiness has promised a safe-conduct. So, Michelotto – I
shall see you again. In Cesena.' He smiled.

Michelotto did not return his smile, but merely bowed
slightly and moved to the door. 'Or yet in hell,' he said.
Then he turned as he reached the door, before going out.
'His Holiness, I'm sure, has a safe-conduct!'

'He gave his word ...' Cesare began, but the door had
already closed behind Michelotto. He reached out a hand
to grasp Vasia by the hair as she knelt and dragged her to
him, pressing her face to his thigh. 'To me. He gave it ...'

*   *   *

'I'll see him before he celebrates Mass! I shall not wait!'
Cesare pushed past protesting guards and chamberlains
into the Pope's apartments, where Rovere was being robed
by attendant priests. 'I'll see him now!' he shouted furiously.

Rovere, his back to him, did not turn, merely saying with
calm authority, 'We are preparing for our devotions, My
Lord Duke ...'

Cesare interrupted him, waving a letter at his impassive
back. 'A safe-conduct has been refused! Florence refuses to
let me pass. You swore ...'

Rovere's voice was cold. 'We refused you nothing. It is
the Florentines who will decide.'

'You have betrayed me!' Cesare shouted at him. 'Under
the terms of our agreement it was sworn – you swore to
confirm me as Captain-General of the Holy See! It was your
oath ...'

'Be silent!' Rovere swung round upon him, cope flying,
hand held high in papal authority. He stepped down from

the dais on which he stood to face Cesare. 'By our divine authority we command you to guard your tongue! Hear what we say, My Lord, for you have forced yourself into the communion between ourselves and God. You ask for confirmation of your appointment and we shall grant it as we agreed ...'

'But you do *not*!' Cesare cried in an agony of exasperation.

Rovere ignored him. 'Upon the instant you submit yourself in obedience to Holy Church. How else can you become her soldier? Therefore, My Lord, as token of this obedience, you will surrender to us the citadels of Cesena and Forlì.'

'Never! I shall never ...'

'Then we have done,' Rovere replied firmly. 'No more! Till God shall purge you of this defiance.' Imperiously, he swept past Cesare, the terrified priests in his wake.

'Serpent and minister of hell!' Cesare shouted after him. 'Liar and hypocrite!' He made as if to follow Rovere out, but stopped as he almost collided with his brother on the threshold. Jofre was accompanied by a Spanish-looking man in riding clothes.

'Cesare ...' Jofre said.

For a moment, Cesare, his features working with rage, seemed almost not to notice them. 'He's cheated me!' he shouted. 'I'll denounce him. Even in the basilica ...' Then he saw the expression on their faces and stopped. 'Don Jaime,' he said, looking at Jofre's companion. Then, sharply, 'What is it?'

'My Lord Duke ...' The man stopped, his voice shook.

Jofre spoke for him. 'He's ridden from Arezzo. Michelotto and his forces were intercepted.'

Don Jaime recovered his voice. 'By a large troop, My Lord, from Florence.'

'Michelotto?'

'They captured the artillery,' Don Jaime told him. 'Don Miguel's arrested ...'

Cesare turned pale as death; for a moment he seemed petrified to the spot. Then he bellowed, 'Under the oath of God ... Treachery!' He pushed past them to fling out of the doors, but guards moved forward to bar his way. 'Let me pass!' he shouted at them. The men, immovable, said nothing. Cesare looked across their halberds lowered in his path, into the face of the Captain of the papal guard. Realisation of his predicament dawned upon him. 'So ...' he said slowly under his breath, 'Michelotto and I ... two caged birds ...'

* * *

Cesare was taken, under guard, to the apartments that had once been Lucrezia's. With grim irony, no doubt intentional on the part of the Pope, he was confined to the very room in the Torre Borgia in which Alfonso Biselli had died at his orders, only three years before. Here, after midnight, Vanozza visited him. 'Cesare?' Her voice was frightened. 'They've confined you to this room?' She could not see her son's expression by the light of the single candle.

'It's enough,' he said shortly. 'You had my letter?' As she nodded, he glanced warningly at the door. 'Keep your voice low,' he told her.

'I've done as you said,' she whispered. 'The deeds of my house in Rome. I've given them to the church of Santa Maria. I have the use of it during my lifetime. But he'd not dare to rob the church ...'

'The chests for Lucrezia?' Cesare asked.

'Two waggonloads for Ferrara. Pray God she'll have them safe.'

'There's still the gold with the bankers of Genoa ...'

'Three hundred thousand ducats. Your father held it for such a moment. But I'd not believe then ...' Vannozza stopped, on the verge of tears.

Cesare took her hands, reassuring her. 'It is not lost,' he told her. 'Nothing is lost yet. Even now I could have my freedom – if I'd yield him Cesena and Forlì. But I shall not!'

'What will you do then?' Vannozza looked at him, wondering.

'Cheat him – as he cheated me,' Cesare said simply. Then he led her over to the bed. 'You see how I sleep here – my sword at my side ... Giuliano lied to me – but I shall make him pay for it. I'll take my freedom and give him nothing in return ...' He bent and picked up the sword, holding it out to her. 'You remember this?'

Vannozza nodded. 'You had it made for France.'

Cesare looked down at the blade, reading out the inscription like an incantation – to himself. '*Aut Caesar aut Nihil* ... Caesar – or nothing. I'll escape from Rome. I'll make an alliance with the Venetians – or with the devil! But I shall win ...' He fell silent, staring at the sword, his symbol.

Vannozza interrupted his reverie with a question of practical interest to herself. 'Jofre? And the children?'

'They've fled to Naples,' Cesare answered shortly, as if their fate were of minor importance compared to his own. He moved over to the window, looking out into the dark winter night. 'I've sent a message to Gonsalvo de Cordoba there. He's a fine soldier, a true Spaniard. If he'd receive me ...' There was a sound outside the room. Vannozza raised her hand in warning. Cesare looked at her briefly. 'They change the guard ...' Then he turned back to the window, facing the darkness again as if he could see the light of dawn. 'I have a plan,' he told her. 'Nothing is lost yet. Do you remember whose room this was?' He turned back to look at her. She shook her head. 'Alfonso Biselli's – when he was married to Lucrezia.'

Vanozza quailed. 'This room?' she whispered.

Cesare nodded. 'You see then. I am confined here for a purpose. It is the room in which he died.'

Vanozza crossed herself. '*Virgo Maria ...*'

'Lucrezia forgave me,' Cesare said quietly. 'I had a reason ... Caesar or nothing ...' He turned again to the window. 'She trusts me still. And I trust her. I have written to her about the waggons. And about my plans. I shall give Giuliano what he wants – the citadels of Cesena and Forlì. He will release me as he promised and I shall ride to Ostia and take ship for Naples – before His Holiness finds out that I have tricked him. The castellans of the fortresses have secret orders not to give them up because my promise to the Pope was given under duress. He turned to her, smiling with satisfaction at the cleverness of his plan. 'I should like to see Giuliano's face when he finds out. But by that time I shall be on the sea bound for Naples ...'

*   *   *

Cesare's plan worked, as he had expected it would. Although the galleys promised from Naples to fetch him could not leave port because of contrary winds, he escaped from Ostia, accompanied by Don Jaime, and took to the sea in a small rowing boat, heading south. By the spring, he was in Naples, riding into the courtyard of Jofre's house, his heart full of hope again to be welcomed by Jofre and Lucrezia's children, Rodrigo and Giovanni. 'My Lord!' Giovanni cried eagerly as Cesare bent to embrace them, 'did you cheat the Pope?'

Cesare smiled. 'He has bought Cesena – for six thousand ducats. The fortress of Forlì is still mine.' He took two ducats from the purse at his belt and gave one to each of the boys.

'Then I *can* be a soldier!' little Rodrigo said, delighted.

'And fight for the name of Borgia,' Cesare told him. As soon as the children had run off to show their coins to their tutor, he turned to Jofre. 'Have you spoken to the Viceroy – Gonsalvo de Cordoba?' he asked eagerly. His manner was excited and nervous, and he paced the hall as though unable to contain his energy. 'He's proved himself to be the greatest soldier under the flag of Spain. I'd rather fight for him than for any man I know of.' He swung round to look at Jofre. 'And I can help him. He can save me.' He noticed Jofre's hesitation. 'You *have* spoken to him. He's refused.' His voice was flat with disappointment.

Jofre shook his head.

'Then what?' Cesare said sharply. 'You're shuffling like a barbary ape! What has Gonsalvo said of me?'

'It isn't you ...'

'Then what?'

'It's Sancia.'

Cesare was surprised. 'Sancia? She came to Naples with Prospero Colonna. What has she ...'

285

'She's left Prospero.' Jofre took Cesare's arm, speaking quickly and angrily, seeking reassurance from his brother. 'I have been humiliated. Everyone in Naples knows. I want you to go to Sancia and tell her ...'

Cesare shook him off impatiently. 'She's a whore! Why do we talk of Sancia? The beggars of Naples may roll her on a dungcart for all I care!' Then he took Jofre by the shoulders as if he would like to shake him. 'It's Gonsalvo I have to speak to. What in the name of lechery has Sancia to do with that?'

Jofre stared back at him. 'She's his mistress.'

'What?' Cesare released Jofre and turned away, his face troubled.

'Yes, it's true,' Jofre went on. 'He's given her an apartment in the Castel Nuovo. Since I'm her husband Gonsalvo won't engage me – Cesare, please,' his voice became pleading, 'if you would only speak to her.'

Cesare seemed to have recovered his confidence. He smiled. 'Don't worry, little brother,' he said, 'I shall speak to her. And soon. Is she still as beautiful ...?'

*   *   *

Sancia lay elegantly composed upon a divan covered with Oriental silks. Below the delicate white marble tracery of the windows, the May sun glittered on the waters of the Bay of Naples, reflections of its light dappling her warm skin. The faintest of smiles played about her sensuous mouth as she watched Cesare, sitting beside her, gallantly peeling a peach with a silver knife. 'Cesare Borgia ...' she mused in her rich voice. She paused to take the peach as he offered it to her, licking a drop of juice from it with a cat-like movement of her tongue before taking a slow bite of the fruit. 'I'm glad you have come to see me. It's been so long...'

'Too long,' Cesare said, smiling.

'But then ... you were away,' she said silkily. 'I was in prison ...'

'Through my father,' Cesare said sympathetically, 'that terrible old man.'

'Yes. He was. Terrible,' Sancia agreed, imperturbable. She indicated the fruit bowl with her eyes. Obediently, Cesare reached for another peach and began to peel it for her. 'Gonsalvo obtains these for me,' she went on. 'I dote on peaches ... How strange that we should meet again in Naples. When you remember ...'

She paused. Cesare looked at her warily. 'When you remember what? he asked.

'That Naples was the cause of everything that's come between us.' She paused again.

Cesare continued to watch her closely. 'You mean your brother's death,' he said.

'Alfonso's murder,' she corrected him. 'Yes. And other things.'

Cesare's face betrayed no emotion. His voice when he spoke was reasonable. 'It wasn't for Naples that I killed my *own* brother,' he said. 'It was the lie you told me that led to the death of Juan.'

Sancia sighed. 'I was very angry with Juan. And with you too. I didn't know it was a lie. I thought it might be true.'

Cesare said earnestly, his tone conciliatory, 'I will forgive you for your part in Juan's death – if you forgive me for Alfonso's. There are things we both regret. Will you?'

Sancia's eyes widened slightly, then returned to their normal rather bored expression. 'Curious ...' she said. Then she reached out to touch Cesare's hair, as if to re-assure herself that he was real. 'That's what I love about you, Cesare,' she went on; 'you make life so simple. Like a little boy. And the games you played – you and Juan and Lucrezia – were only the games of children. Except that naughty children are sent to bed. Which in your case wouldn't ...'

She stopped as he offered her a slice of the peach. When she went on her tone changed again, there was a lazy, sensual note in her voice as she began to unlace her bodice. 'How tight it is. Because I wanted to please you. Now I've eaten too much ...' She pulled at the silk ties with her long fingers, the flesh beginning to show right down to the waist. 'Did you enjoy the sea salad?' Cesare nodded, the slice of peach still poised between his fingers. 'Gonsalvo has found me the best cook in the whole of Naples. And with squid . . .' She settled herself comfortably back on the pillows, her breasts naked in front of him. 'There's really nothing else one could wish for. Do you think?'

For once Cesare was hesitant. 'Yes. There is . . . something else . . .'

'I know. You want me to speak for you to Gonsalvo.'

'Yes.' Then, fearing he had revealed himself too quickly, 'That is . . .'

Sancia's eyebrows arched teasingly. 'And to make love to me of course.' She caught his hand as it went to her breast, warding him off. 'But then. There is Gonsalvo . . .'

'To the devil with Gonsalvo.'

Sancia smiled in mock reproof. 'Impulsive and generous boy. But we must be grown up. And since you can't behave – then I shall.' Graciously, she finally accepted the slice of peach, eating it from his fingers as he held it to her mouth. 'So. I shall ask Gonsalvo to see you. And to be kind. And in return . . . You will do something for me . . .' Cesare looked at her apprehensively. 'Aren't you going to ask me what?' she went on.

'What am I to do for you?'

'Give me a child.'

'No.'

She laughed at his questioning look. 'Not that way. We tried often enough before. The child I want is a little boy you brought to Naples. Alfonso's child.'

'Rodrigo?'

Sancia nodded. 'He is a child of the house of Aragon so he should come to me. Giovanni is a Borgia.' She smiled maliciously. 'Really it's impossible to be more Borgia than Giovanni . . .' Then, as he looked thunderous, 'Well we won't speak of that – for dear Lucrezia's sake. But Rodrigo *should* be mine. Will you give him to me?'

Cesare nodded. Sancia watched him from the pillows, her lids heavy. 'How long I've wanted to have a child,' she went on. 'It could have been yours ...' Her voice took on a caressing tone. 'Did you want very much to make love to me? How sad life is. Once I would have let you love and love me ... And now I can't.'

But Cesare, single-minded and bent on his own concerns, was not interested in such speculation. He leaned towards her, speaking urgently. 'Speak to Gonsalvo. I believe that I can serve him – and the King of Spain. I have a stronghold in the Romagna. All that I need is the ships and guns. I'll find the men. Sancia – you must tell him – for all that there has been between us ...' He grasped her hand and knelt before her.

'Yes,' Sancia said slowly and distinctly. 'For all that. I give my word ...' Cesare looked up at her searchingly, trying to fathom the expression in her eyes. 'Yes,' she said again, 'for all that has passed. Gonsalvo *will* see you ...'

*   *   *

Gonsalvo de Cordoba, Viceroy of the kingdom of Naples for King Ferdinand of Spain, known as *El Gran Capitan* for his military prowess, looked up at Cesare from the table at which he sat writing, his lean, handsome features composed, betraying nothing. 'The Princess Sancia spoke well of you. She's a noble lady.'

Cesare bowed with a courteous smile. 'And beautiful. The Prince her husband begged me to recommend his service to you.'

Gonsalvo looked faintly surprised. 'It would not insult him?' he asked.

'Your relations with his wife will not affect the Prince at all,' Cesare assured him. 'He delights only in her happiness.'

'I see ... I am most grateful to Your Excellency.' Gonsalvo glanced at a paper which he held in his hand. 'As to this letter ...'

'From the citizens of Pisa.' Cesare jumped up and began to pace the room. 'They call on me to release them from the oppression of the Florentines. I need ships. I need artillery.

And if I win ...' he turned and looked at Gonsalvo, 'Pisa will need a Lord.'

Gonsalvo returned his look steadily. 'Yourself?' he asked blandly.

'I am Lord of the Romagna.' Cesare swung himself back into the chair opposite the Viceroy. 'Each of us, Gonsalvo, has conquered Naples. I took it from its King – you from the French. You rule it now for Ferdinand of Spain – as its Viceroy, *El Gran Capitan*, the greatest soldier. What have you for yourself?'

'I was not born a Prince.'

'Then do not serve one – except for your own ends. I never served a man – even a King – for any other cause. I will serve you, Gonsalvo, if you will help me. And make you Lord of Pisa.' He paused, his eyes on Gonsalvo's face. 'What do you say?'

Gonsalvo did not answer directly. He rose from his chair and moved over to the window. 'It's an enterprise that will prove expensive,' was all he said.

'I have the money,' Cesare assured him. 'And I will find the men. Three thousand ...'

Gonsalvo remained standing at the window, his back to Cesare. 'You require ships and artillery ...' Cesare nodded. 'When should they be ready? Gonsalvo asked.

'A month from today.'

'Eight ships will be sufficient.'

'Eight is enough. And guns. You have *them* in plenty.' He got up and strode across the room to stand behind the Viceroy. 'In the devil's name, Gonsalvo,' he pleaded, 'you didn't let me come to Naples to see the view! I've waited long enough. Give me your word!'

Gonsalvo turned to look at him. For a moment he hesitated, as if the decision he was about to take was a hard one for him. Finally he said, 'Come when you are ready. A month from today.'

Cesare's face lit up as he gripped Gonsalvo's hand. 'A month from today then ...'

*   *   *

Faithful to his promise, Cesare went on the appointed day to the Viceroy's palace, the Castel Nuovo, to take his leave of Gonsalvo on the eve of his departure for Pisa. Everything was ready: the galleys provided by Gonsalvo lay at the quayside, the guns, also loaned by the Viceroy, were already aboard; the following morning, Cesare's cavalry and foot-soldiers would embark. Exhilarated at the certain prospect of action after long months of doubt, Cesare entered the Viceroy's room eagerly. He was surprised to find it empty. He turned questioningly to one of Gonsalvo's officers who accompanied him. 'We sail by morning. The Viceroy asked me to call on him before embarking to say farewell. It's the hour agreed on. Two days before the month, it's true ...'

The officer said politely, 'The Viceroy sends his apologies. If you will wait ...'

'I'd wait for no other man,' Cesare told him. 'But he's a soldier of honour. He said he'd be here and *El Gran Capitan* is not a man to break his word.' He made a gesture of dismissal. 'There is no need for you to stay.' But the officer did not move. 'Do you think I'd steal the silver? Cesare asked angrily. Then, a sudden fear gripping him, he glanced quickly round the room, his hand flying to his sword-hilt, sensing a trap. 'I shall not stay to serve his pleasure,' he said shortly and moved towards the door. As he did so, it opened and Prospero Colonna stepped into the room. Cesare fell back in surprise. 'Prospero ... what are you here for? Sancia betrayed you ...'

Prospero did not reply, but made a signal with his head. As he did so, six armed men appeared in the door-way. Cesare gave a fearful shout, '*Santa Maria*! With me alone has My Lord Gonsalvo dealt unfaithfully!' He drew his sword and moved forward threateningly. 'Let me pass.'

'His sword,' Prospero gave the brief order. The armed soldiers seized Cesare, taking his sword from him and pinning him to the wall.

'You'll kill me!' Cesare cried to Prospero.

'No ... but I'll be even with you, Cesare Borgia. You

were to meet me – you remember? At Vespers at the gate of Rome,' Prospero replied.

'Have you Gonsalvo's orders . . .?' Cesare's voice was still unbelieving. He broke off as Sancia appeared in the doorway.

She moved gracefully towards him and stood in front of him, her voice caressing. 'Cesare Borgia . . . who killed my brother. Thank you for his child.' Delicately and accurately, she spat in his face.

*   *   *

Cesare lay sweating and feverish on a pallet in the cell known as 'The Oven' under the leads of the Castel Nuovo, a place specifically designed as a high security prison, being on a rocky islet just offshore, and to make important prisoners especially uncomfortable. It was high summer and the heat was appalling. Vasia wore only a light linen shift as she sponged Cesare's half-naked body, but she too was soaked with sweat. Cesare seemed half-delirious, moaning as he twisted his head from side to side. 'Trust no one . . .' he whispered through fever-cracked lips. 'He gave his word . . . A man of honour . . .' Then he looked at her, recognition in his eyes, but also a rising panic. 'This cell. It's "The Oven" . . . Why do they not release me? They cannot keep me. I'll not endure another *day*!' He struggled to his feet, gripping her wrist. 'He promised – if I'd surrender Forlì. I gave up the fortress to the Pope. What else is mine? They lie! They lie – to torture me!' Brutally, he twisted the girl's arm behind her back so that she screamed in pain. 'Let them hear your screaming . . . Your tears are true. There's nothing else but that!' He crushed her to him – kissing her hair and face, desperate to blot out the horror of the present. 'Vasia . . . they mustn't take you. Alone . . . they'll kill me . . . charge me with crimes. A thousand – murders it may be . . . But I'd give your body to the flames – for freedom. And who will not betray . . .' He released her, a look of terror forming on his face. ' . . . Michelotto . . .' he whispered.

*   *   *

Naked but for a loin-cloth, Michelotto lay in a cell in Sant'Angelo. He too was sweating, but the sweat was not occasioned by the heat, for the underground dungeon was icy cold, but by the agony of his hand which was being deliberately and efficiently mangled in a press by an executioner whose efforts were personally directed by the Pope himself. Giuliano Rovere was particularly anxious that the man who had been Cesare Borgia's executioner should tell him all his secrets, and betray his master into his hands. 'Enough . . .' He made a signal to the executioner to cease the pressure. He bent over Michelotto. 'My son,' he said gently, 'do you hear me? You know my face . . .'

'Yes, Holy Father,' Michelotto breathed through twisted lips.

'The killing of Alfonso Biselli. You were present. Soon you may see God face to face. As you will answer to Him, Michelotto, who gave your orders?' He motioned the executioner to apply the press. Michelotto writhed in agony, as Rovere went on remorselessly, 'Who ordered you to kill the Duke? In youth, unshriven . . .' A cry of pain burst from Michelotto. 'You'll speak?' Rovere asked, then, as his victim nodded, he signalled to the executioner to stop.

'Holy Father . . .' Michelotto's voice was a harsh whisper, ' . . . I will tell you. Before God – the man who gave the order was a villain . . . No greater – since the world began . . .' Rovere bent closer in his eagerness to hear what he was saying, his face almost touching Michelotto's. The tortured voice went on, 'The Pope . . . It was the Holy Father . . . Pray God – he roasts in hell . . .'

Rovere's face clouded with disappointment as he motioned the executioner to turn the press again. But, looking at Michelotto, he knew that he had lost. The secrets of Cesare Borgia would remain secret within that tough, unyielding body.

*   *   *

Cesare looked up apprehensively as the key grated in the lock of his cell door and Prospero Colonna entered. 'I have come for you,' Prospero told him brusquely. 'You are to go with me.'

Cesare rose uncertainly from the bed. 'To freedom?' he asked. Prospero shook his head. 'Then to what?' Then, as he began slowly and painfully pulling on his clothes, he said defiantly, 'I don't want your answer. It would be a lie.'

Prospero shrugged off the insult. 'You sail with me to Villaneuva del Grao.'

A small ray of hope dawned in Cesare's eyes. 'To Spain? King Ferdinand must have a use for me. As a weapon against the Pope . . .' He sat down on the pallet again, lacing his boots. 'You may tell Gonsalvo I bear no grudge. If I go to Spain, he acted under orders from the King. Ferdinand needs the Pope to recognise his rights in Naples. And the Pope wants my life.' He stood up. 'The game is played by the rules I gave it. Honour's a Spanish turd. If I'd remembered that, I'd not have lost.' He buckled on his belt, moving over to Prospero at the door. 'Whom may I see before I go? My little brother?'

'Prince Jofre has entered the service of Lord Gonsalvo.'

'He'll prosper,' Cesare said contemptuously, 'like a Spanish turd.'

Vasia stood timidly beside him, preparing to leave with him. But Prospero shook his head, his expression unyielding. 'You sail to Spain alone,' he told Cesare. 'Only your page goes with you.'

Cesare looked down at Vasia. 'Wait. I'll return,' he said gently. Then he turned away and walked out through the door without a backward glance. Prospero followed, closing the door in the girl's face. As they walked away down the corridor, they could hear her anguished cries and her fists pounding helplessly on the door behind them. Cesare looked straight ahead of him, facing the future. He was about to return to the land of his ancestors.

*   *   *

When they reached Spain, Cesare was confined, with only his page Juanito for company, in the high keep, called the Torre de Homenaje, of the fortress of La Mota at Medina del Campo in the central highlands of Castile. Here he passed his time watching the hawks wheel in the wind over the tawny fields below, and in writing letters to Lucrezia asking her to intercede for him with King Ferdinand.

*   *   *

Lucrezia held his letter in her hand as she sat in her bed-chamber at Ferrara. Cesara, she thought, he looked to her — only to her — for help. And she must help him. If only Alfonso, her husband, were not so hostile — to them both. For him, they were one and the same, both Borgias. She heard her husband approaching and looked up to meet his eyes in the mirror before her. He stood behind her, a candle in his hand. For a moment they looked at each other, then she said softly, 'Do you come to bed, My Lord?' Alfonso nodded, his eyes falling on the letter which she put down as she turned on the stool to face him. Lucrezia looked up at him anxiously. 'Then you'll give a sweeter answer to my pleadings. My brother is not to die in prison?'

Alfonso replied, with more than a trace of irritation, 'Lucrezia. There's no more that I can do.'

'Write to the King of Spain. That's what he asks ...'

'The King will not listen,' Alfonso said coldly. 'He cages Cesare like a savage dog — and threatens the Pope with his release. If he goes free ...'

Lucrezia rose abruptly and started towards the door. Alfonso caught her arm as she passed and held her. 'Let me pass, My Lord.' Lucrezia's tone was as frigid as her husband's. 'You may not share my bed tonight. You show no kindness ...'

'It's not from kindness that I've come,' Alfonso reminded her. 'You have that from others. And kisses too ... ' He maintained his grip on her arm as she tried to break away from him. 'When you can bear me a son, you'll find me less exacting.'

'I have borne a son!' Lucrezia cried at him. 'But not to

295

you!' She pulled her arm away, her face stormy. 'How can I bear you a son – knowing what you deny me?'

Alfonso's voice was gentler, as he replied, 'Rodrigo cannot come to you in Ferrara. He belongs to the house of Aragon. But there's another child in Naples too. Giovanni ...' Lucrezia looked at him, surprised, as he went on, 'If his parentage were proved ...'

'I have the deeds! Under the papal seal, my father acknowledged that Giovanni was his child. By a Roman lady.'

'Then you have proof – he is your brother?'

Lucrezia met his eyes. 'Yes, most surely.' Softened, she moved towards him. 'My Lord ... if you'd allow ...'

'There's no reason I should deny you. Unless *you* deny *me*.'

Lucrezia moved past him to the bed. 'It may be,' she said, 'that I *have* denied you – in my heart before.' She turned to look at him. 'But now ; ...' Alfonso moved towards her. 'If it does nothing ...' she went on, 'still you can write to Spain. He's endured prison for more than a year. Poor Cesare.' She put out her hand to touch her husband's robe, with a little smile. 'Poor savage dog ...'

*   *   *

Cesare stood at the window of his room in the top of the tower of La Mota, looking out over the windswept plains to the south, dreaming of Italy and freedom. Abstractedly he fed scraps of meat to a falcon perched on his wrist. His page, Juanito, seated at the table by his side, looked up in surprise as footsteps sounded on the stone stair leading up to the room, and the door opened to admit a fat priest, accompanied by a guard. The priest bowed slightly to Cesare, who did not turn round. 'My Lord,' he said respectfully, then to the guard, 'Leave me with His Excellency.'

As the guard withdrew, the priest came forward introducing himself. 'My name is Don Diego Ibanez. The governor of La Mota has graciously consented to allow

Your Excellency the services of a chaplain. For which reason I present myself ...'

Cesare continued to stare out of the window, not deigning to spare the priest a glance. 'Leave us,' he said contemptuously, 'unless you have wings.'

'I'm a priest, My Lord. Not an angel.' Don Diego moved closer to Cesare, glancing uncertainly at Juanito. 'However ... if we could be private ...'

Something in the priest's tone made Cesare turn round and look at him consideringly. 'Juanito,' he said, 'what are you doing?'

Juanito was holding something between finger and thumb over the flame of a lighted candle. 'Burning lice, My Lord.'

'Like souls in torment,' Cesare said savagely. 'I shall not make confession. To buy an hour of freedom, I'd hang a hundred priests.'

Don Diego smiled broadly. 'Why then, Excellency,' he replied, 'it's fitting that I've brought the rope!' He raised his robe to reveal a length of rope wound round his body. Cesare and Juanito stared at him in amazement as he went on, 'I come from my master – the Count of Benavente. Letters have passed between him and your sister ...'

Cesare strode forward to grip him by the arm. 'Madonna Lucrezia!'

Don Diego began to uncoil the rope as he spoke. 'In three nights, when the moon is dark, I'll be waiting with your officer, Don Jaime Requerenz, beyond the moat. We shall bring horses ... All that is needed is for Your Excellency to climb from this window unobserved by the guards. Don Jaime and I will conduct you to the coast. From which we hope to reach the kingdom of Navarre ...'

'To raise a rebellion against the house of Aragon,' Cesare interjected. 'Your master's cause.'

'The freedom of Castile, My Lord. If you'll engage your service ...'

'Don Diego, I'd fight for every louse in Juanito's hair ...' he reached out and took the page by the ear, 'to raise an army ...' He released the boy and turned back to the window to hide the madness in his eyes. 'Three days ... three nights ... why do we wait so long?'

*   *   *

Three nights later, the sleeping guard on the bench outside Cesare's room was roused from his slumbers by cries of alarm from the prisoner's room. Fumbling with the key, he opened the door to see a struggling form under a blanket on the bed, whence came muffled cries in the boy's voice. 'My Lord, I shall not ... Let me go! Let me go ...'

Hurrying over, the guard pulled back the blanket to reveal Juanito alone. As he did so, Cesare leapt upon him from behind the door, sinking a knife into the man's back. While Juanito retrieved the torch which the guard had dropped, Cesare knelt over the man's body in a frenzy, stabbing him again and again. 'My Lord, he's dead!' Juanito said anxiously.

Cesare looked up, as if suddenly recalled to reality, his eyes unclouding. He rose slowly to his feet, sheathing the knife at his belt, and strode over to the window. Two bars had been already removed in readiness and the rope tied to the remaining one. Cesare picked up the coil from the floor and threw it out of the window. Then, taking the torch from the page, he motioned for him to go first. 'I saw the signal,' he said. 'Now go. Swim the moat. I'll follow.' Juanito leapt nimbly up onto the sill, grasping the rope. 'Hold fast, Juanito,' Cesare warned.

Juanito grinned. 'It's nothing. I've climbed rigging ...' He swung out through the window, Cesare looking down after him as he slipped into the darkness. The boy's confidence was misplaced, however – the rope was too short from the ground by some thirty feet. Reaching the end, Juanito panicked and scrabbled frantically for a toehold in the crevices of the wall as he dangled in mid-air. Putting out a hand to steady himself, his foot slipped, and, with only one hand on the rope, he lost his hold and fell with a cry to the ground below.

From above, Cesare heard the sickening thud as the boy's body hit the ground; he heard too the footsteps of a guard on the stair, alerted by Juanito's cry. There was no time to lose. He swung his legs over the sill and lowered himself steadily, bracing himself with his legs against the tower wall. By the time the guard burst into the room, stumbling over the body of his colleague, Cesare was half-way down the rope, beyond reach. Calling the alarm, the guard took out his sword and hacked at the rope in a desperate effort to cut it. 'Murdering swine!' he shouted into the darkness. Below him, Cesare, nearing the end of the rope, pushed hard with all his force against the wall to swing himself outwards so that he should not fall, as Juanito had, onto the bank below. As he did so, the guard succeeded in cutting the rope, letting Cesare plummet like a stone into the dark water.

Cesare surfaced to the confused shouts of the castle guard, who were now running along the bank below the wall to where Juanito lay. He swam swiftly to the edge of the moat, where Don Diego and Don Jaime, alerted by the splash, stretched out anxious hands to pull him from the water. 'The boy . . .' Cesare gasped as he stood up panting.

'He fell . . . I think he's dead,' Jaime replied.

Then they heard Juanito's voice in a high cry of pain from the other side of the moat. 'Ah . . . ! Help me! Help me! My legs . . .'

Jaime looked questioningly at Cesare, but he shook his head briefly. 'It's too late. Your horses!'

'Over here . . .' Don Diego's voice came from the darkness. The two men hurried to join him where four horses stood tethered to some stunted trees. Don Diego had to help Cesare, weak from long imprisonment and unaccustomed to such exertion, into the saddle, while Jaime looked across the water from whence Juanito's cries could be heard in frantic appeal.

'Help me . . . My Lord. They're coming . . . Don't leave me here alone . . . Don't leave me!'

Cesare ignored him. Shouting to his companions to follow him, he spurred his horse and galloped into the darkness, Juanito's anguished cries fading away behind him, until they were abruptly ended by a sword-thrust.

*   *   *

Cesare and his companions, travelling by sea and by land, eventually reached the safety of Navarre, the tiny mountain kingdom of Cesare's brother-in-law, Jean d'Albret. Here Cesare was welcomed by the King at his court in Pamplona as an ally against their common enemy, King Ferdinand. Immediately on his arrival, he sat down to send news to Lucrezia. 'Sweet sister,' he wrote, 'know by this that I have reached sanctuary at the court of my brother of Navarre, who has received me gladly and hopes for my aid in the struggle against the tyrant of the house of Aragon who hoped to imprison me for ever from the sight of men. What would I not give to see Giuliano's face when he hears the news ...'

*   *   *

Lucrezia sat in the garden of her palace at Ferrara, her excited face illumined by the pale sun of early spring. Her hand shook with excitement as she held the letter. Cesare – alive – and free! She turned to the boy at her side. 'Giovanni! The Duke is safe. Listen to what he says to you. 'Tell Giovanni that he need not come here to fight for the name of Borgia. Wait but a little, and I shall return to Italy in triumph at the head of an army like my great namesake, and Giovanni shall bear my sword with my motto, 'Caesar or nothing', before me across that very Rubicon which Caesar crossed and into all my cities of the Romagna ...''

'Please,' the child interrupted, 'cannot I go to him now?'

Lucrezia shook her head, smiling at his enthusiasm. 'You would find no glory there, Giovanni. It is but a tiny kingdom. You must wait ... wait here for Cesare. Listen to what he says ...' She held up the letter and began to read it out to him again, '"Here in Navarre there is no enterprise worthy of Giovanni's valour – for I am placed in command of a small army to go against a petty nobleman – a little Count – who has rebelled against the King ... "' She stopped, as a fierce gust of March wind caught her veil, blowing it across her face.

'Go on. Please go on,' Giovanni urged her eagerly.

Lucrezia bent over the letter, trying to make out the unfamiliar names. 'Wait,' she said. 'Yes ... he says he is encamped at a place called Viana on the River Ebro near the borders of Castile, where the rebel Count holds a citadel that is poorly garrisoned and short of food. Listen – "Our position commands the road where I have posted sentinels – so nothing may reach the fortress which will not fall into our hands first. Campaigning in this far country is not like it was in the Romagna. I have no bombards and very little artillery, so, though I am impatient, as you know, I must wait a little until starvation compels the fortress to surrender, which cannot now be long ..."'

Lucrezia raised her head, half closing her eyes and trying to imagine her brother in that distant country. Poor Cesare ... how different it must all be for him, she thought. How he must yearn for Italy. To be in the world again ... A sudden gust of wind shook the dry branches of the willows overhanging the stream by which they sat. She looked up to see dark clouds scudding across the sky. 'Come, Giovanni,' she said, taking his hand and rising from the bench. 'We must go inside. There will be a storm ...'

*　　*　　*

'Do they have springtime in this accursed country?' Cesare asked his Squire, Grasica, as another furious bout of wind and rain shook the tent. The Squire took off his master's surcoat. Cesare held out his hands to the brazier. 'We shall be either blown or washed away!'

'I believe such storms are not uncommon here, My Lord. Even at this time of year,' Grasica replied.

'Then the enemy must starve – before we drown.' Cesare looked up as the draught from the raised tent flap sent the papers on his field table flying. Jaime Requerenz came in, his face and armour streaming.

'My Lord.'

'Yes, Jaime.'

'My Lord. The Captain of the guard has made a request to withdraw his sentinels till morning. There's little the Count can do to send provisions into the castle while the storm lasts. And it's great hardship for the men to keep their watch.'

Cesare nodded. 'It's true . . . nothing will stir tonight.' He paused, considering for a moment, then nodded again in acquiescence. 'Tell the Captain of the guard to stand down the watch till dawn.'

'Very well, My Lord.' Jaime moved to the tent flap to go out into the storm again.

'Jaime . . .'

'My Lord?'

'At first light. Be sure.'

'Yes, My Lord.'

'I should trust no one. God least of all . . .' Cesare said slowly, then he shrugged. 'And yet there is no purpose in a watch tonight. Give them the order.' Requerenz went out, leaving Cesare frowning into the red light of the brazier, listening to the noise of the storm outside.

Cesare slept fitfully that night, until awakened out of a troubled sleep by the sound of confused shouting outside the tent. He sat up, immediately alert. 'Grasica . . .'

The Squire stirred on his pallet on the floor beside the camp litter. 'My Lord . . .?' he mumbled sleepily.

Cesare was listening for another sound. Something was different. Then he realised. 'The rain has ceased!' he shouted, struggling to his feet. As he did so, a guard appeared at the tent flaps.

'My Lord . . . They say there are horsemen on the road – and pack mules – moving towards the castle . . .'

'Pack mules . . .!' Cesare reached for his armour with sudden urgency. 'Call out the guard!' he commanded. 'Rouse the camp! You hear me?' The guard saluted and disappeared. 'Fires of hell!' Cesare raged, struggling with his armour. 'Grasica – where the devil are you?'

'Here, My Lord.' Grasica was at his side holding his helmet.

'Harness my horse. No, stay! I'll call them. Pack mules ... I should have kept the watch. If we can take them before they reach the castle, I'll cut them all to pieces!' Furious in his haste, he turned savagely on Grasica. 'Why do you fumble like a silly whore? Get me in armour!'·

Cesare strode out of the tent to a scene of confusion. Although the rain had stopped the wind still blew, and men were running about shouting in the wild darkness. 'Where's Don Jaime?' Cesare asked the guard on the tent.

'Coming, My Lord!' the man answered promptly.

A groom appeared leading Cesare's charger. Cesare put his foot in the stirrup and, assisted by Grasica, swung himself into the saddle. The Squire handed him his lance. Cesare settled himself into the saddle, lance in hand. 'I shall not stay for anyone. Tell Don Jaime to follow – with as many as are ready. Tell him to wait for no man. Do you hear?'

'Yes, My Lord ...' He strained eyes and ears into the darkness. 'I think Don Jaime is coming now ...'

Cesare ignored him. He was working himself up into a reckless passion in which anger mingled with pent-up frustration at the pettiness of this minor war, blunting his normal wariness. 'Where is this little Count?' he said between his teeth. Then, shouting 'Follow me to the castle ...!' he spurred his horse and rode off headlong into the darkness, leaving Grasica staring after him, until his voice was lost in the noise of the wind.

First light was beginning to break at the edges of the sky as Cesare galloped alone through the desolate country towards the castle, the rough road channelling through a bleak sandstone gorge. Suddenly, six mounted men appeared on the road ahead of him. He pulled his horse to a standstill, jerking its head round to return the way he had come, only to see four more horsemen blocking his retreat. Cesare turned back to look towards the group of men ahead. Slowly, they began to move towards him. He glanced behind him; those four men, too, were moving in.

'Where is the escort?' he shouted. 'I lost them in the dark ... We were escorting pack mules. To relieve the castle ...'

The men did not respond. Menacingly, they continued to move in upon Cesare, trapped by the steep walls of the ravine. 'It's not time ...' Cesare said. 'The Ides of March have not yet come. You hear me?'

The men were now very close before him. Cesare tilted his lance in readiness, and launched himself at them at full gallop with a great shout, 'Caesar! Or nothing ...!'

The group parted before his charge but, as he passed, one of the men thrust at him with a lance, catching him under his upraised arm and unhorsing him. Cesare gave a choking cry as the steel penetrated deep into his chest, but he struggled to his feet, drawing his great sword to defend himself as his attackers closed in on him. Once, twice, his sword hacked at the men surrounding him, before he fell, impaled on their lances, to the mud. Finally all movement ceased; the horsemen dismounted to look at their victim, their eyes lighting up at the sight of his fine armour. 'One of the Duke Valentino's men,' said one. 'We'll take the armour ...'

Naked and bleeding from more than twenty wounds, the body of Cesare Borgia lay in the mud on the lonely road in the uplands of Navarre, the blood staring black against the white skin in the cold light of dawn. It was the morning of 12th March, three days short of the Ides which had been fatal to his hero, Caesar.

Or Caesar – or nothing.

CESARE BORGIA

Sarah Bradford

Almost five centuries have passed since the death of Cesare Borgia, yet his reputation still casts a sinister shadow. He stands accused of treachery, cruelty, rape, incest and murder. But as Sarah Bradford illustrates in this definitive biography, the real Cesare Borgia was a much more complex and fascinating figure than his evil reputation would suggest.

His rise to fame was meteoric. The illegitimate son of Pope Alexander VI, he was, by his twenty-seventh year, the most hated, feared and envied man of Renaissance Europe. His story is the drama of a man of exceptional gifts and a driving lust for power, who was to die at the age of thirty-one as violently and spectacularly as he had lived.

EYE OF THE NEEDLE

Ken Follett

'Top notch thriller, as gripping and persuasive as
THE DAY OF THE JACKAL'
Ira Levin, author of *THE BOYS FROM BRAZIL*.

His weapon is the stiletto, his codename: THE
NEEDLE. He is Henry Faber, coldly professional, a
killer, Germany's most feared deep-cover agent in
Britain. His task: to discover the Allies' plans for
D-Day, and get them to Germany at all costs. A task
he ruthlessly carries through, until Storm Island and
the woman called Lucy.

'An absolutely terrific thriller, so pulse pounding, so
ingenious in its plotting and so frighteningly realistic
that you simply cannot stop reading'
Publishers' Weekly

'A tense, marvellously detailed suspense thriller
built on a solid foundation of fact'
Sunday Times

All Futura Books are available at your bookshop or newsagent, or can be ordered from the following address:
Futura Books, Cash Sales Department,
P.O. Box 11, Falmouth, Cornwall.

Please send cheque or postal order (no currency), and allow 40p for postage and packing for the first book plus 18p for the second book and 13p for each additional book ordered up to a maximum charge of £1.49 in U.K.

Customers in Eire and B.F.P.O. please allow 40p for the first book, 18p for the second book plus 13p per copy for the next 7 books, thereafter 7p per book.

Overseas customers please allow 60p for postage and packing for the first book and 18p per copy for each additional book.